Wait Till Helen Comes

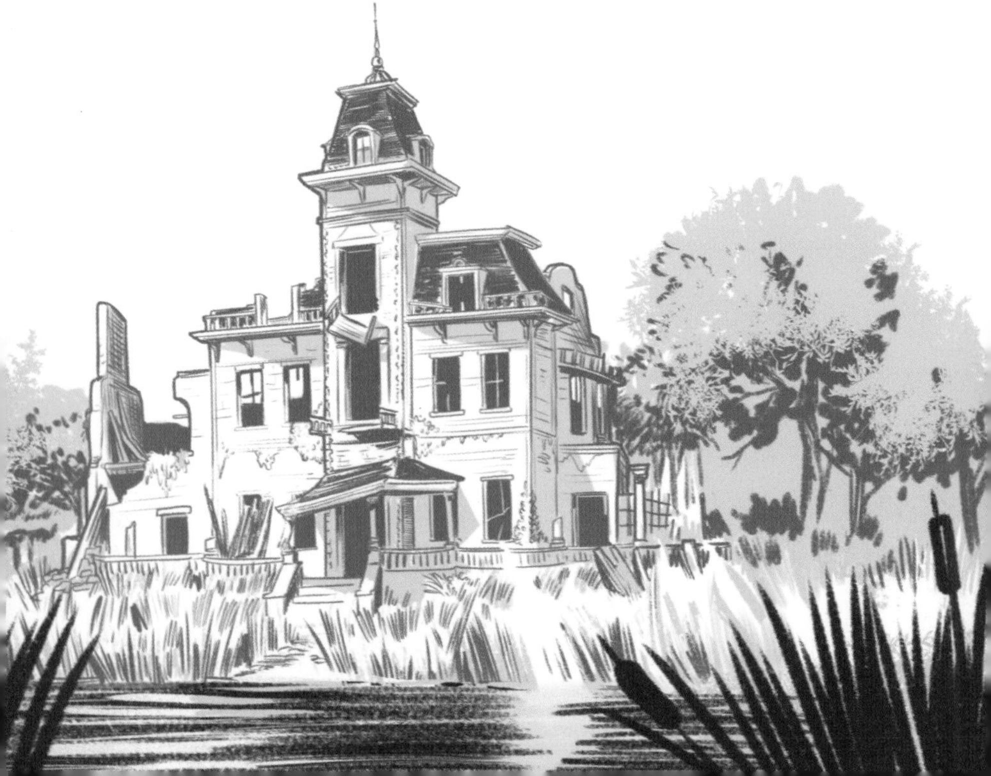

MARY DOWNING HAHN

Wait Till Helen Comes

a ghost story graphic novel

Adapted by Scott Peterson, Meredith Laxton,
and Russ Badgett

Clarion Books
Imprints of HarperCollins*Publishers*

For my kids for being understanding as to why dinner is always late.
And for Meredith for doing such an amazing job on the art.
And, as always, here's to Story.
—S.P.

To my mom, who gives me the courage to face my fears everyday.
Thank you for everything.
—M.L.

Clarion Books is an imprint of HarperCollins Publishers.
HarperAlley is an imprint of HarperCollins Publishers.

Wait Till Helen Comes Graphic Novel
Copyright © 2022 by HarperCollins Publishers LLC
Adapted from *Wait Till Helen Comes* by Mary Downing Hahn
Copyright © 1986 by Mary Downing Hahn
Text copyright © 2022 by Scott Peterson
Illustrations copyright © 2022 by Meredith Laxton

ISBN 978-0-35-853690-1—ISBN 978-0-35-853689-5 (pbk.)

The artist used Clip Studio to create the digital illustrations for this book.
Typography by Bones Leopard and Pete Friedrich

22 23 24 25 26 EP 10 9 8 7 6 5 4 3 2 1

First Edition

Wait Till Helen Comes

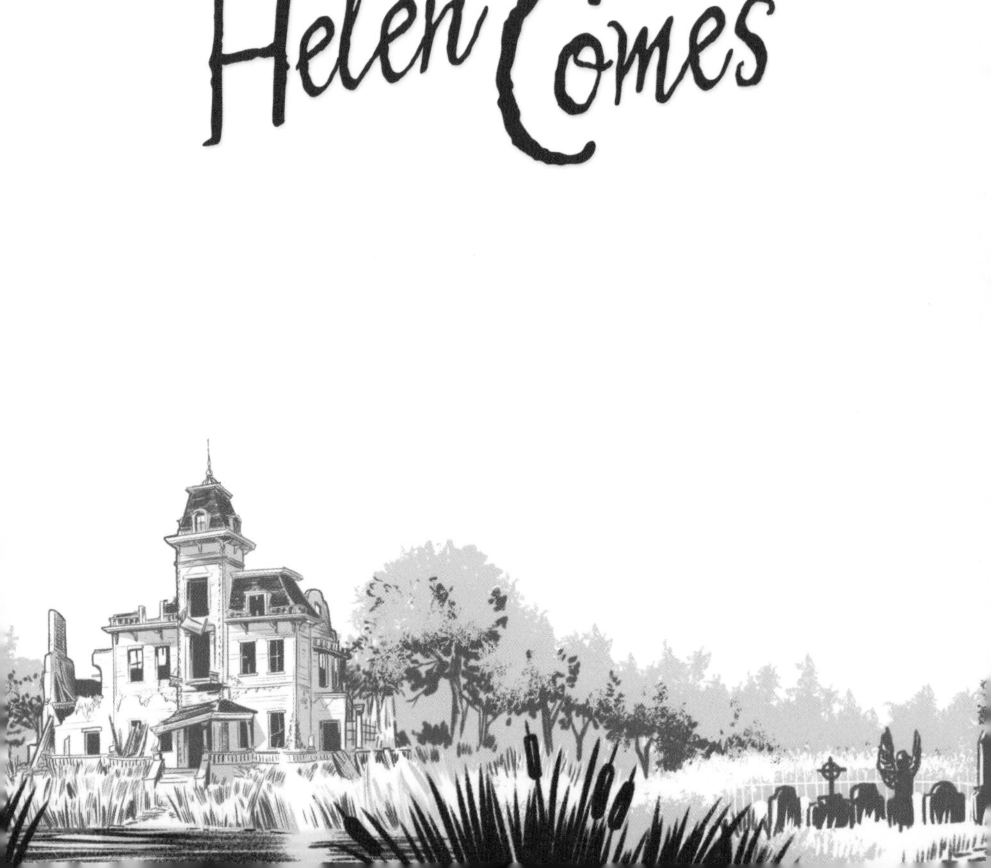

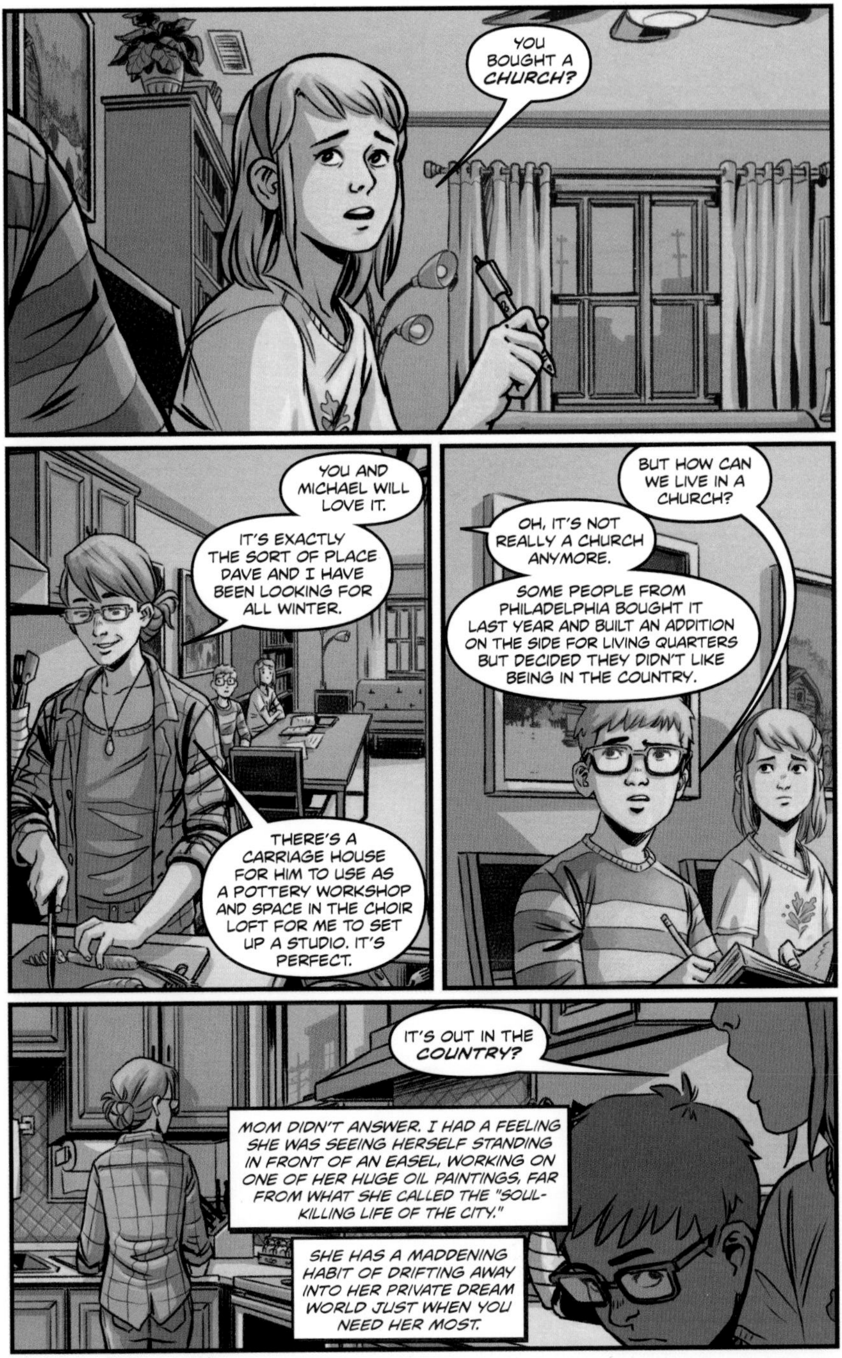
YOU BOUGHT A *CHURCH?*
YOU AND MICHAEL WILL LOVE IT.
IT'S EXACTLY THE SORT OF PLACE DAVE AND I HAVE BEEN LOOKING FOR ALL WINTER.
THERE'S A CARRIAGE HOUSE FOR HIM TO USE AS A POTTERY WORKSHOP AND SPACE IN THE CHOIR LOFT FOR ME TO SET UP A STUDIO. IT'S PERFECT.
BUT HOW CAN WE LIVE IN A CHURCH?
OH, IT'S NOT REALLY A CHURCH ANYMORE.
SOME PEOPLE FROM PHILADELPHIA BOUGHT IT LAST YEAR AND BUILT AN ADDITION ON THE SIDE FOR LIVING QUARTERS BUT DECIDED THEY DIDN'T LIKE BEING IN THE COUNTRY.
IT'S OUT IN THE *COUNTRY?*
MOM DIDN'T ANSWER. I HAD A FEELING SHE WAS SEEING HERSELF STANDING IN FRONT OF AN EASEL, WORKING ON ONE OF HER HUGE OIL PAINTINGS, FAR FROM WHAT SHE CALLED THE "SOUL-KILLING LIFE OF THE CITY."
SHE HAS A MADDENING HABIT OF DRIFTING AWAY INTO HER PRIVATE DREAM WORLD JUST WHEN YOU NEED HER MOST.

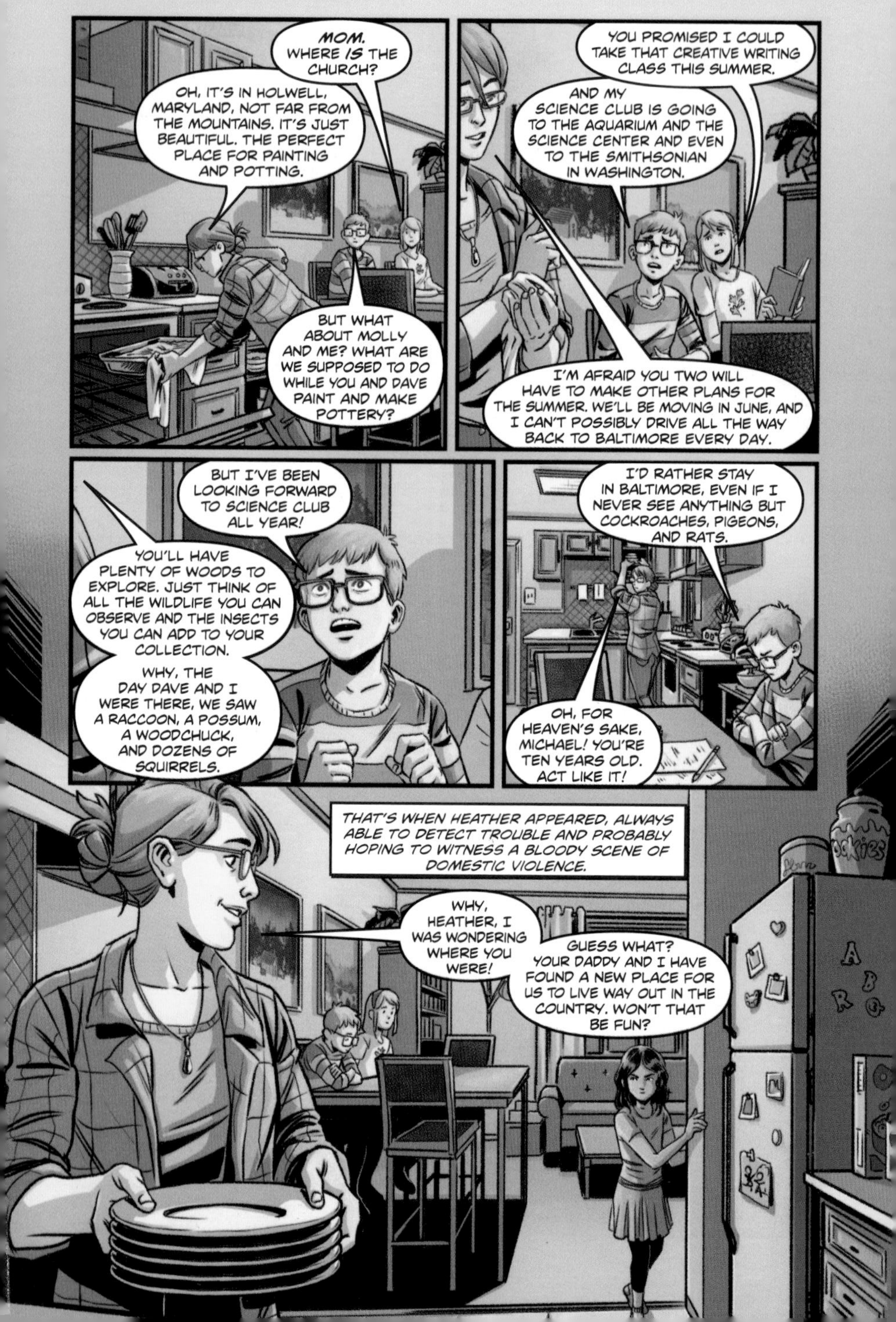
MOM. WHERE IS THE CHURCH?
OH, IT'S IN HOLWELL, MARYLAND, NOT FAR FROM THE MOUNTAINS. IT'S JUST BEAUTIFUL. THE PERFECT PLACE FOR PAINTING AND POTTING.
BUT WHAT ABOUT MOLLY AND ME? WHAT ARE WE SUPPOSED TO DO WHILE YOU AND DAVE PAINT AND MAKE POTTERY?
YOU PROMISED I COULD TAKE THAT CREATIVE WRITING CLASS THIS SUMMER.
AND MY SCIENCE CLUB IS GOING TO THE AQUARIUM AND THE SCIENCE CENTER AND EVEN TO THE SMITHSONIAN IN WASHINGTON.
I'M AFRAID YOU TWO WILL HAVE TO MAKE OTHER PLANS FOR THE SUMMER. WE'LL BE MOVING IN JUNE, AND I CAN'T POSSIBLY DRIVE ALL THE WAY BACK TO BALTIMORE EVERY DAY.
BUT I'VE BEEN LOOKING FORWARD TO SCIENCE CLUB ALL YEAR!
YOU'LL HAVE PLENTY OF WOODS TO EXPLORE. JUST THINK OF ALL THE WILDLIFE YOU CAN OBSERVE AND THE INSECTS YOU CAN ADD TO YOUR COLLECTION.
WHY, THE DAY DAVE AND I WERE THERE, WE SAW A RACCOON, A POSSUM, A WOODCHUCK, AND DOZENS OF SQUIRRELS.
I'D RATHER STAY IN BALTIMORE, EVEN IF I NEVER SEE ANYTHING BUT COCKROACHES, PIGEONS, AND RATS.
OH, FOR HEAVEN'S SAKE, MICHAEL! YOU'RE TEN YEARS OLD. ACT LIKE IT!
THAT'S WHEN HEATHER APPEARED, ALWAYS ABLE TO DETECT TROUBLE AND PROBABLY HOPING TO WITNESS A BLOODY SCENE OF DOMESTIC VIOLENCE.
WHY, HEATHER, I WAS WONDERING WHERE YOU WERE!
GUESS WHAT? YOUR DADDY AND I HAVE FOUND A NEW PLACE FOR US TO LIVE WAY OUT IN THE COUNTRY. WON'T THAT BE FUN?

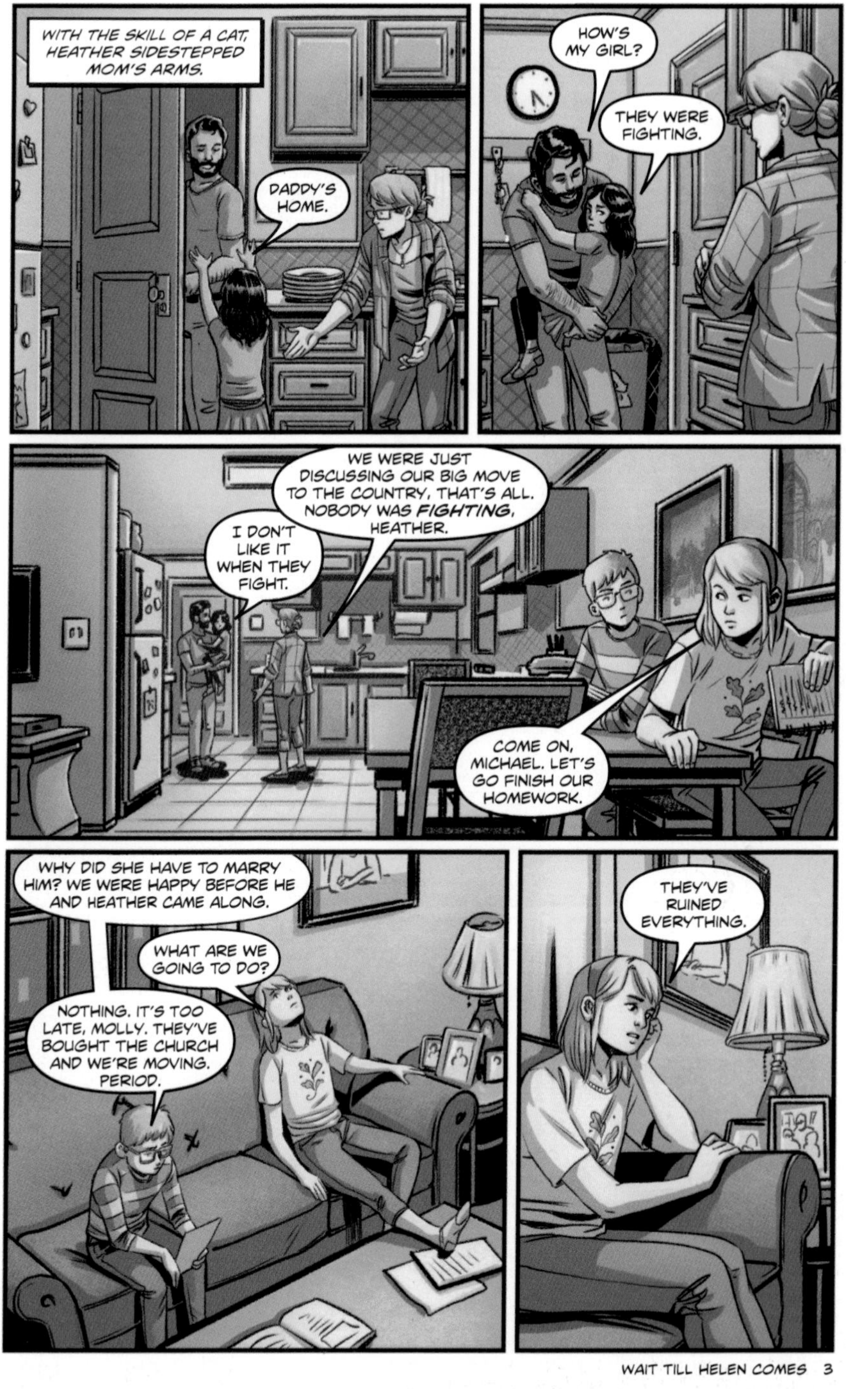
WITH THE SKILL OF A CAT, HEATHER SIDESTEPPED MOM'S ARMS.
DADDY'S HOME.
HOW'S MY GIRL?
THEY WERE FIGHTING.
I DON'T LIKE IT WHEN THEY FIGHT.
WE WERE JUST DISCUSSING OUR BIG MOVE TO THE COUNTRY, THAT'S ALL. NOBODY WAS *FIGHTING*, HEATHER.
COME ON, MICHAEL. LET'S GO FINISH OUR HOMEWORK.
WHY DID SHE HAVE TO MARRY HIM? WE WERE HAPPY BEFORE HE AND HEATHER CAME ALONG.
WHAT ARE WE GOING TO DO?
NOTHING. IT'S TOO LATE, MOLLY. THEY'VE BOUGHT THE CHURCH AND WE'RE MOVING. PERIOD.
THEY'VE RUINED EVERYTHING.

IF ONLY HEATHER WERE A NORMAL KID. SHE ACTS MORE LIKE A TWO-YEAR-OLD THAN A SEVEN-YEAR-OLD.

AND SHE'S MEAN--SHE TATTLES AND LIES AND TRIES TO GET US IN TROUBLE WITH DAVE.

WHY DO THEY *ALWAYS* TAKE HER SIDE--EVEN MOM?

YOU KNOW WHAT DAVE SAYS.

"HEATHER IS AN UNUSUALLY IMAGINATIVE AND SENSITIVE CHILD WHO HAS SUFFERED A GREAT LOSS. YOU TWO MUST BE PATIENT WITH HER."

BUT HOW LONG CAN WE FEEL SORRY FOR HER? I KNOW IT MUST HAVE BEEN HORRIBLE TO SEE HER MOTHER DIE IN A FIRE, BUT SHE WAS ONLY THREE YEARS OLD.

SHE SHOULD'VE GOTTEN OVER IT BY NOW.

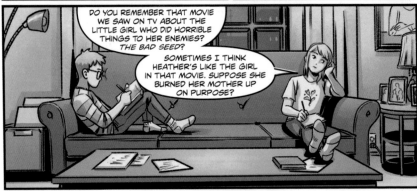

DO YOU REMEMBER THAT MOVIE WE SAW ON TV ABOUT THE LITTLE GIRL WHO DID HORRIBLE THINGS TO HER ENEMIES? *THE BAD SEED?*

SOMETIMES I THINK HEATHER'S LIKE THE GIRL IN THAT MOVIE. SUPPOSE SHE BURNED HER MOTHER UP ON PURPOSE?

YOU'RE CRAZY, MOLLY. NO THREE-YEAR-OLD KID COULD DO ANYTHING LIKE THAT.

I REALIZED HOW RIDICULOUS I SOUNDED.

JUST KIDDING.

BUT I WASN'T. THERE WAS SOMETHING ABOUT HEATHER THAT MADE ME TRULY UNCOMFORTABLE.

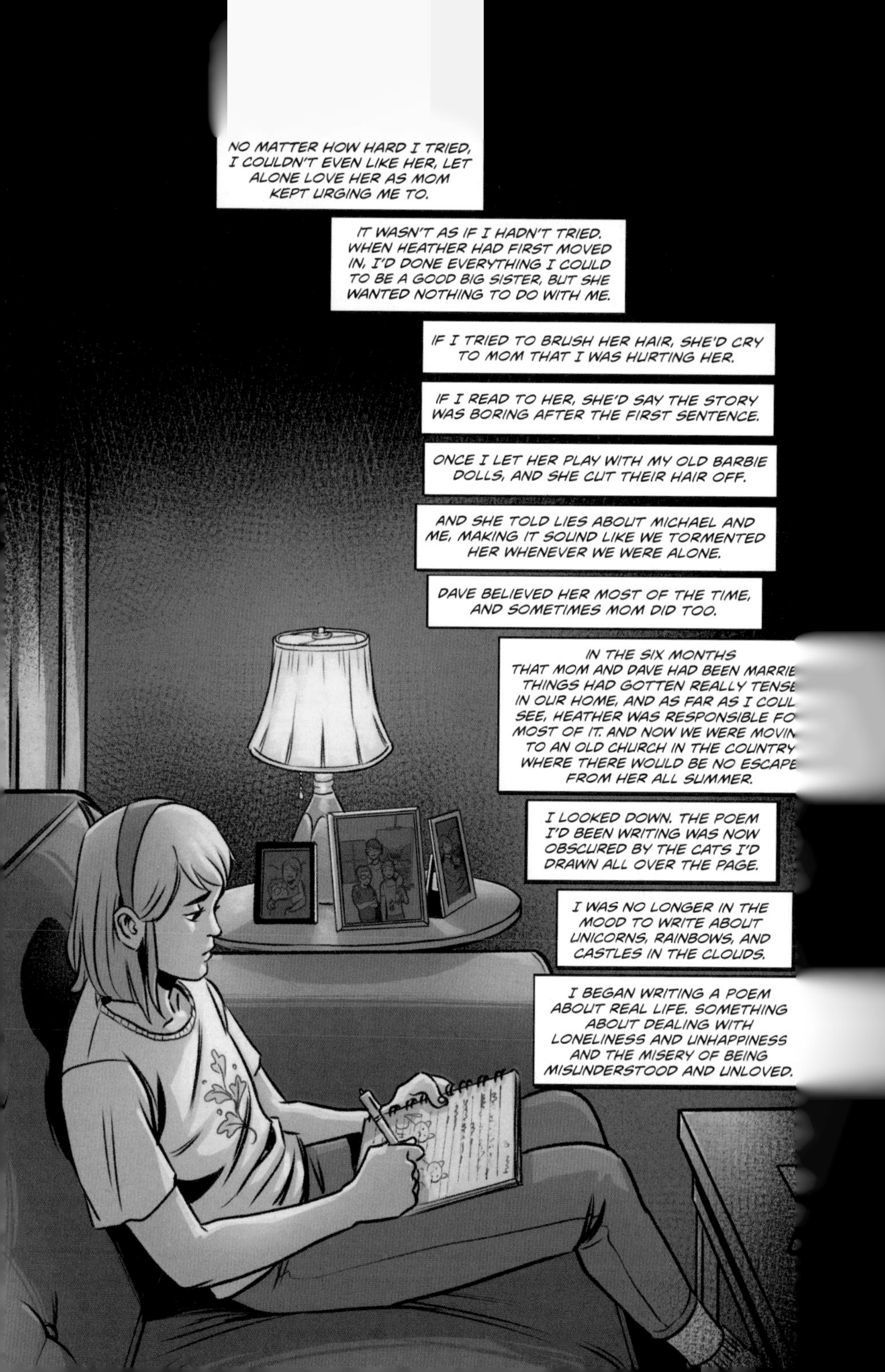
NO MATTER HOW HARD I TRIED, I COULDN'T EVEN LIKE HER, LET ALONE LOVE HER AS MOM KEPT URGING ME TO.
IT WASN'T AS IF I HADN'T TRIED. WHEN HEATHER HAD FIRST MOVED IN, I'D DONE EVERYTHING I COULD TO BE A GOOD BIG SISTER, BUT SHE WANTED NOTHING TO DO WITH ME.
IF I TRIED TO BRUSH HER HAIR, SHE'D CRY TO MOM THAT I WAS HURTING HER.
IF I READ TO HER, SHE'D SAY THE STORY WAS BORING AFTER THE FIRST SENTENCE.
ONCE I LET HER PLAY WITH MY OLD BARBIE DOLLS, AND SHE CUT THEIR HAIR OFF.
AND SHE TOLD LIES ABOUT MICHAEL AND ME, MAKING IT SOUND LIKE WE TORMENTED HER WHENEVER WE WERE ALONE.
DAVE BELIEVED HER MOST OF THE TIME, AND SOMETIMES MOM DID TOO.
IN THE SIX MONTHS THAT MOM AND DAVE HAD BEEN MARRIE THINGS HAD GOTTEN REALLY TENSE IN OUR HOME, AND AS FAR AS I COUL SEE, HEATHER WAS RESPONSIBLE FO MOST OF IT. AND NOW WE WERE MOVIN TO AN OLD CHURCH IN THE COUNTRY WHERE THERE WOULD BE NO ESCAPE FROM HER ALL SUMMER.
I LOOKED DOWN. THE POEM I'D BEEN WRITING WAS NOW OBSCURED BY THE CATS I'D DRAWN ALL OVER THE PAGE.
I WAS NO LONGER IN THE MOOD TO WRITE ABOUT UNICORNS, RAINBOWS, AND CASTLES IN THE CLOUDS.
I BEGAN WRITING A POEM ABOUT REAL LIFE. SOMETHING ABOUT DEALING WITH LONELINESS AND UNHAPPINESS AND THE MISERY OF BEING MISUNDERSTOOD AND UNLOVED.

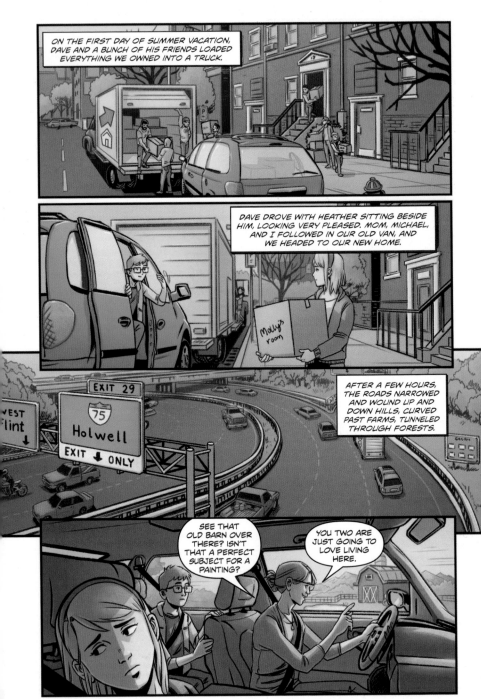

ON THE FIRST DAY OF SUMMER VACATION, DAVE AND A BUNCH OF HIS FRIENDS LOADED EVERYTHING WE OWNED INTO A TRUCK.

DAVE DROVE WITH HEATHER SITTING BESIDE HIM, LOOKING VERY PLEASED. MOM, MICHAEL, AND I FOLLOWED IN OUR OLD VAN, AND WE HEADED TO OUR NEW HOME.

Molly's room

EXIT 29
75
Holwell
EXIT ↓ ONLY

WEST
Flint

AFTER A FEW HOURS, THE ROADS NARROWED AND WOUND UP AND DOWN HILLS, CURVED PAST FARMS, TUNNELED THROUGH FORESTS.

SEE THAT OLD BARN OVER THERE? ISN'T THAT A PERFECT SUBJECT FOR A PAINTING?

YOU TWO ARE JUST GOING TO LOVE LIVING HERE.

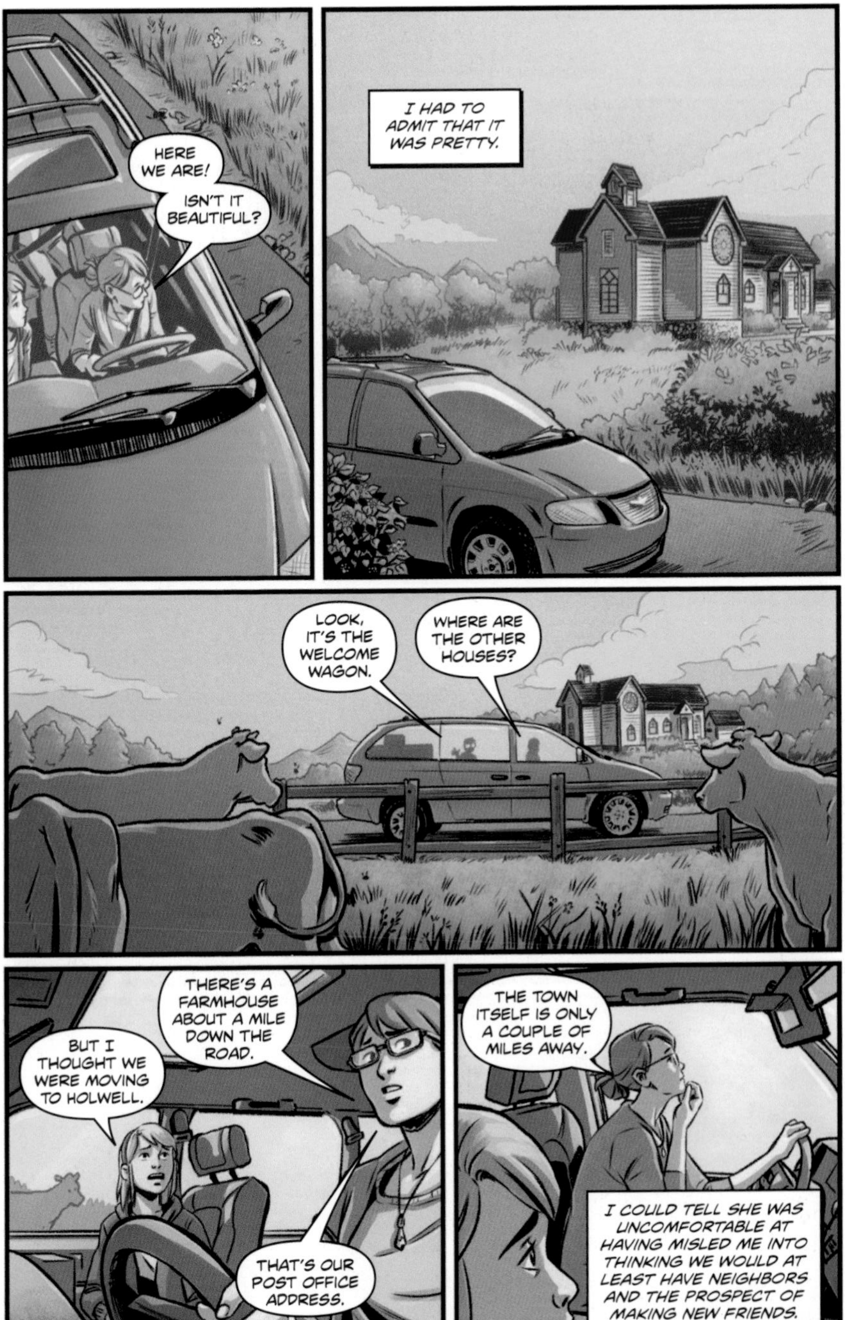
HERE WE ARE!
ISN'T IT BEAUTIFUL?
I HAD TO ADMIT THAT IT WAS PRETTY.
LOOK, IT'S THE WELCOME WAGON.
WHERE ARE THE OTHER HOUSES?
BUT I THOUGHT WE WERE MOVING TO HOLWELL.
THERE'S A FARMHOUSE ABOUT A MILE DOWN THE ROAD.
THAT'S OUR POST OFFICE ADDRESS.
THE TOWN ITSELF IS ONLY A COUPLE OF MILES AWAY.
I COULD TELL SHE WAS UNCOMFORTABLE AT HAVING MISLED ME INTO THINKING WE WOULD AT LEAST HAVE NEIGHBORS AND THE PROSPECT OF MAKING NEW FRIENDS.

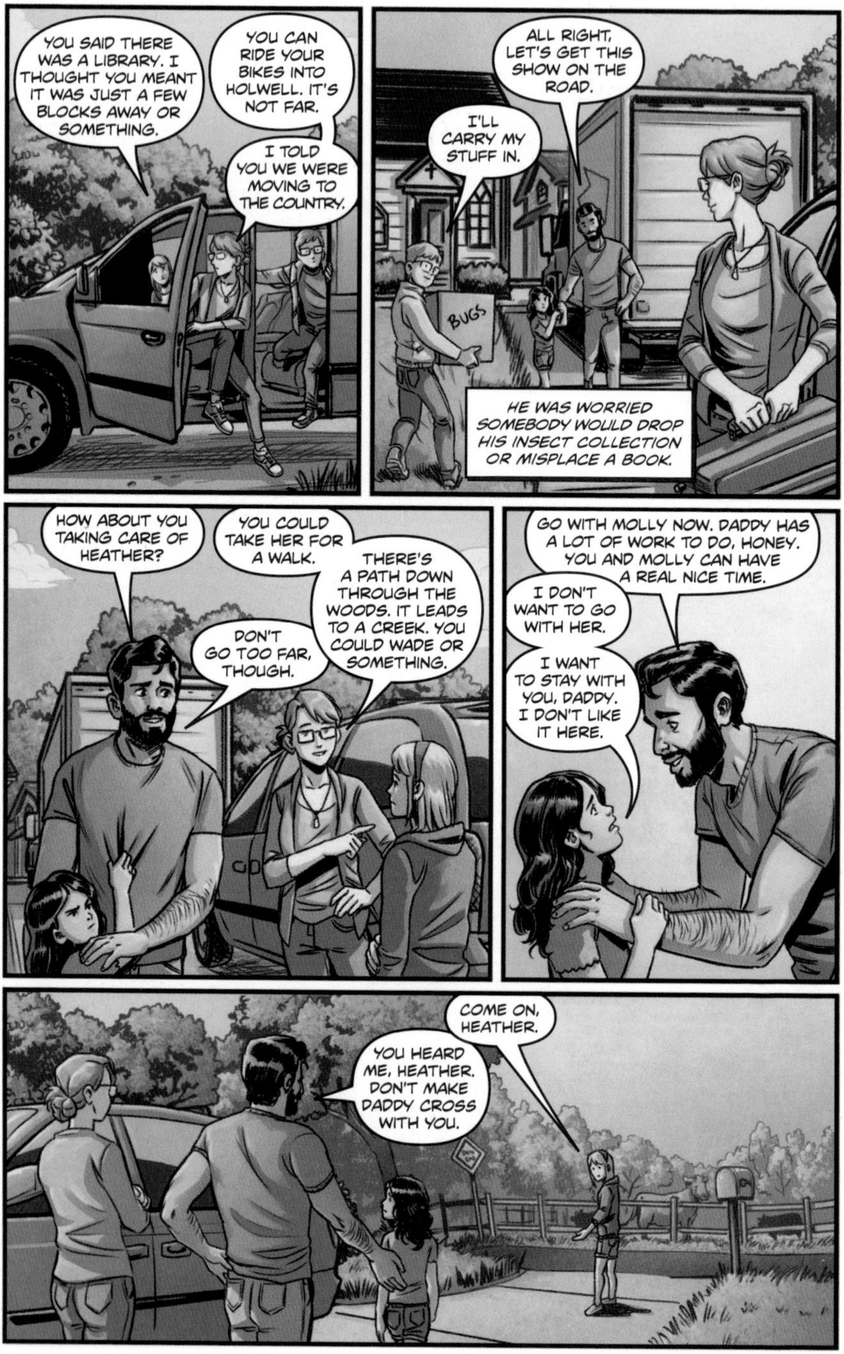
YOU SAID THERE WAS A LIBRARY. I THOUGHT YOU MEANT IT WAS JUST A FEW BLOCKS AWAY OR SOMETHING.
YOU CAN RIDE YOUR BIKES INTO HOLWELL. IT'S NOT FAR.
I TOLD YOU WE WERE MOVING TO THE COUNTRY.
ALL RIGHT, LET'S GET THIS SHOW ON THE ROAD.
I'LL CARRY MY STUFF IN.
BUGS
HE WAS WORRIED SOMEBODY WOULD DROP HIS INSECT COLLECTION OR MISPLACE A BOOK.
HOW ABOUT YOU TAKING CARE OF HEATHER?
YOU COULD TAKE HER FOR A WALK.
THERE'S A PATH DOWN THROUGH THE WOODS. IT LEADS TO A CREEK. YOU COULD WADE OR SOMETHING.
DON'T GO TOO FAR, THOUGH.
GO WITH MOLLY NOW. DADDY HAS A LOT OF WORK TO DO, HONEY. YOU AND MOLLY CAN HAVE A REAL NICE TIME.
I DON'T WANT TO GO WITH HER.
I WANT TO STAY WITH YOU, DADDY. I DON'T LIKE IT HERE.
COME ON, HEATHER.
YOU HEARD ME, HEATHER. DON'T MAKE DADDY CROSS WITH YOU.

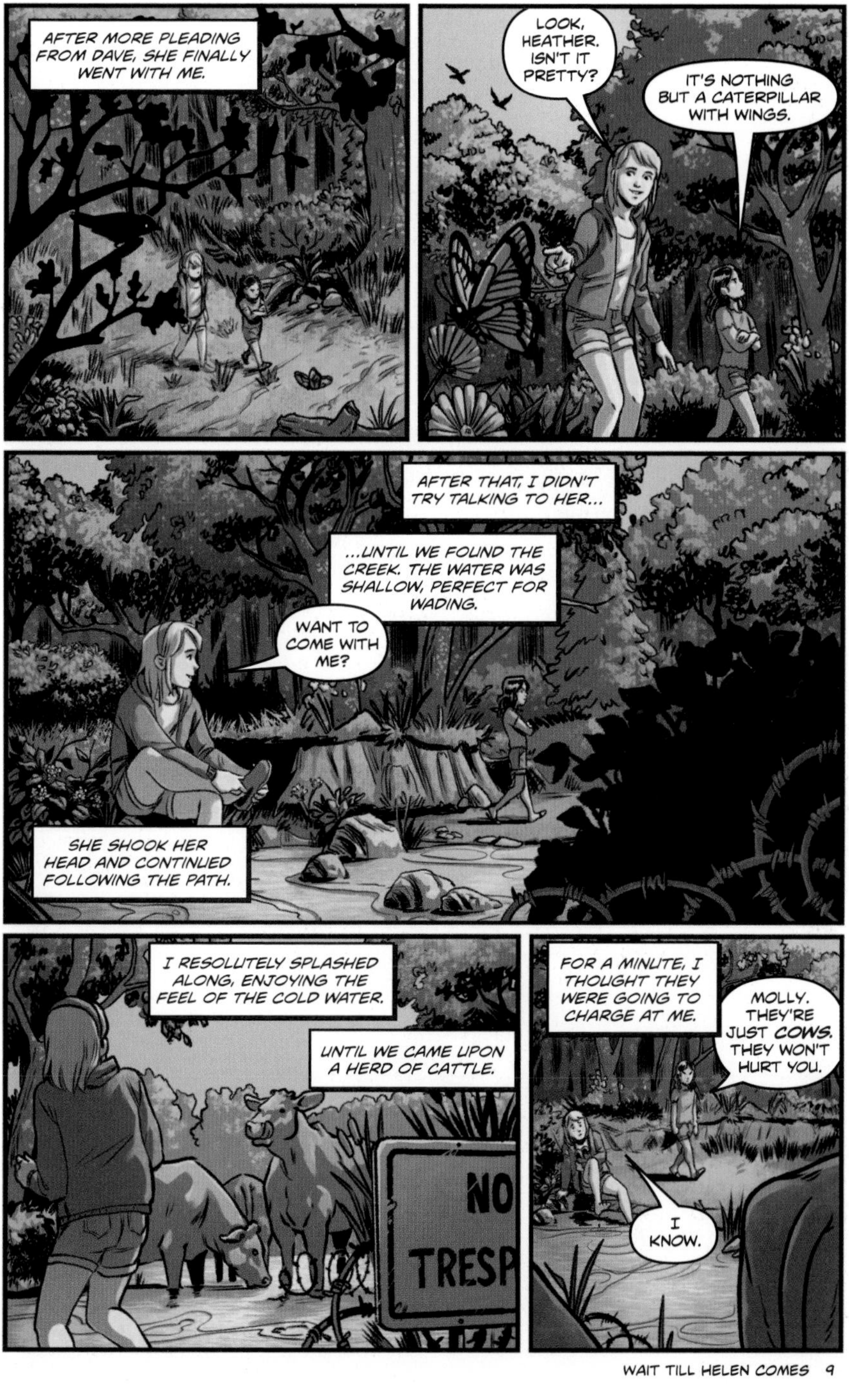
AFTER MORE PLEADING FROM DAVE, SHE FINALLY WENT WITH ME.
LOOK, HEATHER. ISN'T IT PRETTY?
IT'S NOTHING BUT A CATERPILLAR WITH WINGS.
AFTER THAT, I DIDN'T TRY TALKING TO HER...
...UNTIL WE FOUND THE CREEK. THE WATER WAS SHALLOW, PERFECT FOR WADING.
WANT TO COME WITH ME?
SHE SHOOK HER HEAD AND CONTINUED FOLLOWING THE PATH.
I RESOLUTELY SPLASHED ALONG, ENJOYING THE FEEL OF THE COLD WATER.
UNTIL WE CAME UPON A HERD OF CATTLE.
NO
TRESP
FOR A MINUTE, I THOUGHT THEY WERE GOING TO CHARGE AT ME.
MOLLY. THEY'RE JUST COWS. THEY WON'T HURT YOU.
I KNOW.

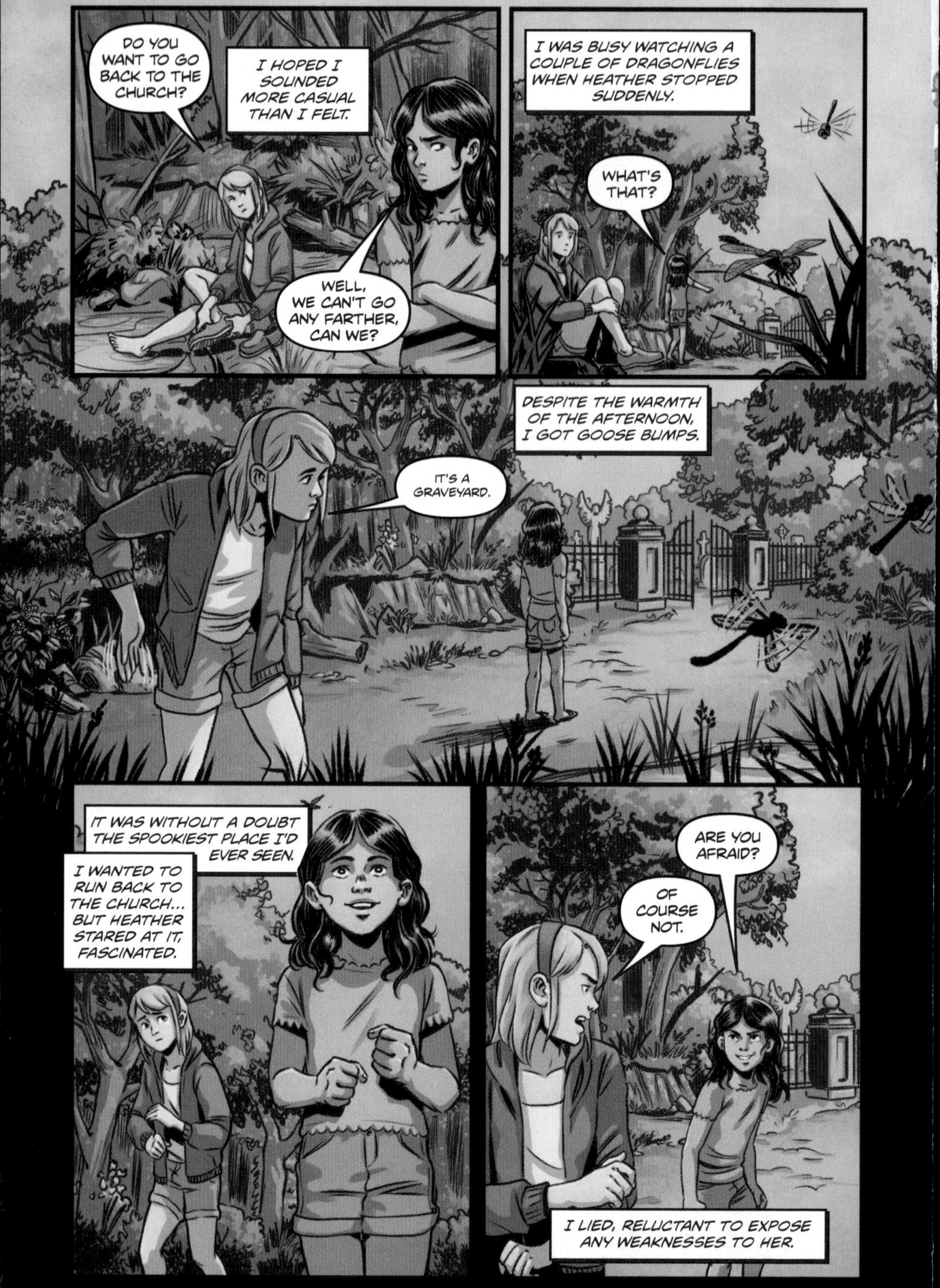
DO YOU WANT TO GO BACK TO THE CHURCH?
I HOPED I SOUNDED MORE CASUAL THAN I FELT.
WELL, WE CAN'T GO ANY FARTHER, CAN WE?
I WAS BUSY WATCHING A COUPLE OF DRAGONFLIES WHEN HEATHER STOPPED SUDDENLY.
WHAT'S THAT?
DESPITE THE WARMTH OF THE AFTERNOON, I GOT GOOSE BUMPS.
IT'S A GRAVEYARD.
IT WAS WITHOUT A DOUBT THE SPOOKIEST PLACE I'D EVER SEEN.
I WANTED TO RUN BACK TO THE CHURCH... BUT HEATHER STARED AT IT, FASCINATED.
ARE YOU AFRAID?
OF COURSE NOT.
I LIED, RELUCTANT TO EXPOSE ANY WEAKNESSES TO HER.

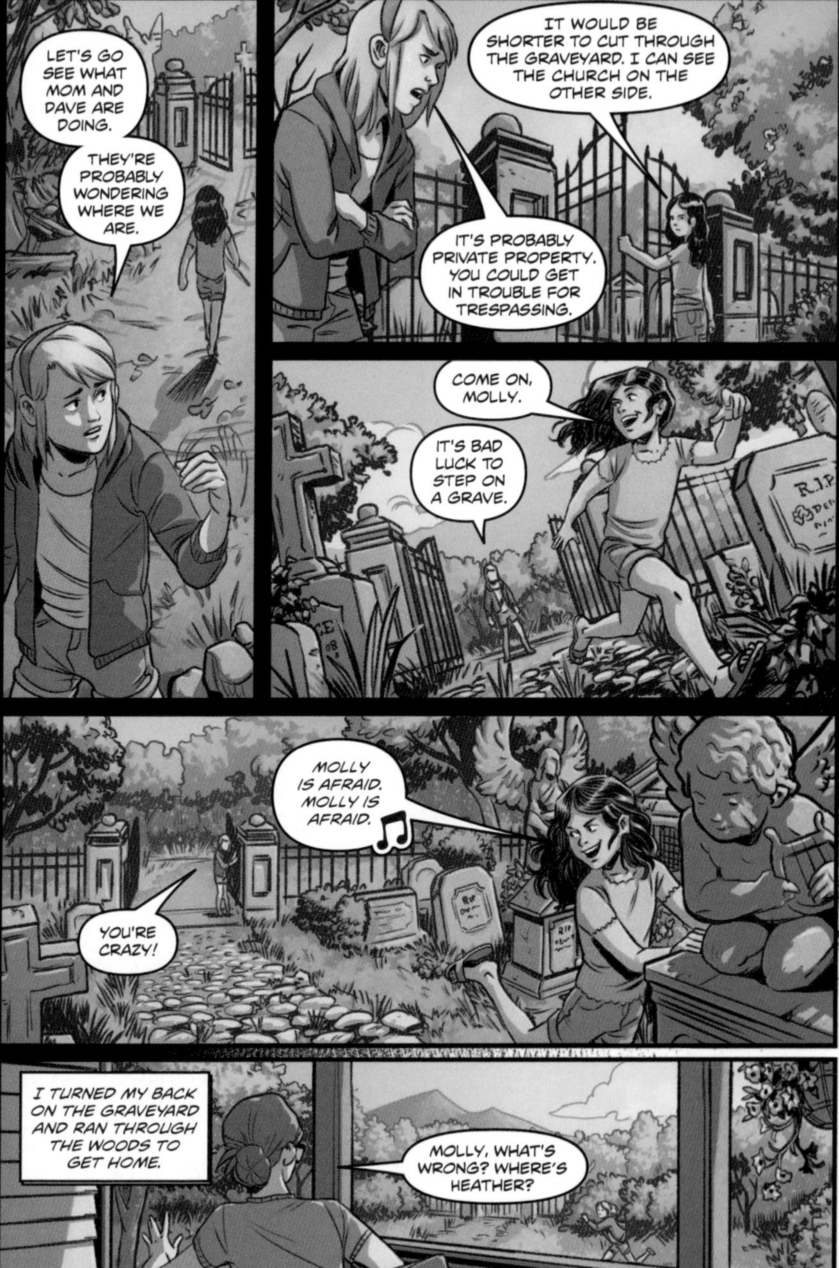
LET'S GO SEE WHAT MOM AND DAVE ARE DOING.
THEY'RE PROBABLY WONDERING WHERE WE ARE.
IT WOULD BE SHORTER TO CUT THROUGH THE GRAVEYARD. I CAN SEE THE CHURCH ON THE OTHER SIDE.
IT'S PROBABLY PRIVATE PROPERTY. YOU COULD GET IN TROUBLE FOR TRESPASSING.
COME ON, MOLLY.
IT'S BAD LUCK TO STEP ON A GRAVE.
R.I.P.
MOLLY IS AFRAID. MOLLY IS AFRAID.
YOU'RE CRAZY!
I TURNED MY BACK ON THE GRAVEYARD AND RAN THROUGH THE WOODS TO GET HOME.
MOLLY, WHAT'S WRONG? WHERE'S HEATHER?
KITCHEN

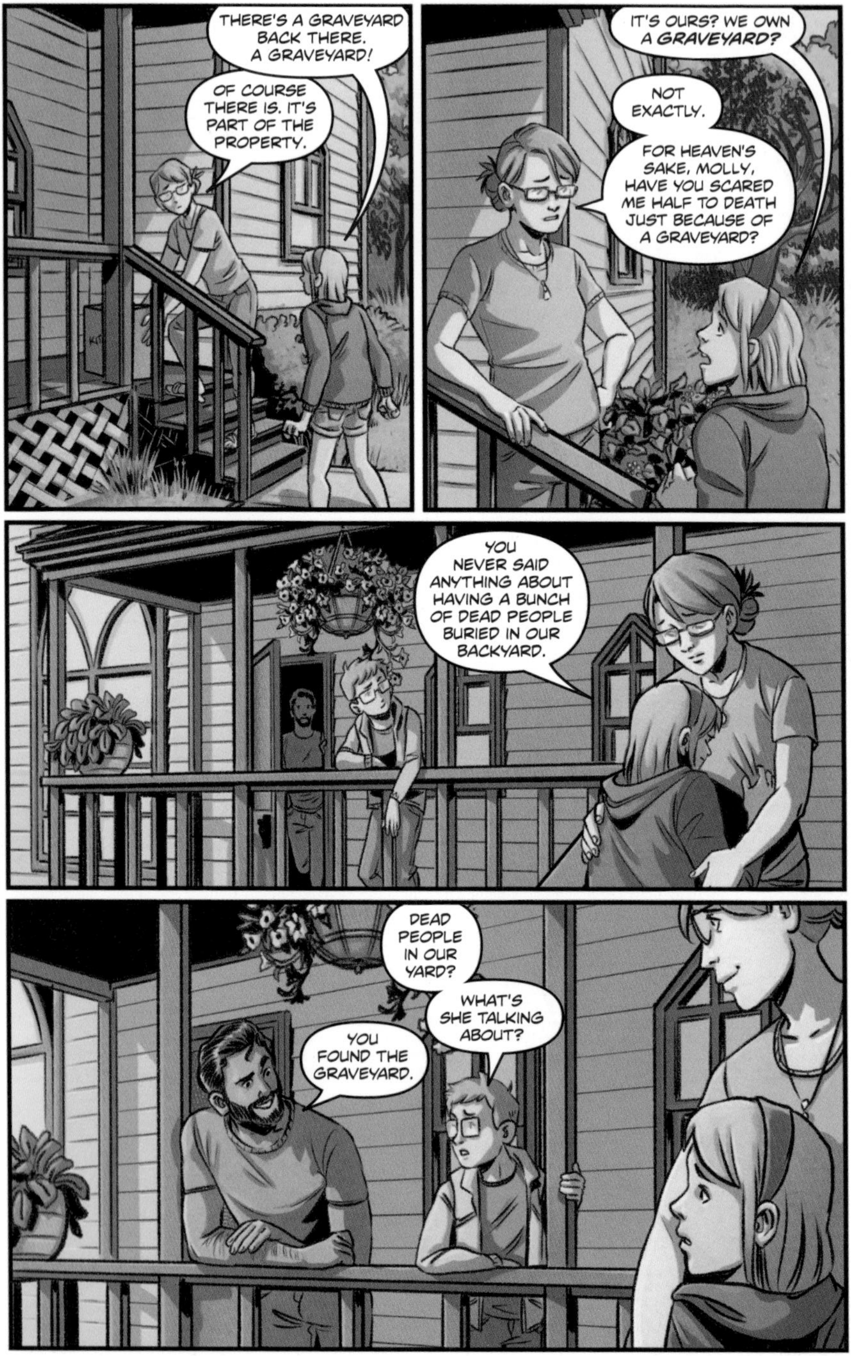
THERE'S A GRAVEYARD BACK THERE. A GRAVEYARD!
OF COURSE THERE IS. IT'S PART OF THE PROPERTY.
IT'S OURS? WE OWN A **GRAVEYARD?**
NOT EXACTLY.
FOR HEAVEN'S SAKE, MOLLY, HAVE YOU SCARED ME HALF TO DEATH JUST BECAUSE OF A GRAVEYARD?
YOU NEVER SAID ANYTHING ABOUT HAVING A BUNCH OF DEAD PEOPLE BURIED IN OUR BACKYARD.
DEAD PEOPLE IN OUR YARD?
WHAT'S SHE TALKING ABOUT?
YOU FOUND THE GRAVEYARD.

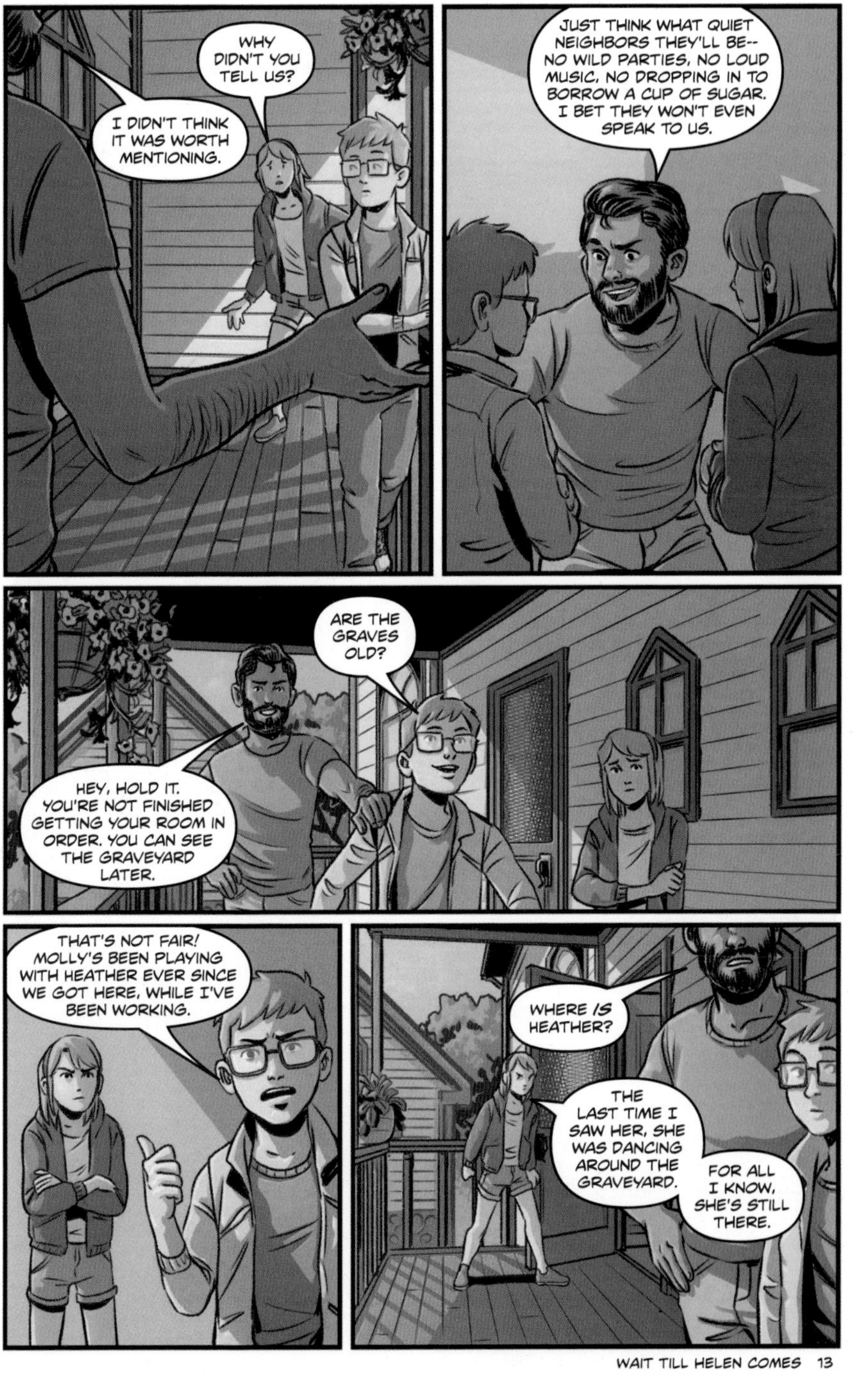
WHY DIDN'T YOU TELL US?
I DIDN'T THINK IT WAS WORTH MENTIONING.
JUST THINK WHAT QUIET NEIGHBORS THEY'LL BE-- NO WILD PARTIES, NO LOUD MUSIC, NO DROPPING IN TO BORROW A CUP OF SUGAR. I BET THEY WON'T EVEN SPEAK TO US.
ARE THE GRAVES OLD?
HEY, HOLD IT. YOU'RE NOT FINISHED GETTING YOUR ROOM IN ORDER. YOU CAN SEE THE GRAVEYARD LATER.
THAT'S NOT FAIR! MOLLY'S BEEN PLAYING WITH HEATHER EVER SINCE WE GOT HERE, WHILE I'VE BEEN WORKING.
WHERE *IS* HEATHER?
THE LAST TIME I SAW HER, SHE WAS DANCING AROUND THE GRAVEYARD.
FOR ALL I KNOW, SHE'S STILL THERE.

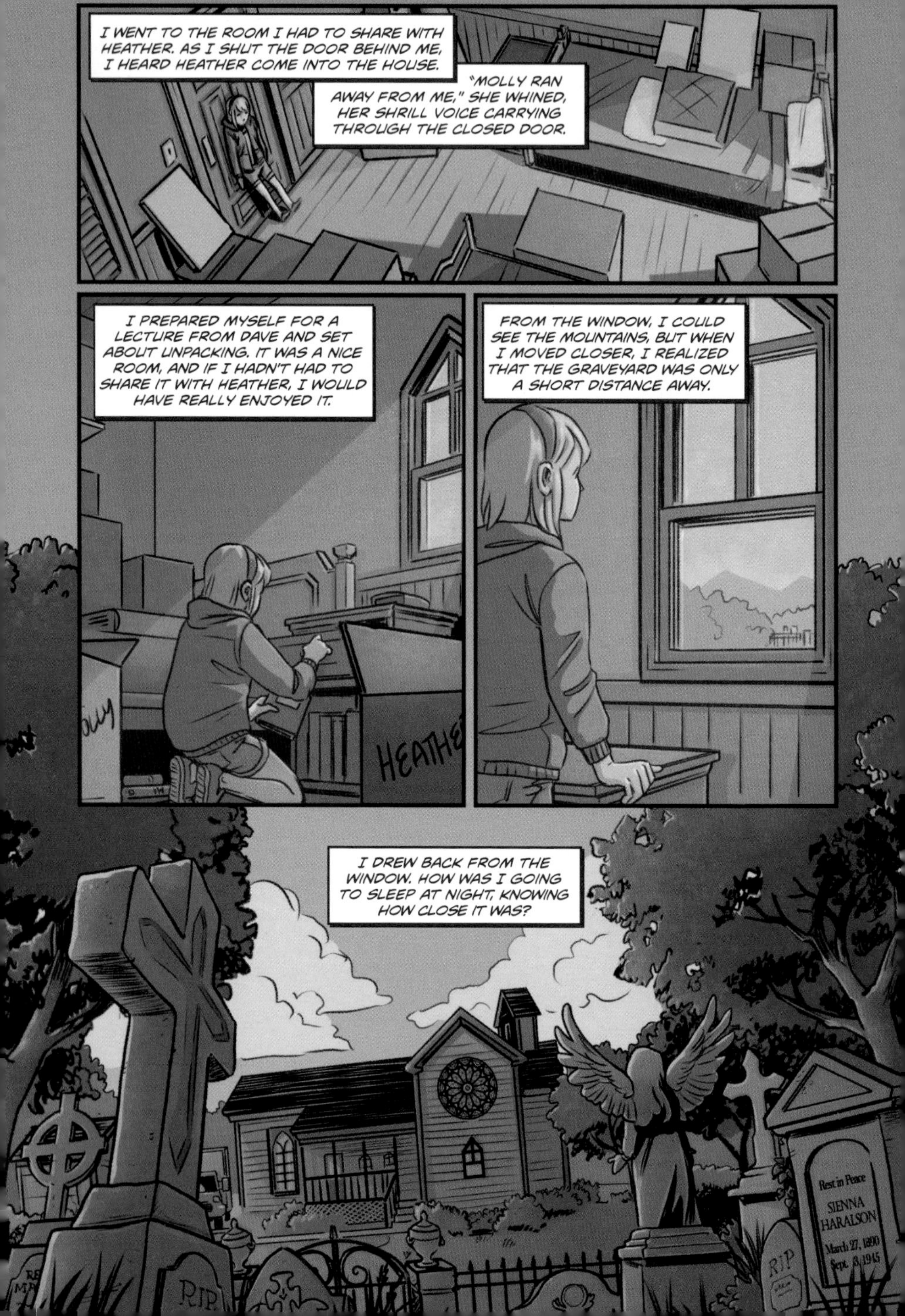
I WENT TO THE ROOM I HAD TO SHARE WITH HEATHER. AS I SHUT THE DOOR BEHIND ME, I HEARD HEATHER COME INTO THE HOUSE.
"MOLLY RAN AWAY FROM ME," SHE WHINED, HER SHRILL VOICE CARRYING THROUGH THE CLOSED DOOR.
I PREPARED MYSELF FOR A LECTURE FROM DAVE AND SET ABOUT UNPACKING. IT WAS A NICE ROOM, AND IF I HADN'T HAD TO SHARE IT WITH HEATHER, I WOULD HAVE REALLY ENJOYED IT.
FROM THE WINDOW, I COULD SEE THE MOUNTAINS, BUT WHEN I MOVED CLOSER, I REALIZED THAT THE GRAVEYARD WAS ONLY A SHORT DISTANCE AWAY.
I DREW BACK FROM THE WINDOW. HOW WAS I GOING TO SLEEP AT NIGHT, KNOWING HOW CLOSE IT WAS?
Rest in Peace
SIENNA HARALSON
March 27, 1890
Sept. 3, 1945
RIP
RIP

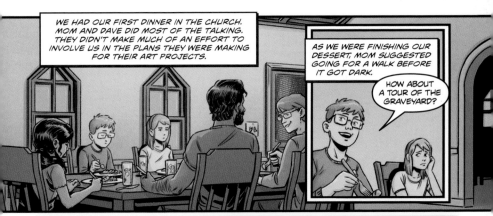

WE HAD OUR FIRST DINNER IN THE CHURCH. MOM AND DAVE DID MOST OF THE TALKING. THEY DIDN'T MAKE MUCH OF AN EFFORT TO INVOLVE US IN THE PLANS THEY WERE MAKING FOR THEIR ART PROJECTS.

AS WE WERE FINISHING OUR DESSERT, MOM SUGGESTED GOING FOR A WALK BEFORE IT GOT DARK.

HOW ABOUT A TOUR OF THE GRAVEYARD?

I CONSIDERED STAYING HOME BUT DECIDED IT MIGHT BE WORSE TO BE ALL ALONE IN THE HOUSE.

WHEN I TOOK MOM'S HAND, HEATHER SMILED MOCKINGLY.

MOLLY'S SCARED OF THE GRAVEYARD, BUT I'M NOT.

TO PROVE HOW BRAVE SHE WAS, SHE SCRAMBLED UP ON A TOMBSTONE.

LOOK AT ME, DADDY. I'M AN ANGEL.

HEY, GET DOWN FROM THERE.

THESE ARE TOO OLD FOR YOU TO CLIMB ON, HONEY. THEY COULD TOPPLE RIGHT OVER.

I WAS JUST PLAYING.

AT LEAST I'M NOT A SCAREDY-CAT.

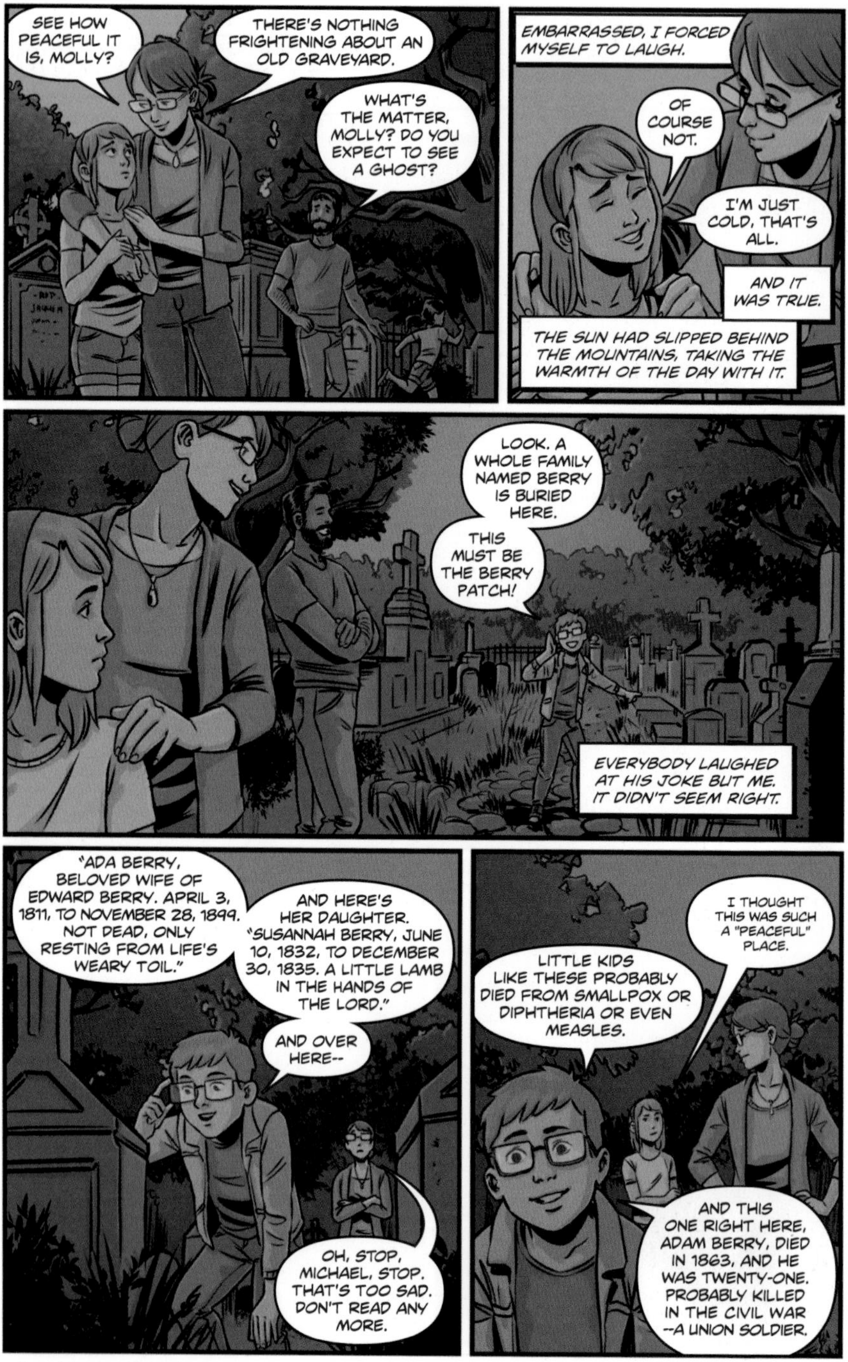
SEE HOW PEACEFUL IT IS, MOLLY?
THERE'S NOTHING FRIGHTENING ABOUT AN OLD GRAVEYARD.
WHAT'S THE MATTER, MOLLY? DO YOU EXPECT TO SEE A GHOST?
EMBARRASSED, I FORCED MYSELF TO LAUGH.
OF COURSE NOT.
I'M JUST COLD, THAT'S ALL.
AND IT WAS TRUE.
THE SUN HAD SLIPPED BEHIND THE MOUNTAINS, TAKING THE WARMTH OF THE DAY WITH IT.
LOOK. A WHOLE FAMILY NAMED BERRY IS BURIED HERE.
THIS MUST BE THE BERRY PATCH!
EVERYBODY LAUGHED AT HIS JOKE BUT ME. IT DIDN'T SEEM RIGHT.
"ADA BERRY, BELOVED WIFE OF EDWARD BERRY. APRIL 3, 1811, TO NOVEMBER 28, 1899. NOT DEAD, ONLY RESTING FROM LIFE'S WEARY TOIL."
AND HERE'S HER DAUGHTER. "SUSANNAH BERRY, JUNE 10, 1832, TO DECEMBER 30, 1835. A LITTLE LAMB IN THE HANDS OF THE LORD."
AND OVER HERE--
OH, STOP, MICHAEL, STOP. THAT'S TOO SAD. DON'T READ ANY MORE.
I THOUGHT THIS WAS SUCH A "PEACEFUL" PLACE.
LITTLE KIDS LIKE THESE PROBABLY DIED FROM SMALLPOX OR DIPHTHERIA OR EVEN MEASLES.
AND THIS ONE RIGHT HERE, ADAM BERRY, DIED IN 1863, AND HE WAS TWENTY-ONE. PROBABLY KILLED IN THE CIVIL WAR --A UNION SOLDIER.

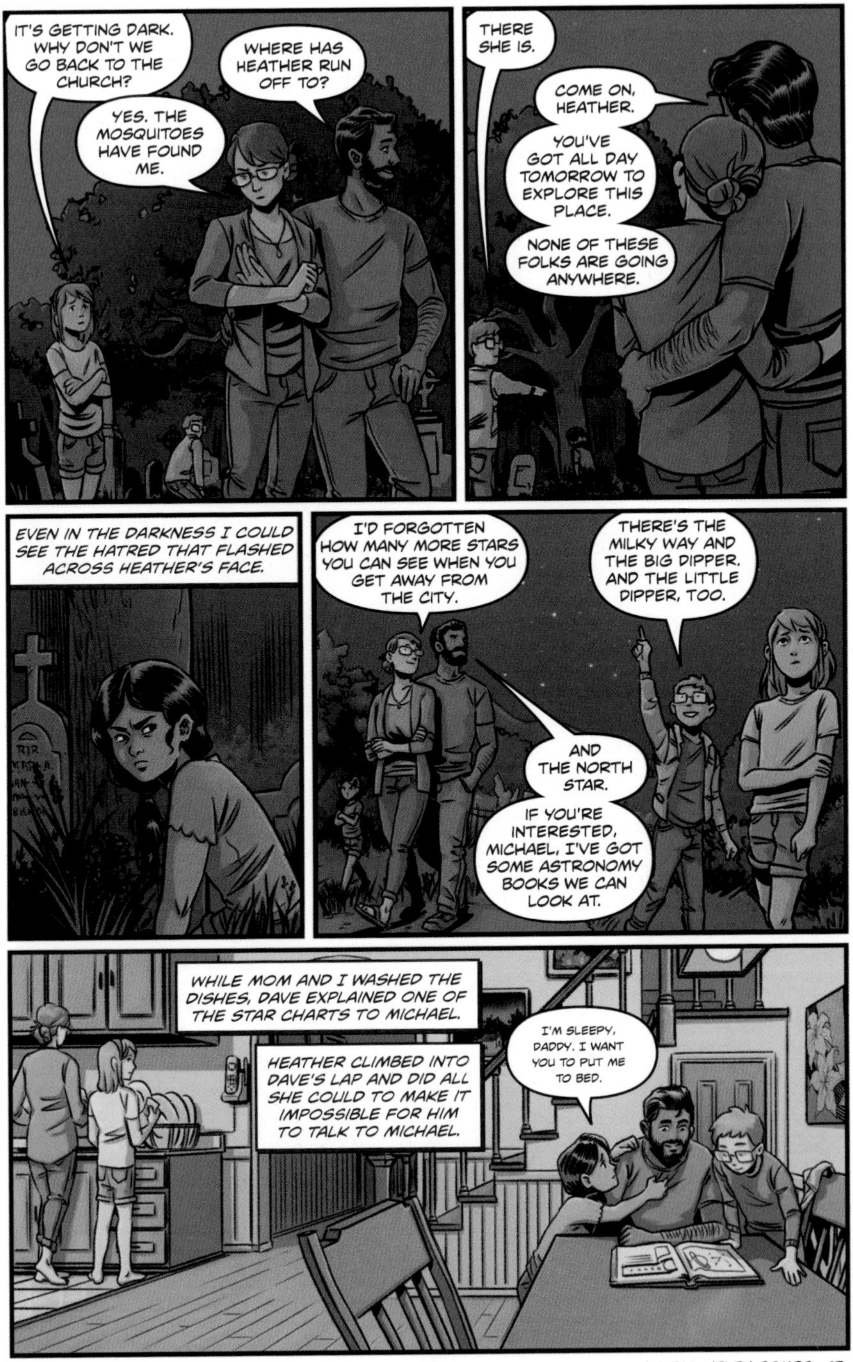
IT'S GETTING DARK. WHY DON'T WE GO BACK TO THE CHURCH?
WHERE HAS HEATHER RUN OFF TO?
YES. THE MOSQUITOES HAVE FOUND ME.
THERE SHE IS.
COME ON, HEATHER.
YOU'VE GOT ALL DAY TOMORROW TO EXPLORE THIS PLACE.
NONE OF THESE FOLKS ARE GOING ANYWHERE.
EVEN IN THE DARKNESS I COULD SEE THE HATRED THAT FLASHED ACROSS HEATHER'S FACE.
I'D FORGOTTEN HOW MANY MORE STARS YOU CAN SEE WHEN YOU GET AWAY FROM THE CITY.
THERE'S THE MILKY WAY AND THE BIG DIPPER. AND THE LITTLE DIPPER, TOO.
AND THE NORTH STAR.
IF YOU'RE INTERESTED, MICHAEL, I'VE GOT SOME ASTRONOMY BOOKS WE CAN LOOK AT.
WHILE MOM AND I WASHED THE DISHES, DAVE EXPLAINED ONE OF THE STAR CHARTS TO MICHAEL.
HEATHER CLIMBED INTO DAVE'S LAP AND DID ALL SHE COULD TO MAKE IT IMPOSSIBLE FOR HIM TO TALK TO MICHAEL.
I'M SLEEPY, DADDY. I WANT YOU TO PUT ME TO BED.

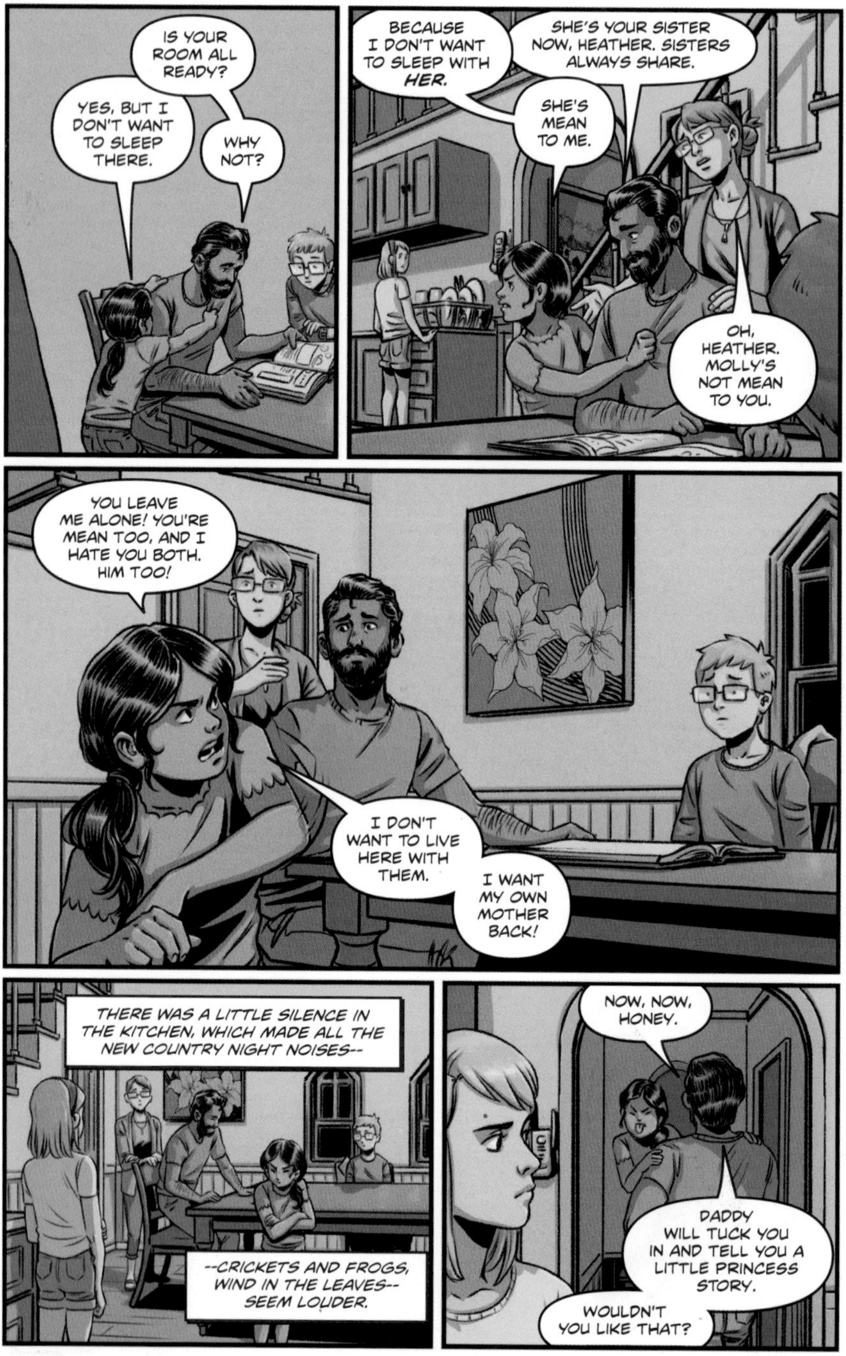
IS YOUR ROOM ALL READY?
YES, BUT I DON'T WANT TO SLEEP THERE.
WHY NOT?
BECAUSE I DON'T WANT TO SLEEP WITH HER.
SHE'S YOUR SISTER NOW, HEATHER. SISTERS ALWAYS SHARE.
SHE'S MEAN TO ME.
OH, HEATHER. MOLLY'S NOT MEAN TO YOU.
YOU LEAVE ME ALONE! YOU'RE MEAN TOO, AND I HATE YOU BOTH. HIM TOO!
I DON'T WANT TO LIVE HERE WITH THEM.
I WANT MY OWN MOTHER BACK!
THERE WAS A LITTLE SILENCE IN THE KITCHEN, WHICH MADE ALL THE NEW COUNTRY NIGHT NOISES--
--CRICKETS AND FROGS, WIND IN THE LEAVES-- SEEM LOUDER.
NOW, NOW, HONEY.
DADDY WILL TUCK YOU IN AND TELL YOU A LITTLE PRINCESS STORY.
WOULDN'T YOU LIKE THAT?

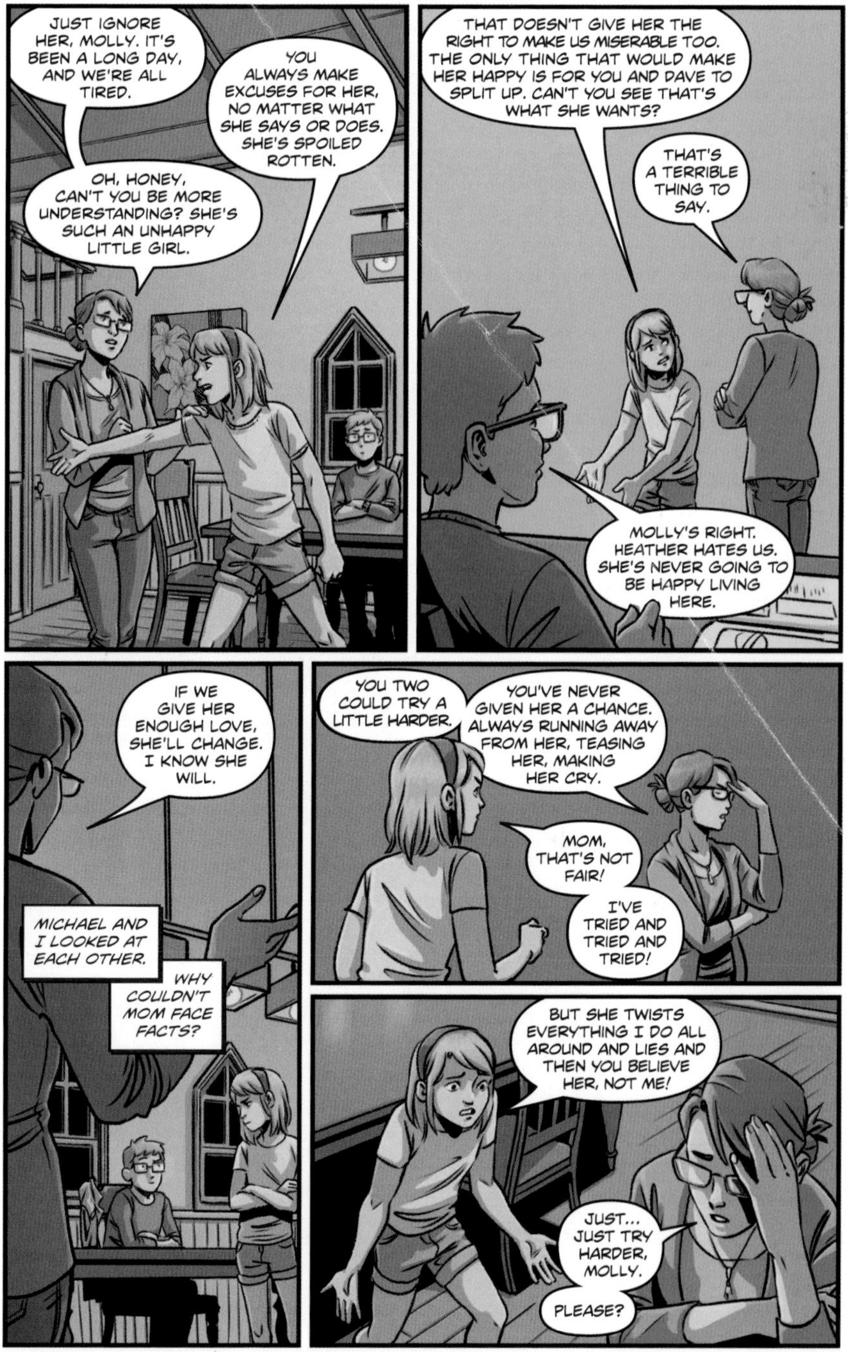
JUST IGNORE HER, MOLLY. IT'S BEEN A LONG DAY, AND WE'RE ALL TIRED.
OH, HONEY, CAN'T YOU BE MORE UNDERSTANDING? SHE'S SUCH AN UNHAPPY LITTLE GIRL.
YOU ALWAYS MAKE EXCUSES FOR HER, NO MATTER WHAT SHE SAYS OR DOES. SHE'S SPOILED ROTTEN.
THAT DOESN'T GIVE HER THE RIGHT TO MAKE US MISERABLE TOO. THE ONLY THING THAT WOULD MAKE HER HAPPY IS FOR YOU AND DAVE TO SPLIT UP. CAN'T YOU SEE THAT'S WHAT SHE WANTS?
THAT'S A TERRIBLE THING TO SAY.
MOLLY'S RIGHT. HEATHER HATES US. SHE'S NEVER GOING TO BE HAPPY LIVING HERE.
IF WE GIVE HER ENOUGH LOVE, SHE'LL CHANGE. I KNOW SHE WILL.
MICHAEL AND I LOOKED AT EACH OTHER.
WHY COULDN'T MOM FACE FACTS?
YOU TWO COULD TRY A LITTLE HARDER.
YOU'VE NEVER GIVEN HER A CHANCE. ALWAYS RUNNING AWAY FROM HER, TEASING HER, MAKING HER CRY.
MOM, THAT'S NOT FAIR!
I'VE TRIED AND TRIED AND TRIED!
BUT SHE TWISTS EVERYTHING I DO ALL AROUND AND LIES AND THEN YOU BELIEVE HER, NOT ME!
JUST... JUST TRY HARDER, MOLLY.
PLEASE?

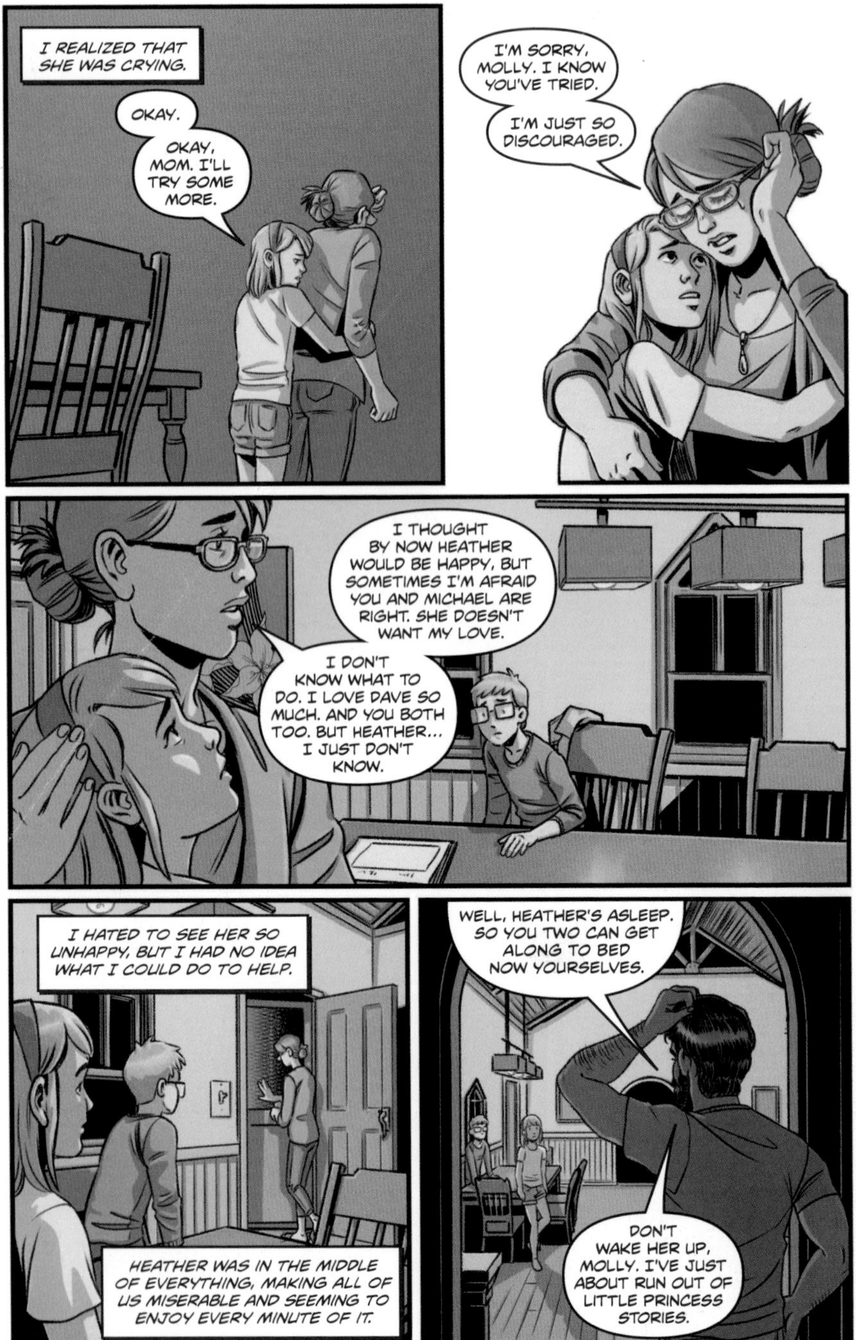
I REALIZED THAT SHE WAS CRYING.
OKAY.
OKAY, MOM. I'LL TRY SOME MORE.
I'M SORRY, MOLLY. I KNOW YOU'VE TRIED.
I'M JUST SO DISCOURAGED.
I THOUGHT BY NOW HEATHER WOULD BE HAPPY, BUT SOMETIMES I'M AFRAID YOU AND MICHAEL ARE RIGHT. SHE DOESN'T WANT MY LOVE.
I DON'T KNOW WHAT TO DO. I LOVE DAVE SO MUCH. AND YOU BOTH TOO. BUT HEATHER... I JUST DON'T KNOW.
I HATED TO SEE HER SO UNHAPPY, BUT I HAD NO IDEA WHAT I COULD DO TO HELP.
HEATHER WAS IN THE MIDDLE OF EVERYTHING, MAKING ALL OF US MISERABLE AND SEEMING TO ENJOY EVERY MINUTE OF IT.
WELL, HEATHER'S ASLEEP. SO YOU TWO CAN GET ALONG TO BED NOW YOURSELVES.
DON'T WAKE HER UP, MOLLY. I'VE JUST ABOUT RUN OUT OF LITTLE PRINCESS STORIES.

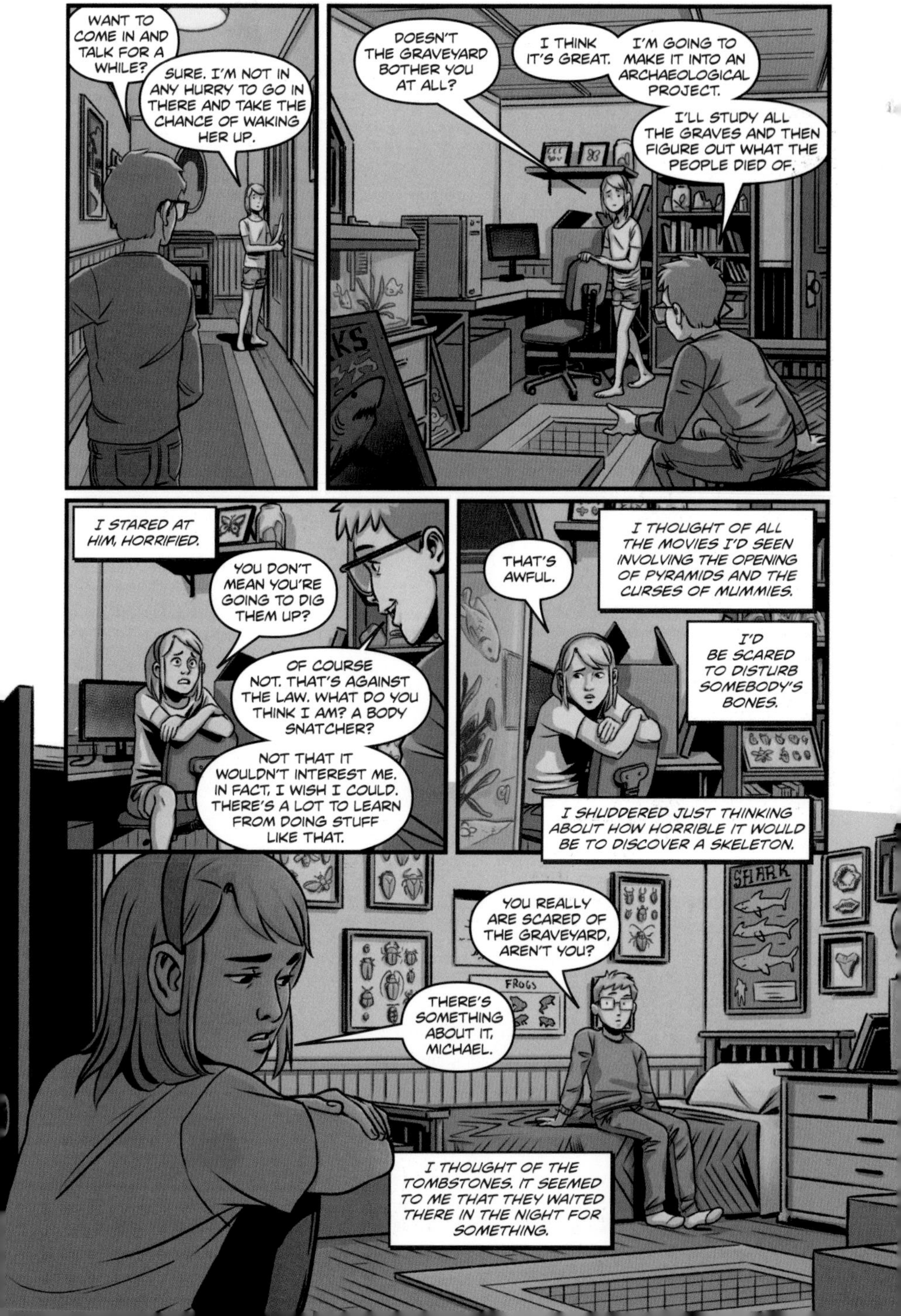

WANT TO COME IN AND TALK FOR A WHILE?
SURE. I'M NOT IN ANY HURRY TO GO IN THERE AND TAKE THE CHANCE OF WAKING HER UP.
DOESN'T THE GRAVEYARD BOTHER YOU AT ALL?
I THINK IT'S GREAT.
I'M GOING TO MAKE IT INTO AN ARCHAEOLOGICAL PROJECT.
I'LL STUDY ALL THE GRAVES AND THEN FIGURE OUT WHAT THE PEOPLE DIED OF.
I STARED AT HIM, HORRIFIED.
YOU DON'T MEAN YOU'RE GOING TO DIG THEM UP?
OF COURSE NOT. THAT'S AGAINST THE LAW. WHAT DO YOU THINK I AM? A BODY SNATCHER?
NOT THAT IT WOULDN'T INTEREST ME. IN FACT, I WISH I COULD. THERE'S A LOT TO LEARN FROM DOING STUFF LIKE THAT.
THAT'S AWFUL.
I THOUGHT OF ALL THE MOVIES I'D SEEN INVOLVING THE OPENING OF PYRAMIDS AND THE CURSES OF MUMMIES.
I'D BE SCARED TO DISTURB SOMEBODY'S BONES.
I SHUDDERED JUST THINKING ABOUT HOW HORRIBLE IT WOULD BE TO DISCOVER A SKELETON.
YOU REALLY ARE SCARED OF THE GRAVEYARD, AREN'T YOU?
THERE'S SOMETHING ABOUT IT, MICHAEL.
I THOUGHT OF THE TOMBSTONES. IT SEEMED TO ME THAT THEY WAITED THERE IN THE NIGHT FOR SOMETHING.

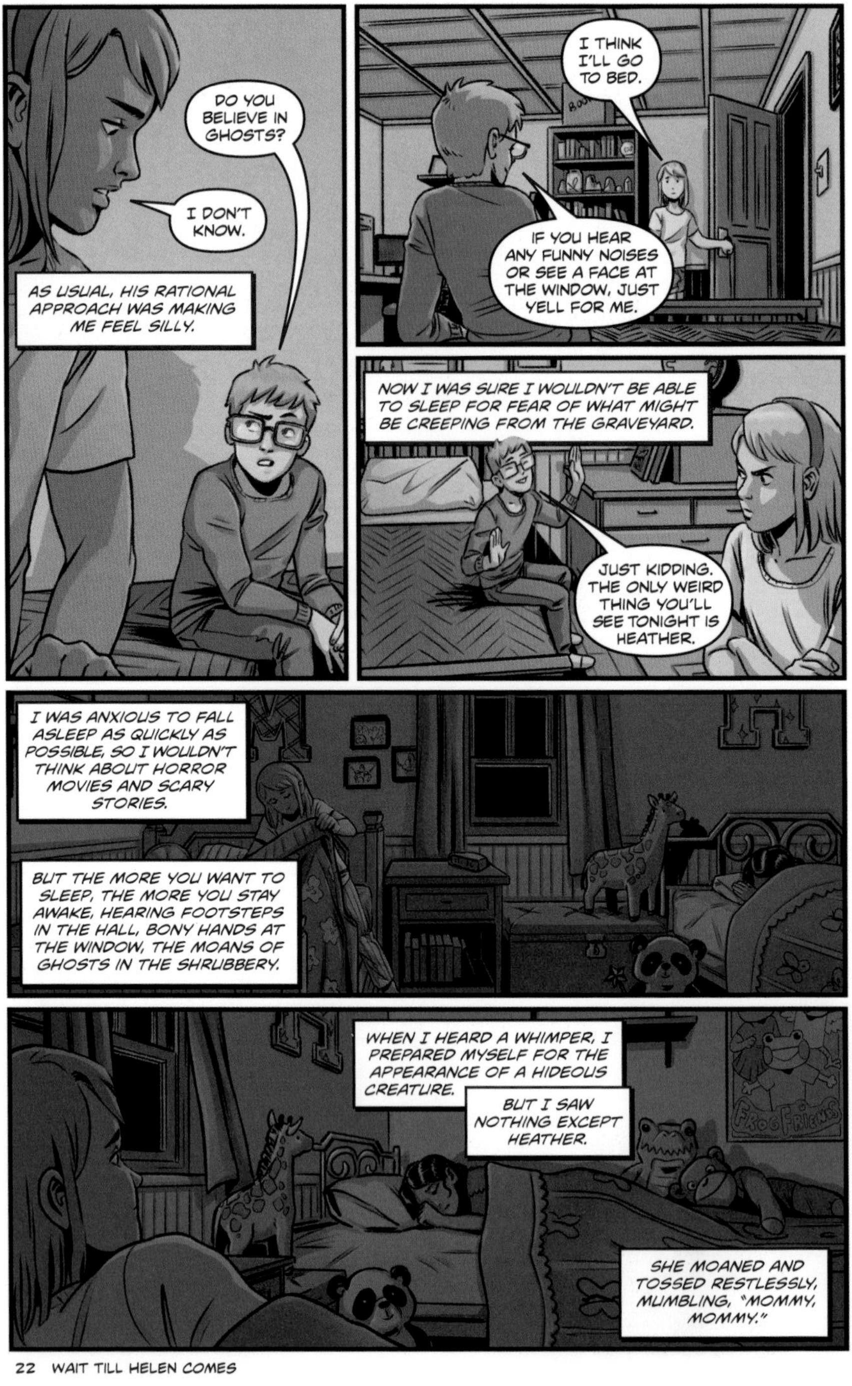
DO YOU BELIEVE IN GHOSTS?
I DON'T KNOW.
AS USUAL, HIS RATIONAL APPROACH WAS MAKING ME FEEL SILLY.
I THINK I'LL GO TO BED.
IF YOU HEAR ANY FUNNY NOISES OR SEE A FACE AT THE WINDOW, JUST YELL FOR ME.
NOW I WAS SURE I WOULDN'T BE ABLE TO SLEEP FOR FEAR OF WHAT MIGHT BE CREEPING FROM THE GRAVEYARD.
JUST KIDDING. THE ONLY WEIRD THING YOU'LL SEE TONIGHT IS HEATHER.
I WAS ANXIOUS TO FALL ASLEEP AS QUICKLY AS POSSIBLE, SO I WOULDN'T THINK ABOUT HORROR MOVIES AND SCARY STORIES.
BUT THE MORE YOU WANT TO SLEEP, THE MORE YOU STAY AWAKE, HEARING FOOTSTEPS IN THE HALL, BONY HANDS AT THE WINDOW, THE MOANS OF GHOSTS IN THE SHRUBBERY.
WHEN I HEARD A WHIMPER, I PREPARED MYSELF FOR THE APPEARANCE OF A HIDEOUS CREATURE.
BUT I SAW NOTHING EXCEPT HEATHER.
FROG FRIENDS
SHE MOANED AND TOSSED RESTLESSLY, MUMBLING, "MOMMY, MOMMY."

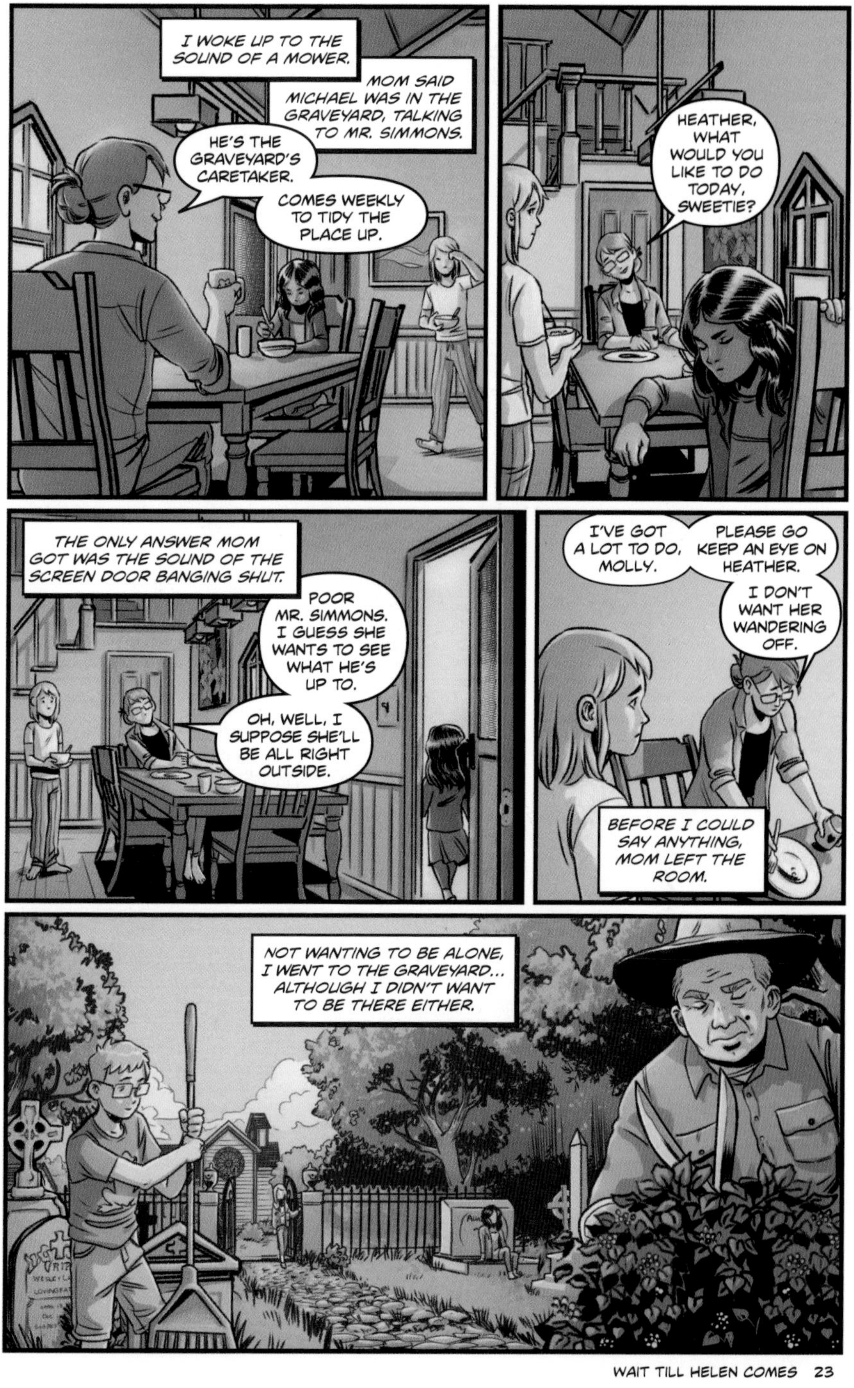
I WOKE UP TO THE SOUND OF A MOWER.
MOM SAID MICHAEL WAS IN THE GRAVEYARD, TALKING TO MR. SIMMONS.
HE'S THE GRAVEYARD'S CARETAKER.
COMES WEEKLY TO TIDY THE PLACE UP.
HEATHER, WHAT WOULD YOU LIKE TO DO TODAY, SWEETIE?
THE ONLY ANSWER MOM GOT WAS THE SOUND OF THE SCREEN DOOR BANGING SHUT.
POOR MR. SIMMONS. I GUESS SHE WANTS TO SEE WHAT HE'S UP TO.
OH, WELL, I SUPPOSE SHE'LL BE ALL RIGHT OUTSIDE.
I'VE GOT A LOT TO DO, MOLLY.
PLEASE GO KEEP AN EYE ON HEATHER.
I DON'T WANT HER WANDERING OFF.
BEFORE I COULD SAY ANYTHING, MOM LEFT THE ROOM.
NOT WANTING TO BE ALONE, I WENT TO THE GRAVEYARD... ALTHOUGH I DIDN'T WANT TO BE THERE EITHER.

HEATHER SAW ME HESITATING AT THE GATE.

MOLLY'S AFRAID TO COME IN HERE.

SHE THINKS SOMETHING'S GOING TO GET HER.

R.I.P.
ALLIE PIPIT
BELOVED FRIE
AND
LEADER

WELL, GOOD MORNING, MOLLY.

WON'T YOU JOIN US?

MR. SIMMONS SAYS THIS IS A REAL OLD GRAVEYARD. THE CHURCH WAS BUILT WAY BACK IN 1825, SO SOME OF THE GRAVES ARE NEARLY 200 YEARS OLD.

THE CIVIL WAR HADN'T EVEN HAPPENED YET.

BUT NOBODY'S BEEN BURIED HERE SINCE 1950. ISN'T THAT RIGHT?

THEY FILLED THE GRAVEYARD UP. OLD MRS. PERKINS THERE WAS THE LAST ONE TO GET IN. MY FIRST-GRADE TEACHER.

NOT HANDING OUT ANY MORE REPORT CARDS NOW, IS SHE?

DEAR DEPARTED
CAROLINE PERKINS
WIFE OF JOHN ALBERT PERKINS
SHE WILL LONG BE MISSED

MICHAEL LAUGHED, BUT I FELT SAD JUST THINKING ABOUT MRS. PERKINS.

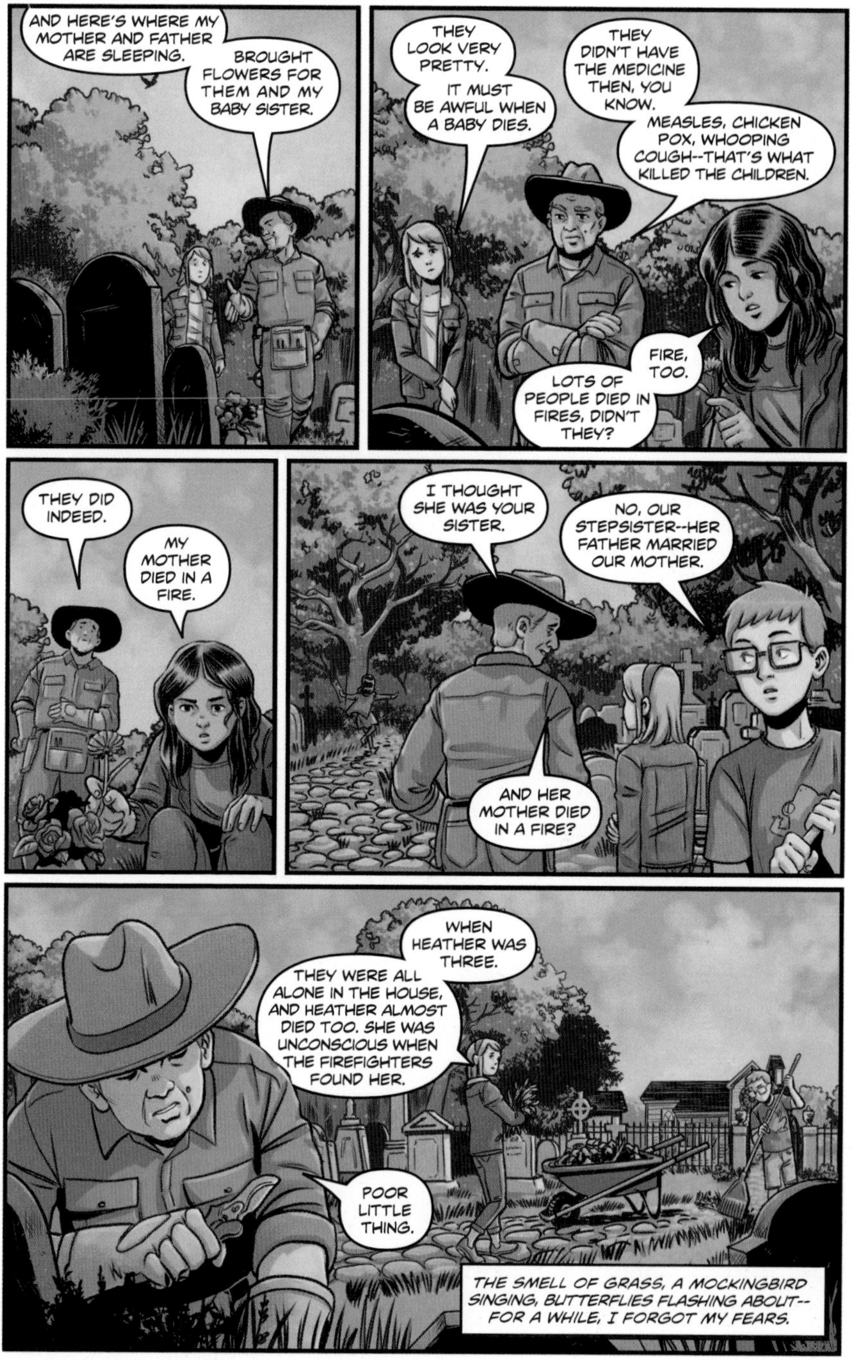
AND HERE'S WHERE MY MOTHER AND FATHER ARE SLEEPING.
BROUGHT FLOWERS FOR THEM AND MY BABY SISTER.
THEY LOOK VERY PRETTY.
IT MUST BE AWFUL WHEN A BABY DIES.
THEY DIDN'T HAVE THE MEDICINE THEN, YOU KNOW.
MEASLES, CHICKEN POX, WHOOPING COUGH--THAT'S WHAT KILLED THE CHILDREN.
FIRE, TOO.
LOTS OF PEOPLE DIED IN FIRES, DIDN'T THEY?
THEY DID INDEED.
MY MOTHER DIED IN A FIRE.
I THOUGHT SHE WAS YOUR SISTER.
NO, OUR STEPSISTER--HER FATHER MARRIED OUR MOTHER.
AND HER MOTHER DIED IN A FIRE?
WHEN HEATHER WAS THREE.
THEY WERE ALL ALONE IN THE HOUSE, AND HEATHER ALMOST DIED TOO. SHE WAS UNCONSCIOUS WHEN THE FIREFIGHTERS FOUND HER.
POOR LITTLE THING.
THE SMELL OF GRASS, A MOCKINGBIRD SINGING, BUTTERFLIES FLASHING ABOUT-- FOR A WHILE, I FORGOT MY FEARS.

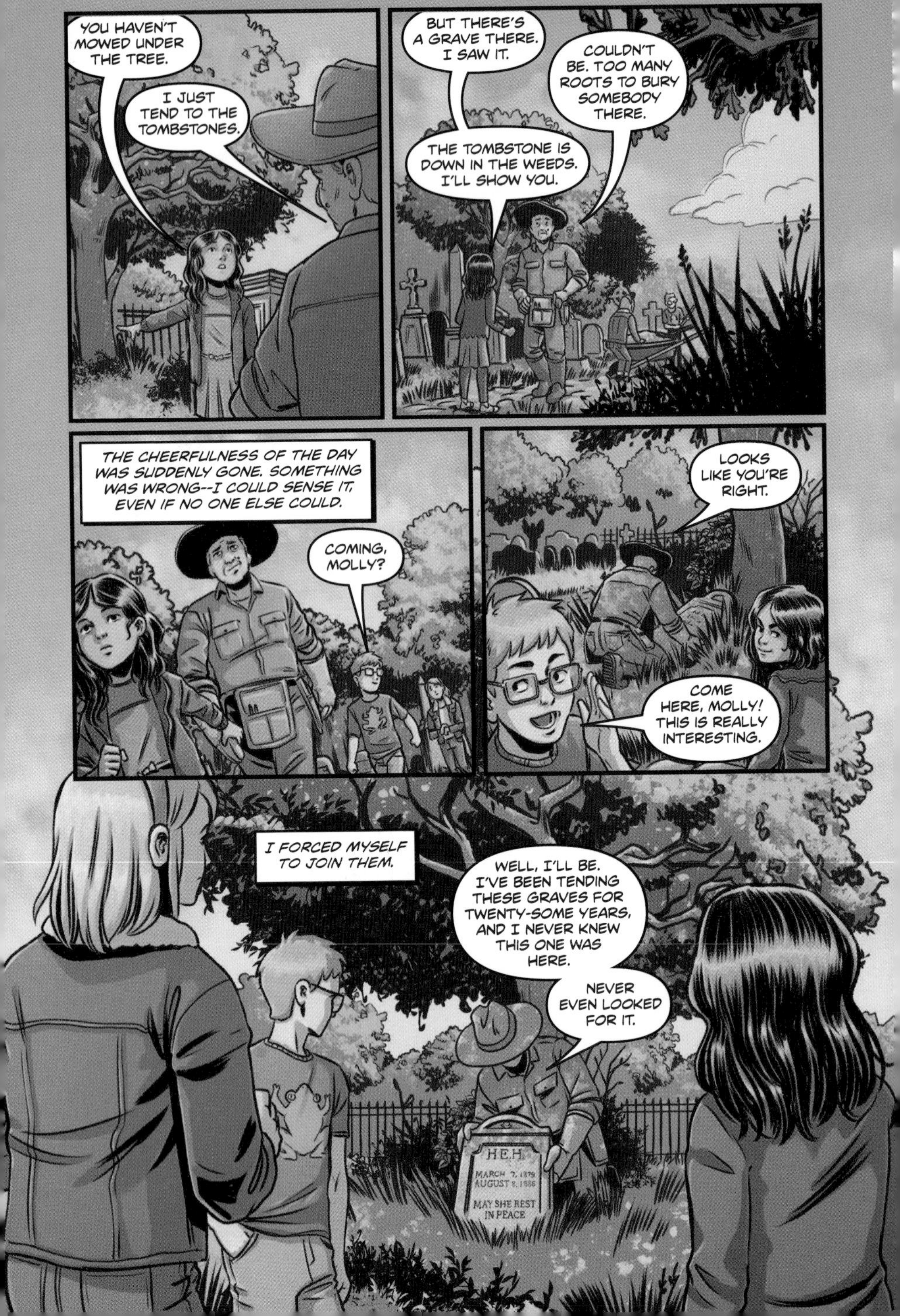
YOU HAVEN'T MOWED UNDER THE TREE.
I JUST TEND TO THE TOMBSTONES.
BUT THERE'S A GRAVE THERE. I SAW IT.
COULDN'T BE. TOO MANY ROOTS TO BURY SOMEBODY THERE.
THE TOMBSTONE IS DOWN IN THE WEEDS. I'LL SHOW YOU.
THE CHEERFULNESS OF THE DAY WAS SUDDENLY GONE. SOMETHING WAS WRONG--I COULD SENSE IT, EVEN IF NO ONE ELSE COULD.
COMING, MOLLY?
LOOKS LIKE YOU'RE RIGHT.
COME HERE, MOLLY! THIS IS REALLY INTERESTING.
I FORCED MYSELF TO JOIN THEM.
WELL, I'LL BE. I'VE BEEN TENDING THESE GRAVES FOR TWENTY-SOME YEARS, AND I NEVER KNEW THIS ONE WAS HERE.
NEVER EVEN LOOKED FOR IT.
H.E.H.
MARCH 7, 1879
AUGUST 8, 1886
MAY SHE REST IN PEACE

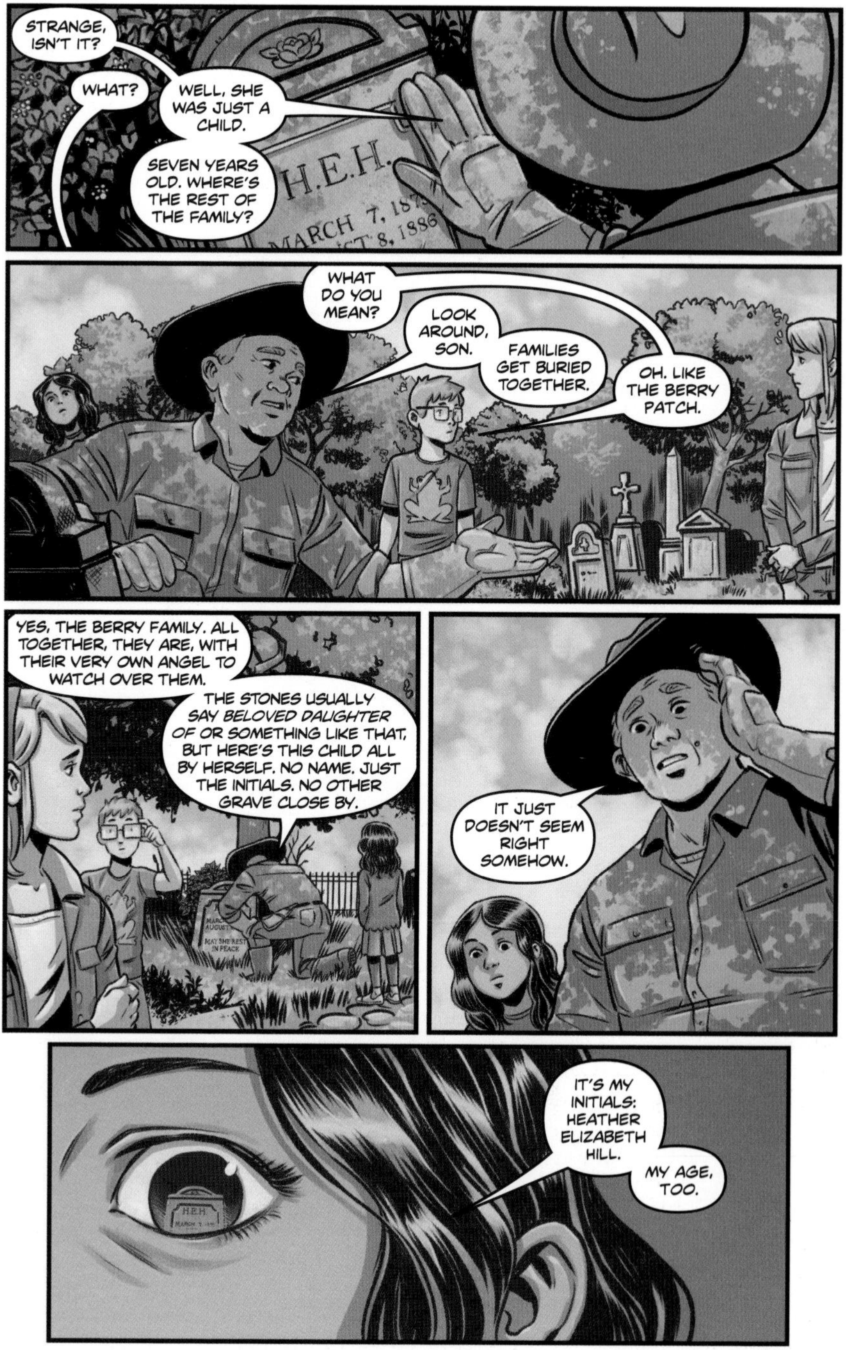
STRANGE, ISN'T IT?
WHAT?
WELL, SHE WAS JUST A CHILD.
SEVEN YEARS OLD. WHERE'S THE REST OF THE FAMILY?
H.E.H.
MARCH 7, 187
ST 8, 1886
WHAT DO YOU MEAN?
LOOK AROUND, SON.
FAMILIES GET BURIED TOGETHER.
OH. LIKE THE BERRY PATCH.
YES, THE BERRY FAMILY. ALL TOGETHER, THEY ARE, WITH THEIR VERY OWN ANGEL TO WATCH OVER THEM.
THE STONES USUALLY SAY *BELOVED DAUGHTER OF* OR SOMETHING LIKE THAT, BUT HERE'S THIS CHILD ALL BY HERSELF. NO NAME. JUST THE INITIALS. NO OTHER GRAVE CLOSE BY.
MAY SHE REST IN PEACE
IT JUST DOESN'T SEEM RIGHT SOMEHOW.
IT'S MY INITIALS: HEATHER ELIZABETH HILL.
MY AGE, TOO.

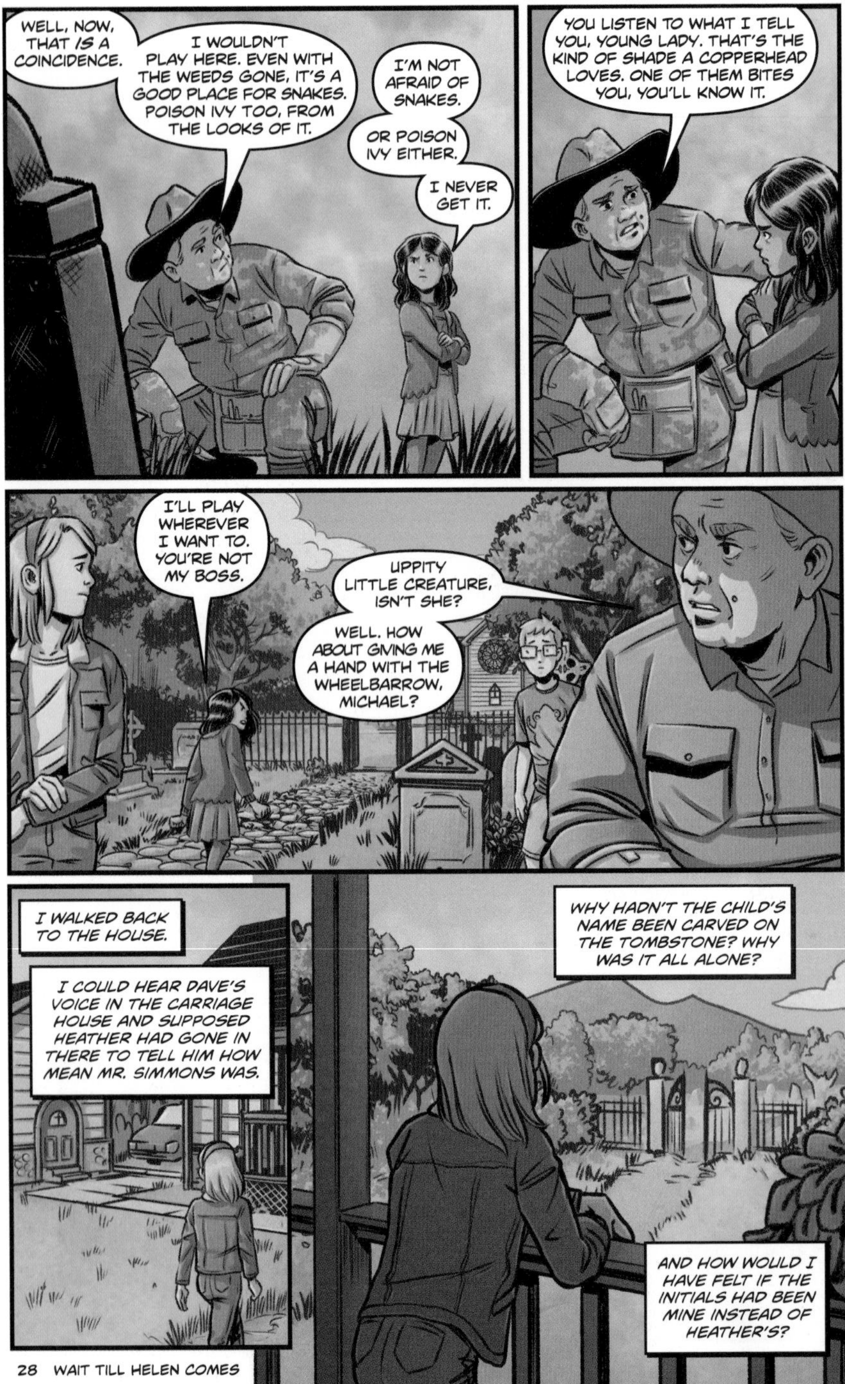
WELL, NOW, THAT *IS* A COINCIDENCE.
I WOULDN'T PLAY HERE. EVEN WITH THE WEEDS GONE, IT'S A GOOD PLACE FOR SNAKES. POISON IVY TOO, FROM THE LOOKS OF IT.
I'M NOT AFRAID OF SNAKES.
OR POISON IVY EITHER.
I NEVER GET IT.
YOU LISTEN TO WHAT I TELL YOU, YOUNG LADY. THAT'S THE KIND OF SHADE A COPPERHEAD LOVES. ONE OF THEM BITES YOU, YOU'LL KNOW IT.
I'LL PLAY WHEREVER I WANT TO. YOU'RE NOT MY BOSS.
UPPITY LITTLE CREATURE, ISN'T SHE?
WELL. HOW ABOUT GIVING ME A HAND WITH THE WHEELBARROW, MICHAEL?
I WALKED BACK TO THE HOUSE.
I COULD HEAR DAVE'S VOICE IN THE CARRIAGE HOUSE AND SUPPOSED HEATHER HAD GONE IN THERE TO TELL HIM HOW MEAN MR. SIMMONS WAS.
WHY HADN'T THE CHILD'S NAME BEEN CARVED ON THE TOMBSTONE? WHY WAS IT ALL ALONE?
AND HOW WOULD I HAVE FELT IF THE INITIALS HAD BEEN MINE INSTEAD OF HEATHER'S?

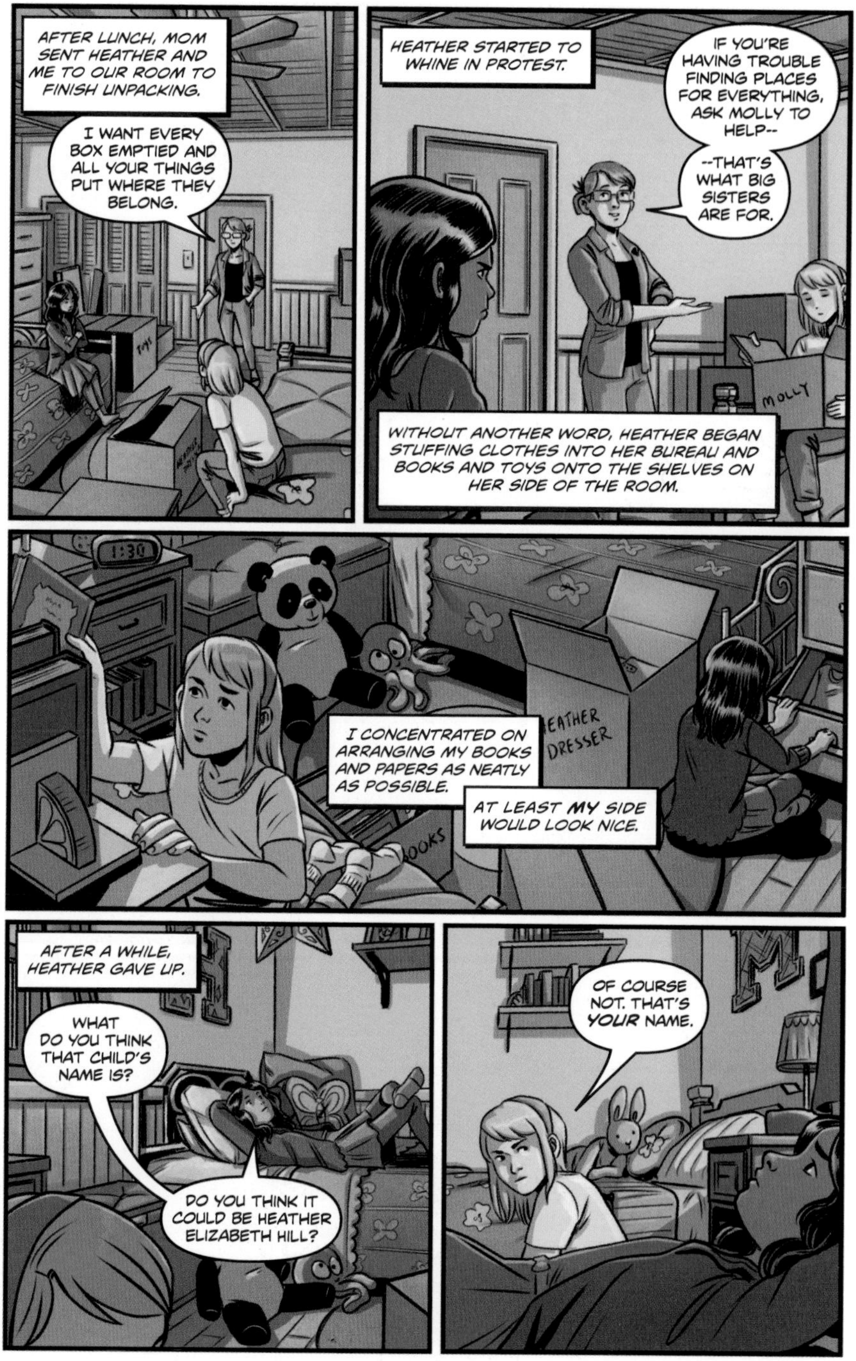
AFTER LUNCH, MOM SENT HEATHER AND ME TO OUR ROOM TO FINISH UNPACKING.
I WANT EVERY BOX EMPTIED AND ALL YOUR THINGS PUT WHERE THEY BELONG.
HEATHER STARTED TO WHINE IN PROTEST.
IF YOU'RE HAVING TROUBLE FINDING PLACES FOR EVERYTHING, ASK MOLLY TO HELP--
--THAT'S WHAT BIG SISTERS ARE FOR.
MOLLY
WITHOUT ANOTHER WORD, HEATHER BEGAN STUFFING CLOTHES INTO HER BUREAU AND BOOKS AND TOYS ONTO THE SHELVES ON HER SIDE OF THE ROOM.
1:30
HEATHER DRESSER
I CONCENTRATED ON ARRANGING MY BOOKS AND PAPERS AS NEATLY AS POSSIBLE.
AT LEAST MY SIDE WOULD LOOK NICE.
BOOKS
AFTER A WHILE, HEATHER GAVE UP.
WHAT DO YOU THINK THAT CHILD'S NAME IS?
DO YOU THINK IT COULD BE HEATHER ELIZABETH HILL?
OF COURSE NOT. THAT'S YOUR NAME.

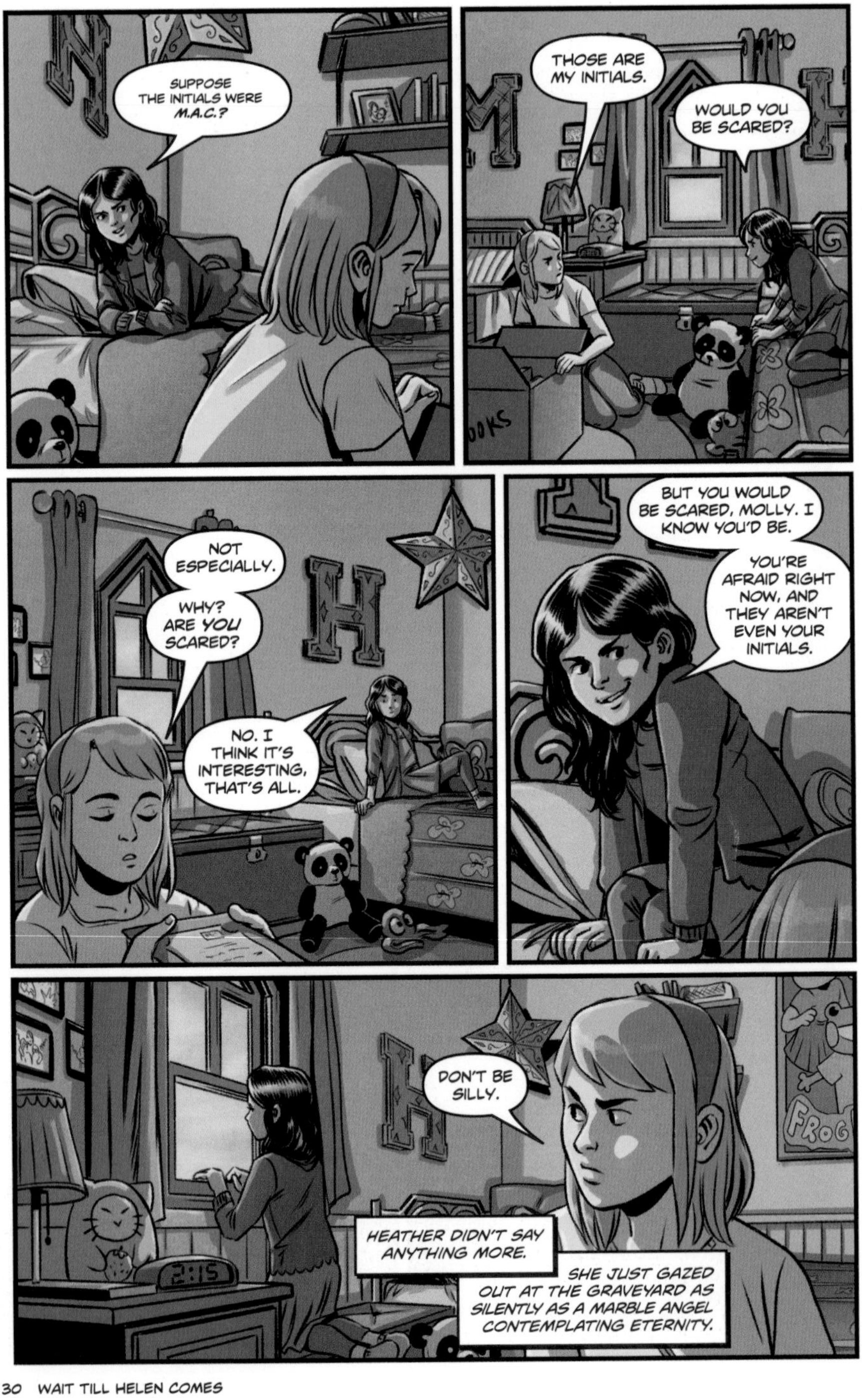
SUPPOSE THE INITIALS WERE *M.A.C.*?
THOSE ARE MY INITIALS.
WOULD YOU BE SCARED?
NOT ESPECIALLY.
WHY? ARE *YOU* SCARED?
NO. I THINK IT'S INTERESTING, THAT'S ALL.
BUT YOU WOULD BE SCARED, MOLLY. I KNOW YOU'D BE.
YOU'RE AFRAID RIGHT NOW, AND THEY AREN'T EVEN YOUR INITIALS.
DON'T BE SILLY.
HEATHER DIDN'T SAY ANYTHING MORE.
SHE JUST GAZED OUT AT THE GRAVEYARD AS SILENTLY AS A MARBLE ANGEL CONTEMPLATING ETERNITY.

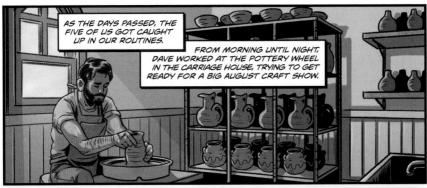

AS THE DAYS PASSED, THE FIVE OF US GOT CAUGHT UP IN OUR ROUTINES.

FROM MORNING UNTIL NIGHT, DAVE WORKED AT THE POTTERY WHEEL IN THE CARRIAGE HOUSE, TRYING TO GET READY FOR A BIG AUGUST CRAFT SHOW.

MOM WAS EXCITED ABOUT HAVING A REAL STUDIO AFTER SO MANY YEARS OF SETTING UP HER EASEL WHEREVER SHE COULD FIND SOME UNOCCUPIED SPACE.

BUT SHE DIDN'T LIKE TO BE WATCHED WHILE SHE WAS PAINTING--IT MADE HER SELF-CONSCIOUS.

SHE'D ALWAYS TELL ME TO GO OUTSIDE AND PLAY. I GUESS SHE FELT THAT WE WERE ALL SAFE OUT HERE IN THE COUNTRY.

THE ONLY THING SHE EVER ASKED ME TO DO WAS TO KEEP AN EYE ON HEATHER. SHE THOUGHT MICHAEL AND I SHOULD TAKE CARE OF HER.

OF COURSE, THAT WAS THE ONE THING NEITHER OF US DID.

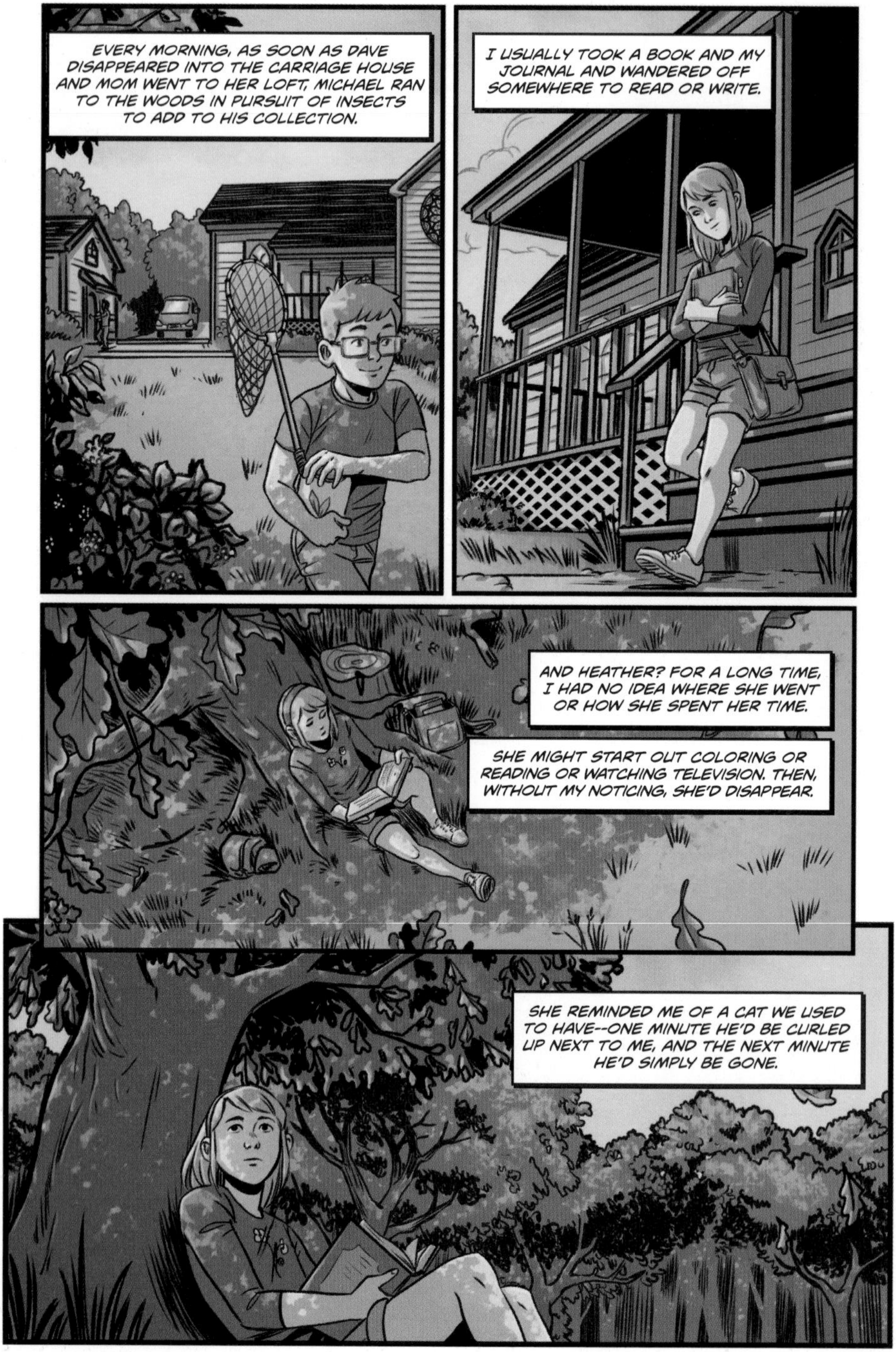
EVERY MORNING, AS SOON AS DAVE DISAPPEARED INTO THE CARRIAGE HOUSE AND MOM WENT TO HER LOFT, MICHAEL RAN TO THE WOODS IN PURSUIT OF INSECTS TO ADD TO HIS COLLECTION.
I USUALLY TOOK A BOOK AND MY JOURNAL AND WANDERED OFF SOMEWHERE TO READ OR WRITE.
AND HEATHER? FOR A LONG TIME, I HAD NO IDEA WHERE SHE WENT OR HOW SHE SPENT HER TIME.
SHE MIGHT START OUT COLORING OR READING OR WATCHING TELEVISION. THEN, WITHOUT MY NOTICING, SHE'D DISAPPEAR.
SHE REMINDED ME OF A CAT WE USED TO HAVE--ONE MINUTE HE'D BE CURLED UP NEXT TO ME, AND THE NEXT MINUTE HE'D SIMPLY BE GONE.

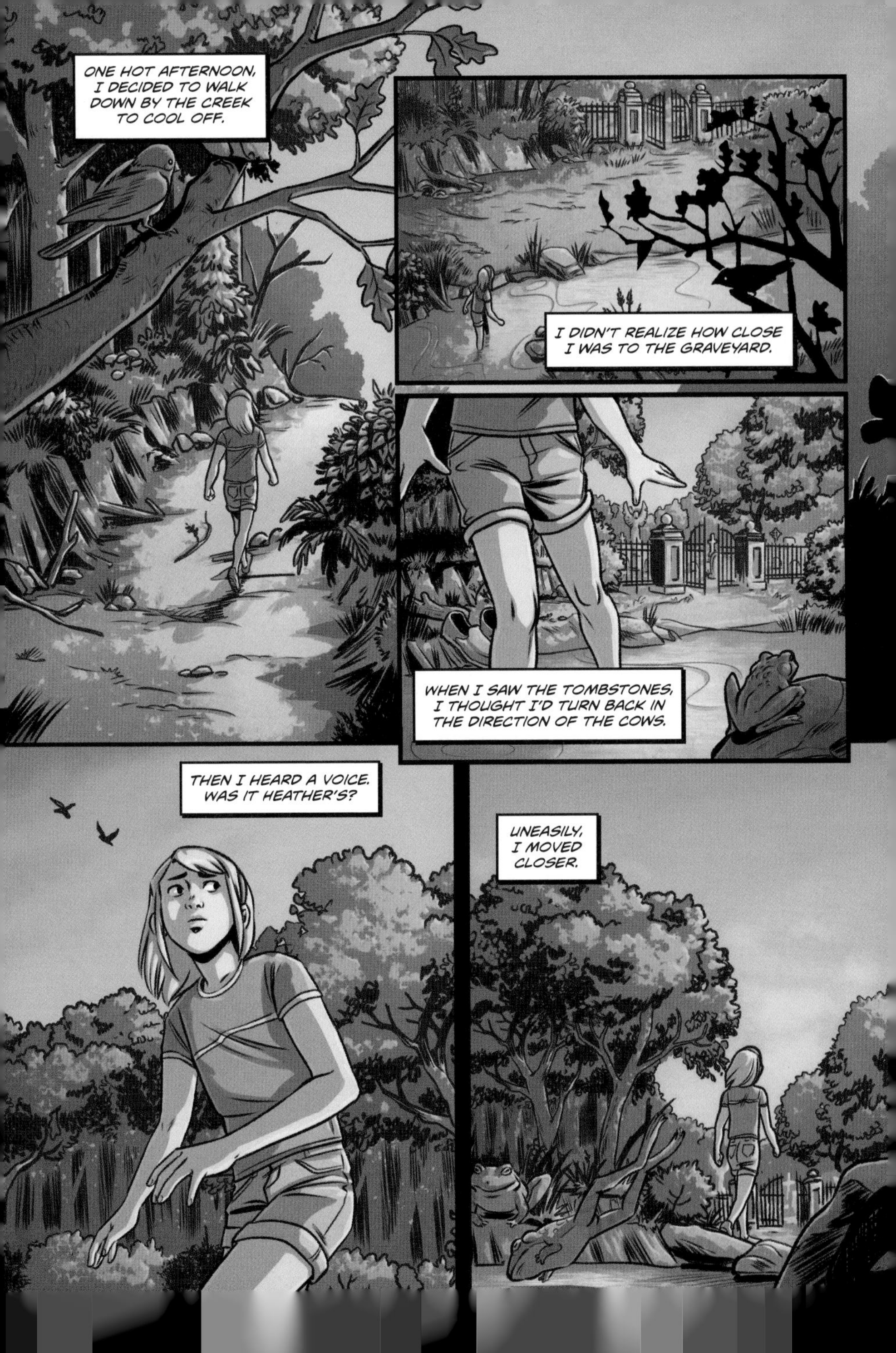
ONE HOT AFTERNOON, I DECIDED TO WALK DOWN BY THE CREEK TO COOL OFF.
I DIDN'T REALIZE HOW CLOSE I WAS TO THE GRAVEYARD.
WHEN I SAW THE TOMBSTONES, I THOUGHT I'D TURN BACK IN THE DIRECTION OF THE COWS.
THEN I HEARD A VOICE. WAS IT HEATHER'S?
UNEASILY, I MOVED CLOSER.

I FOUND HEATHER STARING AT THE SMALL TOMBSTONE UNDER THE OAK.

SHE SEEMED TO BE LISTENING TO SOMETHING...OR SOMEONE.

H.E.H.
MARCH 7, 1879
AUGUST 8, 1886
MAY SHE REST
IN PEACE

OH, HELEN... WILL YOU REALLY BE MY FRIEND?

I'LL DO ANYTHING YOU SAY--I PROMISE I WILL--IF YOU'LL BE MY FRIEND.

THE BREEZE BLEW AGAIN, MAKING A DRY SOUND, A WHISPERING, AND HEATHER NODDED.

I'LL WAIT FOR YOU, HELEN.

WHEN YOU COME, I'LL BE THE BEST FRIEND YOU EVER HAD.

H.E.H.
ARC
UGU
MAY SHE
IN PEACE

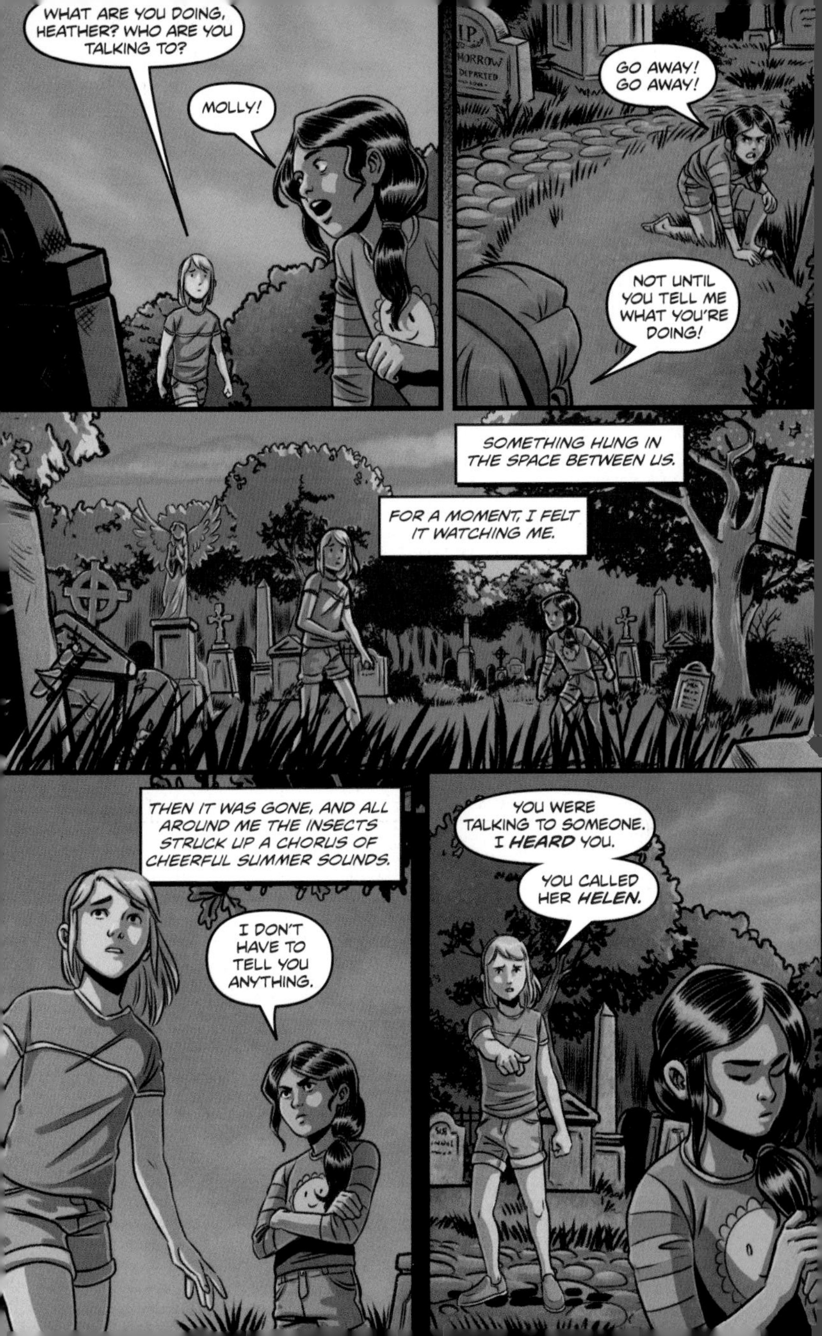
WHAT ARE YOU DOING, HEATHER? WHO ARE YOU TALKING TO?
MOLLY!
GO AWAY! GO AWAY!
NOT UNTIL YOU TELL ME WHAT YOU'RE DOING!
SOMETHING HUNG IN THE SPACE BETWEEN US.
FOR A MOMENT, I FELT IT WATCHING ME.
THEN IT WAS GONE, AND ALL AROUND ME THE INSECTS STRUCK UP A CHORUS OF CHEERFUL SUMMER SOUNDS.
I DON'T HAVE TO TELL YOU ANYTHING.
YOU WERE TALKING TO SOMEONE. I **HEARD** YOU.
YOU CALLED HER **HELEN**.

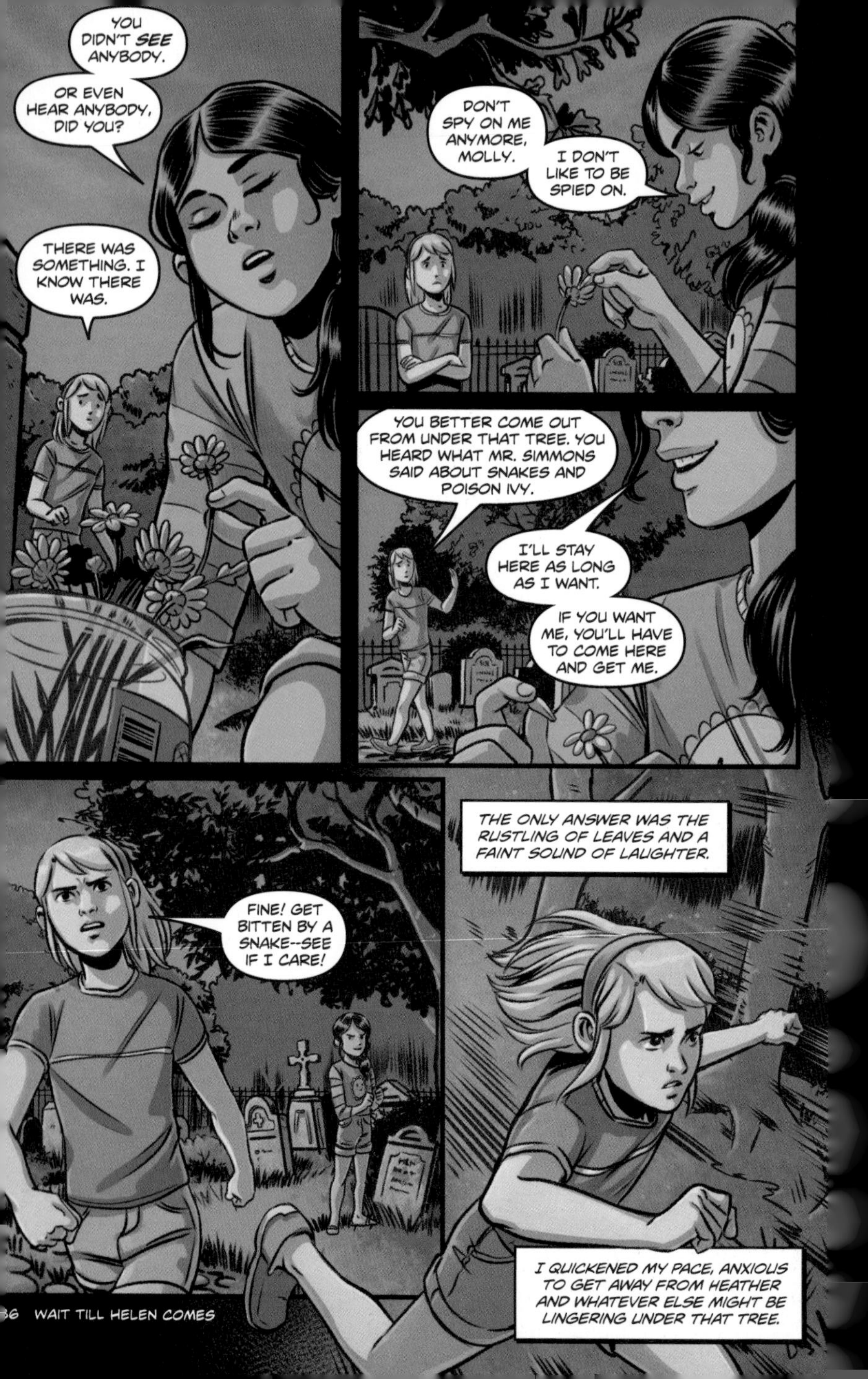
YOU DIDN'T SEE ANYBODY.
OR EVEN HEAR ANYBODY, DID YOU?
THERE WAS SOMETHING. I KNOW THERE WAS.
DON'T SPY ON ME ANYMORE, MOLLY.
I DON'T LIKE TO BE SPIED ON.
YOU BETTER COME OUT FROM UNDER THAT TREE. YOU HEARD WHAT MR. SIMMONS SAID ABOUT SNAKES AND POISON IVY.
I'LL STAY HERE AS LONG AS I WANT.
IF YOU WANT ME, YOU'LL HAVE TO COME HERE AND GET ME.
FINE! GET BITTEN BY A SNAKE--SEE IF I CARE!
THE ONLY ANSWER WAS THE RUSTLING OF LEAVES AND A FAINT SOUND OF LAUGHTER.
I QUICKENED MY PACE, ANXIOUS TO GET AWAY FROM HEATHER AND WHATEVER ELSE MIGHT BE LINGERING UNDER THAT TREE.

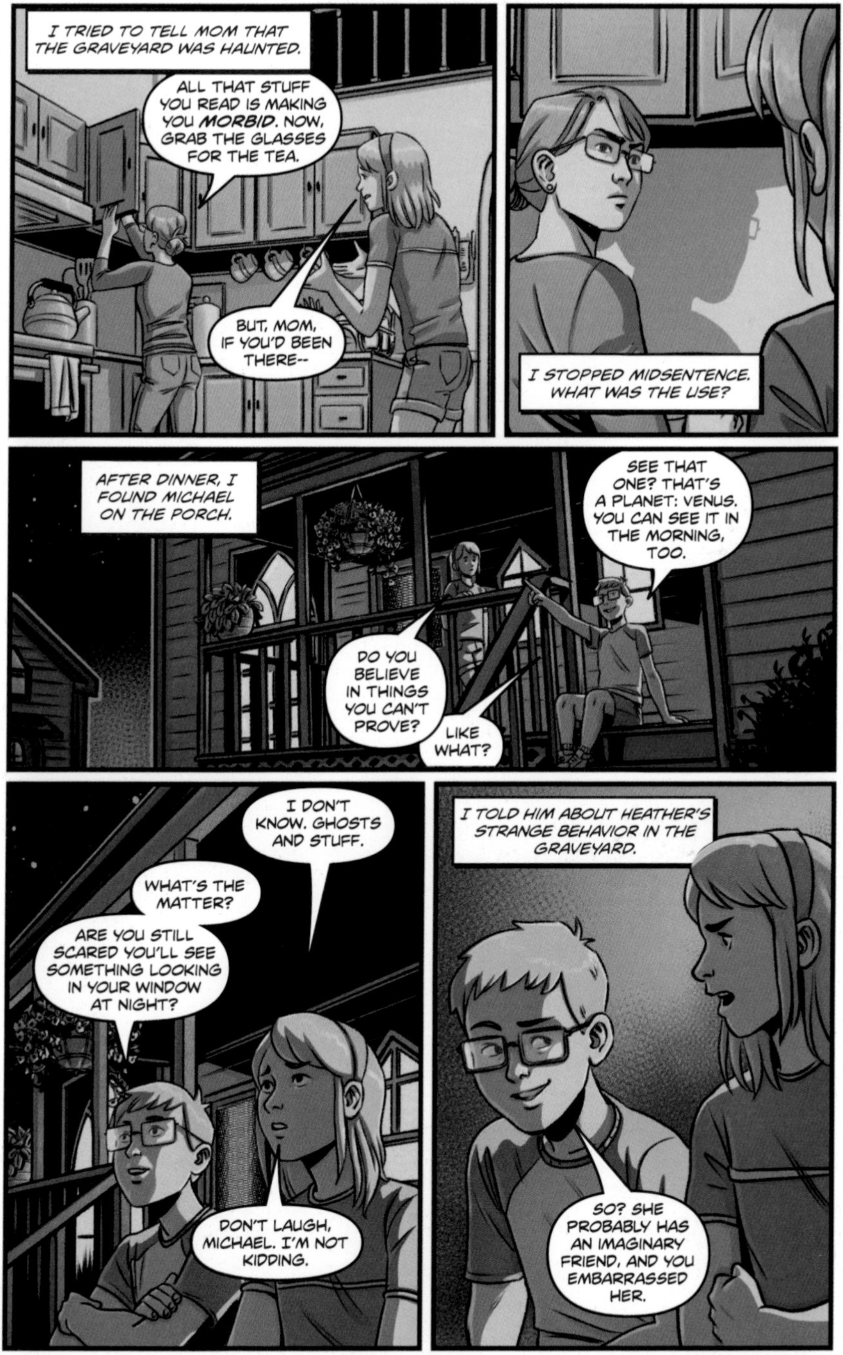
I TRIED TO TELL MOM THAT THE GRAVEYARD WAS HAUNTED.
ALL THAT STUFF YOU READ IS MAKING YOU *MORBID*. NOW, GRAB THE GLASSES FOR THE TEA.
BUT, MOM, IF YOU'D BEEN THERE--
I STOPPED MIDSENTENCE. WHAT WAS THE USE?
AFTER DINNER, I FOUND MICHAEL ON THE PORCH.
SEE THAT ONE? THAT'S A PLANET: VENUS. YOU CAN SEE IT IN THE MORNING, TOO.
DO YOU BELIEVE IN THINGS YOU CAN'T PROVE?
LIKE WHAT?
I DON'T KNOW. GHOSTS AND STUFF.
WHAT'S THE MATTER?
ARE YOU STILL SCARED YOU'LL SEE SOMETHING LOOKING IN YOUR WINDOW AT NIGHT?
DON'T LAUGH, MICHAEL. I'M NOT KIDDING.
I TOLD HIM ABOUT HEATHER'S STRANGE BEHAVIOR IN THE GRAVEYARD.
SO? SHE PROBABLY HAS AN IMAGINARY FRIEND, AND YOU EMBARRASSED HER.

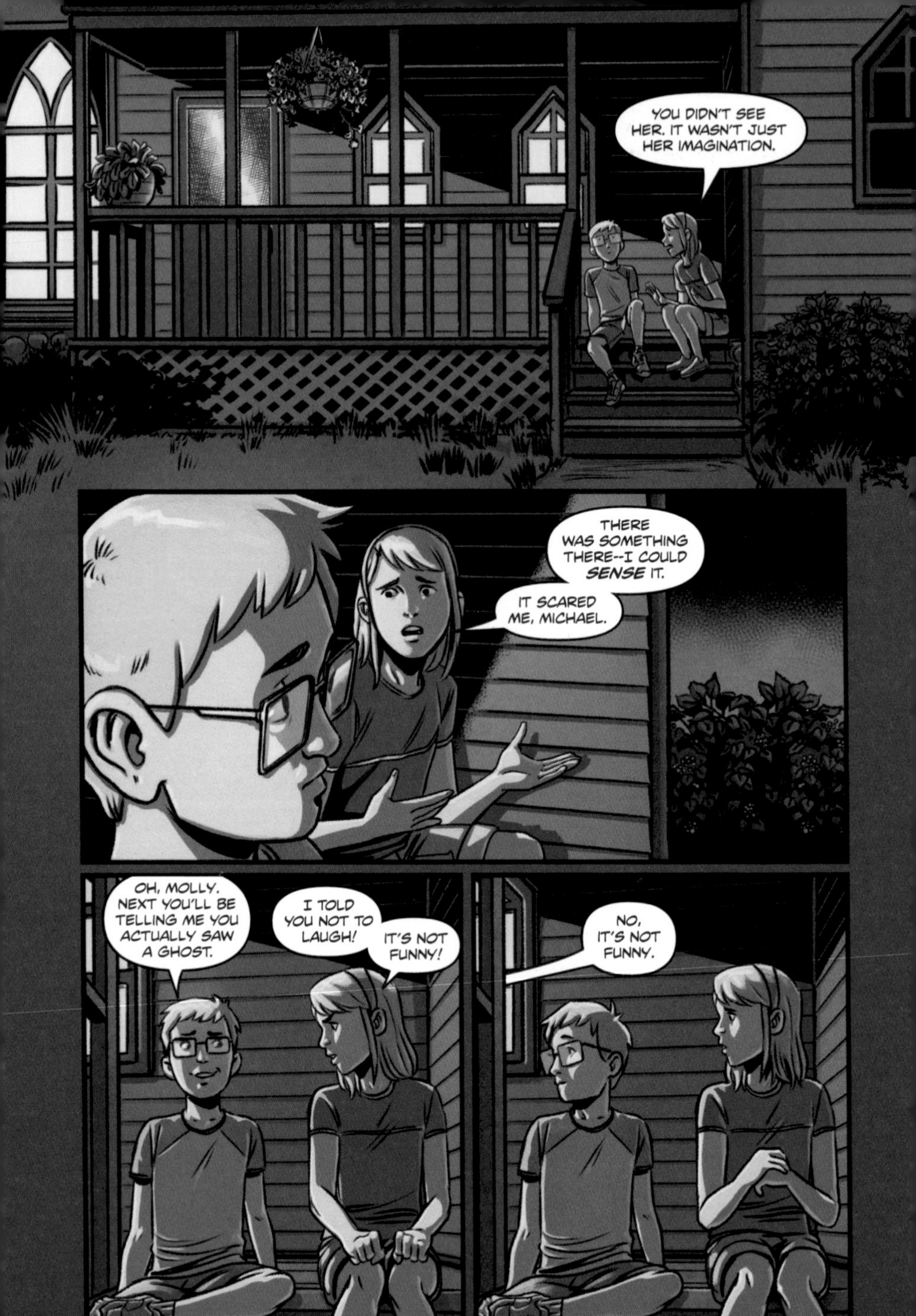
YOU DIDN'T SEE HER. IT WASN'T JUST HER IMAGINATION.
THERE WAS SOMETHING THERE--I COULD *SENSE* IT.
IT SCARED ME, MICHAEL.
OH, MOLLY. NEXT YOU'LL BE TELLING ME YOU ACTUALLY SAW A GHOST.
I TOLD YOU NOT TO LAUGH!
IT'S NOT FUNNY!
NO, IT'S NOT FUNNY.

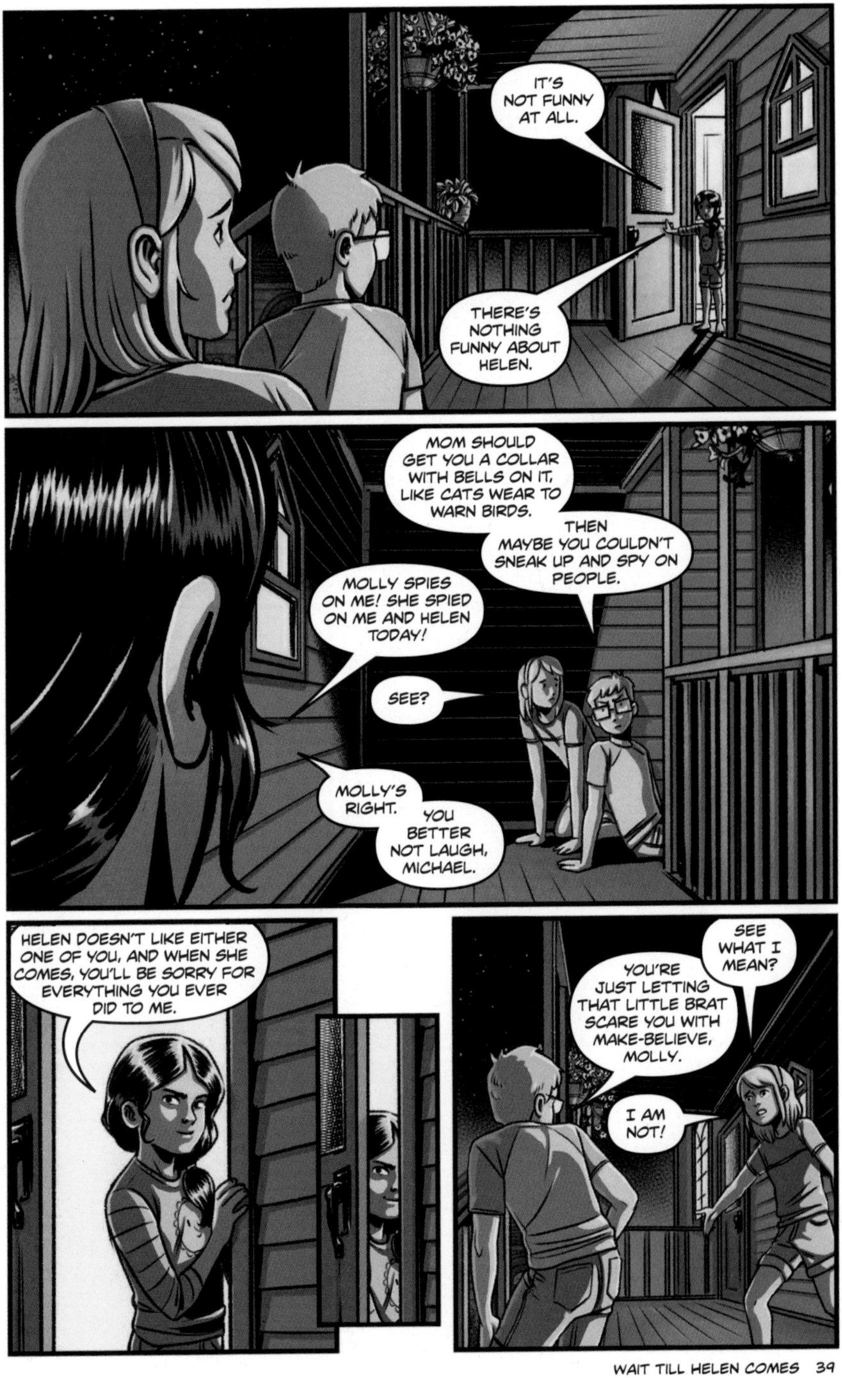
IT'S NOT FUNNY AT ALL.
THERE'S NOTHING FUNNY ABOUT HELEN.
MOM SHOULD GET YOU A COLLAR WITH BELLS ON IT, LIKE CATS WEAR TO WARN BIRDS.
THEN MAYBE YOU COULDN'T SNEAK UP AND SPY ON PEOPLE.
MOLLY SPIES ON ME! SHE SPIED ON ME AND HELEN TODAY!
SEE?
MOLLY'S RIGHT.
YOU BETTER NOT LAUGH, MICHAEL.
HELEN DOESN'T LIKE EITHER ONE OF YOU, AND WHEN SHE COMES, YOU'LL BE SORRY FOR EVERYTHING YOU EVER DID TO ME.
SEE WHAT I MEAN?
YOU'RE JUST LETTING THAT LITTLE BRAT SCARE YOU WITH MAKE-BELIEVE, MOLLY.
I AM NOT!

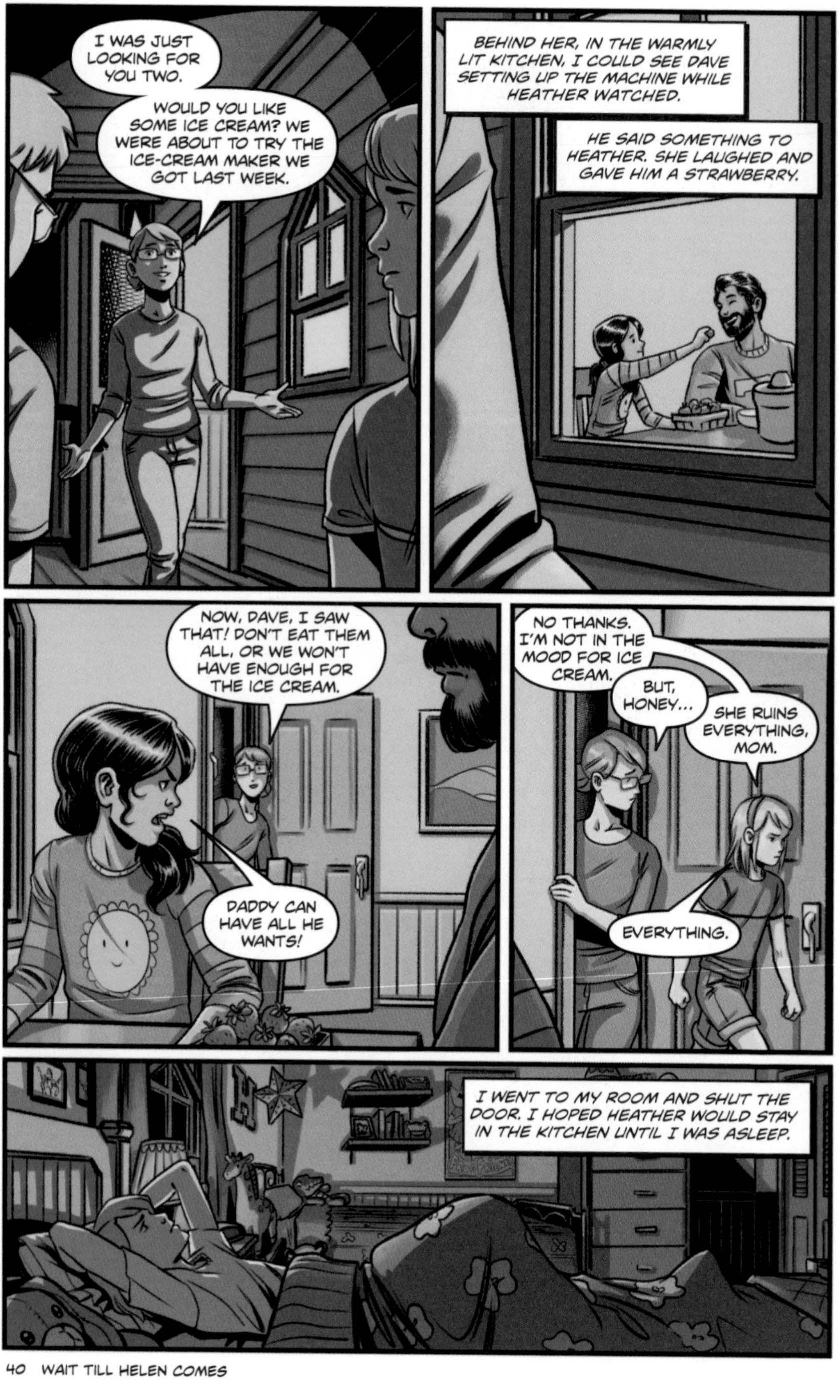
I WAS JUST LOOKING FOR YOU TWO.
WOULD YOU LIKE SOME ICE CREAM? WE WERE ABOUT TO TRY THE ICE-CREAM MAKER WE GOT LAST WEEK.
BEHIND HER, IN THE WARMLY LIT KITCHEN, I COULD SEE DAVE SETTING UP THE MACHINE WHILE HEATHER WATCHED.
HE SAID SOMETHING TO HEATHER. SHE LAUGHED AND GAVE HIM A STRAWBERRY.
NOW, DAVE, I SAW THAT! DON'T EAT THEM ALL, OR WE WON'T HAVE ENOUGH FOR THE ICE CREAM.
DADDY CAN HAVE ALL HE WANTS!
NO THANKS. I'M NOT IN THE MOOD FOR ICE CREAM.
BUT, HONEY...
SHE RUINS EVERYTHING, MOM.
EVERYTHING.
I WENT TO MY ROOM AND SHUT THE DOOR. I HOPED HEATHER WOULD STAY IN THE KITCHEN UNTIL I WAS ASLEEP.

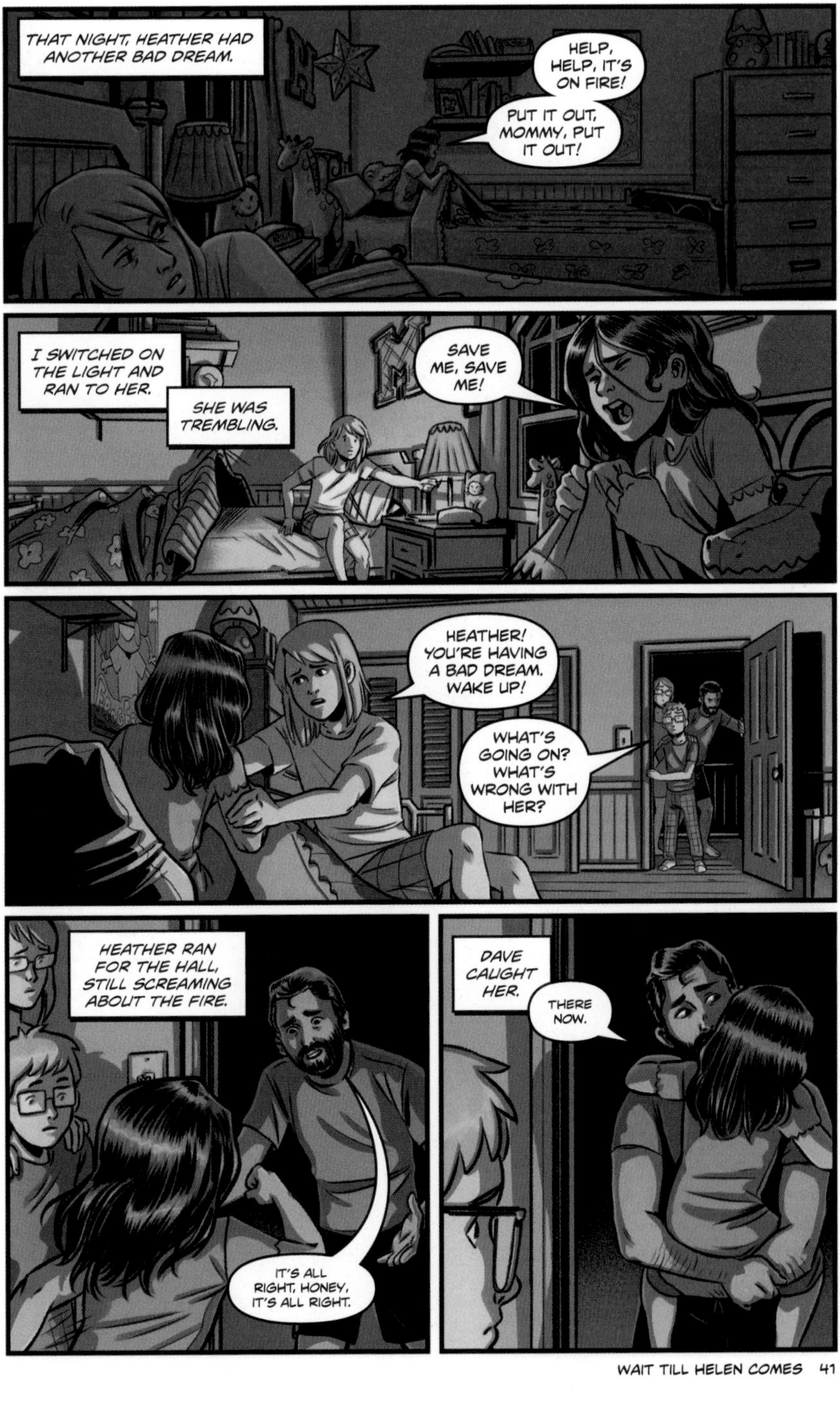
THAT NIGHT, HEATHER HAD ANOTHER BAD DREAM.
HELP, HELP, IT'S ON FIRE!
PUT IT OUT, MOMMY, PUT IT OUT!
I SWITCHED ON THE LIGHT AND RAN TO HER.
SHE WAS TREMBLING.
SAVE ME, SAVE ME!
HEATHER! YOU'RE HAVING A BAD DREAM. WAKE UP!
WHAT'S GOING ON? WHAT'S WRONG WITH HER?
HEATHER RAN FOR THE HALL, STILL SCREAMING ABOUT THE FIRE.
IT'S ALL RIGHT, HONEY, IT'S ALL RIGHT.
DAVE CAUGHT HER.
THERE NOW.

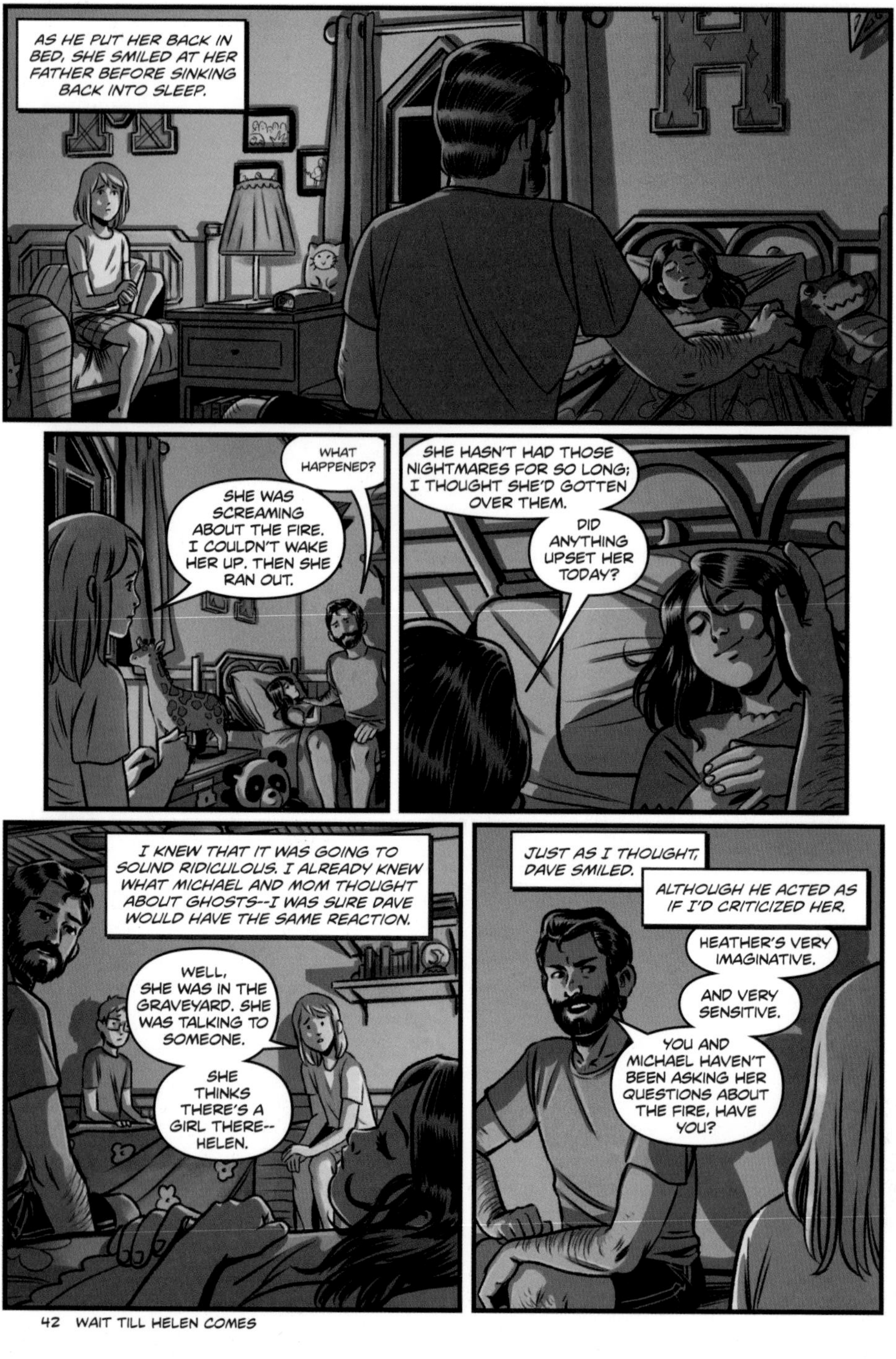
AS HE PUT HER BACK IN BED, SHE SMILED AT HER FATHER BEFORE SINKING BACK INTO SLEEP.
WHAT HAPPENED?
SHE WAS SCREAMING ABOUT THE FIRE. I COULDN'T WAKE HER UP. THEN SHE RAN OUT.
SHE HASN'T HAD THOSE NIGHTMARES FOR SO LONG; I THOUGHT SHE'D GOTTEN OVER THEM.
DID ANYTHING UPSET HER TODAY?
I KNEW THAT IT WAS GOING TO SOUND RIDICULOUS. I ALREADY KNEW WHAT MICHAEL AND MOM THOUGHT ABOUT GHOSTS--I WAS SURE DAVE WOULD HAVE THE SAME REACTION.
WELL, SHE WAS IN THE GRAVEYARD. SHE WAS TALKING TO SOMEONE.
SHE THINKS THERE'S A GIRL THERE-- HELEN.
JUST AS I THOUGHT, DAVE SMILED.
ALTHOUGH HE ACTED AS IF I'D CRITICIZED HER.
HEATHER'S VERY IMAGINATIVE.
AND VERY SENSITIVE.
YOU AND MICHAEL HAVEN'T BEEN ASKING HER QUESTIONS ABOUT THE FIRE, HAVE YOU?

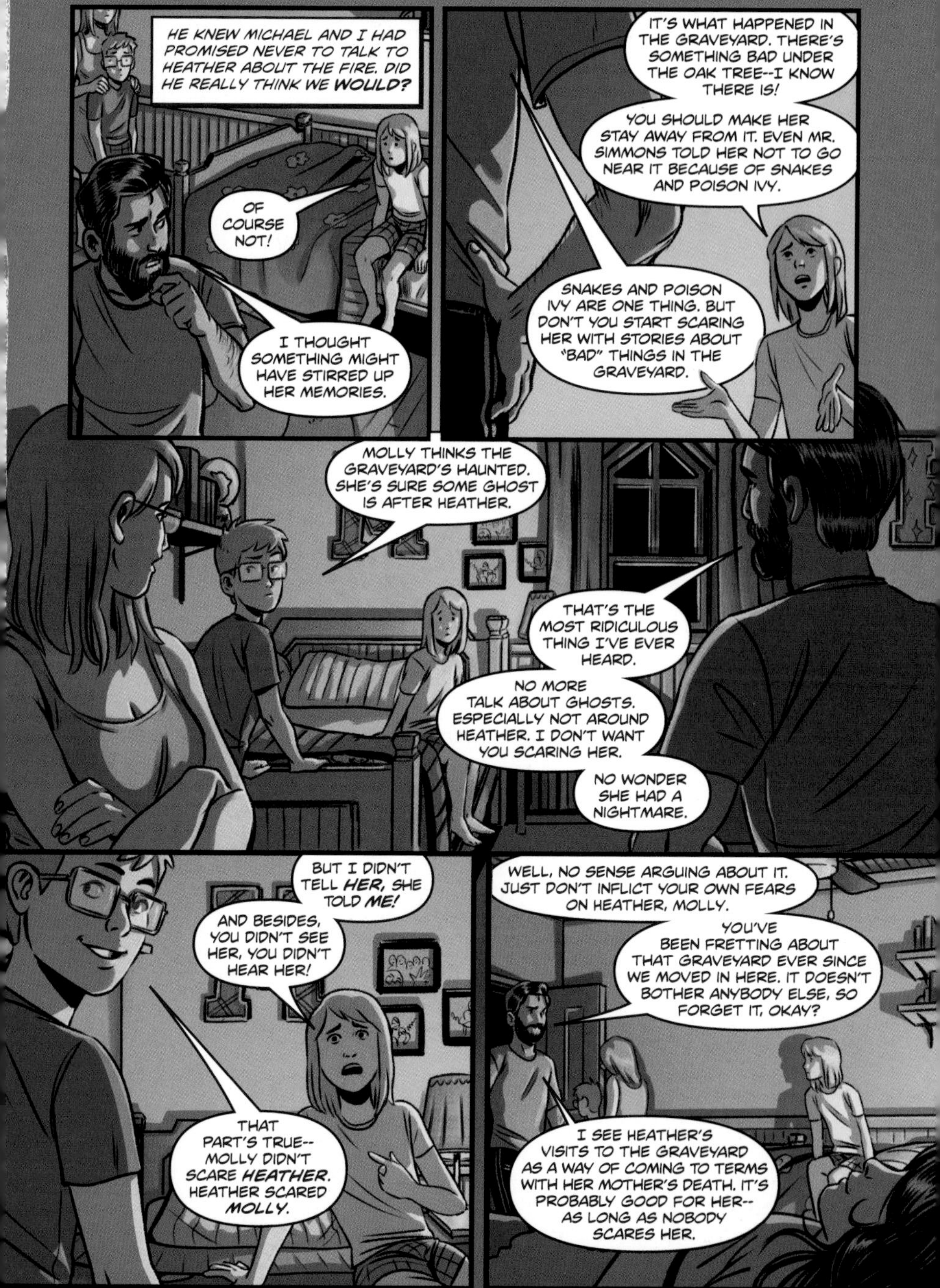
HE KNEW MICHAEL AND I HAD PROMISED NEVER TO TALK TO HEATHER ABOUT THE FIRE. DID HE REALLY THINK WE WOULD?
OF COURSE NOT!
I THOUGHT SOMETHING MIGHT HAVE STIRRED UP HER MEMORIES.
IT'S WHAT HAPPENED IN THE GRAVEYARD. THERE'S SOMETHING BAD UNDER THE OAK TREE--I KNOW THERE IS!
YOU SHOULD MAKE HER STAY AWAY FROM IT. EVEN MR. SIMMONS TOLD HER NOT TO GO NEAR IT BECAUSE OF SNAKES AND POISON IVY.
SNAKES AND POISON IVY ARE ONE THING. BUT DON'T YOU START SCARING HER WITH STORIES ABOUT "BAD" THINGS IN THE GRAVEYARD.
MOLLY THINKS THE GRAVEYARD'S HAUNTED. SHE'S SURE SOME GHOST IS AFTER HEATHER.
THAT'S THE MOST RIDICULOUS THING I'VE EVER HEARD.
NO MORE TALK ABOUT GHOSTS. ESPECIALLY NOT AROUND HEATHER. I DON'T WANT YOU SCARING HER.
NO WONDER SHE HAD A NIGHTMARE.
BUT I DIDN'T TELL HER, SHE TOLD ME!
AND BESIDES, YOU DIDN'T SEE HER, YOU DIDN'T HEAR HER!
THAT PART'S TRUE-- MOLLY DIDN'T SCARE HEATHER. HEATHER SCARED MOLLY.
WELL, NO SENSE ARGUING ABOUT IT. JUST DON'T INFLICT YOUR OWN FEARS ON HEATHER, MOLLY.
YOU'VE BEEN FRETTING ABOUT THAT GRAVEYARD EVER SINCE WE MOVED IN HERE. IT DOESN'T BOTHER ANYBODY ELSE, SO FORGET IT, OKAY?
I SEE HEATHER'S VISITS TO THE GRAVEYARD AS A WAY OF COMING TO TERMS WITH HER MOTHER'S DEATH. IT'S PROBABLY GOOD FOR HER-- AS LONG AS NOBODY SCARES HER.

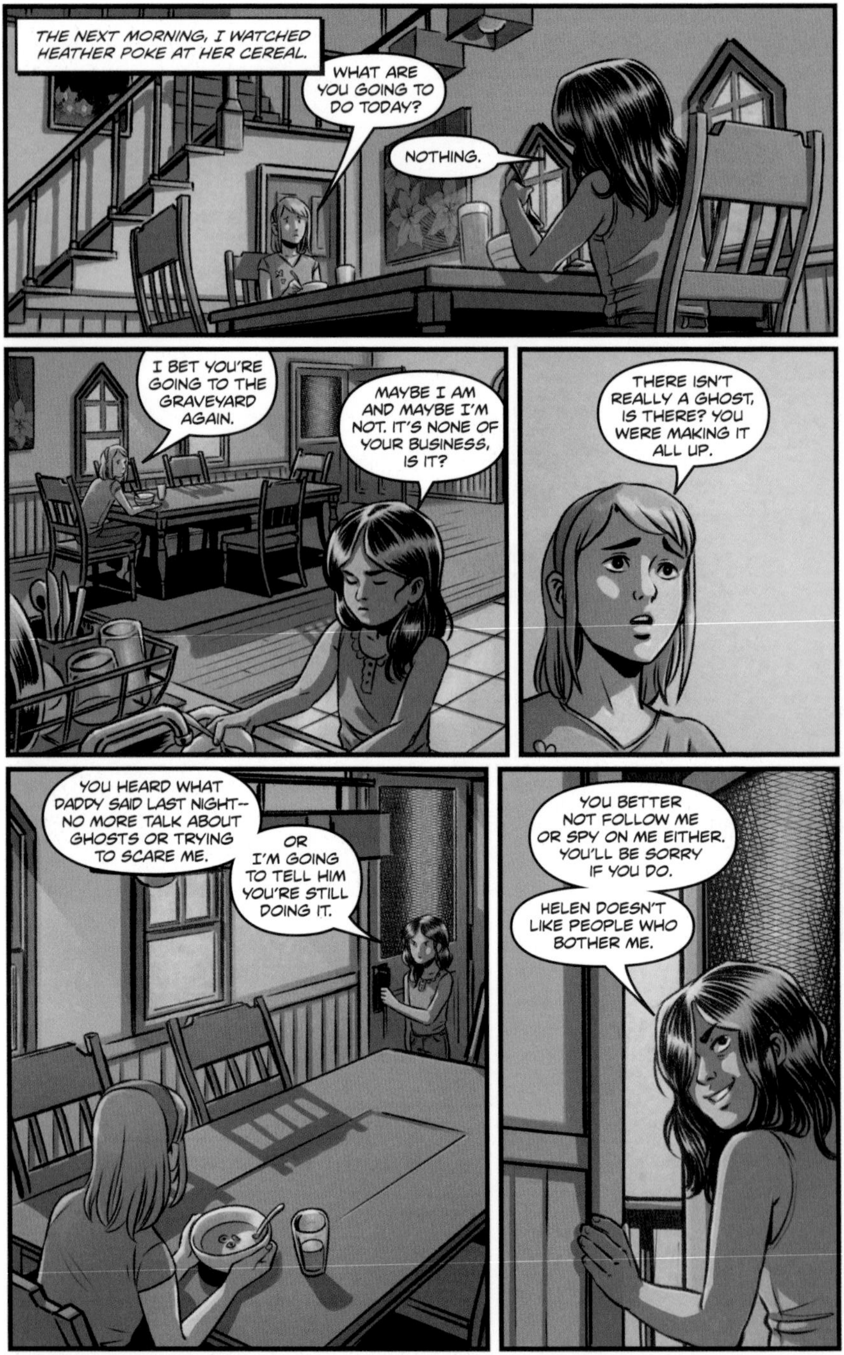
THE NEXT MORNING, I WATCHED HEATHER POKE AT HER CEREAL.
WHAT ARE YOU GOING TO DO TODAY?
NOTHING.
I BET YOU'RE GOING TO THE GRAVEYARD AGAIN.
MAYBE I AM AND MAYBE I'M NOT. IT'S NONE OF YOUR BUSINESS, IS IT?
THERE ISN'T REALLY A GHOST, IS THERE? YOU WERE MAKING IT ALL UP.
YOU HEARD WHAT DADDY SAID LAST NIGHT-- NO MORE TALK ABOUT GHOSTS OR TRYING TO SCARE ME.
OR I'M GOING TO TELL HIM YOU'RE STILL DOING IT.
YOU BETTER NOT FOLLOW ME OR SPY ON ME EITHER. YOU'LL BE SORRY IF YOU DO.
HELEN DOESN'T LIKE PEOPLE WHO BOTHER ME.

I WATCHED HER DISAPPEAR THROUGH THE GRAVEYARD GATE. I WONDERED WHAT I SHOULD DO ABOUT HER AND THE GHOST. IF THERE **WAS** A GHOST. IN THE MORNING SUN, IT SEEMED LIKELY I HAD IMAGINED THE PRESENCE OF SOMETHING INHUMAN UNDER THE OAK.

I WENT OUTSIDE TO READ. BUT THE WARMTH OF SUMMER MADE IT HARD TO CONCENTRATE.

I IMAGINED I HEARD HELEN'S VOICE WHISPERING TO HEATHER, CALLING HER, PROMISING HER THINGS.

I WENT TO THE GRAVEYARD, EXPECTING TO SEE HEATHER. ALL I SAW WAS A PEANUT BUTTER JAR, FILLED WITH FRESH FLOWERS.

H.E.H, I READ. MARCH 7, 1879– AUGUST 8, 1886.

SHE HAD BEEN DEAD FOR OVER A HUNDRED YEARS, MUCH LONGER THAN SHE'D BEEN ALIVE.

WHAT WAS LEFT OF HER NOW? A TANGLE OF BONES? MAYBE NOTHING BUT DUST. I SHIVERED.

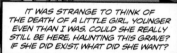

IT WAS STRANGE TO THINK OF THE DEATH OF A LITTLE GIRL, YOUNGER EVEN THAN I WAS. COULD SHE REALLY STILL BE HERE, HAUNTING THIS GRAVE? IF SHE DID EXIST, WHAT DID SHE WANT?

OVERWHELMED WITH SADNESS AND DESPAIR, I RAN AWAY FROM THE GRAVEYARD.

I DECIDED TO LOOK FOR MICHAEL. I GUESSED HE WAS SOMEWHERE IN THE WOODS, MAYBE TRYING TO CATCH CRAWFISH IN THE CREEK.

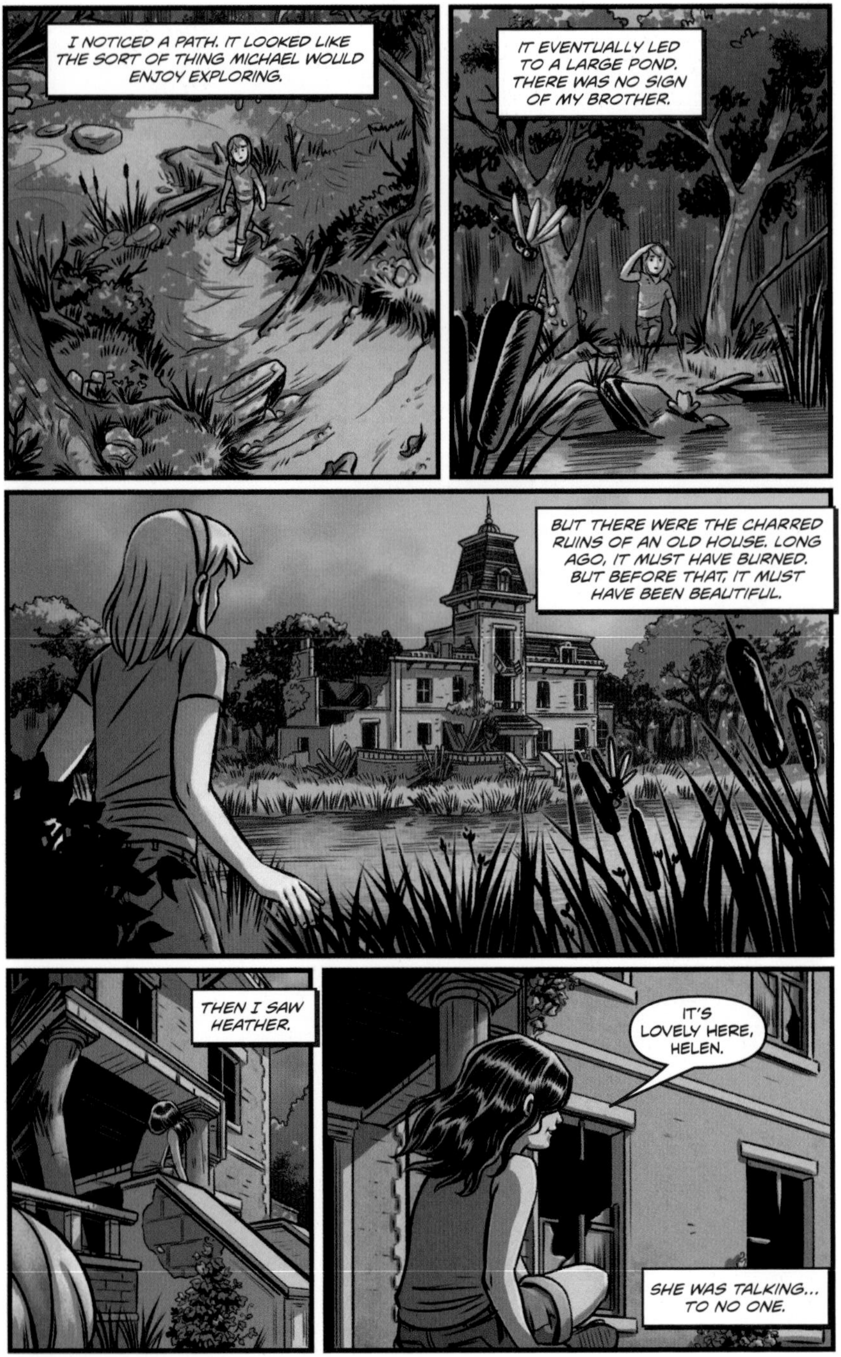
I NOTICED A PATH. IT LOOKED LIKE THE SORT OF THING MICHAEL WOULD ENJOY EXPLORING.
IT EVENTUALLY LED TO A LARGE POND. THERE WAS NO SIGN OF MY BROTHER.
BUT THERE WERE THE CHARRED RUINS OF AN OLD HOUSE. LONG AGO, IT MUST HAVE BURNED. BUT BEFORE THAT, IT MUST HAVE BEEN BEAUTIFUL.
THEN I SAW HEATHER.
IT'S LOVELY HERE, HELEN.
SHE WAS TALKING... TO NO ONE.

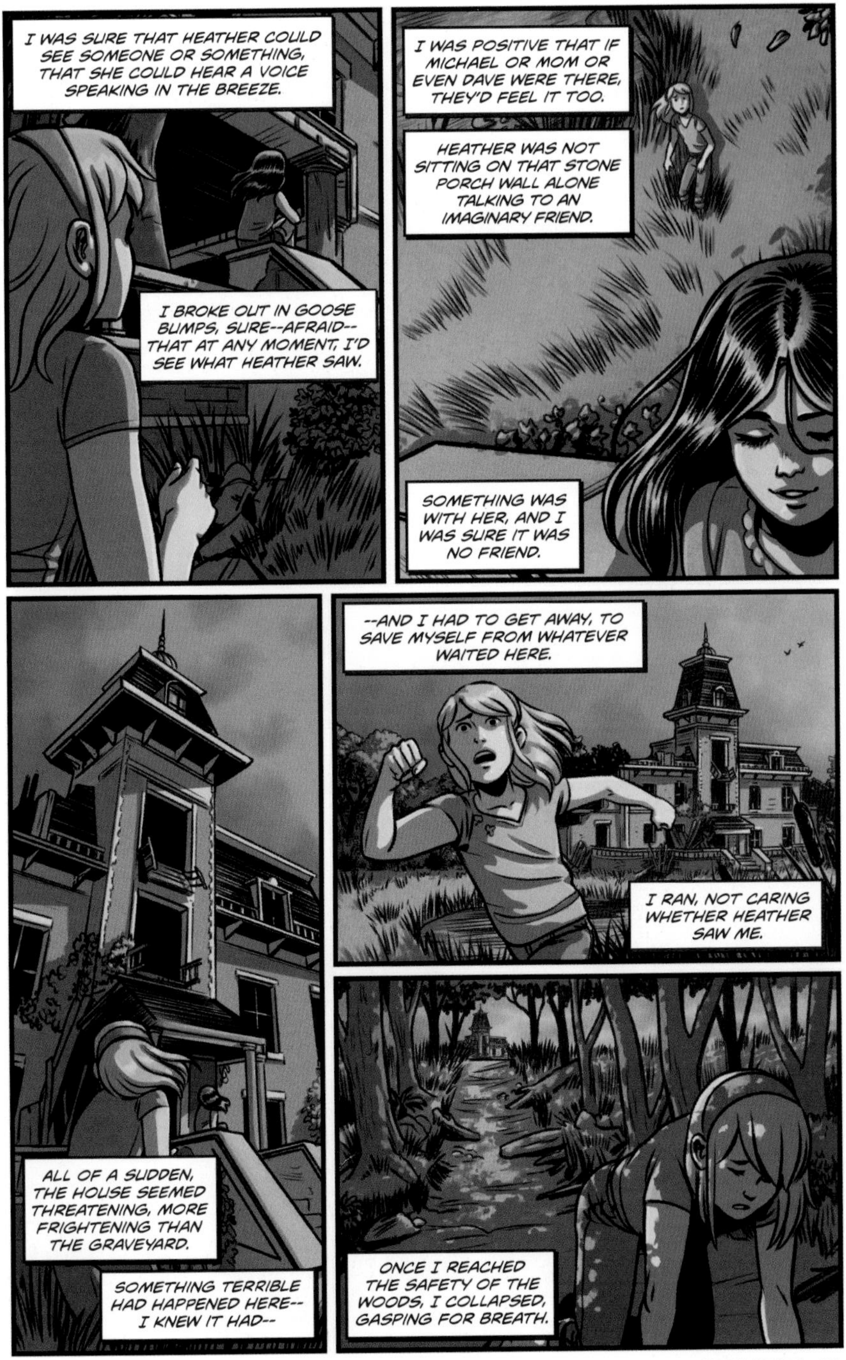
I WAS SURE THAT HEATHER COULD SEE SOMEONE OR SOMETHING, THAT SHE COULD HEAR A VOICE SPEAKING IN THE BREEZE.
I BROKE OUT IN GOOSE BUMPS, SURE--AFRAID--THAT AT ANY MOMENT, I'D SEE WHAT HEATHER SAW.
I WAS POSITIVE THAT IF MICHAEL OR MOM OR EVEN DAVE WERE THERE, THEY'D FEEL IT TOO.
HEATHER WAS NOT SITTING ON THAT STONE PORCH WALL ALONE TALKING TO AN IMAGINARY FRIEND.
SOMETHING WAS WITH HER, AND I WAS SURE IT WAS NO FRIEND.
ALL OF A SUDDEN, THE HOUSE SEEMED THREATENING, MORE FRIGHTENING THAN THE GRAVEYARD.
SOMETHING TERRIBLE HAD HAPPENED HERE--I KNEW IT HAD--
--AND I HAD TO GET AWAY, TO SAVE MYSELF FROM WHATEVER WAITED HERE.
I RAN, NOT CARING WHETHER HEATHER SAW ME.
ONCE I REACHED THE SAFETY OF THE WOODS, I COLLAPSED, GASPING FOR BREATH.

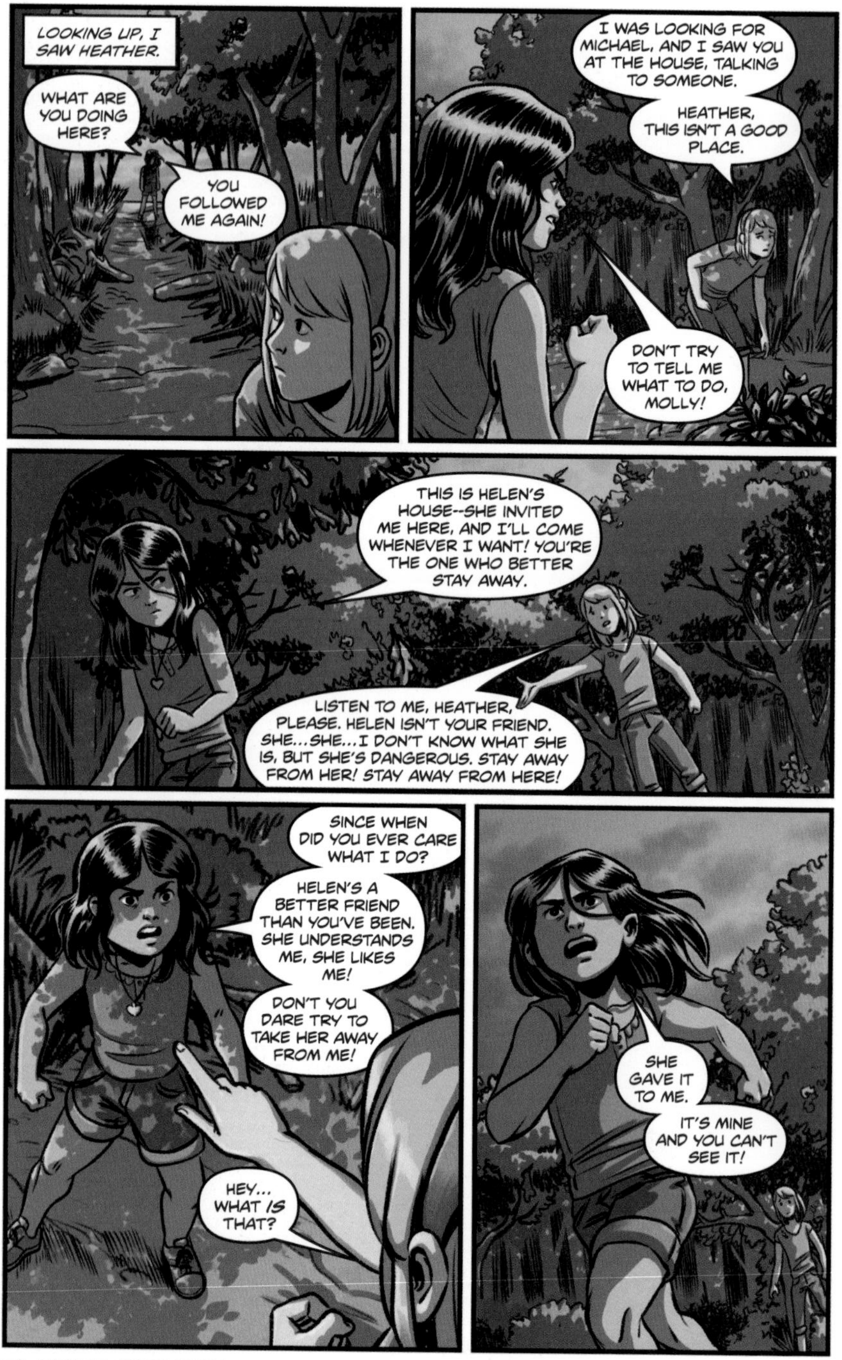
LOOKING UP, I SAW HEATHER.
WHAT ARE YOU DOING HERE?
YOU FOLLOWED ME AGAIN!
I WAS LOOKING FOR MICHAEL, AND I SAW YOU AT THE HOUSE, TALKING TO SOMEONE.
HEATHER, THIS ISN'T A GOOD PLACE.
DON'T TRY TO TELL ME WHAT TO DO, MOLLY!
THIS IS HELEN'S HOUSE--SHE INVITED ME HERE, AND I'LL COME WHENEVER I WANT! YOU'RE THE ONE WHO BETTER STAY AWAY.
LISTEN TO ME, HEATHER, PLEASE. HELEN ISN'T YOUR FRIEND. SHE...SHE...I DON'T KNOW WHAT SHE IS, BUT SHE'S DANGEROUS. STAY AWAY FROM HER! STAY AWAY FROM HERE!
SINCE WHEN DID YOU EVER CARE WHAT I DO?
HELEN'S A BETTER FRIEND THAN YOU'VE BEEN. SHE UNDERSTANDS ME, SHE LIKES ME!
DON'T YOU DARE TRY TO TAKE HER AWAY FROM ME!
HEY... WHAT IS THAT?
SHE GAVE IT TO ME.
IT'S MINE AND YOU CAN'T SEE IT!

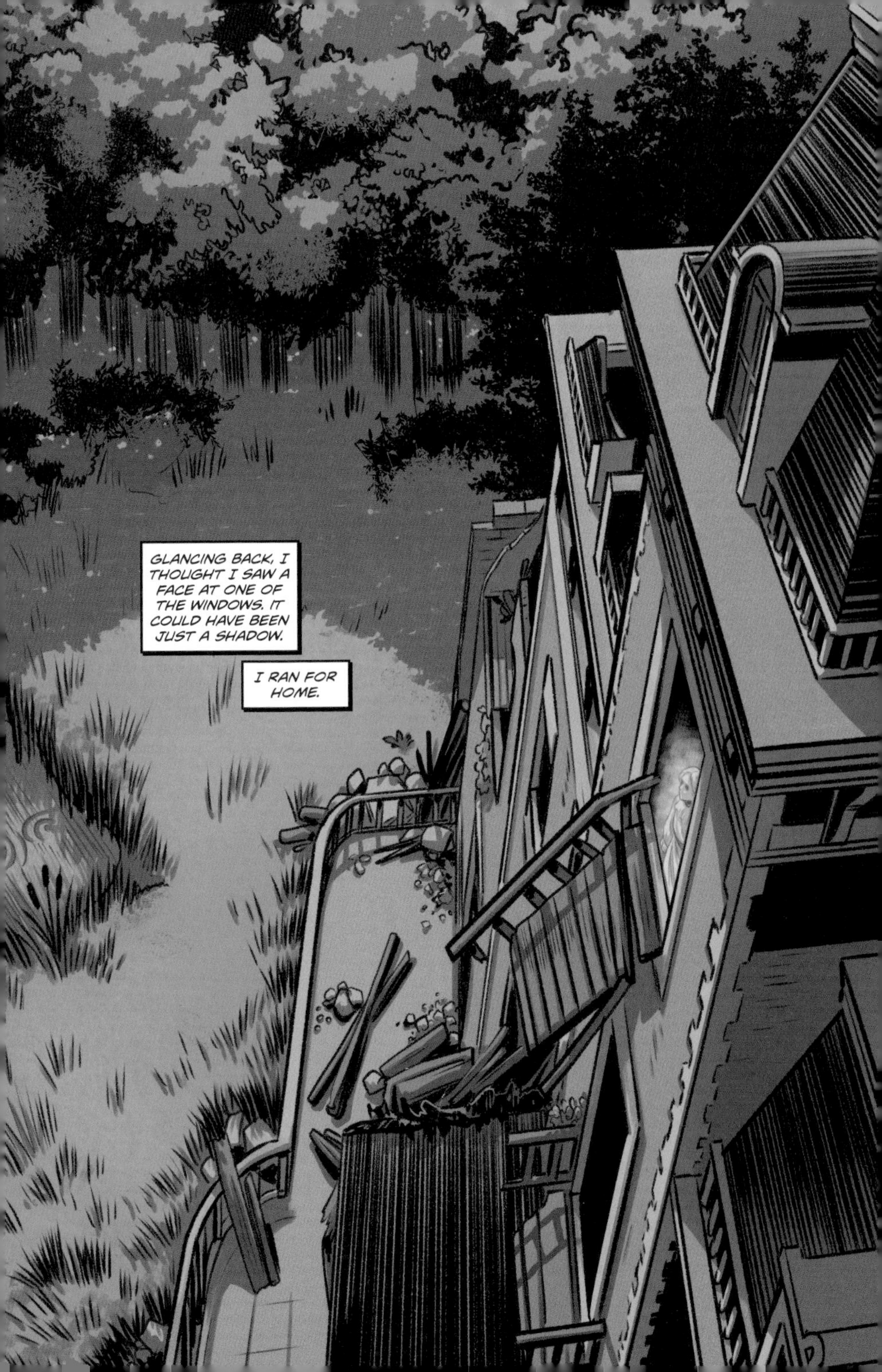
GLANCING BACK, I THOUGHT I SAW A FACE AT ONE OF THE WINDOWS. IT COULD HAVE BEEN JUST A SHADOW.
I RAN FOR HOME.

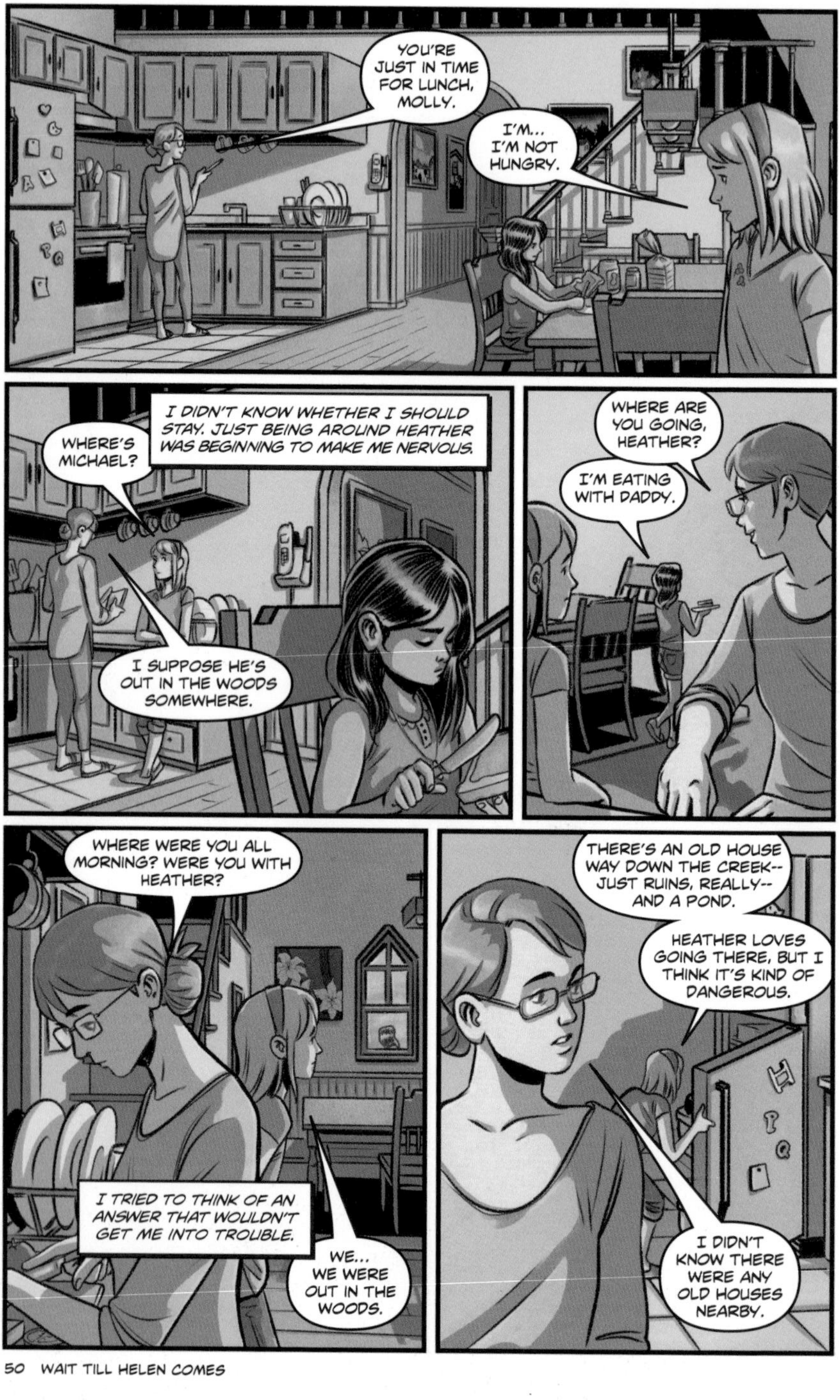
YOU'RE JUST IN TIME FOR LUNCH, MOLLY.
I'M... I'M NOT HUNGRY.
I DIDN'T KNOW WHETHER I SHOULD STAY. JUST BEING AROUND HEATHER WAS BEGINNING TO MAKE ME NERVOUS.
WHERE'S MICHAEL?
I SUPPOSE HE'S OUT IN THE WOODS SOMEWHERE.
WHERE ARE YOU GOING, HEATHER?
I'M EATING WITH DADDY.
WHERE WERE YOU ALL MORNING? WERE YOU WITH HEATHER?
I TRIED TO THINK OF AN ANSWER THAT WOULDN'T GET ME INTO TROUBLE.
WE... WE WERE OUT IN THE WOODS.
THERE'S AN OLD HOUSE WAY DOWN THE CREEK-- JUST RUINS, REALLY-- AND A POND.
HEATHER LOVES GOING THERE, BUT I THINK IT'S KIND OF DANGEROUS.
I DIDN'T KNOW THERE WERE ANY OLD HOUSES NEARBY.

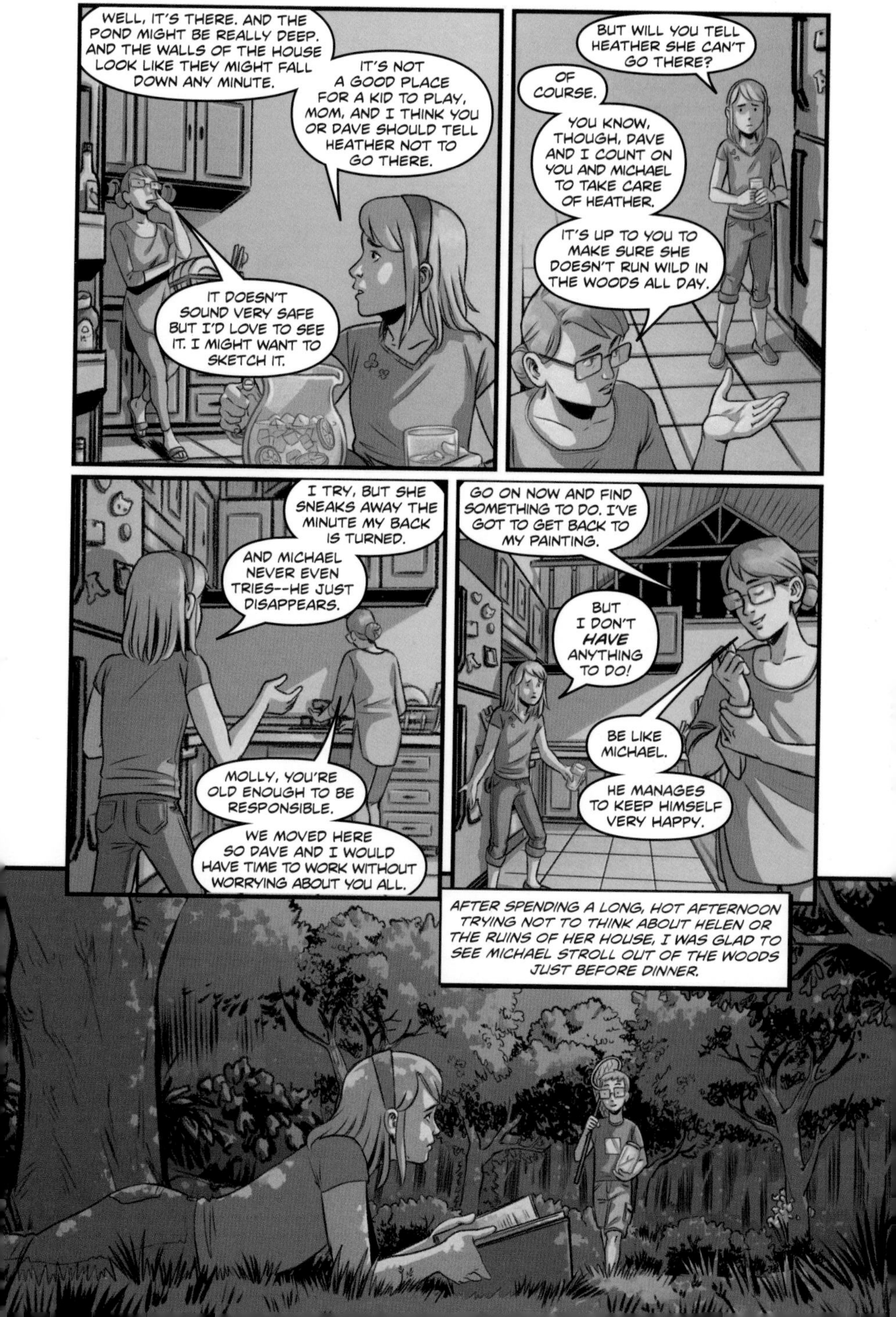
WELL, IT'S THERE. AND THE POND MIGHT BE REALLY DEEP. AND THE WALLS OF THE HOUSE LOOK LIKE THEY MIGHT FALL DOWN ANY MINUTE.
IT'S NOT A GOOD PLACE FOR A KID TO PLAY, MOM, AND I THINK YOU OR DAVE SHOULD TELL HEATHER NOT TO GO THERE.
IT DOESN'T SOUND VERY SAFE BUT I'D LOVE TO SEE IT. I MIGHT WANT TO SKETCH IT.
BUT WILL YOU TELL HEATHER SHE CAN'T GO THERE?
OF COURSE.
YOU KNOW, THOUGH, DAVE AND I COUNT ON YOU AND MICHAEL TO TAKE CARE OF HEATHER.
IT'S UP TO YOU TO MAKE SURE SHE DOESN'T RUN WILD IN THE WOODS ALL DAY.
I TRY, BUT SHE SNEAKS AWAY THE MINUTE MY BACK IS TURNED.
AND MICHAEL NEVER EVEN TRIES--HE JUST DISAPPEARS.
MOLLY, YOU'RE OLD ENOUGH TO BE RESPONSIBLE.
WE MOVED HERE SO DAVE AND I WOULD HAVE TIME TO WORK WITHOUT WORRYING ABOUT YOU ALL.
GO ON NOW AND FIND SOMETHING TO DO. I'VE GOT TO GET BACK TO MY PAINTING.
BUT I DON'T *HAVE* ANYTHING TO DO!
BE LIKE MICHAEL.
HE MANAGES TO KEEP HIMSELF VERY HAPPY.
AFTER SPENDING A LONG, HOT AFTERNOON TRYING NOT TO THINK ABOUT HELEN OR THE RUINS OF HER HOUSE, I WAS GLAD TO SEE MICHAEL STROLL OUT OF THE WOODS JUST BEFORE DINNER.

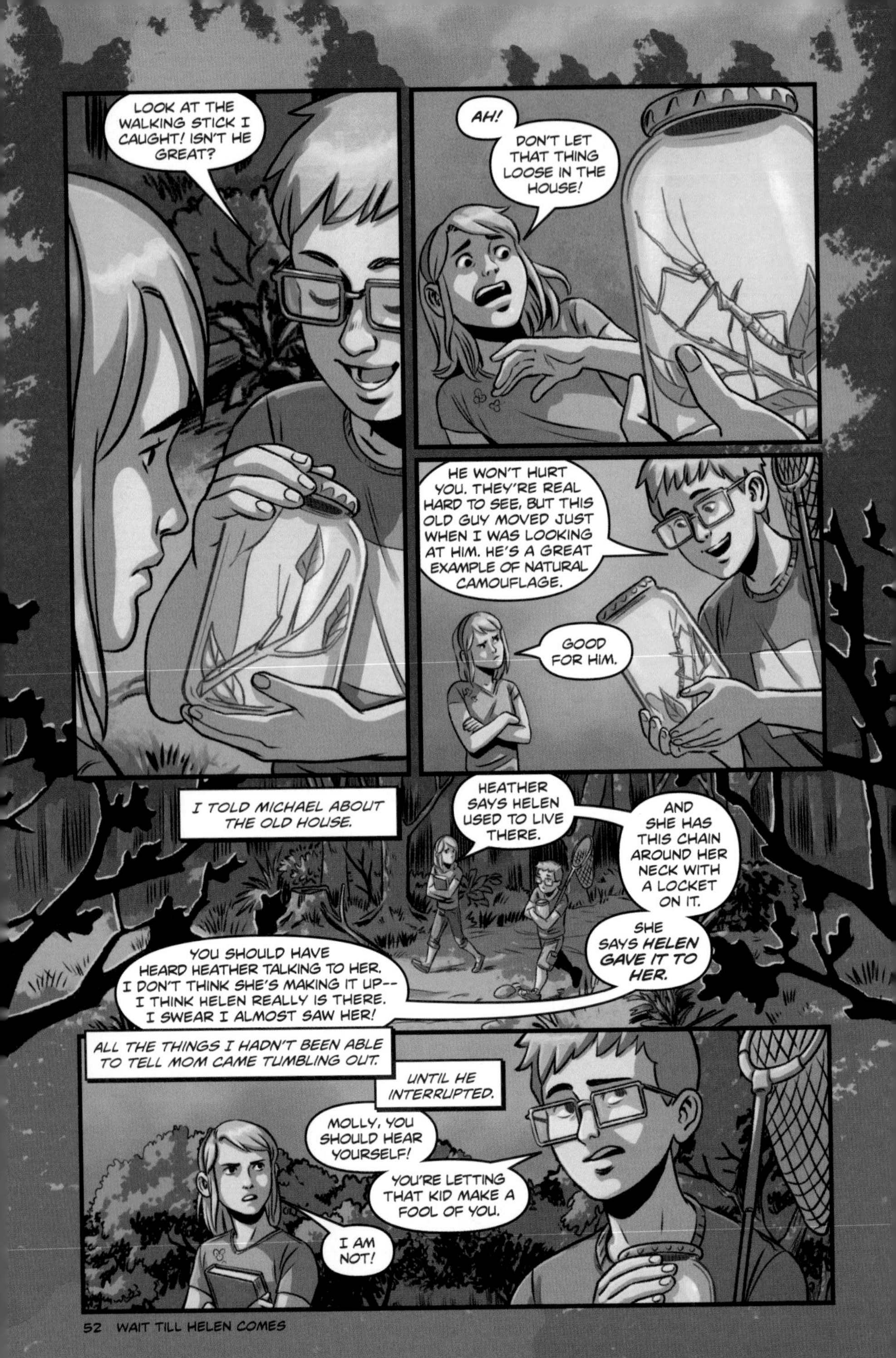

LOOK AT THE WALKING STICK I CAUGHT! ISN'T HE GREAT?
AH!
DON'T LET THAT THING LOOSE IN THE HOUSE!
HE WON'T HURT YOU. THEY'RE REAL HARD TO SEE, BUT THIS OLD GUY MOVED JUST WHEN I WAS LOOKING AT HIM. HE'S A GREAT EXAMPLE OF NATURAL CAMOUFLAGE.
GOOD FOR HIM.
I TOLD MICHAEL ABOUT THE OLD HOUSE.
HEATHER SAYS HELEN USED TO LIVE THERE.
AND SHE HAS THIS CHAIN AROUND HER NECK WITH A LOCKET ON IT.
SHE SAYS HELEN GAVE IT TO HER.
YOU SHOULD HAVE HEARD HEATHER TALKING TO HER. I DON'T THINK SHE'S MAKING IT UP-- I THINK HELEN REALLY IS THERE. I SWEAR I ALMOST SAW HER!
ALL THE THINGS I HADN'T BEEN ABLE TO TELL MOM CAME TUMBLING OUT.
UNTIL HE INTERRUPTED.
MOLLY, YOU SHOULD HEAR YOURSELF!
YOU'RE LETTING THAT KID MAKE A FOOL OF YOU.
I AM NOT!

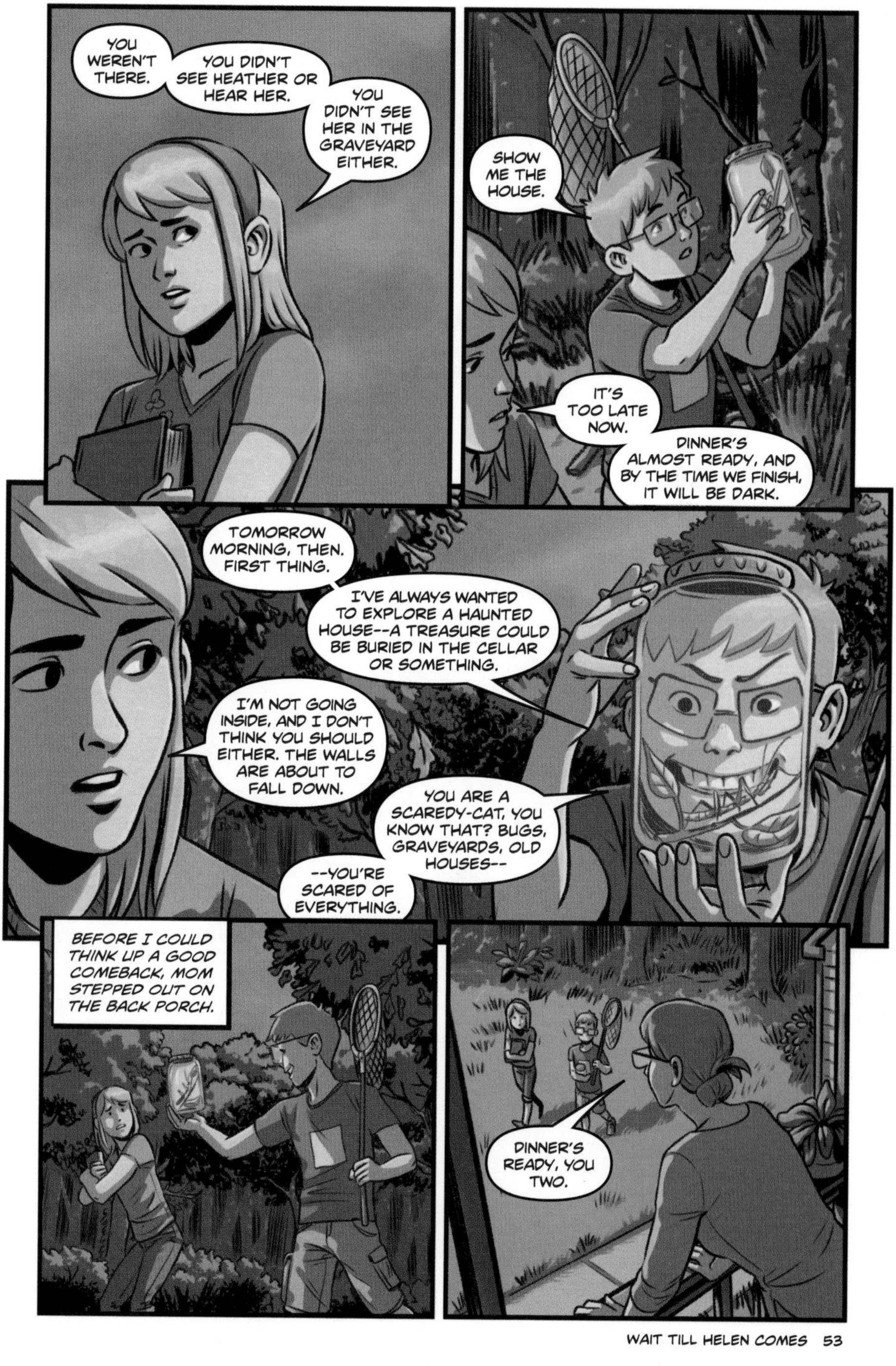
YOU WEREN'T THERE.
YOU DIDN'T SEE HEATHER OR HEAR HER.
YOU DIDN'T SEE HER IN THE GRAVEYARD EITHER.
SHOW ME THE HOUSE.
IT'S TOO LATE NOW.
DINNER'S ALMOST READY, AND BY THE TIME WE FINISH, IT WILL BE DARK.
TOMORROW MORNING, THEN. FIRST THING.
I'VE ALWAYS WANTED TO EXPLORE A HAUNTED HOUSE--A TREASURE COULD BE BURIED IN THE CELLAR OR SOMETHING.
I'M NOT GOING INSIDE, AND I DON'T THINK YOU SHOULD EITHER. THE WALLS ARE ABOUT TO FALL DOWN.
YOU ARE A SCAREDY-CAT, YOU KNOW THAT? BUGS, GRAVEYARDS, OLD HOUSES--
--YOU'RE SCARED OF EVERYTHING.
BEFORE I COULD THINK UP A GOOD COMEBACK, MOM STEPPED OUT ON THE BACK PORCH.
DINNER'S READY, YOU TWO.

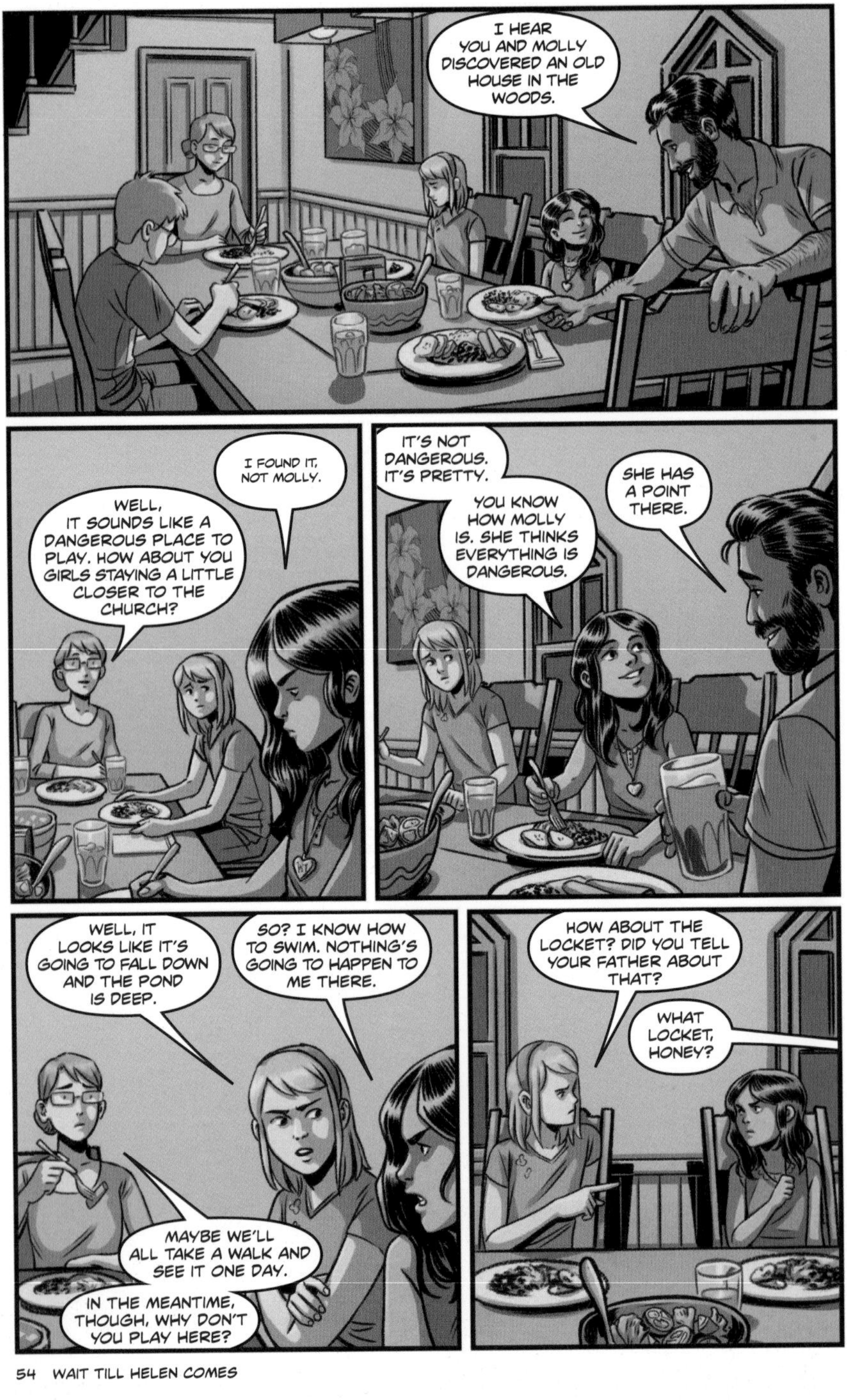
I HEAR YOU AND MOLLY DISCOVERED AN OLD HOUSE IN THE WOODS.
I FOUND IT, NOT MOLLY.
WELL, IT SOUNDS LIKE A DANGEROUS PLACE TO PLAY. HOW ABOUT YOU GIRLS STAYING A LITTLE CLOSER TO THE CHURCH?
IT'S NOT DANGEROUS. IT'S PRETTY.
YOU KNOW HOW MOLLY IS. SHE THINKS EVERYTHING IS DANGEROUS.
SHE HAS A POINT THERE.
WELL, IT LOOKS LIKE IT'S GOING TO FALL DOWN AND THE POND IS DEEP.
SO? I KNOW HOW TO SWIM. NOTHING'S GOING TO HAPPEN TO ME THERE.
MAYBE WE'LL ALL TAKE A WALK AND SEE IT ONE DAY.
IN THE MEANTIME, THOUGH, WHY DON'T YOU PLAY HERE?
HOW ABOUT THE LOCKET? DID YOU TELL YOUR FATHER ABOUT THAT?
WHAT LOCKET, HONEY?

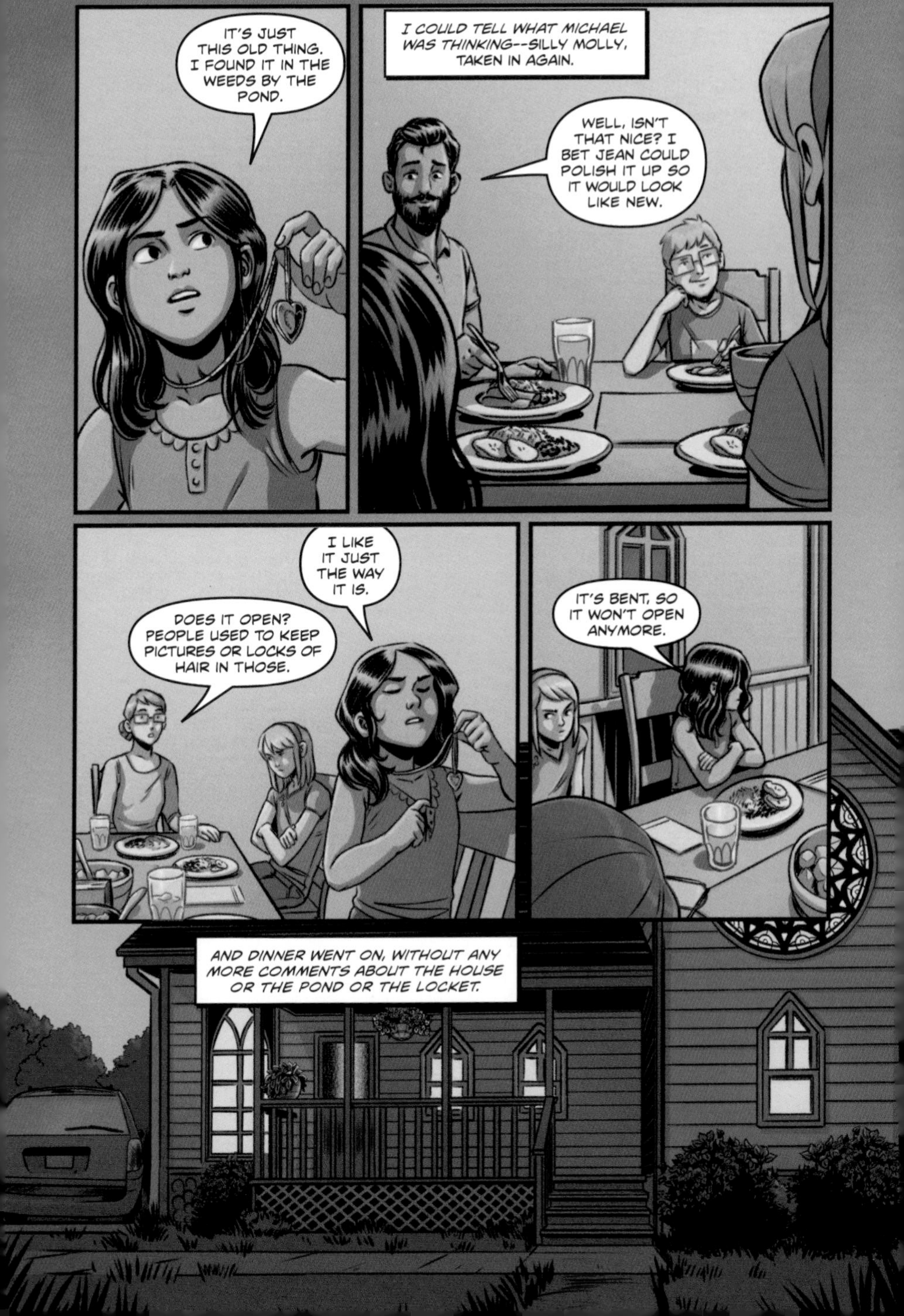
IT'S JUST THIS OLD THING. I FOUND IT IN THE WEEDS BY THE POND.
I COULD TELL WHAT MICHAEL WAS THINKING--SILLY MOLLY, TAKEN IN AGAIN.
WELL, ISN'T THAT NICE? I BET JEAN COULD POLISH IT UP SO IT WOULD LOOK LIKE NEW.
I LIKE IT JUST THE WAY IT IS.
DOES IT OPEN? PEOPLE USED TO KEEP PICTURES OR LOCKS OF HAIR IN THOSE.
IT'S BENT, SO IT WON'T OPEN ANYMORE.
AND DINNER WENT ON, WITHOUT ANY MORE COMMENTS ABOUT THE HOUSE OR THE POND OR THE LOCKET.

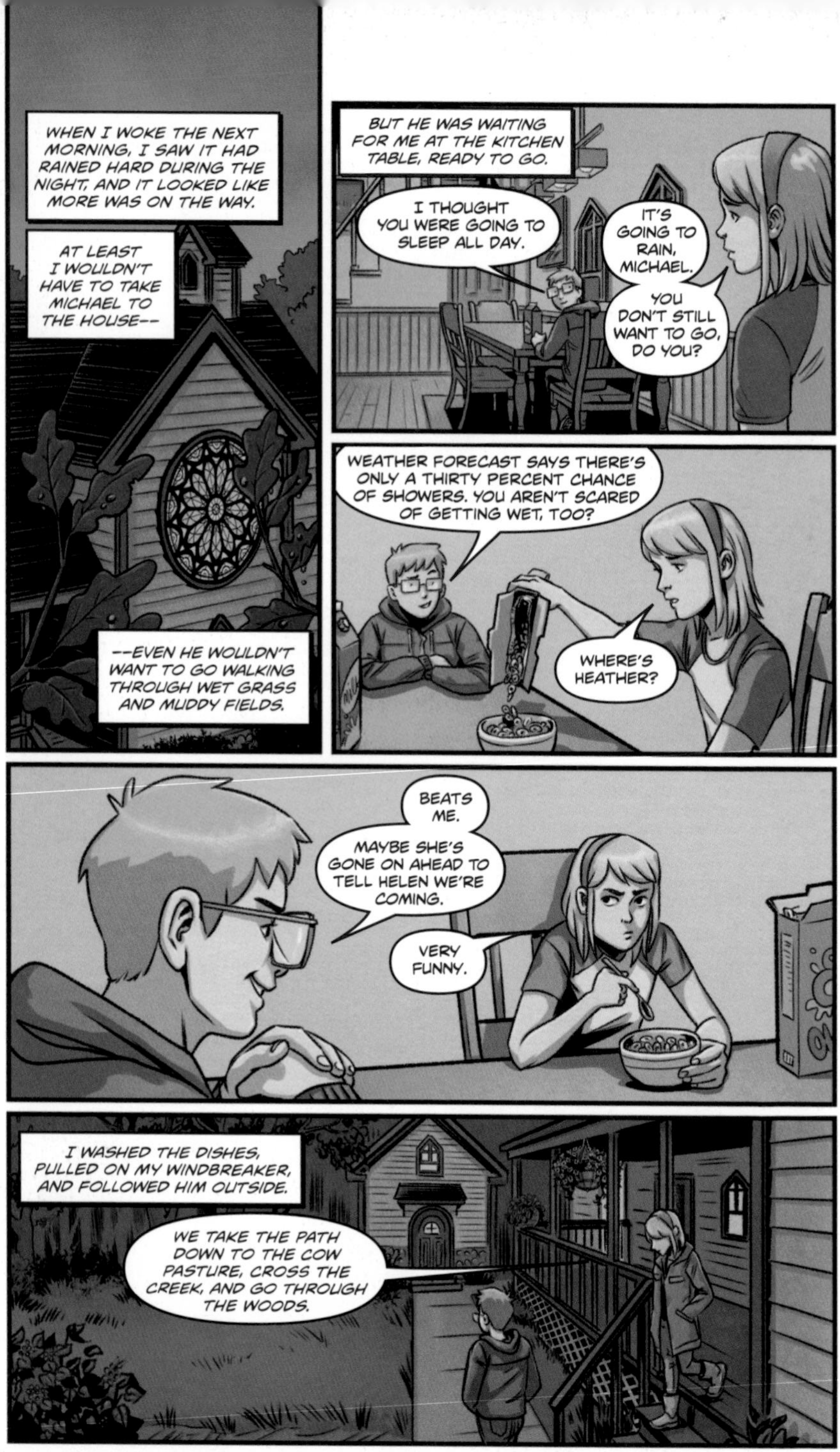
WHEN I WOKE THE NEXT MORNING, I SAW IT HAD RAINED HARD DURING THE NIGHT, AND IT LOOKED LIKE MORE WAS ON THE WAY.
AT LEAST I WOULDN'T HAVE TO TAKE MICHAEL TO THE HOUSE--
--EVEN HE WOULDN'T WANT TO GO WALKING THROUGH WET GRASS AND MUDDY FIELDS.
BUT HE WAS WAITING FOR ME AT THE KITCHEN TABLE, READY TO GO.
I THOUGHT YOU WERE GOING TO SLEEP ALL DAY.
IT'S GOING TO RAIN, MICHAEL.
YOU DON'T STILL WANT TO GO, DO YOU?
WEATHER FORECAST SAYS THERE'S ONLY A THIRTY PERCENT CHANCE OF SHOWERS. YOU AREN'T SCARED OF GETTING WET, TOO?
WHERE'S HEATHER?
BEATS ME.
MAYBE SHE'S GONE ON AHEAD TO TELL HELEN WE'RE COMING.
VERY FUNNY.
I WASHED THE DISHES, PULLED ON MY WINDBREAKER, AND FOLLOWED HIM OUTSIDE.
WE TAKE THE PATH DOWN TO THE COW PASTURE, CROSS THE CREEK, AND GO THROUGH THE WOODS.

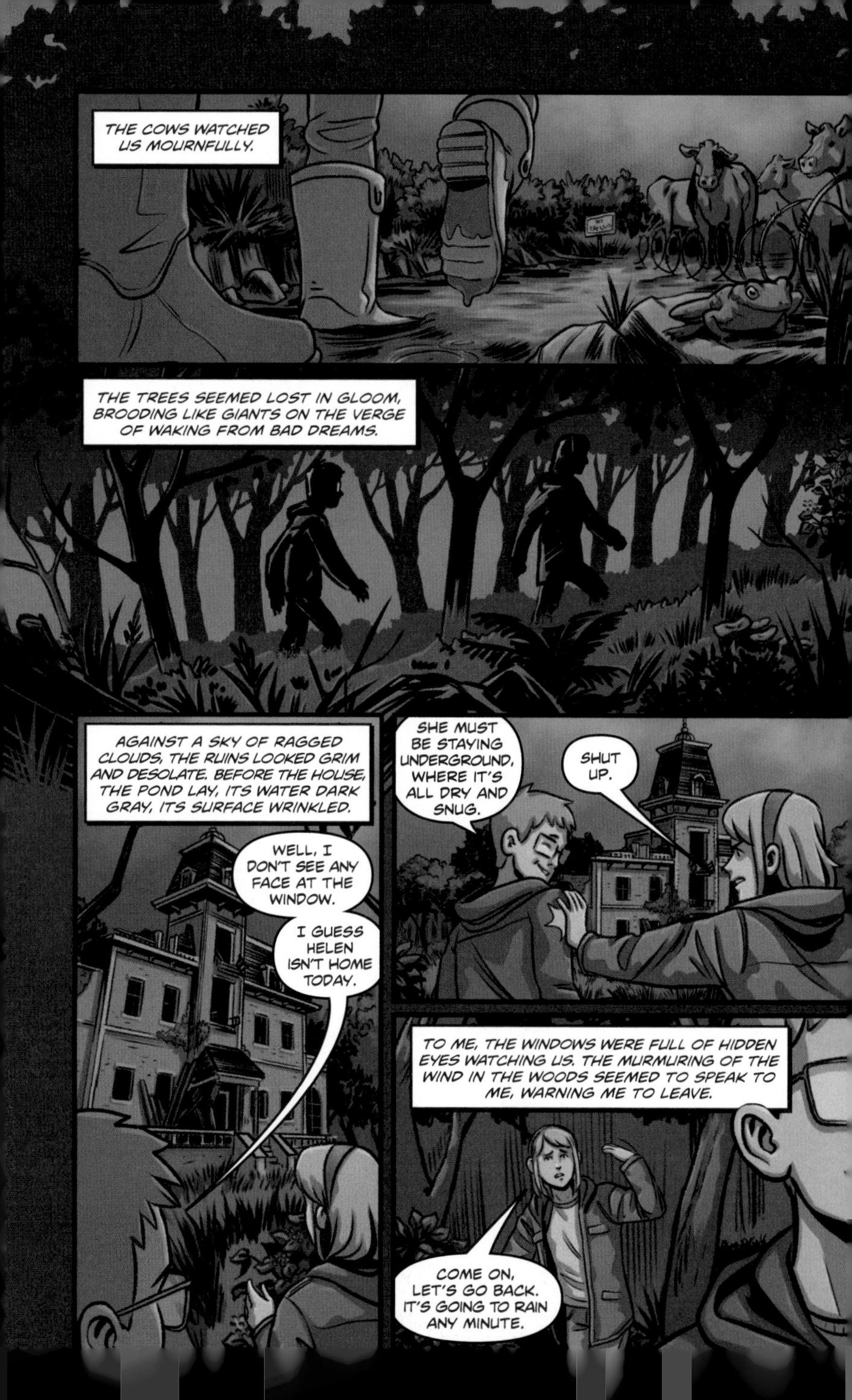
THE COWS WATCHED US MOURNFULLY.
THE TREES SEEMED LOST IN GLOOM, BROODING LIKE GIANTS ON THE VERGE OF WAKING FROM BAD DREAMS.
AGAINST A SKY OF RAGGED CLOUDS, THE RUINS LOOKED GRIM AND DESOLATE. BEFORE THE HOUSE, THE POND LAY, ITS WATER DARK GRAY, ITS SURFACE WRINKLED.
WELL, I DON'T SEE ANY FACE AT THE WINDOW.
I GUESS HELEN ISN'T HOME TODAY.
SHE MUST BE STAYING UNDERGROUND, WHERE IT'S ALL DRY AND SNUG.
SHUT UP.
TO ME, THE WINDOWS WERE FULL OF HIDDEN EYES WATCHING US. THE MURMURING OF THE WIND IN THE WOODS SEEMED TO SPEAK TO ME, WARNING ME TO LEAVE.
COME ON, LET'S GO BACK. IT'S GOING TO RAIN ANY MINUTE.

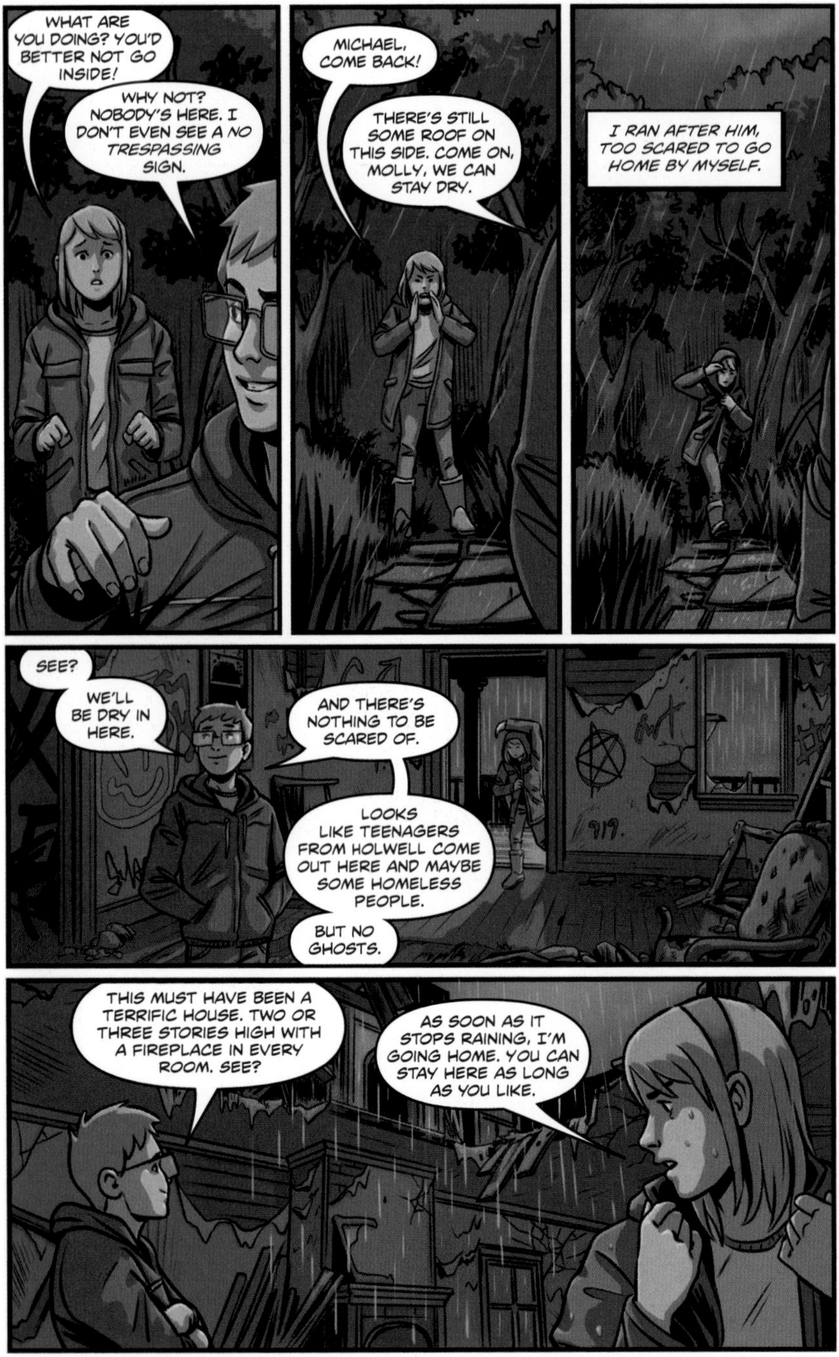
WHAT ARE YOU DOING? YOU'D BETTER NOT GO INSIDE!
WHY NOT? NOBODY'S HERE. I DON'T EVEN SEE A NO *TRESPASSING* SIGN.
MICHAEL, COME BACK!
THERE'S STILL SOME ROOF ON THIS SIDE. COME ON, MOLLY, WE CAN STAY DRY.
I RAN AFTER HIM, TOO SCARED TO GO HOME BY MYSELF.
SEE?
WE'LL BE DRY IN HERE.
AND THERE'S NOTHING TO BE SCARED OF.
LOOKS LIKE TEENAGERS FROM HOLWELL COME OUT HERE AND MAYBE SOME HOMELESS PEOPLE.
BUT NO GHOSTS.
THIS MUST HAVE BEEN A TERRIFIC HOUSE. TWO OR THREE STORIES HIGH WITH A FIREPLACE IN EVERY ROOM. SEE?
AS SOON AS IT STOPS RAINING, I'M GOING HOME. YOU CAN STAY HERE AS LONG AS YOU LIKE.

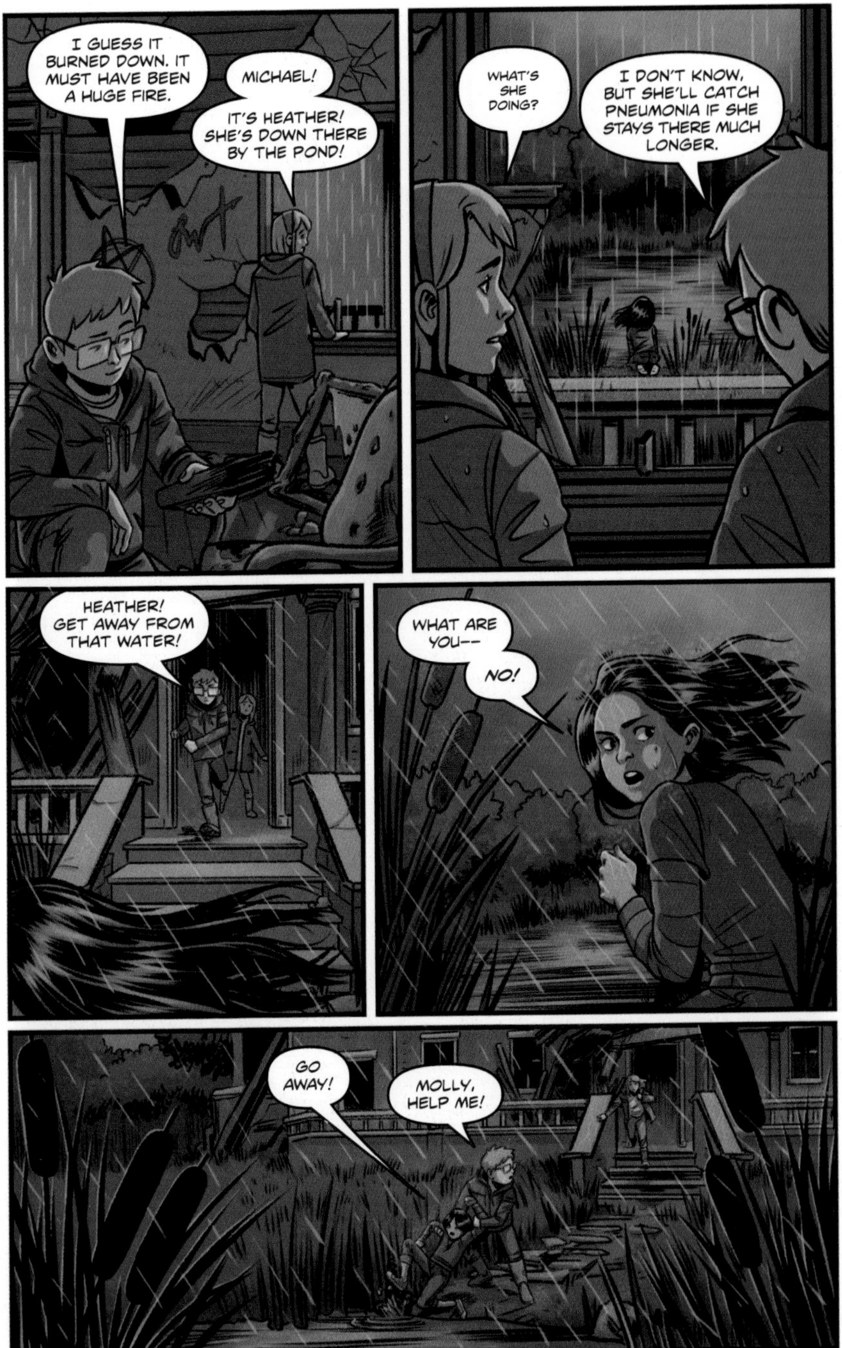
I GUESS IT BURNED DOWN. IT MUST HAVE BEEN A HUGE FIRE.
MICHAEL!
IT'S HEATHER! SHE'S DOWN THERE BY THE POND!
WHAT'S SHE DOING?
I DON'T KNOW, BUT SHE'LL CATCH PNEUMONIA IF SHE STAYS THERE MUCH LONGER.
HEATHER! GET AWAY FROM THAT WATER!
WHAT ARE YOU--
NO!
GO AWAY!
MOLLY, HELP ME!

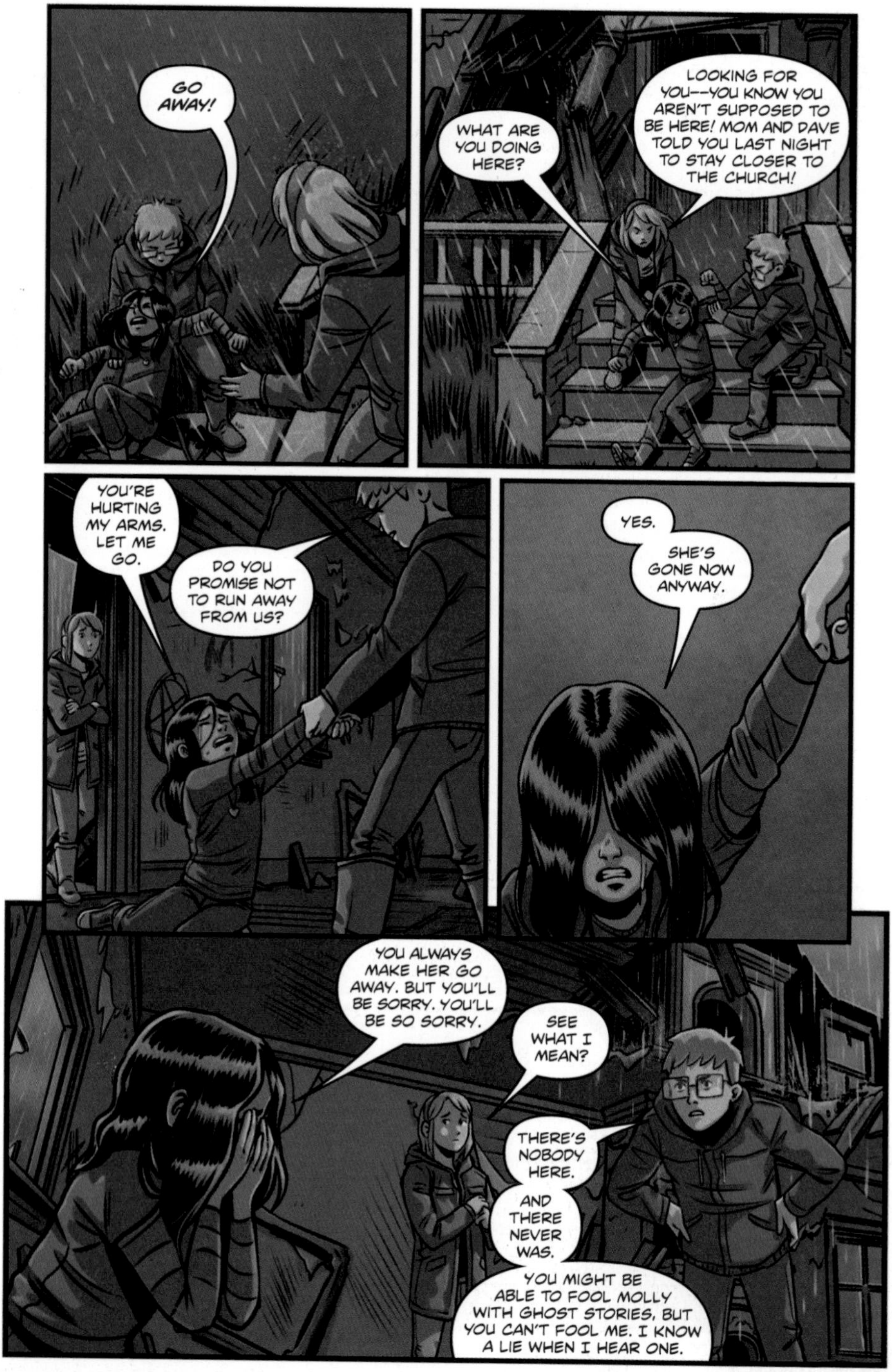
GO AWAY!
WHAT ARE YOU DOING HERE?
LOOKING FOR YOU--YOU KNOW YOU AREN'T SUPPOSED TO BE HERE! MOM AND DAVE TOLD YOU LAST NIGHT TO STAY CLOSER TO THE CHURCH!
YOU'RE HURTING MY ARMS. LET ME GO.
DO YOU PROMISE NOT TO RUN AWAY FROM US?
YES.
SHE'S GONE NOW ANYWAY.
YOU ALWAYS MAKE HER GO AWAY. BUT YOU'LL BE SORRY. YOU'LL BE SO SORRY.
SEE WHAT I MEAN?
THERE'S NOBODY HERE.
AND THERE NEVER WAS.
YOU MIGHT BE ABLE TO FOOL MOLLY WITH GHOST STORIES, BUT YOU CAN'T FOOL ME. I KNOW A LIE WHEN I HEAR ONE.

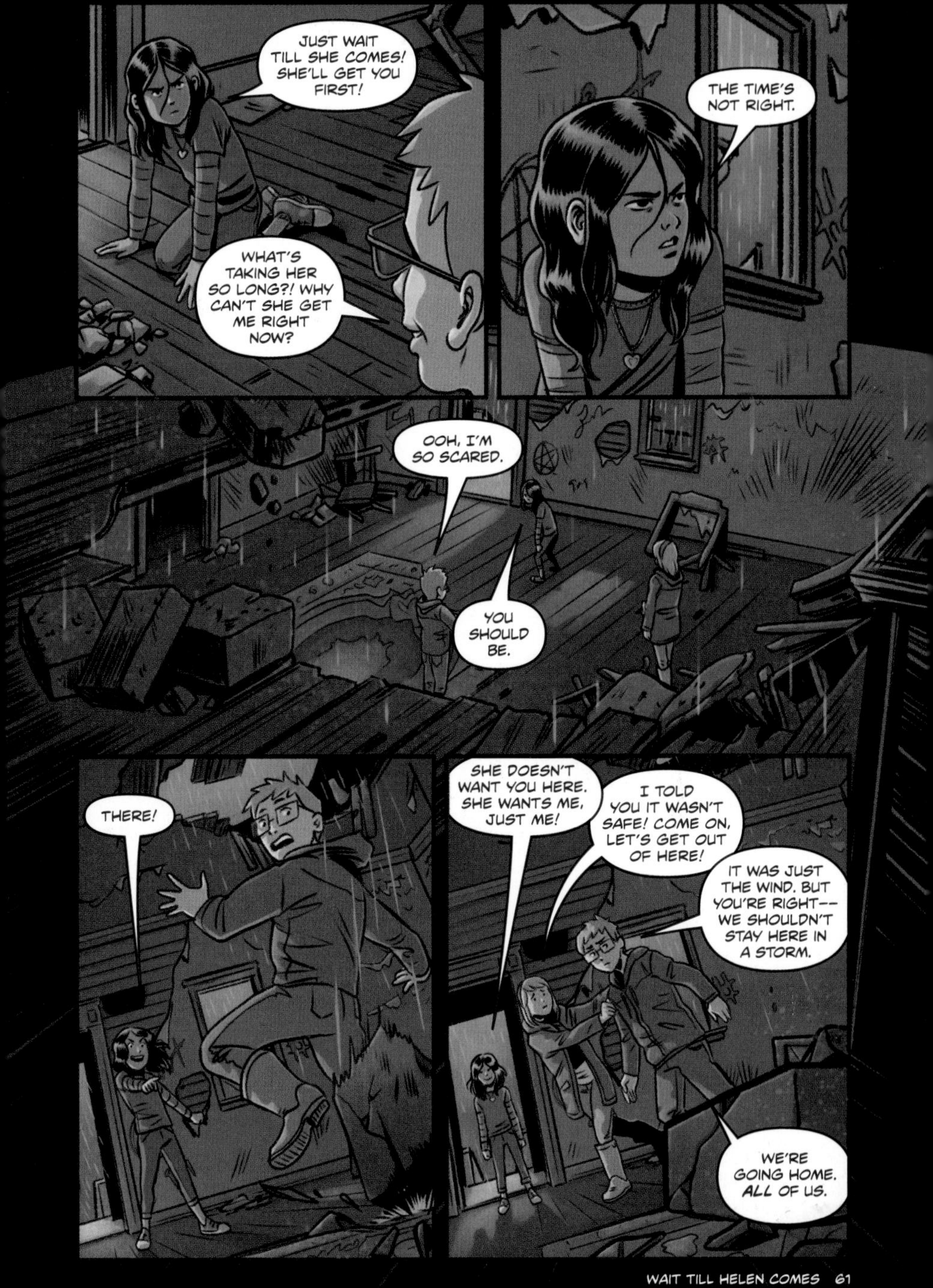
JUST WAIT TILL SHE COMES! SHE'LL GET YOU FIRST!
WHAT'S TAKING HER SO LONG?! WHY CAN'T SHE GET ME RIGHT NOW?
THE TIME'S NOT RIGHT.
OOH, I'M SO SCARED.
YOU SHOULD BE.
THERE!
SHE DOESN'T WANT YOU HERE. SHE WANTS ME, JUST ME!
I TOLD YOU IT WASN'T SAFE! COME ON, LET'S GET OUT OF HERE!
IT WAS JUST THE WIND. BUT YOU'RE RIGHT-- WE SHOULDN'T STAY HERE IN A STORM.
WE'RE GOING HOME. *ALL* OF US.

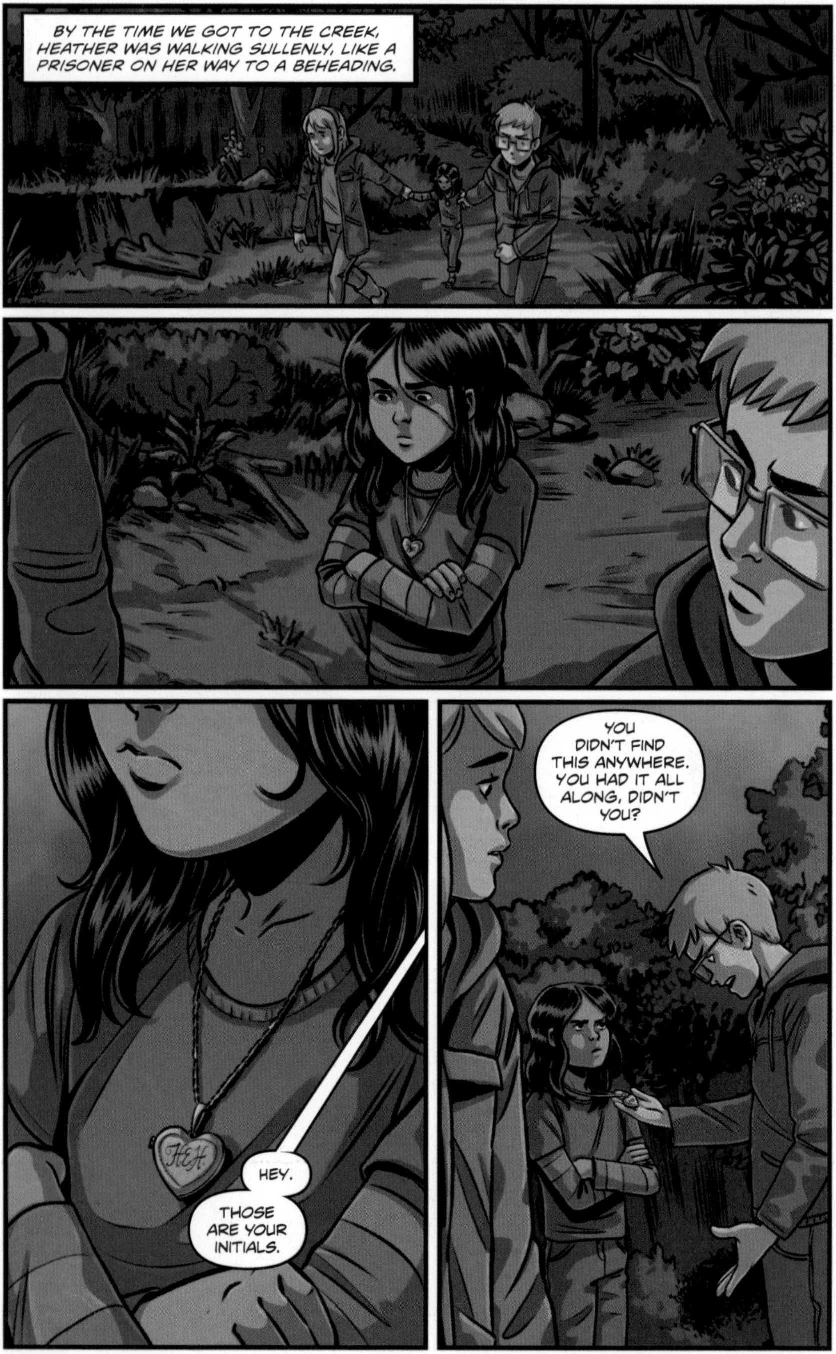
BY THE TIME WE GOT TO THE CREEK, HEATHER WAS WALKING SULLENLY, LIKE A PRISONER ON HER WAY TO A BEHEADING.
HEY.
THOSE ARE YOUR INITIALS.
YOU DIDN'T FIND THIS ANYWHERE. YOU HAD IT ALL ALONG, DIDN'T YOU?

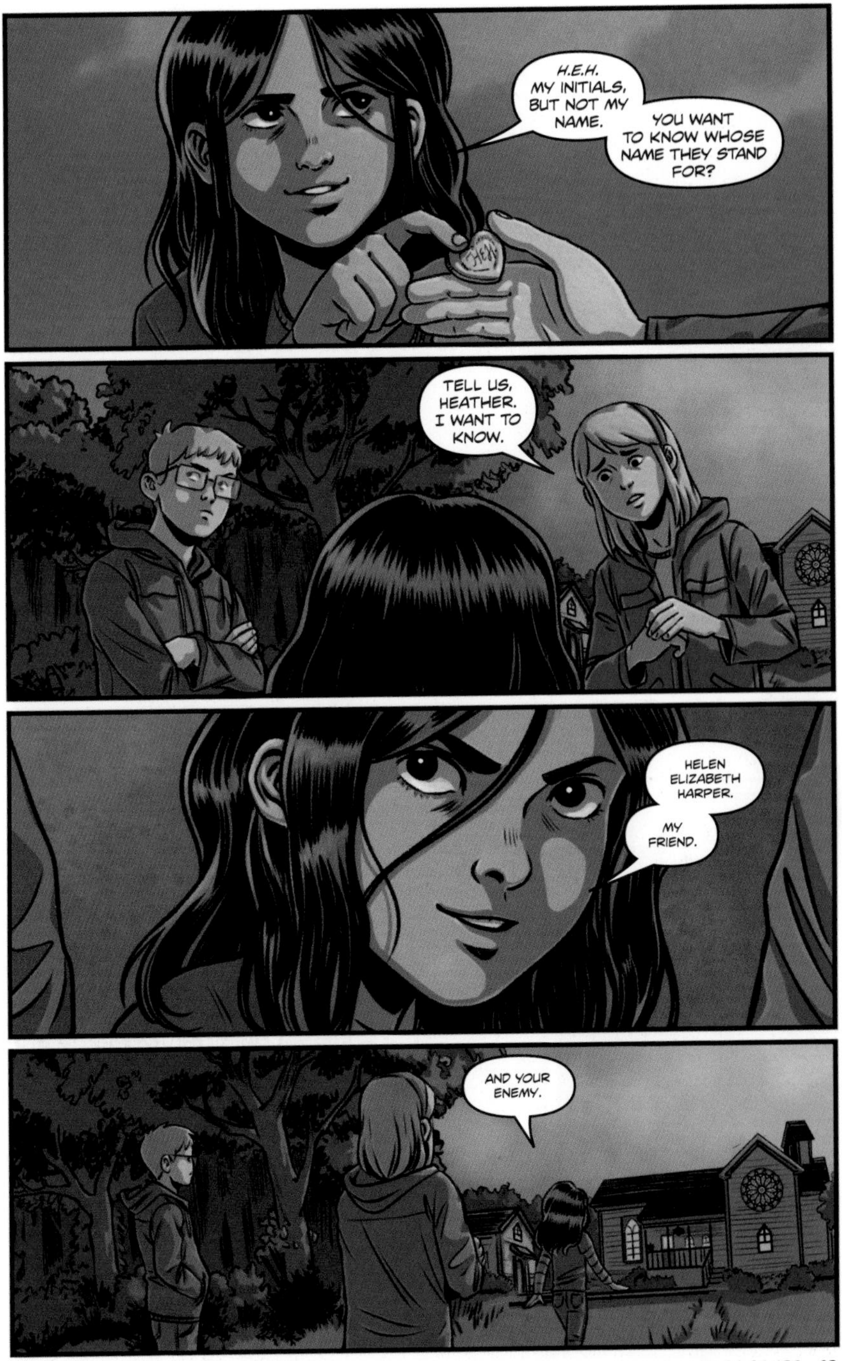
H.E.H. MY INITIALS, BUT NOT MY NAME.
YOU WANT TO KNOW WHOSE NAME THEY STAND FOR?
TELL US, HEATHER. I WANT TO KNOW.
HELEN ELIZABETH HARPER.
MY FRIEND.
AND YOUR ENEMY.

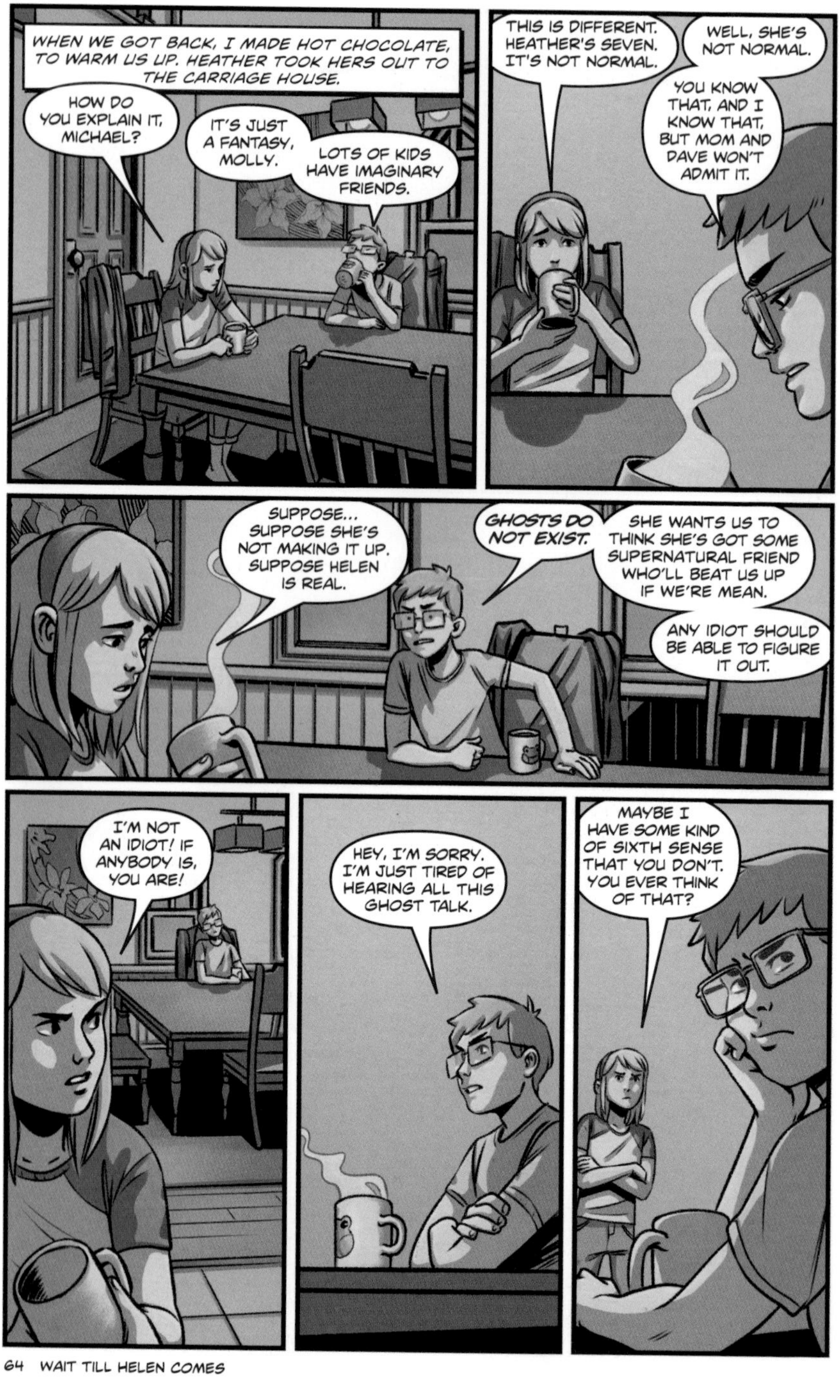
WHEN WE GOT BACK, I MADE HOT CHOCOLATE, TO WARM US UP. HEATHER TOOK HERS OUT TO THE CARRIAGE HOUSE.
HOW DO YOU EXPLAIN IT, MICHAEL?
IT'S JUST A FANTASY, MOLLY.
LOTS OF KIDS HAVE IMAGINARY FRIENDS.
THIS IS DIFFERENT. HEATHER'S SEVEN. IT'S NOT NORMAL.
WELL, SHE'S NOT NORMAL.
YOU KNOW THAT, AND I KNOW THAT, BUT MOM AND DAVE WON'T ADMIT IT.
SUPPOSE... SUPPOSE SHE'S NOT MAKING IT UP. SUPPOSE HELEN IS REAL.
GHOSTS DO NOT EXIST.
SHE WANTS US TO THINK SHE'S GOT SOME SUPERNATURAL FRIEND WHO'LL BEAT US UP IF WE'RE MEAN.
ANY IDIOT SHOULD BE ABLE TO FIGURE IT OUT.
I'M NOT AN IDIOT! IF ANYBODY IS, YOU ARE!
HEY, I'M SORRY. I'M JUST TIRED OF HEARING ALL THIS GHOST TALK.
MAYBE I HAVE SOME KIND OF SIXTH SENSE THAT YOU DON'T. YOU EVER THINK OF THAT?

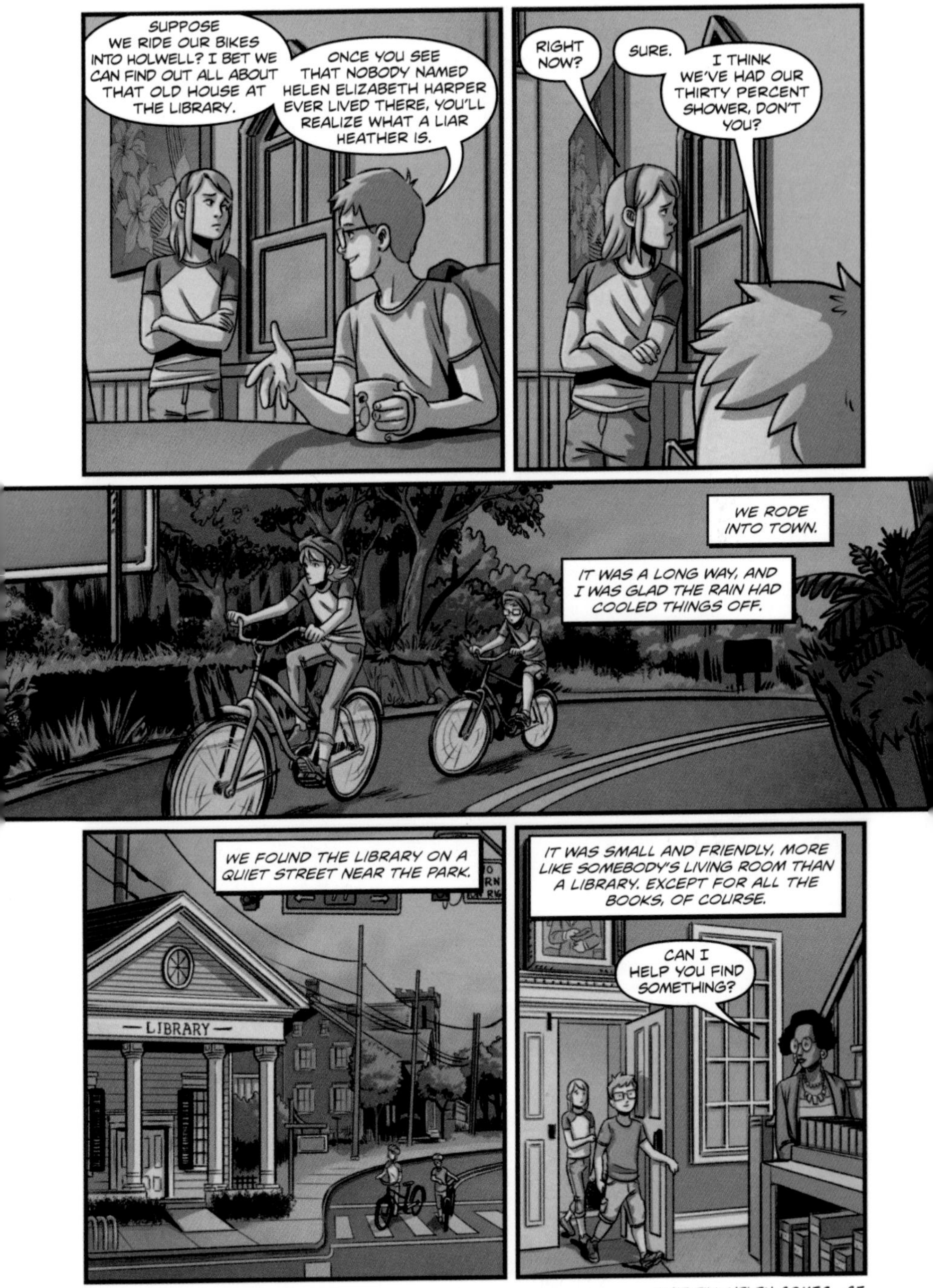
SUPPOSE WE RIDE OUR BIKES INTO HOLWELL? I BET WE CAN FIND OUT ALL ABOUT THAT OLD HOUSE AT THE LIBRARY.
ONCE YOU SEE THAT NOBODY NAMED HELEN ELIZABETH HARPER EVER LIVED THERE, YOU'LL REALIZE WHAT A LIAR HEATHER IS.
RIGHT NOW?
SURE.
I THINK WE'VE HAD OUR THIRTY PERCENT SHOWER, DON'T YOU?
WE RODE INTO TOWN.
IT WAS A LONG WAY, AND I WAS GLAD THE RAIN HAD COOLED THINGS OFF.
WE FOUND THE LIBRARY ON A QUIET STREET NEAR THE PARK.
LIBRARY
IT WAS SMALL AND FRIENDLY, MORE LIKE SOMEBODY'S LIVING ROOM THAN A LIBRARY. EXCEPT FOR ALL THE BOOKS, OF COURSE.
CAN I HELP YOU FIND SOMETHING?

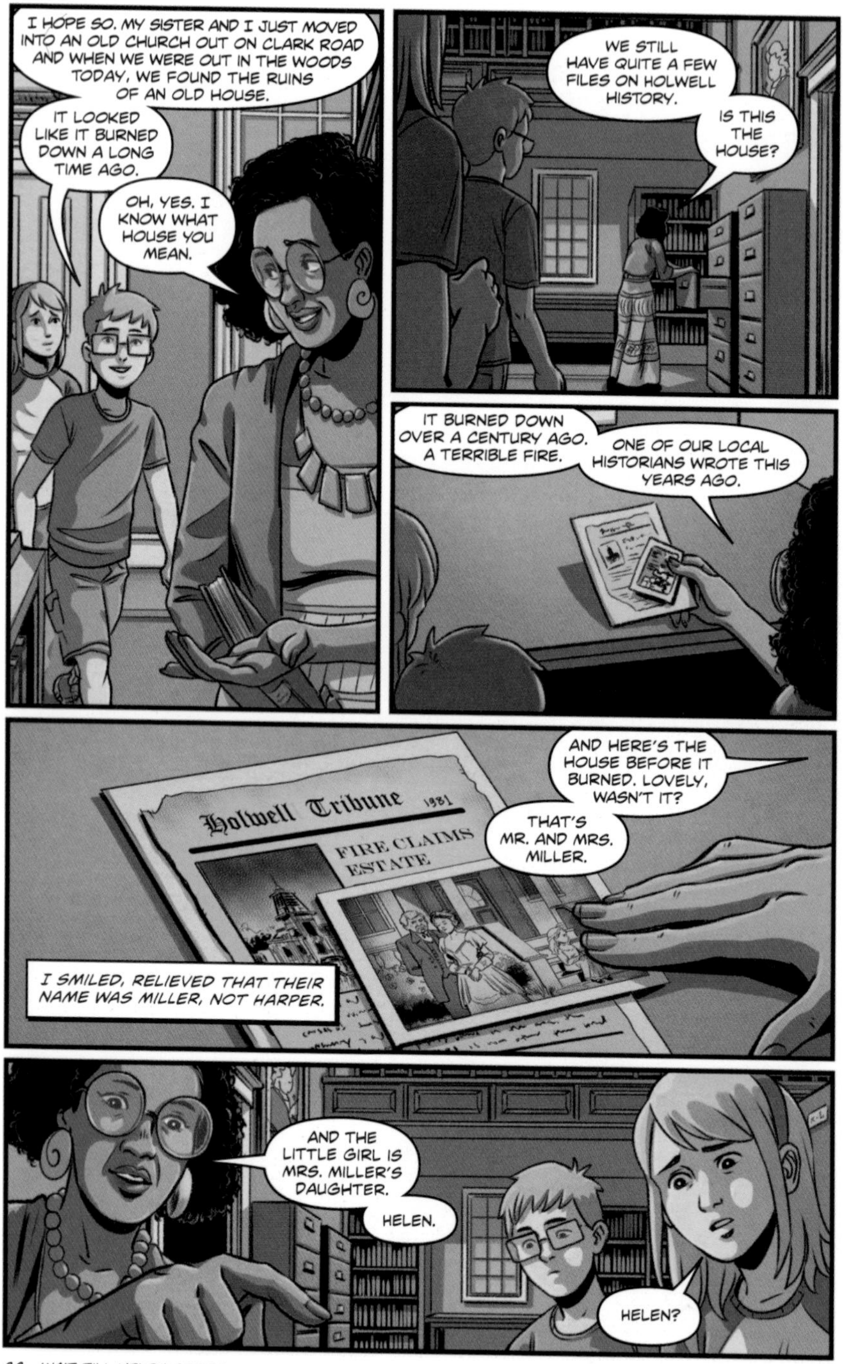
I HOPE SO. MY SISTER AND I JUST MOVED INTO AN OLD CHURCH OUT ON CLARK ROAD AND WHEN WE WERE OUT IN THE WOODS TODAY, WE FOUND THE RUINS OF AN OLD HOUSE.
IT LOOKED LIKE IT BURNED DOWN A LONG TIME AGO.
OH, YES. I KNOW WHAT HOUSE YOU MEAN.
WE STILL HAVE QUITE A FEW FILES ON HOLWELL HISTORY.
IS THIS THE HOUSE?
IT BURNED DOWN OVER A CENTURY AGO. A TERRIBLE FIRE.
ONE OF OUR LOCAL HISTORIANS WROTE THIS YEARS AGO.
Holwell Tribune 1981
FIRE CLAIMS ESTATE
AND HERE'S THE HOUSE BEFORE IT BURNED. LOVELY, WASN'T IT?
THAT'S MR. AND MRS. MILLER.
I SMILED, RELIEVED THAT THEIR NAME WAS MILLER, NOT HARPER.
AND THE LITTLE GIRL IS MRS. MILLER'S DAUGHTER.
HELEN.
HELEN?

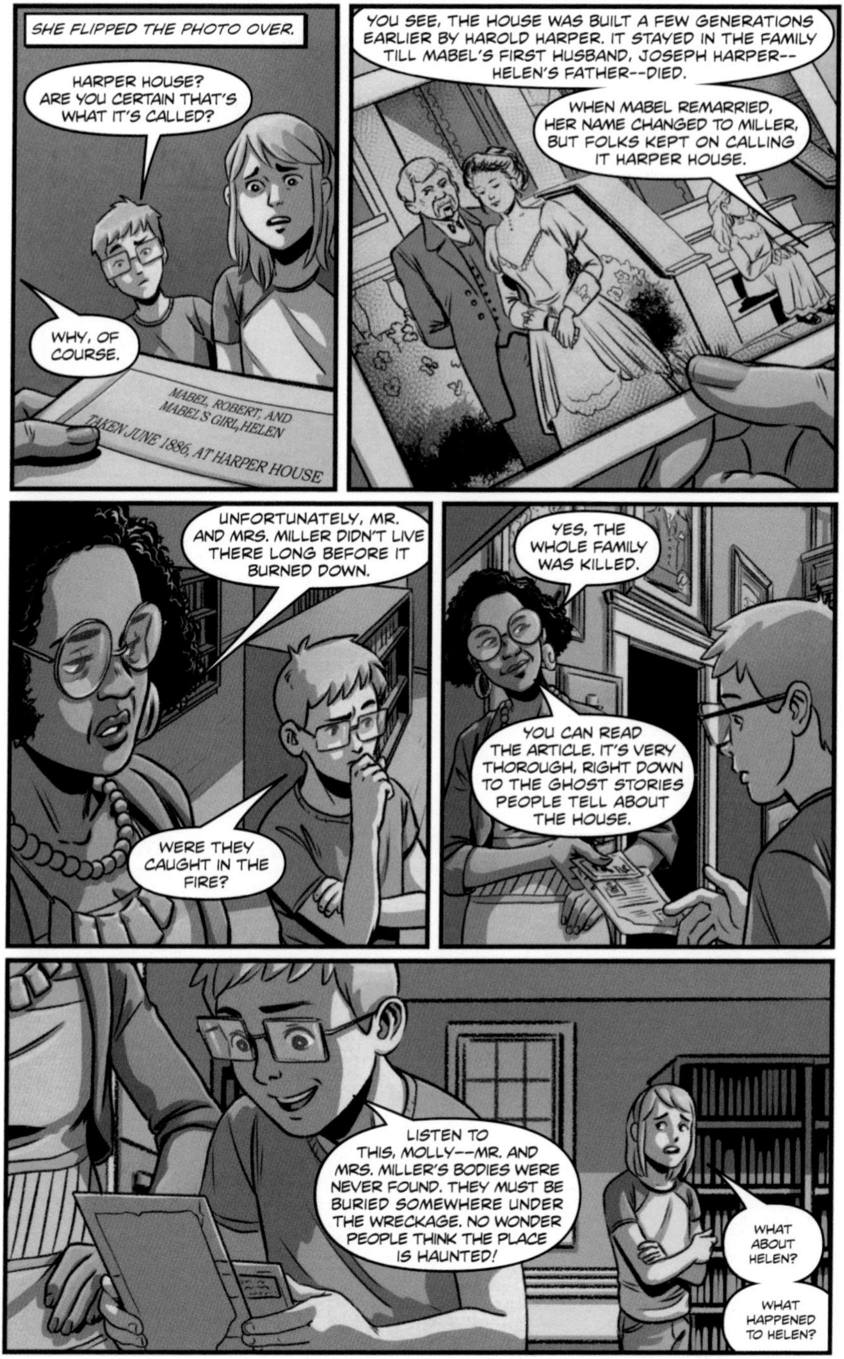
SHE FLIPPED THE PHOTO OVER.
HARPER HOUSE? ARE YOU CERTAIN THAT'S WHAT IT'S CALLED?
WHY, OF COURSE.
MABEL, ROBERT, AND MABEL'S GIRL, HELEN
TAKEN JUNE 1886, AT HARPER HOUSE
YOU SEE, THE HOUSE WAS BUILT A FEW GENERATIONS EARLIER BY HAROLD HARPER. IT STAYED IN THE FAMILY TILL MABEL'S FIRST HUSBAND, JOSEPH HARPER-- HELEN'S FATHER--DIED.
WHEN MABEL REMARRIED, HER NAME CHANGED TO MILLER, BUT FOLKS KEPT ON CALLING IT HARPER HOUSE.
UNFORTUNATELY, MR. AND MRS. MILLER DIDN'T LIVE THERE LONG BEFORE IT BURNED DOWN.
WERE THEY CAUGHT IN THE FIRE?
YES, THE WHOLE FAMILY WAS KILLED.
YOU CAN READ THE ARTICLE. IT'S VERY THOROUGH, RIGHT DOWN TO THE GHOST STORIES PEOPLE TELL ABOUT THE HOUSE.
LISTEN TO THIS, MOLLY--MR. AND MRS. MILLER'S BODIES WERE NEVER FOUND. THEY MUST BE BURIED SOMEWHERE UNDER THE WRECKAGE. NO WONDER PEOPLE THINK THE PLACE IS HAUNTED!
WHAT ABOUT HELEN?
WHAT HAPPENED TO HELEN?

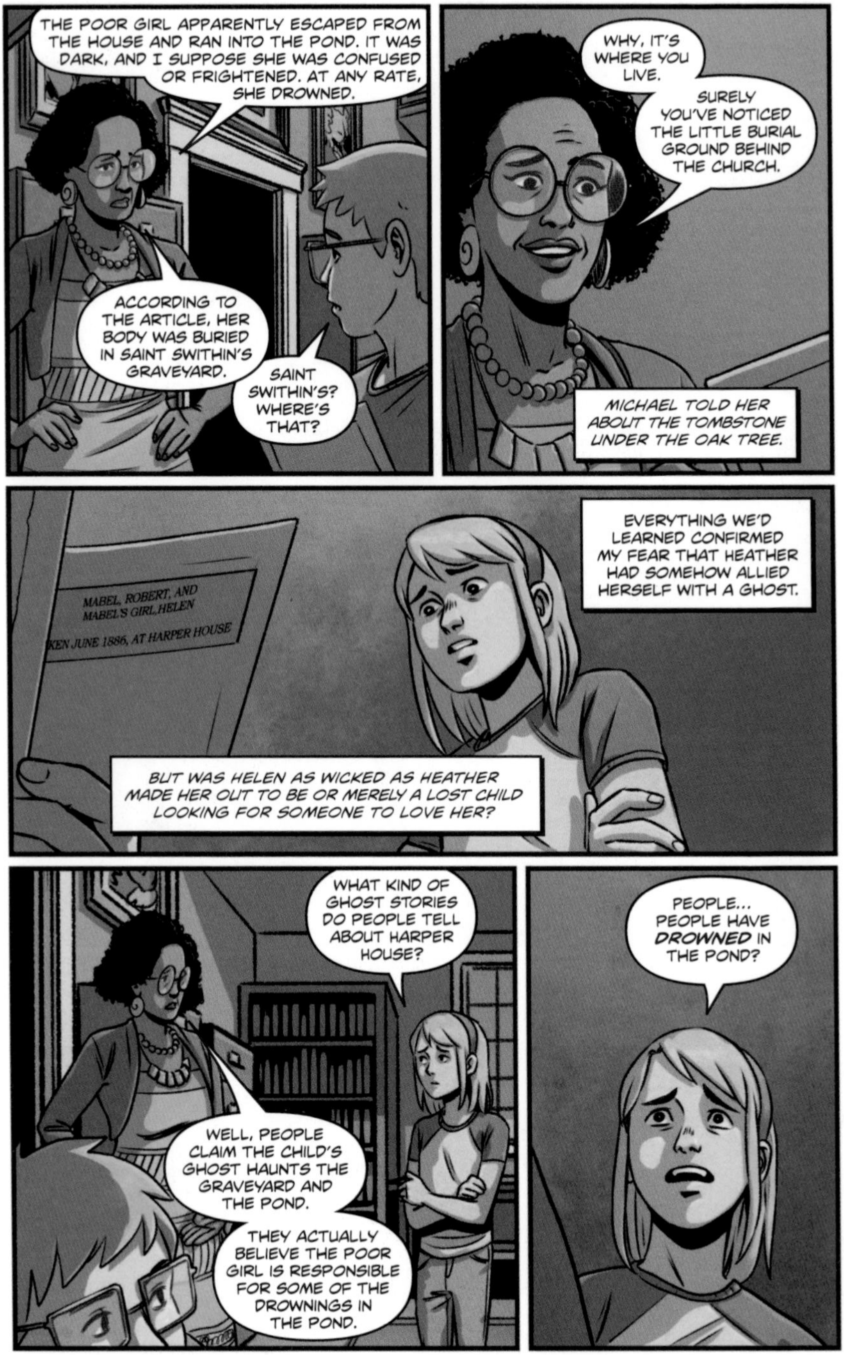
THE POOR GIRL APPARENTLY ESCAPED FROM THE HOUSE AND RAN INTO THE POND. IT WAS DARK, AND I SUPPOSE SHE WAS CONFUSED OR FRIGHTENED. AT ANY RATE, SHE DROWNED.
ACCORDING TO THE ARTICLE, HER BODY WAS BURIED IN SAINT SWITHIN'S GRAVEYARD.
SAINT SWITHIN'S? WHERE'S THAT?
WHY, IT'S WHERE YOU LIVE.
SURELY YOU'VE NOTICED THE LITTLE BURIAL GROUND BEHIND THE CHURCH.
MICHAEL TOLD HER ABOUT THE TOMBSTONE UNDER THE OAK TREE.
MABEL, ROBERT, AND MABEL'S GIRL, HELEN
KEN JUNE 1886, AT HARPER HOUSE
EVERYTHING WE'D LEARNED CONFIRMED MY FEAR THAT HEATHER HAD SOMEHOW ALLIED HERSELF WITH A GHOST.
BUT WAS HELEN AS WICKED AS HEATHER MADE HER OUT TO BE OR MERELY A LOST CHILD LOOKING FOR SOMEONE TO LOVE HER?
WHAT KIND OF GHOST STORIES DO PEOPLE TELL ABOUT HARPER HOUSE?
WELL, PEOPLE CLAIM THE CHILD'S GHOST HAUNTS THE GRAVEYARD AND THE POND.
THEY ACTUALLY BELIEVE THE POOR GIRL IS RESPONSIBLE FOR SOME OF THE DROWNINGS IN THE POND.
PEOPLE... PEOPLE HAVE **DROWNED** IN THE POND?

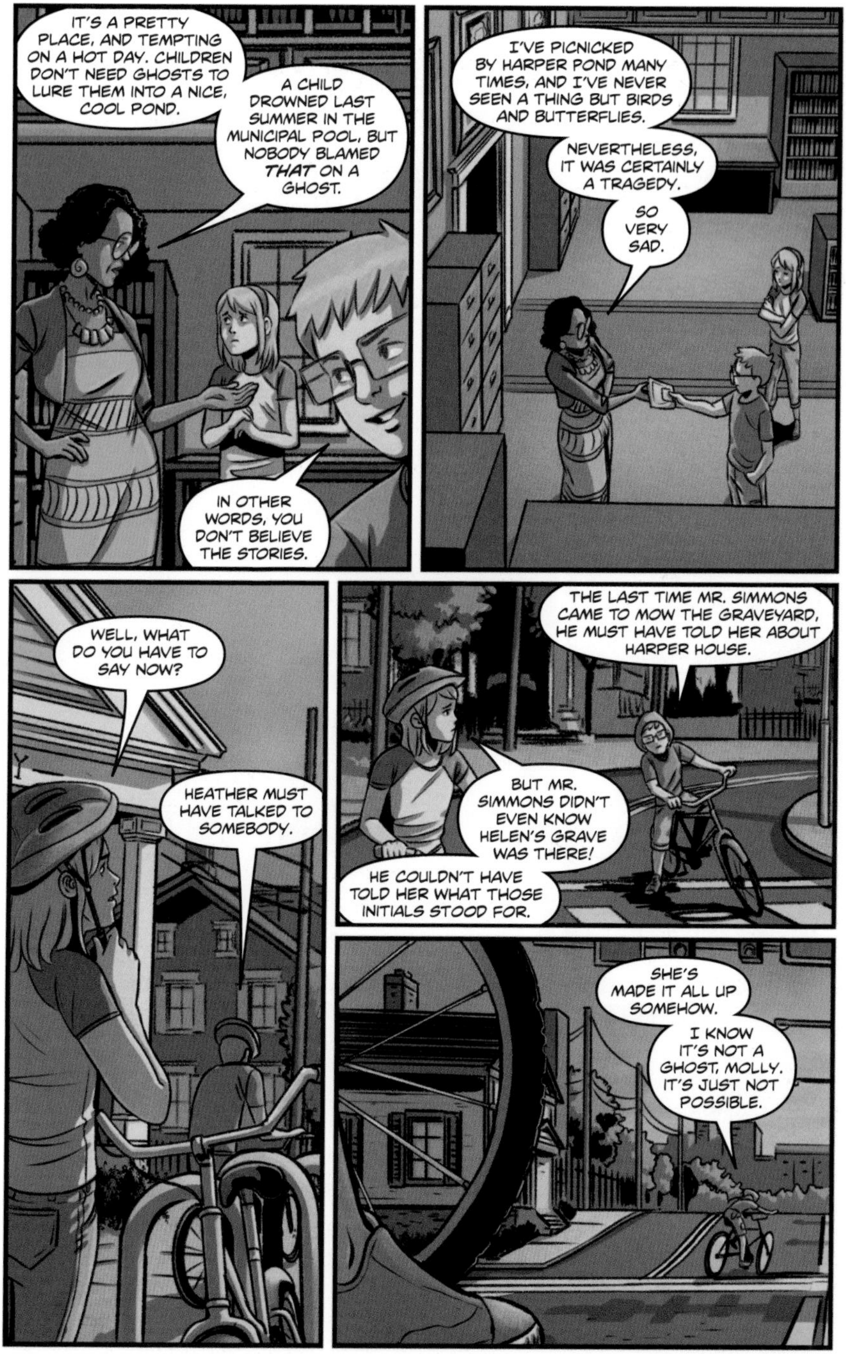
IT'S A PRETTY PLACE, AND TEMPTING ON A HOT DAY. CHILDREN DON'T NEED GHOSTS TO LURE THEM INTO A NICE, COOL POND.
A CHILD DROWNED LAST SUMMER IN THE MUNICIPAL POOL, BUT NOBODY BLAMED *THAT* ON A GHOST.
IN OTHER WORDS, YOU DON'T BELIEVE THE STORIES.
I'VE PICNICKED BY HARPER POND MANY TIMES, AND I'VE NEVER SEEN A THING BUT BIRDS AND BUTTERFLIES.
NEVERTHELESS, IT WAS CERTAINLY A TRAGEDY.
SO VERY SAD.
WELL, WHAT DO YOU HAVE TO SAY NOW?
HEATHER MUST HAVE TALKED TO SOMEBODY.
THE LAST TIME MR. SIMMONS CAME TO MOW THE GRAVEYARD, HE MUST HAVE TOLD HER ABOUT HARPER HOUSE.
BUT MR. SIMMONS DIDN'T EVEN KNOW HELEN'S GRAVE WAS THERE!
HE COULDN'T HAVE TOLD HER WHAT THOSE INITIALS STOOD FOR.
SHE'S MADE IT ALL UP SOMEHOW.
I KNOW IT'S NOT A GHOST, MOLLY. IT'S JUST NOT POSSIBLE.

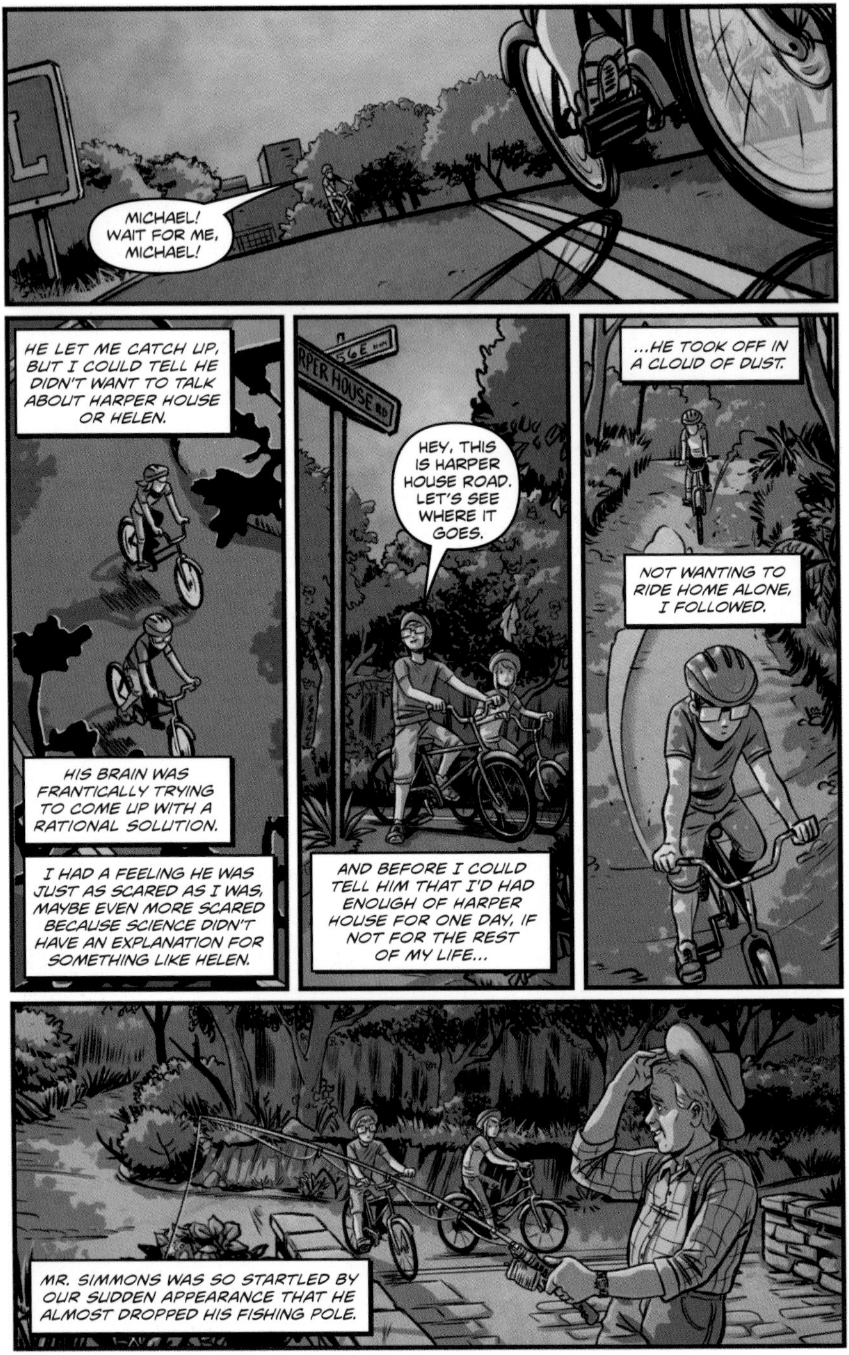
MICHAEL! WAIT FOR ME, MICHAEL!
HE LET ME CATCH UP, BUT I COULD TELL HE DIDN'T WANT TO TALK ABOUT HARPER HOUSE OR HELEN.
HIS BRAIN WAS FRANTICALLY TRYING TO COME UP WITH A RATIONAL SOLUTION.
I HAD A FEELING HE WAS JUST AS SCARED AS I WAS, MAYBE EVEN MORE SCARED BECAUSE SCIENCE DIDN'T HAVE AN EXPLANATION FOR SOMETHING LIKE HELEN.
HARPER HOUSE RD
HEY, THIS IS HARPER HOUSE ROAD. LET'S SEE WHERE IT GOES.
AND BEFORE I COULD TELL HIM THAT I'D HAD ENOUGH OF HARPER HOUSE FOR ONE DAY, IF NOT FOR THE REST OF MY LIFE...
...HE TOOK OFF IN A CLOUD OF DUST.
NOT WANTING TO RIDE HOME ALONE, I FOLLOWED.
MR. SIMMONS WAS SO STARTLED BY OUR SUDDEN APPEARANCE THAT HE ALMOST DROPPED HIS FISHING POLE.

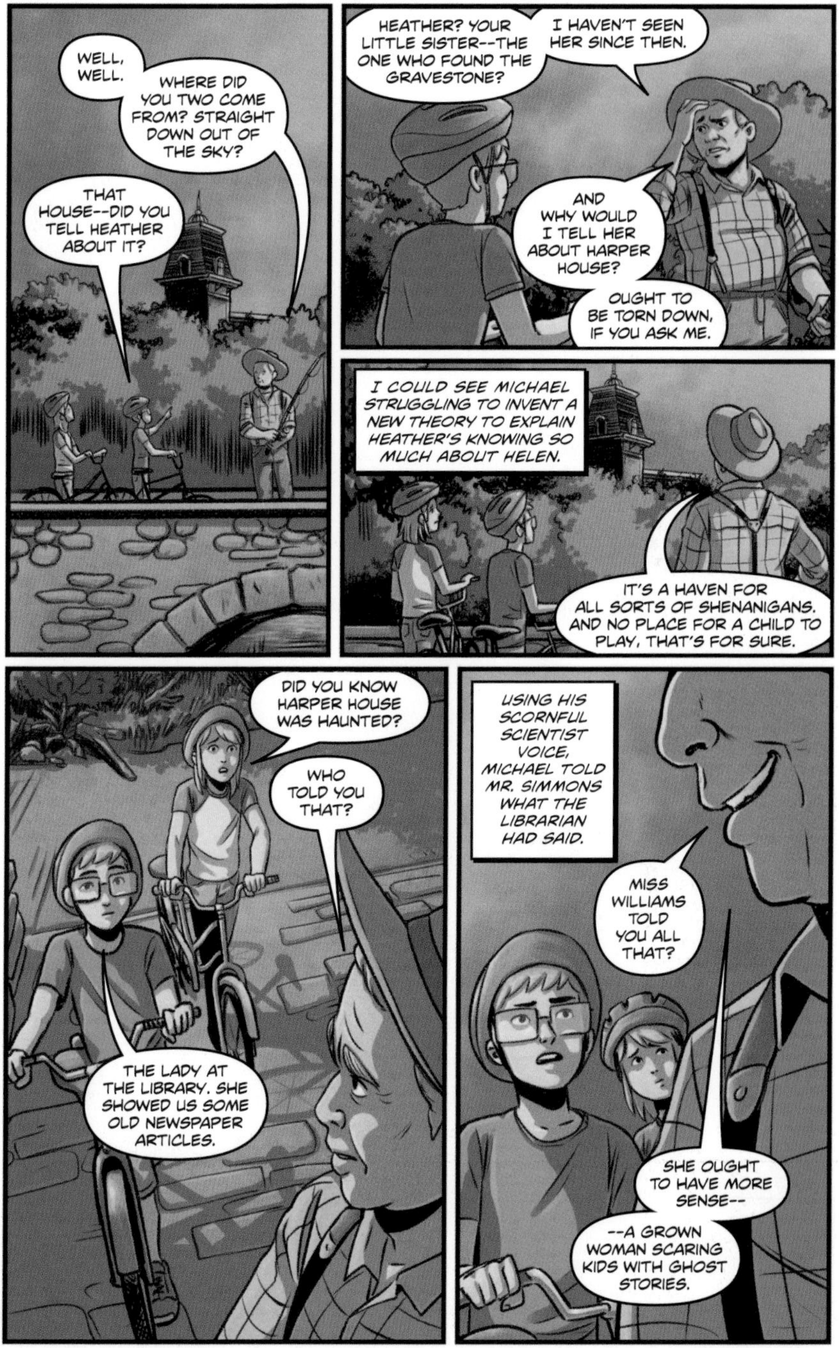
WELL, WELL.
WHERE DID YOU TWO COME FROM? STRAIGHT DOWN OUT OF THE SKY?
THAT HOUSE--DID YOU TELL HEATHER ABOUT IT?
HEATHER? YOUR LITTLE SISTER--THE ONE WHO FOUND THE GRAVESTONE?
I HAVEN'T SEEN HER SINCE THEN.
AND WHY WOULD I TELL HER ABOUT HARPER HOUSE?
OUGHT TO BE TORN DOWN, IF YOU ASK ME.
I COULD SEE MICHAEL STRUGGLING TO INVENT A NEW THEORY TO EXPLAIN HEATHER'S KNOWING SO MUCH ABOUT HELEN.
IT'S A HAVEN FOR ALL SORTS OF SHENANIGANS. AND NO PLACE FOR A CHILD TO PLAY, THAT'S FOR SURE.
DID YOU KNOW HARPER HOUSE WAS HAUNTED?
WHO TOLD YOU THAT?
THE LADY AT THE LIBRARY. SHE SHOWED US SOME OLD NEWSPAPER ARTICLES.
USING HIS SCORNFUL SCIENTIST VOICE, MICHAEL TOLD MR. SIMMONS WHAT THE LIBRARIAN HAD SAID.
MISS WILLIAMS TOLD YOU ALL THAT?
SHE OUGHT TO HAVE MORE SENSE--
--A GROWN WOMAN SCARING KIDS WITH GHOST STORIES.

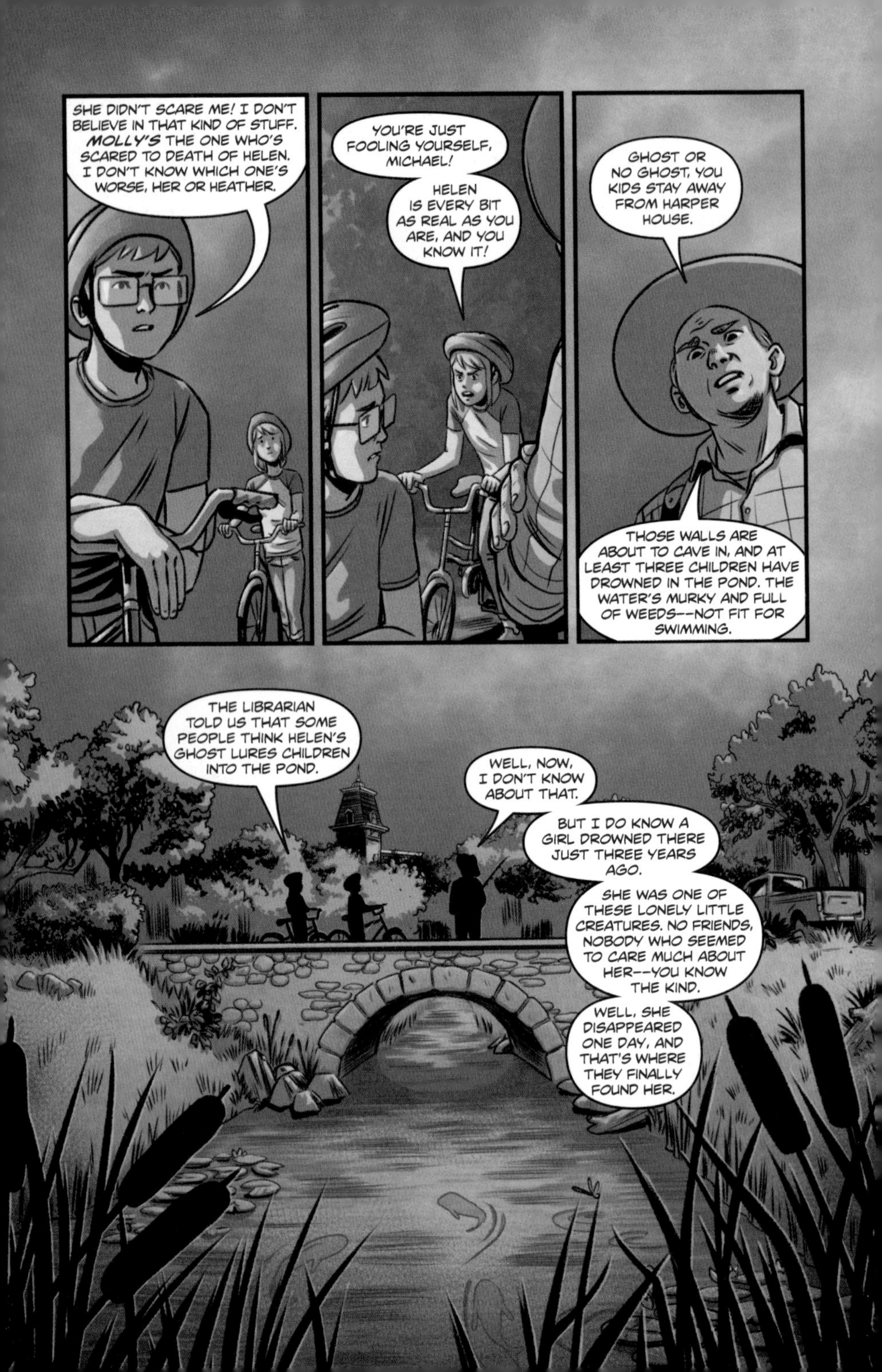
SHE DIDN'T SCARE ME! I DON'T BELIEVE IN THAT KIND OF STUFF. MOLLY'S THE ONE WHO'S SCARED TO DEATH OF HELEN. I DON'T KNOW WHICH ONE'S WORSE, HER OR HEATHER.
YOU'RE JUST FOOLING YOURSELF, MICHAEL!
HELEN IS EVERY BIT AS REAL AS YOU ARE, AND YOU KNOW IT!
GHOST OR NO GHOST, YOU KIDS STAY AWAY FROM HARPER HOUSE.
THOSE WALLS ARE ABOUT TO CAVE IN, AND AT LEAST THREE CHILDREN HAVE DROWNED IN THE POND. THE WATER'S MURKY AND FULL OF WEEDS--NOT FIT FOR SWIMMING.
THE LIBRARIAN TOLD US THAT SOME PEOPLE THINK HELEN'S GHOST LURES CHILDREN INTO THE POND.
WELL, NOW, I DON'T KNOW ABOUT THAT.
BUT I DO KNOW A GIRL DROWNED THERE JUST THREE YEARS AGO.
SHE WAS ONE OF THESE LONELY LITTLE CREATURES. NO FRIENDS, NOBODY WHO SEEMED TO CARE MUCH ABOUT HER--YOU KNOW THE KIND.
WELL, SHE DISAPPEARED ONE DAY, AND THAT'S WHERE THEY FINALLY FOUND HER.

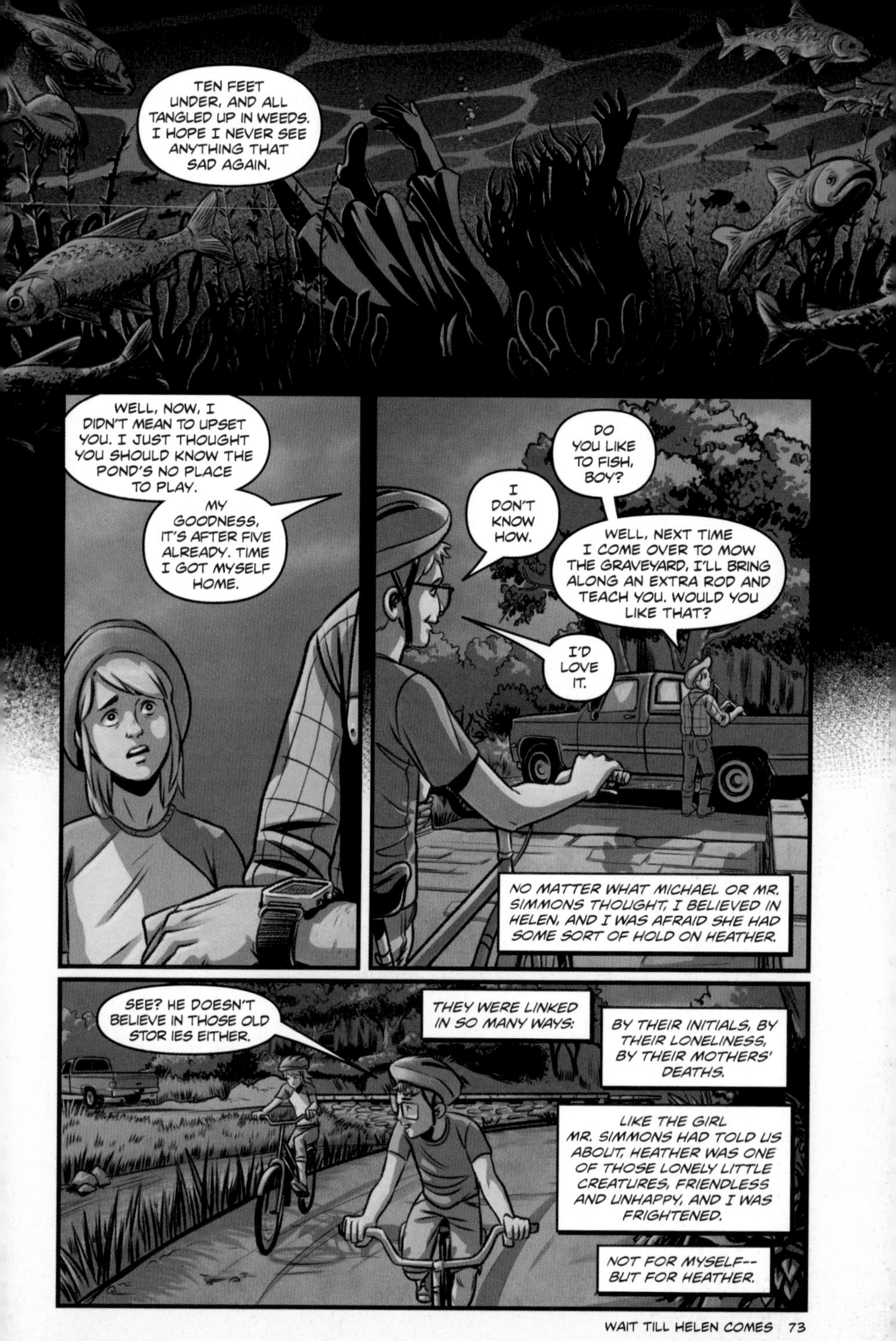
TEN FEET UNDER, AND ALL TANGLED UP IN WEEDS. I HOPE I NEVER SEE ANYTHING THAT SAD AGAIN.
WELL, NOW, I DIDN'T MEAN TO UPSET YOU. I JUST THOUGHT YOU SHOULD KNOW THE POND'S NO PLACE TO PLAY.
MY GOODNESS, IT'S AFTER FIVE ALREADY. TIME I GOT MYSELF HOME.
DO YOU LIKE TO FISH, BOY?
I DON'T KNOW HOW.
WELL, NEXT TIME I COME OVER TO MOW THE GRAVEYARD, I'LL BRING ALONG AN EXTRA ROD AND TEACH YOU. WOULD YOU LIKE THAT?
I'D LOVE IT.
NO MATTER WHAT MICHAEL OR MR. SIMMONS THOUGHT, I BELIEVED IN HELEN, AND I WAS AFRAID SHE HAD SOME SORT OF HOLD ON HEATHER.
SEE? HE DOESN'T BELIEVE IN THOSE OLD STOR IES EITHER.
THEY WERE LINKED IN SO MANY WAYS:
BY THEIR INITIALS, BY THEIR LONELINESS, BY THEIR MOTHERS' DEATHS.
LIKE THE GIRL MR. SIMMONS HAD TOLD US ABOUT, HEATHER WAS ONE OF THOSE LONELY LITTLE CREATURES, FRIENDLESS AND UNHAPPY, AND I WAS FRIGHTENED.
NOT FOR MYSELF-- BUT FOR HEATHER.

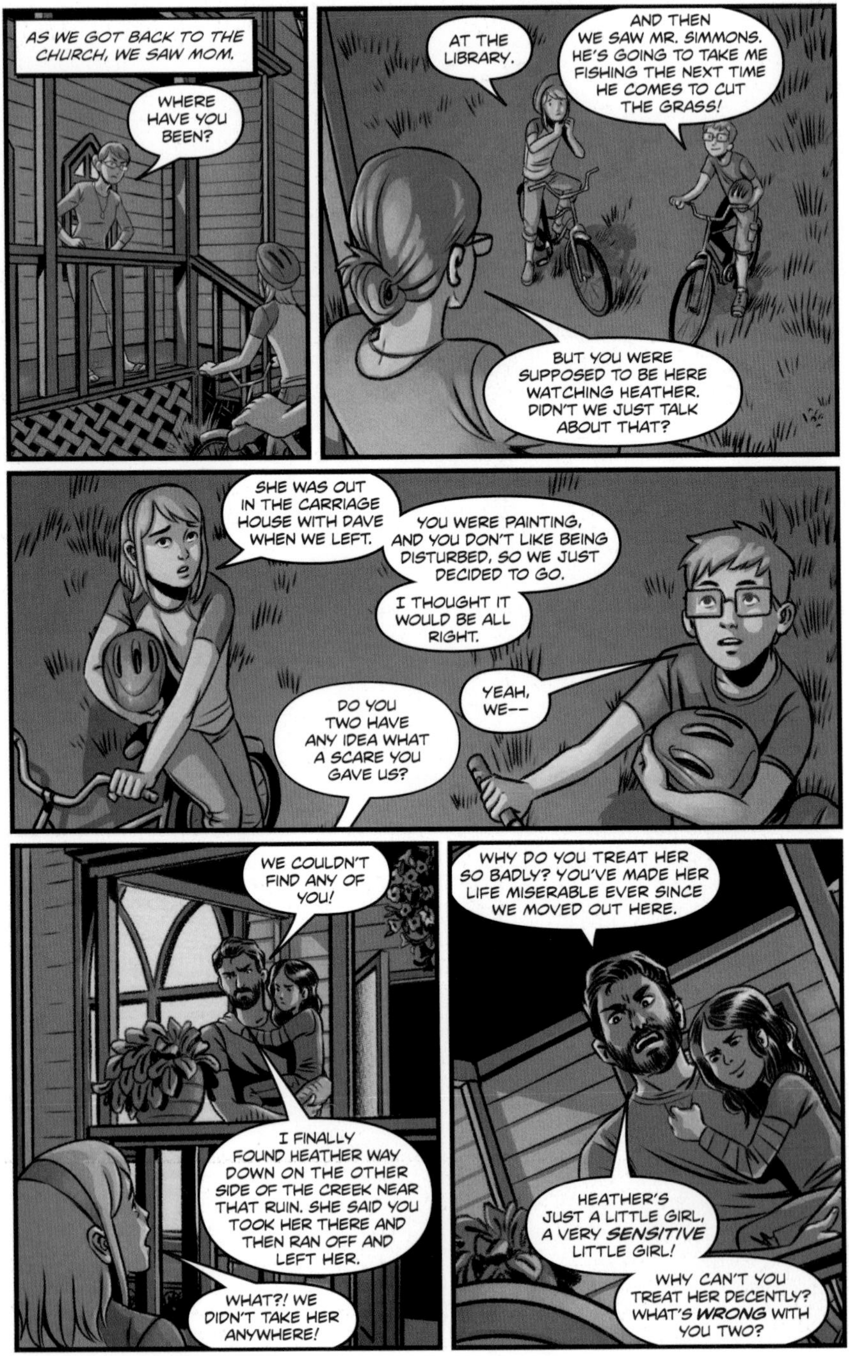
AS WE GOT BACK TO THE CHURCH, WE SAW MOM.
WHERE HAVE YOU BEEN?
AT THE LIBRARY.
AND THEN WE SAW MR. SIMMONS. HE'S GOING TO TAKE ME FISHING THE NEXT TIME HE COMES TO CUT THE GRASS!
BUT YOU WERE SUPPOSED TO BE HERE WATCHING HEATHER. DIDN'T WE JUST TALK ABOUT THAT?
SHE WAS OUT IN THE CARRIAGE HOUSE WITH DAVE WHEN WE LEFT.
YOU WERE PAINTING, AND YOU DON'T LIKE BEING DISTURBED, SO WE JUST DECIDED TO GO.
I THOUGHT IT WOULD BE ALL RIGHT.
YEAH, WE--
DO YOU TWO HAVE ANY IDEA WHAT A SCARE YOU GAVE US?
WE COULDN'T FIND ANY OF YOU!
I FINALLY FOUND HEATHER WAY DOWN ON THE OTHER SIDE OF THE CREEK NEAR THAT RUIN. SHE SAID YOU TOOK HER THERE AND THEN RAN OFF AND LEFT HER.
WHAT?! WE DIDN'T TAKE HER ANYWHERE!
WHY DO YOU TREAT HER SO BADLY? YOU'VE MADE HER LIFE MISERABLE EVER SINCE WE MOVED OUT HERE.
HEATHER'S JUST A LITTLE GIRL, A VERY SENSITIVE LITTLE GIRL!
WHY CAN'T YOU TREAT HER DECENTLY? WHAT'S WRONG WITH YOU TWO?

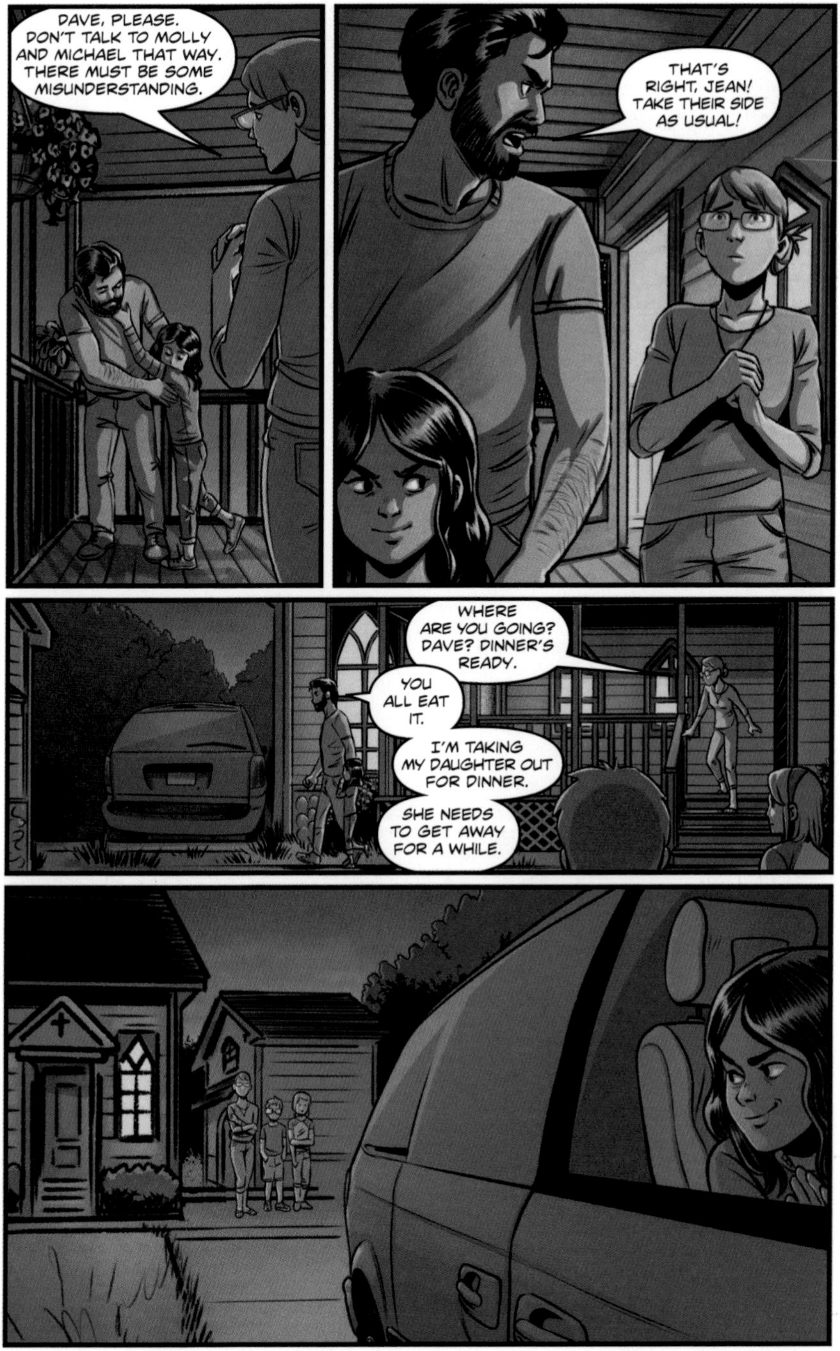
DAVE, PLEASE. DON'T TALK TO MOLLY AND MICHAEL THAT WAY. THERE MUST BE SOME MISUNDERSTANDING.
THAT'S RIGHT, JEAN! TAKE THEIR SIDE AS USUAL!
WHERE ARE YOU GOING? DAVE? DINNER'S READY.
YOU ALL EAT IT.
I'M TAKING MY DAUGHTER OUT FOR DINNER.
SHE NEEDS TO GET AWAY FOR A WHILE.

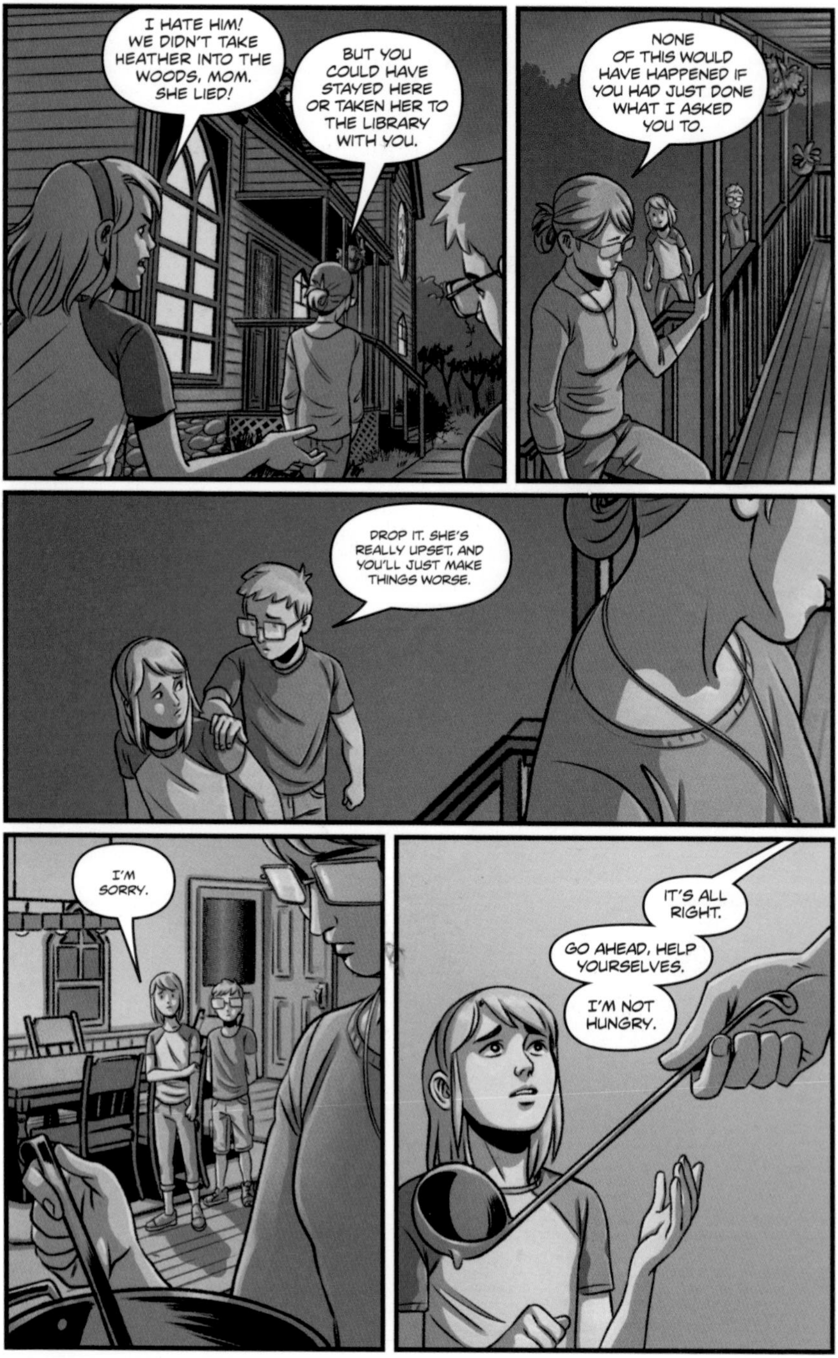
I HATE HIM! WE DIDN'T TAKE HEATHER INTO THE WOODS, MOM. SHE LIED!
BUT YOU COULD HAVE STAYED HERE OR TAKEN HER TO THE LIBRARY WITH YOU.
NONE OF THIS WOULD HAVE HAPPENED IF YOU HAD JUST DONE WHAT I ASKED YOU TO.
DROP IT. SHE'S REALLY UPSET, AND YOU'LL JUST MAKE THINGS WORSE.
I'M SORRY.
IT'S ALL RIGHT.
GO AHEAD, HELP YOURSELVES.
I'M NOT HUNGRY.

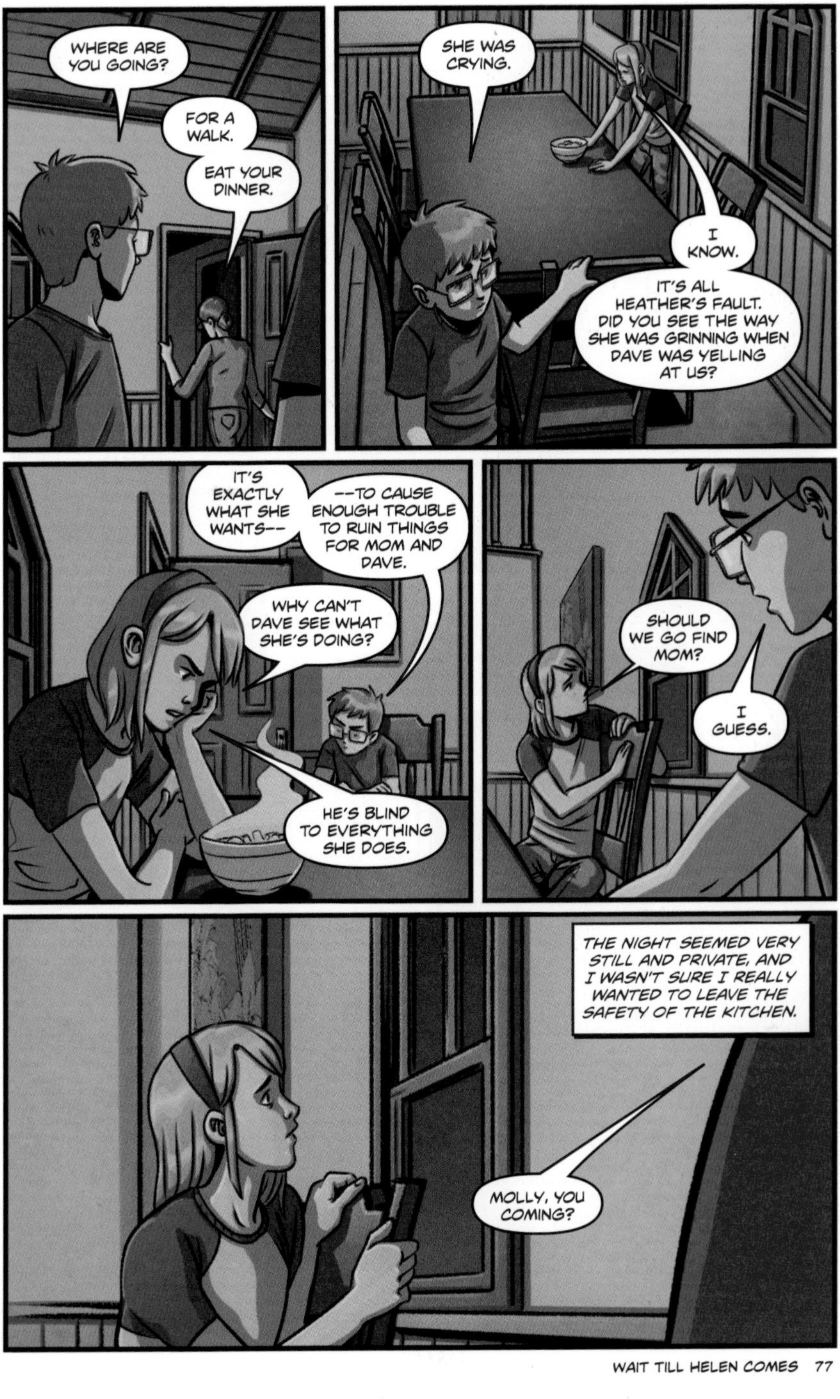
WHERE ARE YOU GOING?
FOR A WALK.
EAT YOUR DINNER.
SHE WAS CRYING.
I KNOW.
IT'S ALL HEATHER'S FAULT. DID YOU SEE THE WAY SHE WAS GRINNING WHEN DAVE WAS YELLING AT US?
IT'S EXACTLY WHAT SHE WANTS--
--TO CAUSE ENOUGH TROUBLE TO RUIN THINGS FOR MOM AND DAVE.
WHY CAN'T DAVE SEE WHAT SHE'S DOING?
HE'S BLIND TO EVERYTHING SHE DOES.
SHOULD WE GO FIND MOM?
I GUESS.
THE NIGHT SEEMED VERY STILL AND PRIVATE, AND I WASN'T SURE I REALLY WANTED TO LEAVE THE SAFETY OF THE KITCHEN.
MOLLY, YOU COMING?

THE GRASS WAS COLD AND WET, SOAKING THROUGH MY SHOES. I FELT HOMESICK FOR BALTIMORE.

MICHAEL...IT WAS NEVER THIS BAD BEFORE WE CAME HERE.

HEATHER WAS PRETTY AWFUL BUT NOTHING LIKE SHE IS NOW.

AND WE GOT ALONG WITH DAVE ALL RIGHT. AND HE AND MOM NEVER FOUGHT.

I KNOW. IT'S LIVING OUT HERE.

IT WAS HELEN'S INFLUENCE, I THOUGHT.

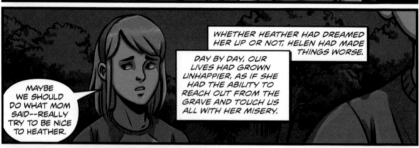

MAYBE WE SHOULD DO WHAT MOM SAID--REALLY TRY TO BE NICE TO HEATHER.

WHETHER HEATHER HAD DREAMED HER UP OR NOT, HELEN HAD MADE THINGS WORSE.

DAY BY DAY, OUR LIVES HAD GROWN UNHAPPIER, AS IF SHE HAD THE ABILITY TO REACH OUT FROM THE GRAVE AND TOUCH US ALL WITH HER MISERY.

ARE YOU KIDDING?

I'M WORRIED ABOUT HER, MICHAEL.

SHE WENT BACK TO THE POND--BACK TO HARPER HOUSE.

I KNOW YOU DON'T BELIEVE SHE REALLY SEES A GHOST, BUT THAT'S NOT THE POINT. WHATEVER MAKES HER GO THERE IS DANGEROUS.

EVEN MR. SIMMONS THINKS IT'S A BAD PLACE TO PLAY.

HE DOESN'T BELIEVE IN GHOSTS-- HE JUST KNOWS KIDS HAVE DROWNED THERE.

KIDS HAVE DROWNED THERE.

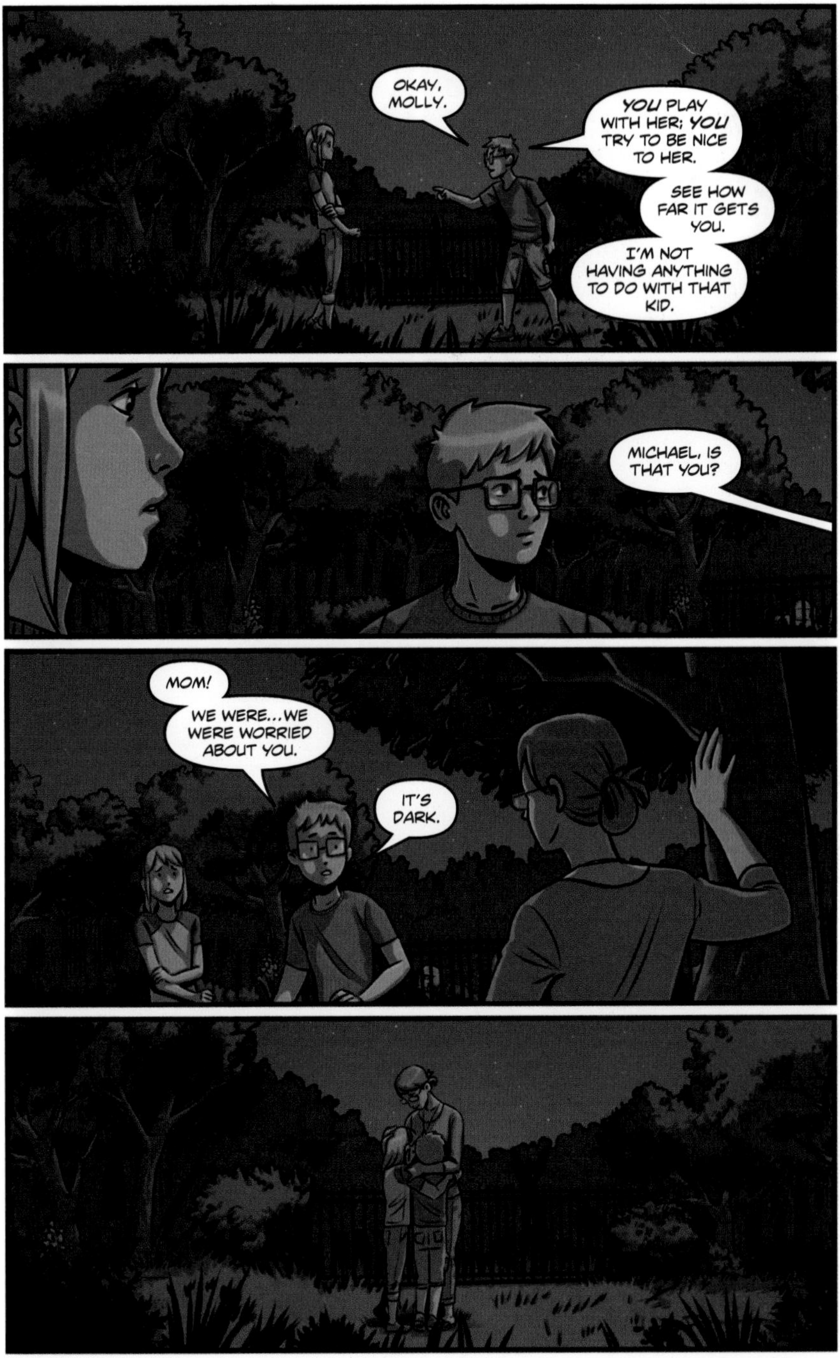
OKAY, MOLLY.
YOU PLAY WITH HER; YOU TRY TO BE NICE TO HER.
SEE HOW FAR IT GETS YOU.
I'M NOT HAVING ANYTHING TO DO WITH THAT KID.
MICHAEL, IS THAT YOU?
MOM!
WE WERE...WE WERE WORRIED ABOUT YOU.
IT'S DARK.

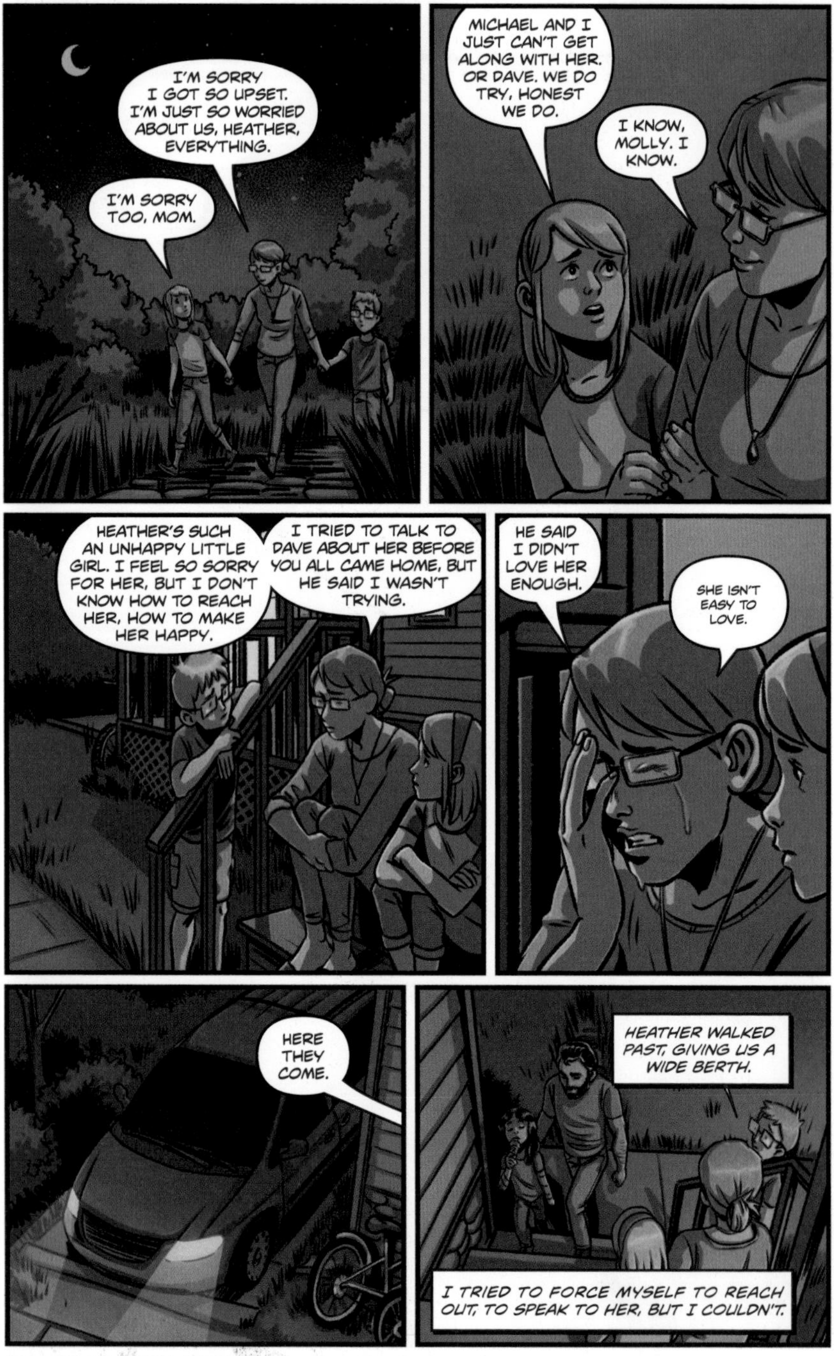
I'M SORRY I GOT SO UPSET. I'M JUST SO WORRIED ABOUT US, HEATHER, EVERYTHING.
I'M SORRY TOO, MOM.
MICHAEL AND I JUST CAN'T GET ALONG WITH HER. OR DAVE. WE DO TRY, HONEST WE DO.
I KNOW, MOLLY. I KNOW.
HEATHER'S SUCH AN UNHAPPY LITTLE GIRL. I FEEL SO SORRY FOR HER, BUT I DON'T KNOW HOW TO REACH HER, HOW TO MAKE HER HAPPY.
I TRIED TO TALK TO DAVE ABOUT HER BEFORE YOU ALL CAME HOME, BUT HE SAID I WASN'T TRYING.
HE SAID I DIDN'T LOVE HER ENOUGH.
SHE ISN'T EASY TO LOVE.
HERE THEY COME.
HEATHER WALKED PAST, GIVING US A WIDE BERTH.
I TRIED TO FORCE MYSELF TO REACH OUT, TO SPEAK TO HER, BUT I COULDN'T.

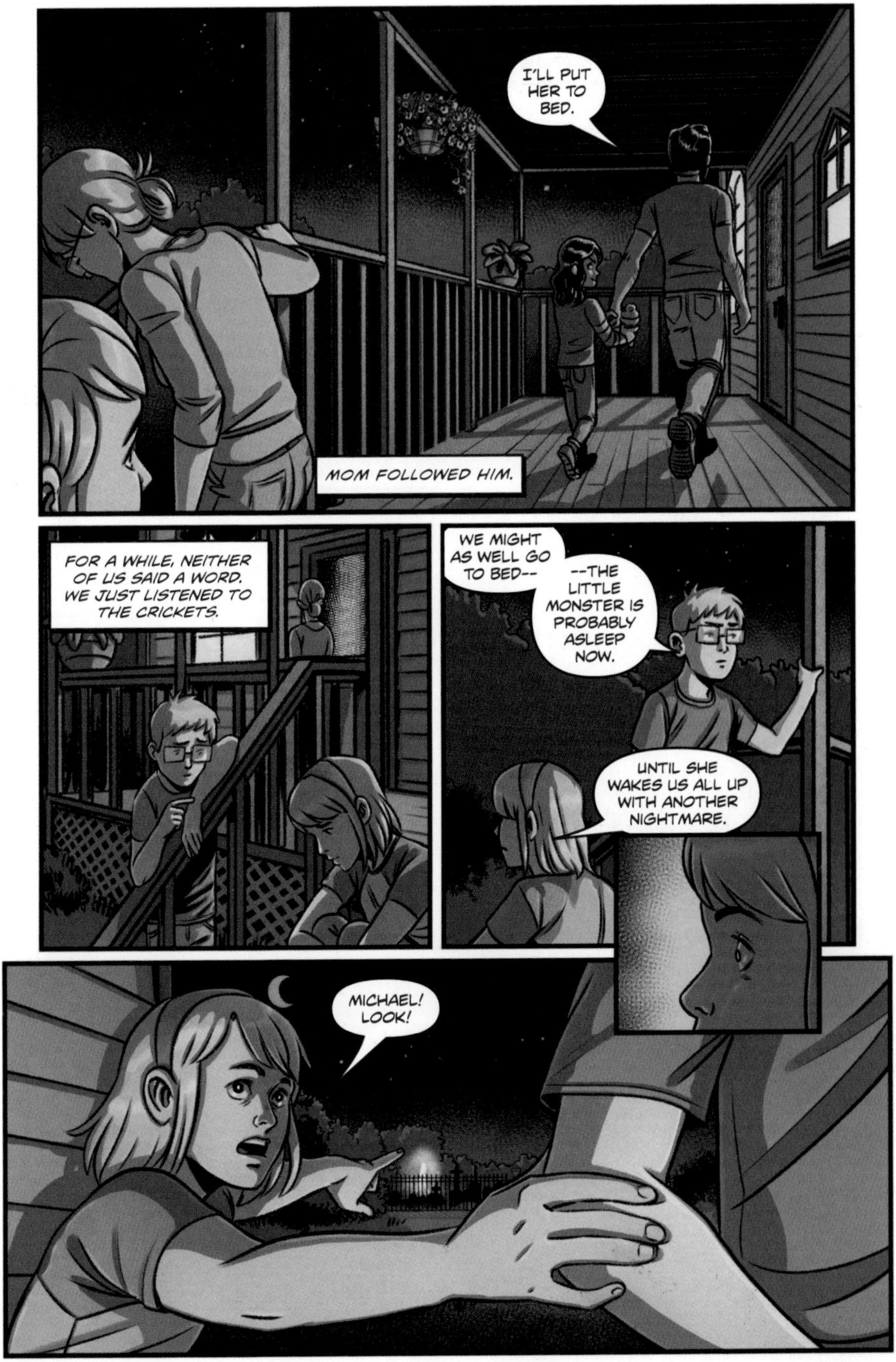
I'LL PUT HER TO BED.
MOM FOLLOWED HIM.
FOR A WHILE, NEITHER OF US SAID A WORD. WE JUST LISTENED TO THE CRICKETS.
WE MIGHT AS WELL GO TO BED--
--THE LITTLE MONSTER IS PROBABLY ASLEEP NOW.
UNTIL SHE WAKES US ALL UP WITH ANOTHER NIGHTMARE.
MICHAEL! LOOK!

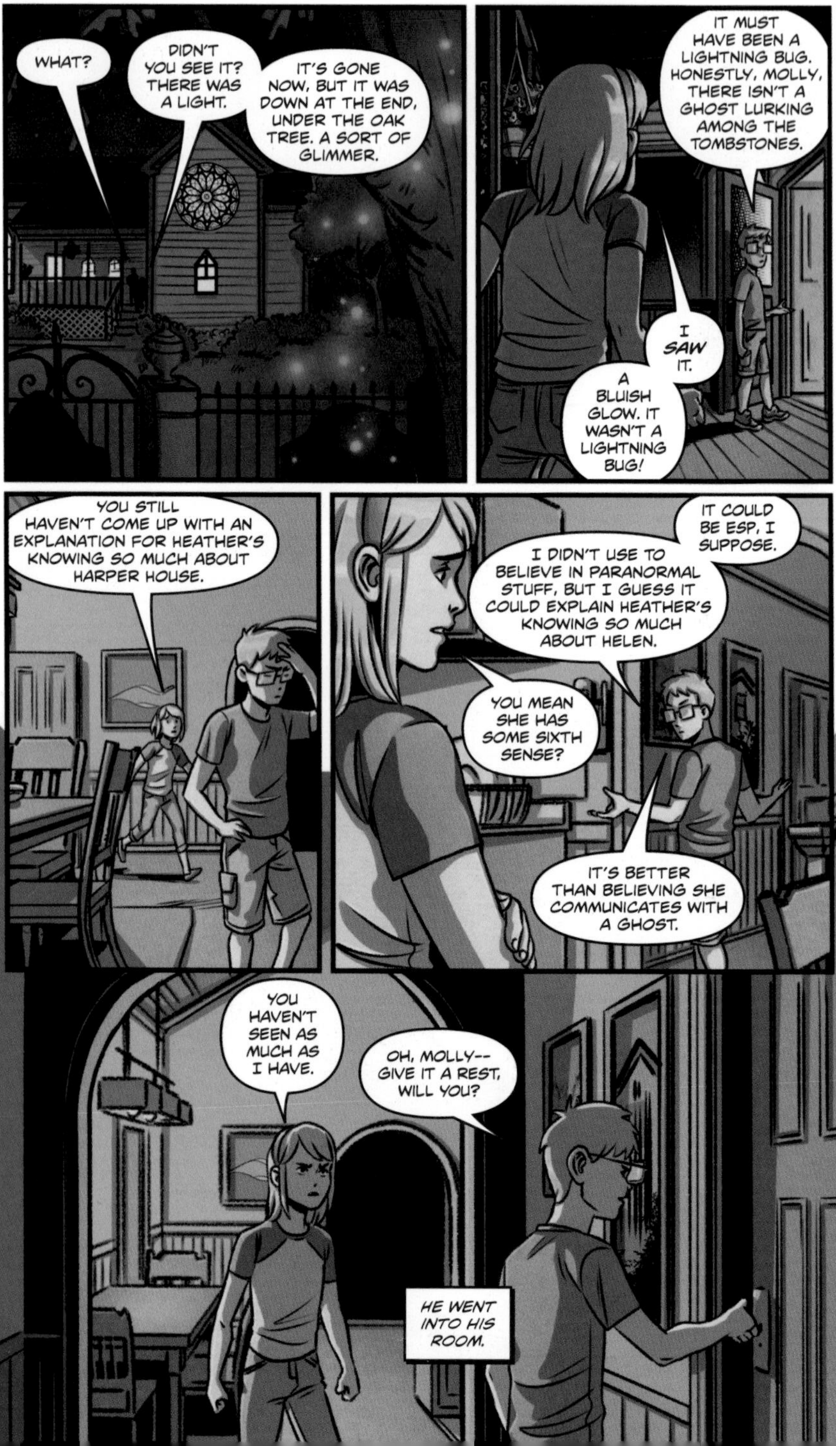
WHAT?
DIDN'T YOU SEE IT? THERE WAS A LIGHT.
IT'S GONE NOW, BUT IT WAS DOWN AT THE END, UNDER THE OAK TREE. A SORT OF GLIMMER.
IT MUST HAVE BEEN A LIGHTNING BUG. HONESTLY, MOLLY, THERE ISN'T A GHOST LURKING AMONG THE TOMBSTONES.
I *SAW* IT.
A BLUISH GLOW. IT WASN'T A LIGHTNING BUG!
YOU STILL HAVEN'T COME UP WITH AN EXPLANATION FOR HEATHER'S KNOWING SO MUCH ABOUT HARPER HOUSE.
IT COULD BE ESP, I SUPPOSE.
I DIDN'T USE TO BELIEVE IN PARANORMAL STUFF, BUT I GUESS IT COULD EXPLAIN HEATHER'S KNOWING SO MUCH ABOUT HELEN.
YOU MEAN SHE HAS SOME SIXTH SENSE?
IT'S BETTER THAN BELIEVING SHE COMMUNICATES WITH A GHOST.
YOU HAVEN'T SEEN AS MUCH AS I HAVE.
OH, MOLLY-- GIVE IT A REST, WILL YOU?
HE WENT INTO HIS ROOM.

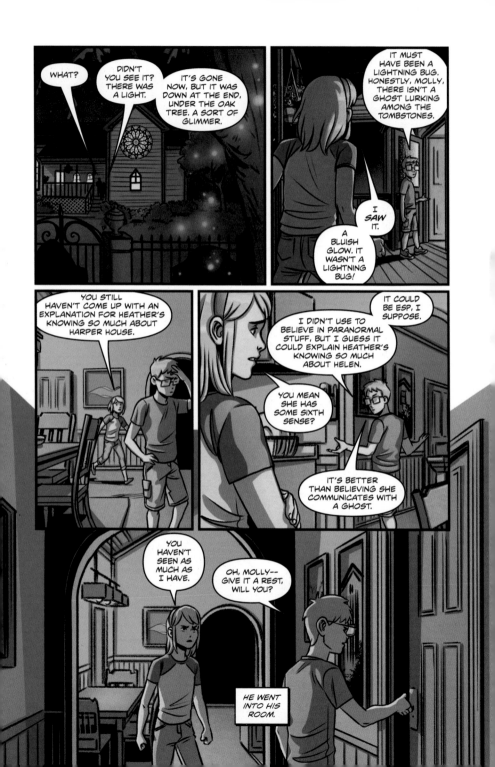

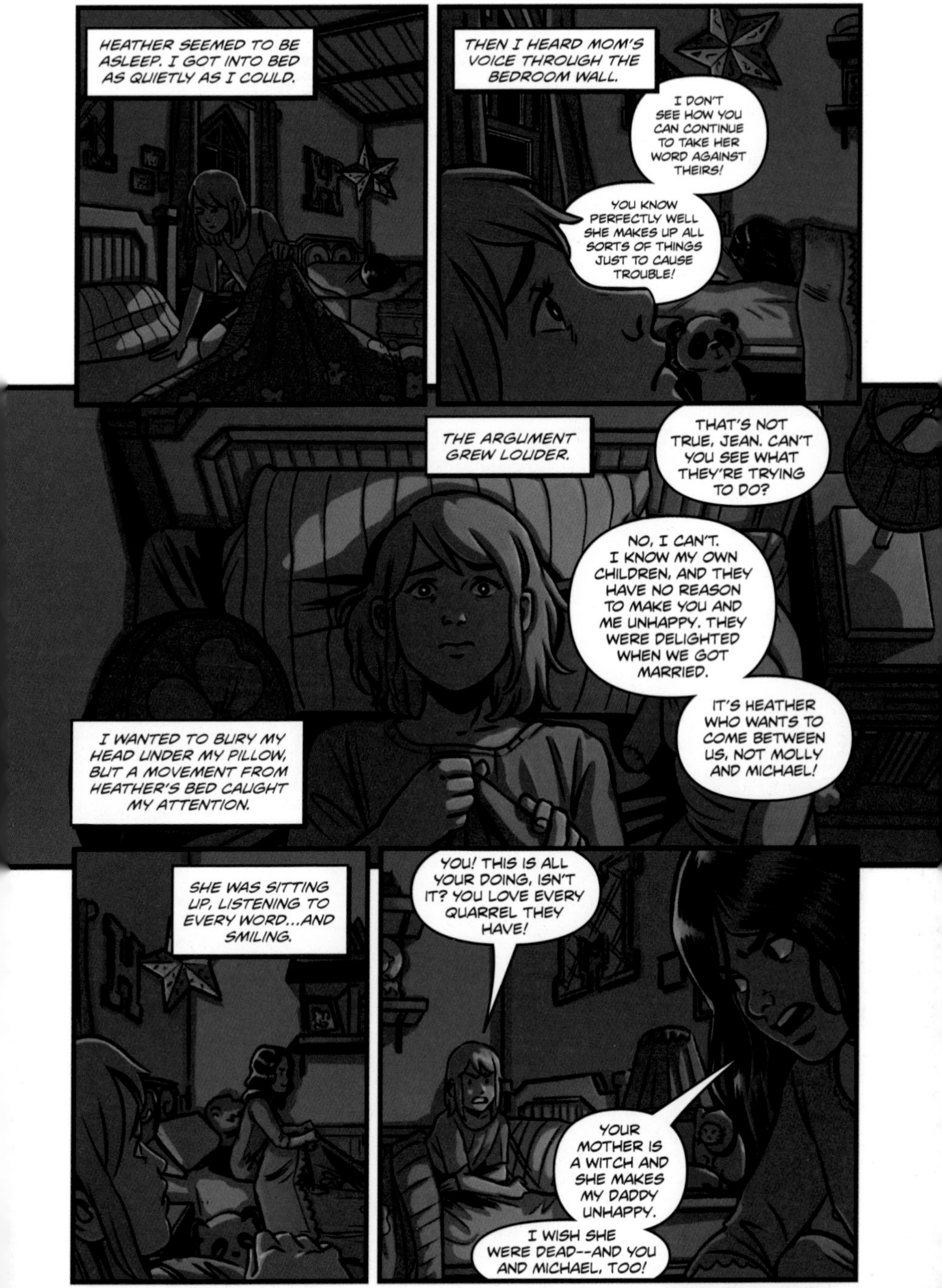
HEATHER SEEMED TO BE ASLEEP. I GOT INTO BED AS QUIETLY AS I COULD.
THEN I HEARD MOM'S VOICE THROUGH THE BEDROOM WALL.
I DON'T SEE HOW YOU CAN CONTINUE TO TAKE HER WORD AGAINST THEIRS!
YOU KNOW PERFECTLY WELL SHE MAKES UP ALL SORTS OF THINGS JUST TO CAUSE TROUBLE!
THE ARGUMENT GREW LOUDER.
THAT'S NOT TRUE, JEAN. CAN'T YOU SEE WHAT THEY'RE TRYING TO DO?
NO, I CAN'T. I KNOW MY OWN CHILDREN, AND THEY HAVE NO REASON TO MAKE YOU AND ME UNHAPPY. THEY WERE DELIGHTED WHEN WE GOT MARRIED.
IT'S HEATHER WHO WANTS TO COME BETWEEN US, NOT MOLLY AND MICHAEL!
I WANTED TO BURY MY HEAD UNDER MY PILLOW, BUT A MOVEMENT FROM HEATHER'S BED CAUGHT MY ATTENTION.
SHE WAS SITTING UP, LISTENING TO EVERY WORD...AND SMILING.
YOU! THIS IS ALL YOUR DOING, ISN'T IT? YOU LOVE EVERY QUARREL THEY HAVE!
YOUR MOTHER IS A WITCH AND SHE MAKES MY DADDY UNHAPPY.
I WISH SHE WERE DEAD--AND YOU AND MICHAEL, TOO!

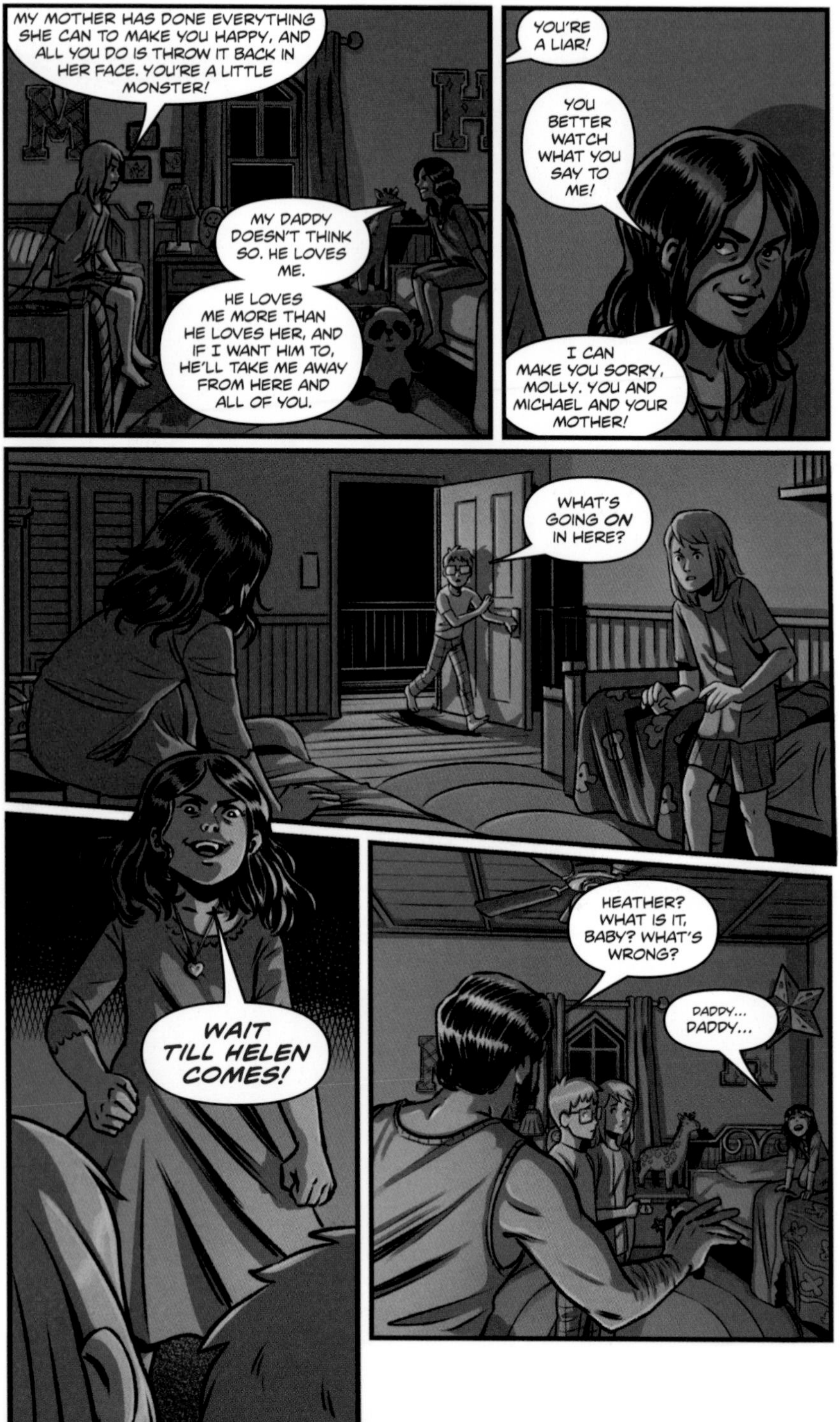
MY MOTHER HAS DONE EVERYTHING SHE CAN TO MAKE YOU HAPPY, AND ALL YOU DO IS THROW IT BACK IN HER FACE. YOU'RE A LITTLE MONSTER!
MY DADDY DOESN'T THINK SO. HE LOVES ME.
HE LOVES ME MORE THAN HE LOVES HER, AND IF I WANT HIM TO, HE'LL TAKE ME AWAY FROM HERE AND ALL OF YOU.
YOU'RE A LIAR!
YOU BETTER WATCH WHAT YOU SAY TO ME!
I CAN MAKE YOU SORRY, MOLLY. YOU AND MICHAEL AND YOUR MOTHER!
WHAT'S GOING ON IN HERE?
WAIT TILL HELEN COMES!
HEATHER? WHAT IS IT, BABY? WHAT'S WRONG?
DADDY... DADDY...

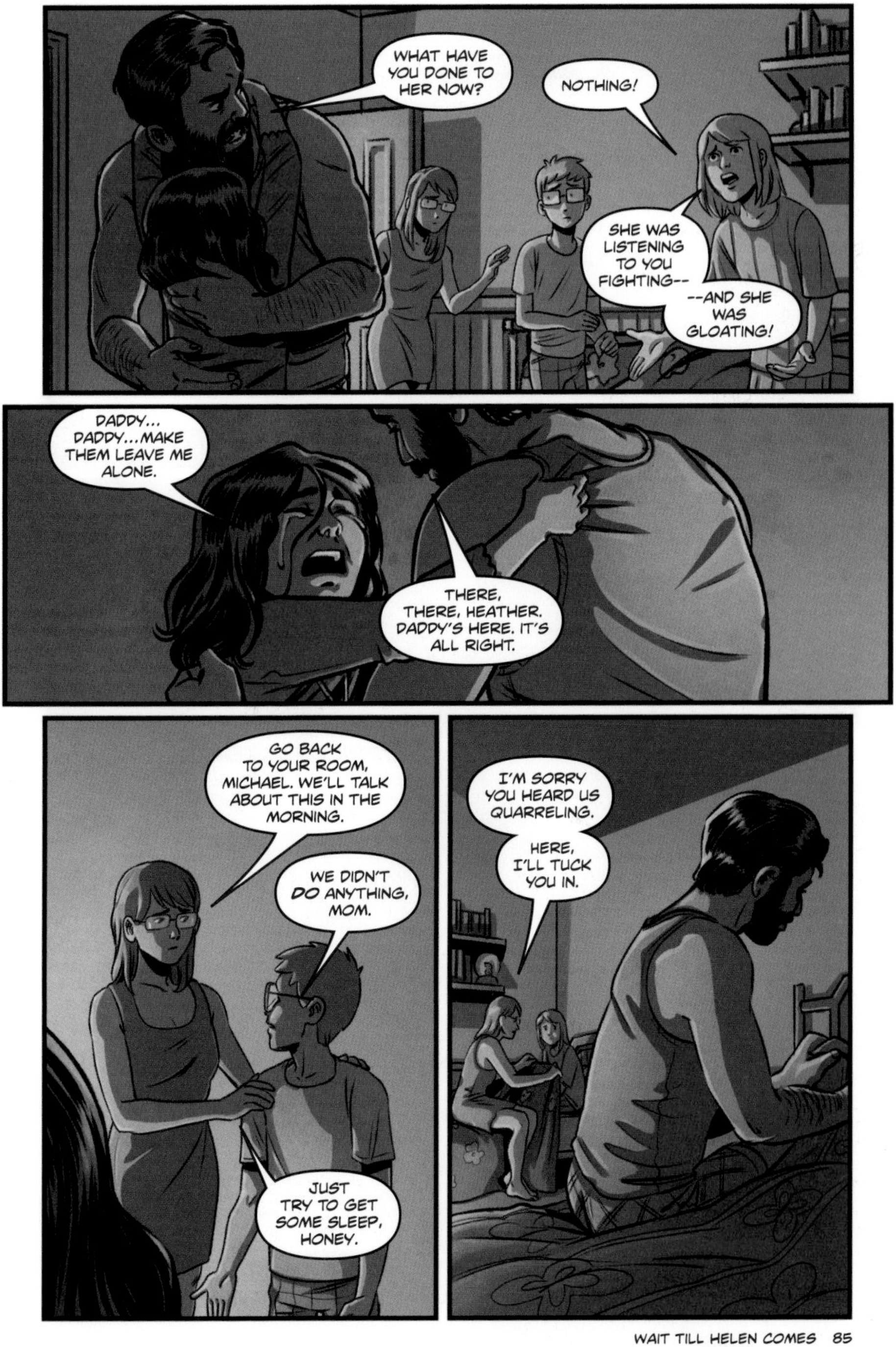
WHAT HAVE YOU DONE TO HER NOW?
NOTHING!
SHE WAS LISTENING TO YOU FIGHTING--
--AND SHE WAS GLOATING!
DADDY... DADDY...MAKE THEM LEAVE ME ALONE.
THERE, THERE, HEATHER. DADDY'S HERE. IT'S ALL RIGHT.
GO BACK TO YOUR ROOM, MICHAEL. WE'LL TALK ABOUT THIS IN THE MORNING.
WE DIDN'T *DO* ANYTHING, MOM.
JUST TRY TO GET SOME SLEEP, HONEY.
I'M SORRY YOU HEARD US QUARRELING.
HERE, I'LL TUCK YOU IN.

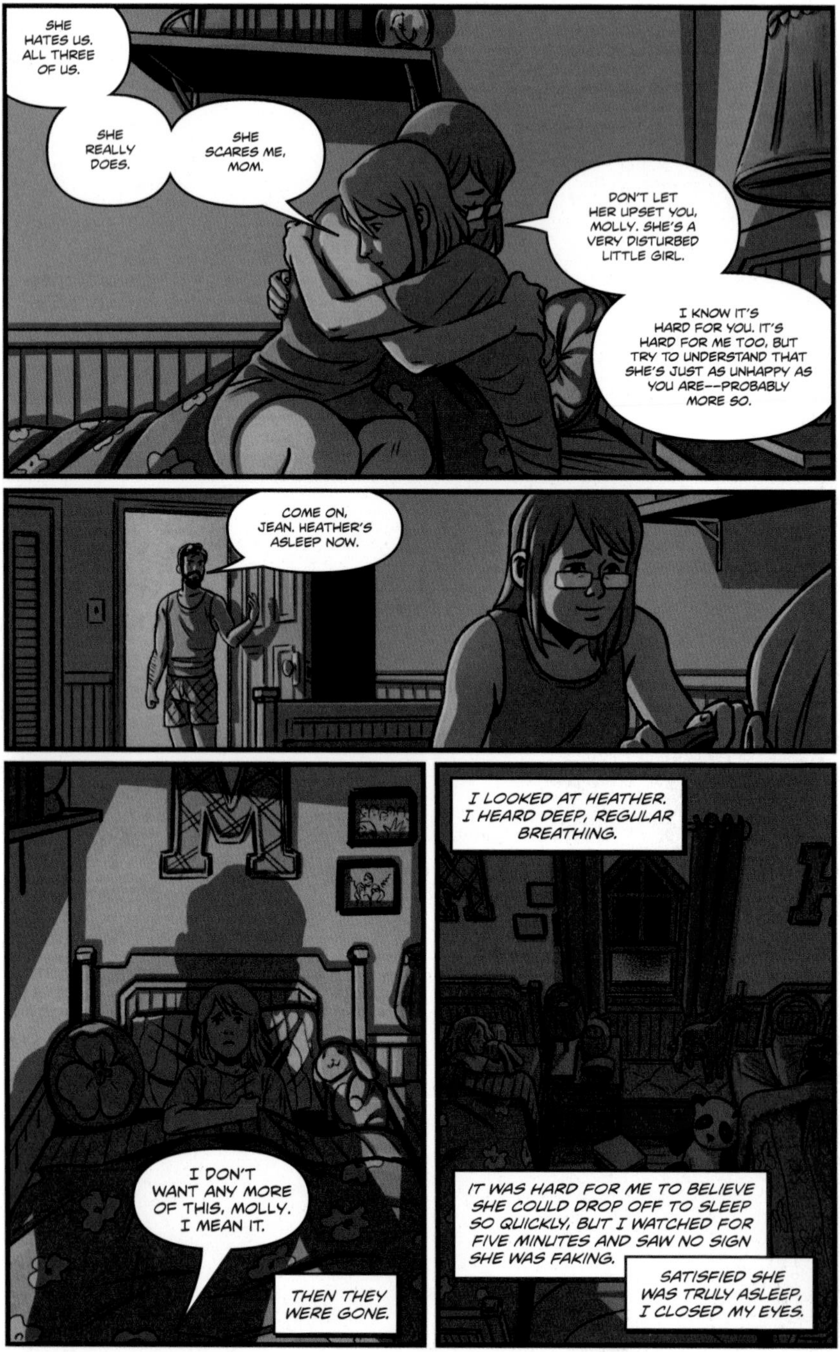
SHE HATES US. ALL THREE OF US.
SHE REALLY DOES.
SHE SCARES ME, MOM.
DON'T LET HER UPSET YOU, MOLLY. SHE'S A VERY DISTURBED LITTLE GIRL.
I KNOW IT'S HARD FOR YOU. IT'S HARD FOR ME TOO, BUT TRY TO UNDERSTAND THAT SHE'S JUST AS UNHAPPY AS YOU ARE--PROBABLY MORE SO.
COME ON, JEAN. HEATHER'S ASLEEP NOW.
I DON'T WANT ANY MORE OF THIS, MOLLY. I MEAN IT.
THEN THEY WERE GONE.
I LOOKED AT HEATHER. I HEARD DEEP, REGULAR BREATHING.
IT WAS HARD FOR ME TO BELIEVE SHE COULD DROP OFF TO SLEEP SO QUICKLY, BUT I WATCHED FOR FIVE MINUTES AND SAW NO SIGN SHE WAS FAKING.
SATISFIED SHE WAS TRULY ASLEEP, I CLOSED MY EYES.

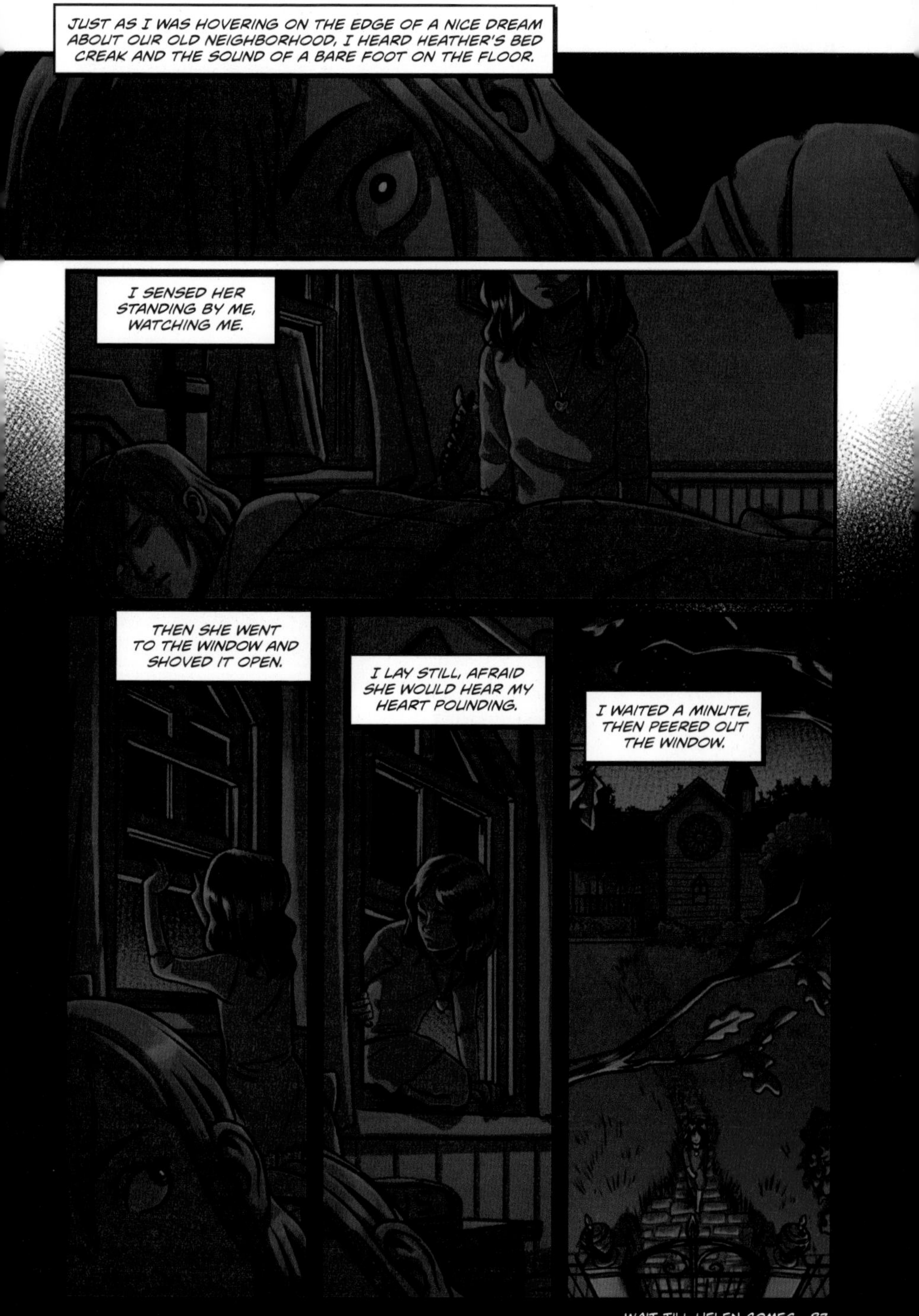
JUST AS I WAS HOVERING ON THE EDGE OF A NICE DREAM ABOUT OUR OLD NEIGHBORHOOD, I HEARD HEATHER'S BED CREAK AND THE SOUND OF A BARE FOOT ON THE FLOOR.
I SENSED HER STANDING BY ME, WATCHING ME.
THEN SHE WENT TO THE WINDOW AND SHOVED IT OPEN.
I LAY STILL, AFRAID SHE WOULD HEAR MY HEART POUNDING.
I WAITED A MINUTE, THEN PEERED OUT THE WINDOW.

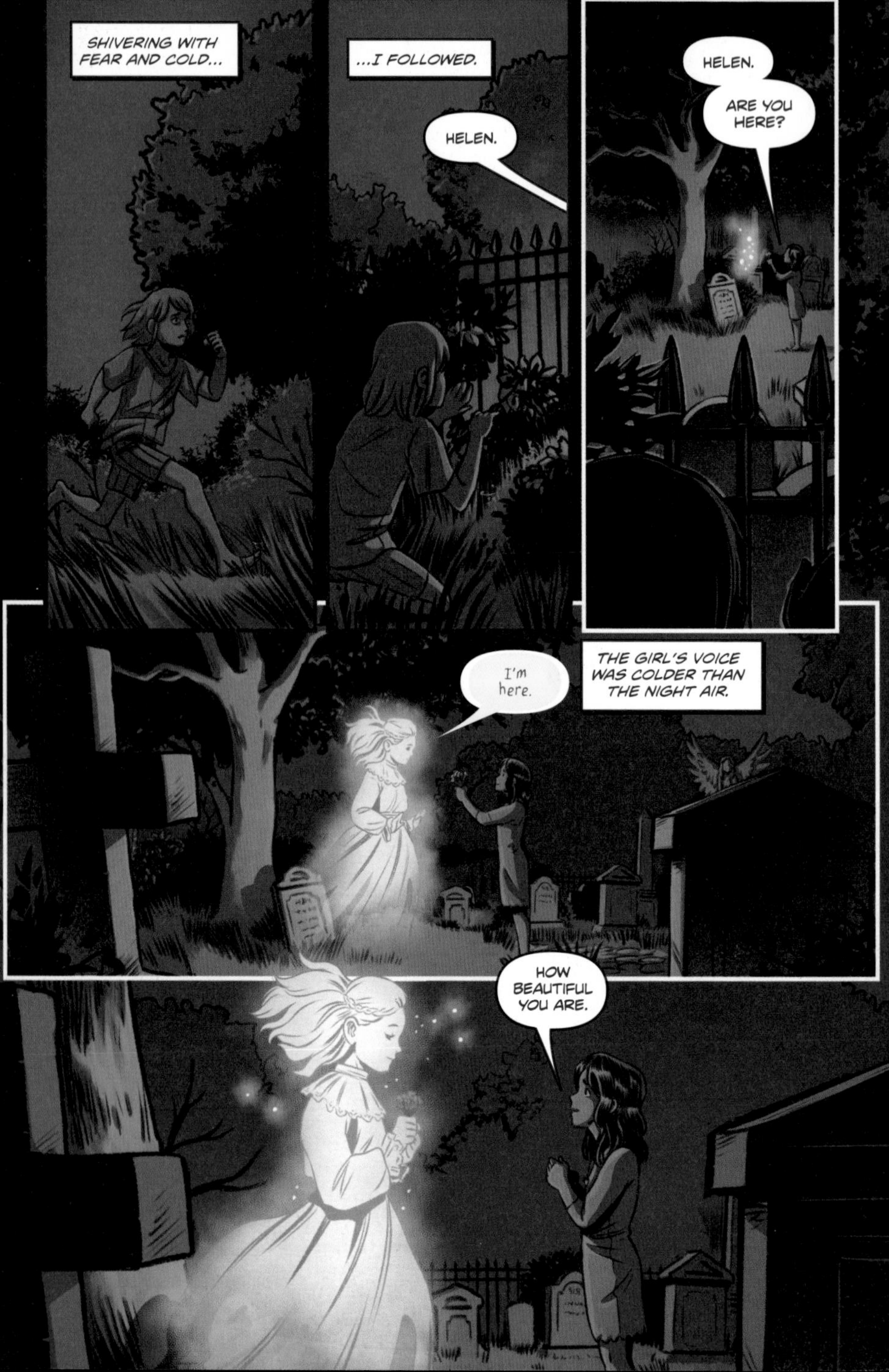
SHIVERING WITH FEAR AND COLD...
...I FOLLOWED.
HELEN.
HELEN.
ARE YOU HERE?
I'm here.
THE GIRL'S VOICE WAS COLDER THAN THE NIGHT AIR.
HOW BEAUTIFUL YOU ARE.

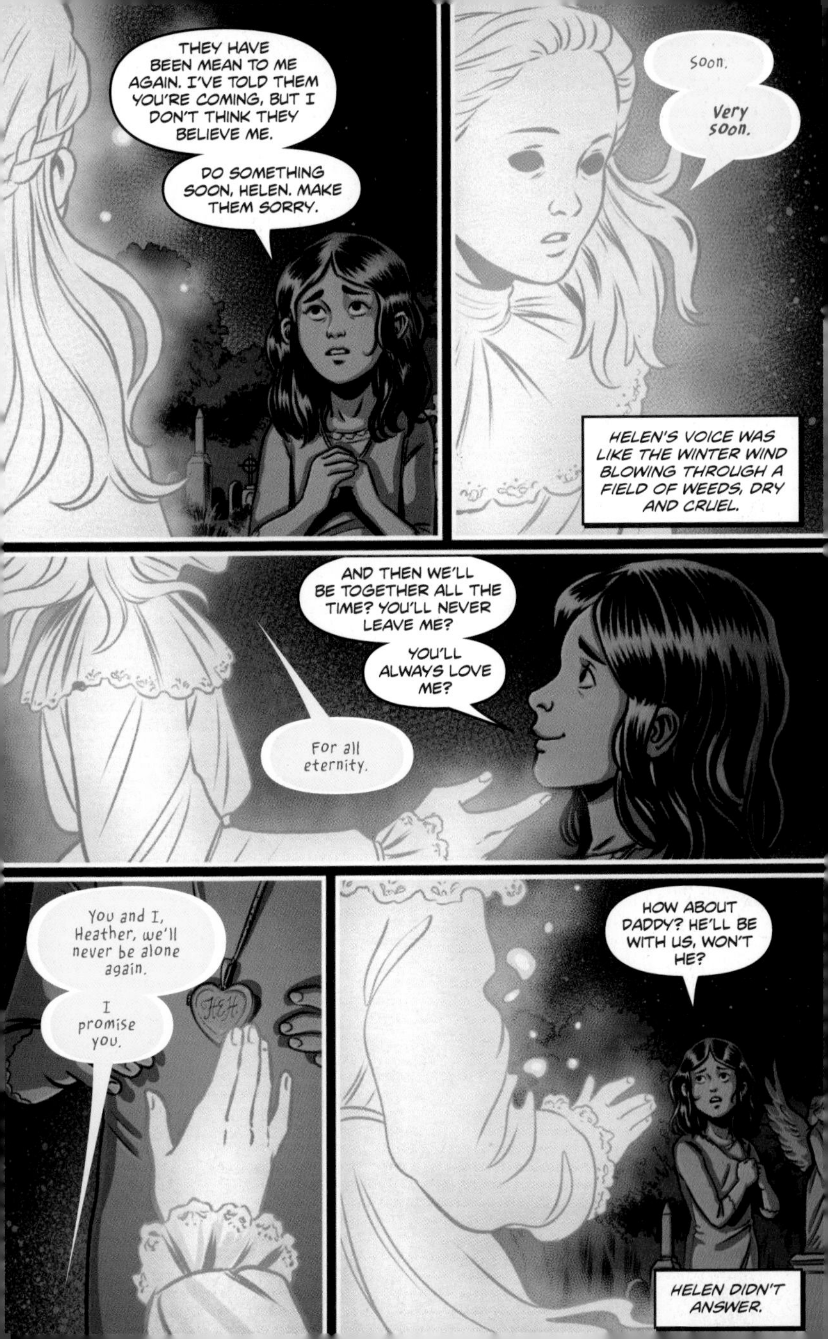
THEY HAVE BEEN MEAN TO ME AGAIN. I'VE TOLD THEM YOU'RE COMING, BUT I DON'T THINK THEY BELIEVE ME.
DO SOMETHING SOON, HELEN. MAKE THEM SORRY.
Soon.
Very soon.
HELEN'S VOICE WAS LIKE THE WINTER WIND BLOWING THROUGH A FIELD OF WEEDS, DRY AND CRUEL.
AND THEN WE'LL BE TOGETHER ALL THE TIME? YOU'LL NEVER LEAVE ME?
YOU'LL ALWAYS LOVE ME?
For all eternity.
You and I, Heather, we'll never be alone again.
I promise you.
HOW ABOUT DADDY? HE'LL BE WITH US, WON'T HE?
HELEN DIDN'T ANSWER.

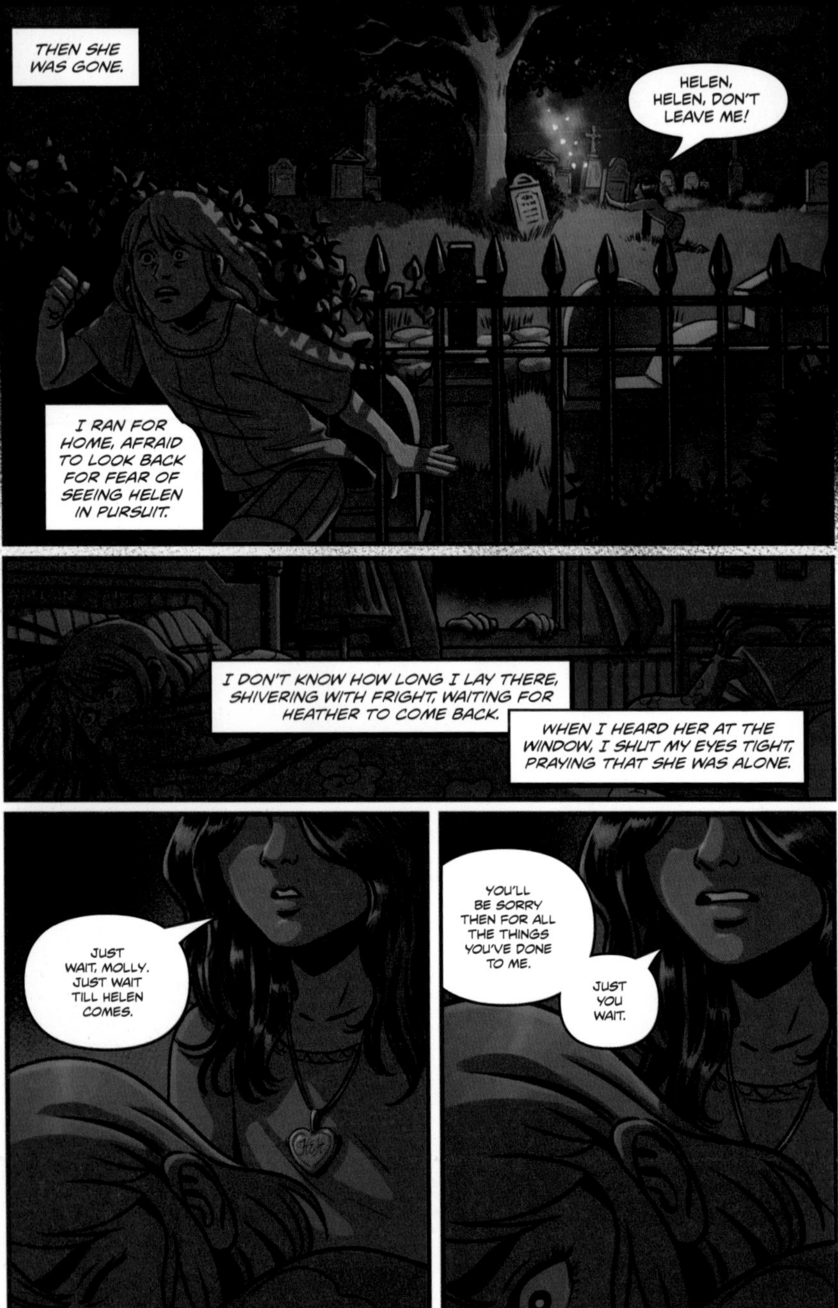
THEN SHE WAS GONE.
HELEN, HELEN, DON'T LEAVE ME!
I RAN FOR HOME, AFRAID TO LOOK BACK FOR FEAR OF SEEING HELEN IN PURSUIT.
I DON'T KNOW HOW LONG I LAY THERE, SHIVERING WITH FRIGHT, WAITING FOR HEATHER TO COME BACK.
WHEN I HEARD HER AT THE WINDOW, I SHUT MY EYES TIGHT, PRAYING THAT SHE WAS ALONE.
JUST WAIT, MOLLY. JUST WAIT TILL HELEN COMES.
YOU'LL BE SORRY THEN FOR ALL THE THINGS YOU'VE DONE TO ME.
JUST YOU WAIT.

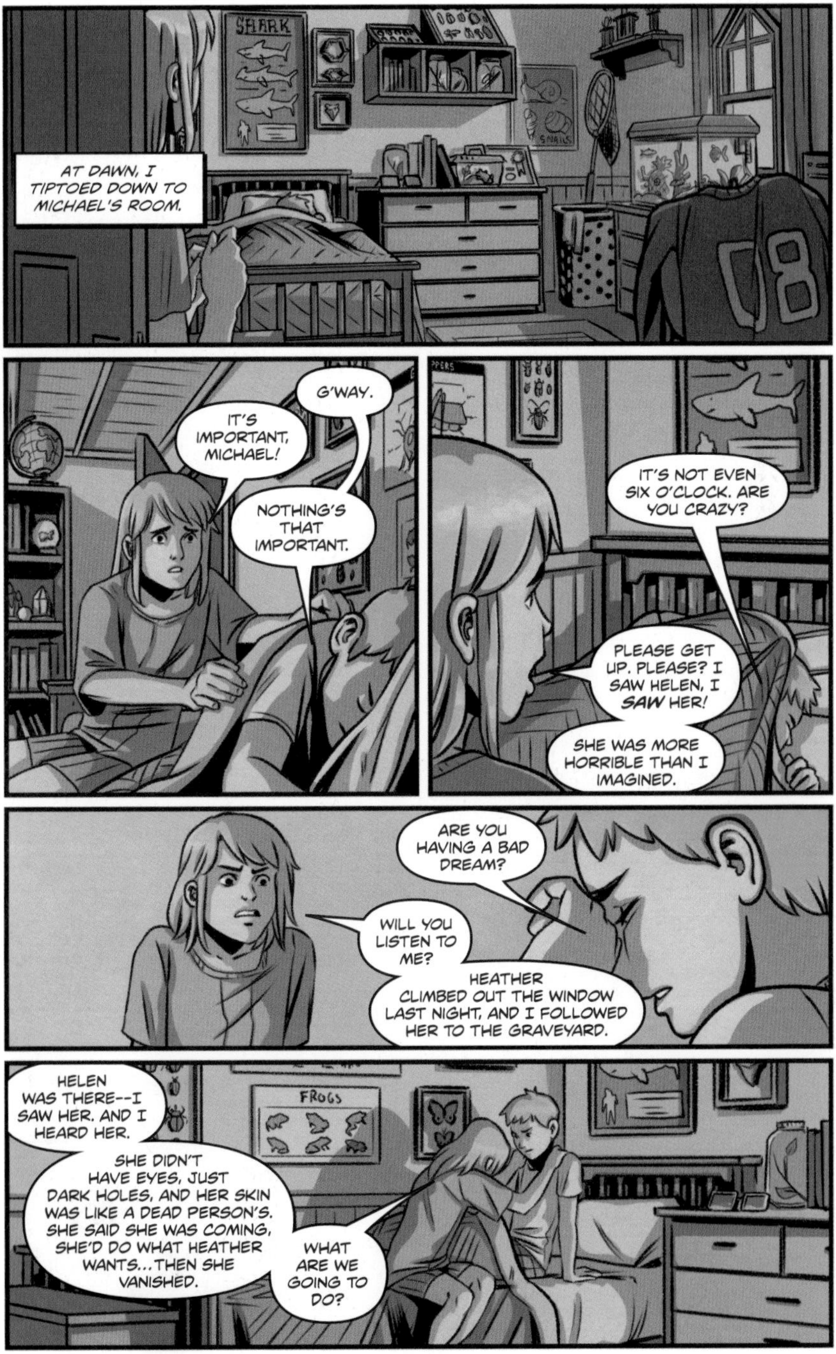
AT DAWN, I TIPTOED DOWN TO MICHAEL'S ROOM.
SHARK
SNAILS
IT'S IMPORTANT, MICHAEL!
G'WAY.
NOTHING'S THAT IMPORTANT.
IT'S NOT EVEN SIX O'CLOCK. ARE YOU CRAZY?
PLEASE GET UP. PLEASE? I SAW HELEN, I *SAW* HER!
SHE WAS MORE HORRIBLE THAN I IMAGINED.
ARE YOU HAVING A BAD DREAM?
WILL YOU LISTEN TO ME?
HEATHER CLIMBED OUT THE WINDOW LAST NIGHT, AND I FOLLOWED HER TO THE GRAVEYARD.
HELEN WAS THERE--I SAW HER. AND I HEARD HER.
FROGS
SHE DIDN'T HAVE EYES, JUST DARK HOLES, AND HER SKIN WAS LIKE A DEAD PERSON'S. SHE SAID SHE WAS COMING, SHE'D DO WHAT HEATHER WANTS...THEN SHE VANISHED.
WHAT ARE WE GOING TO DO?

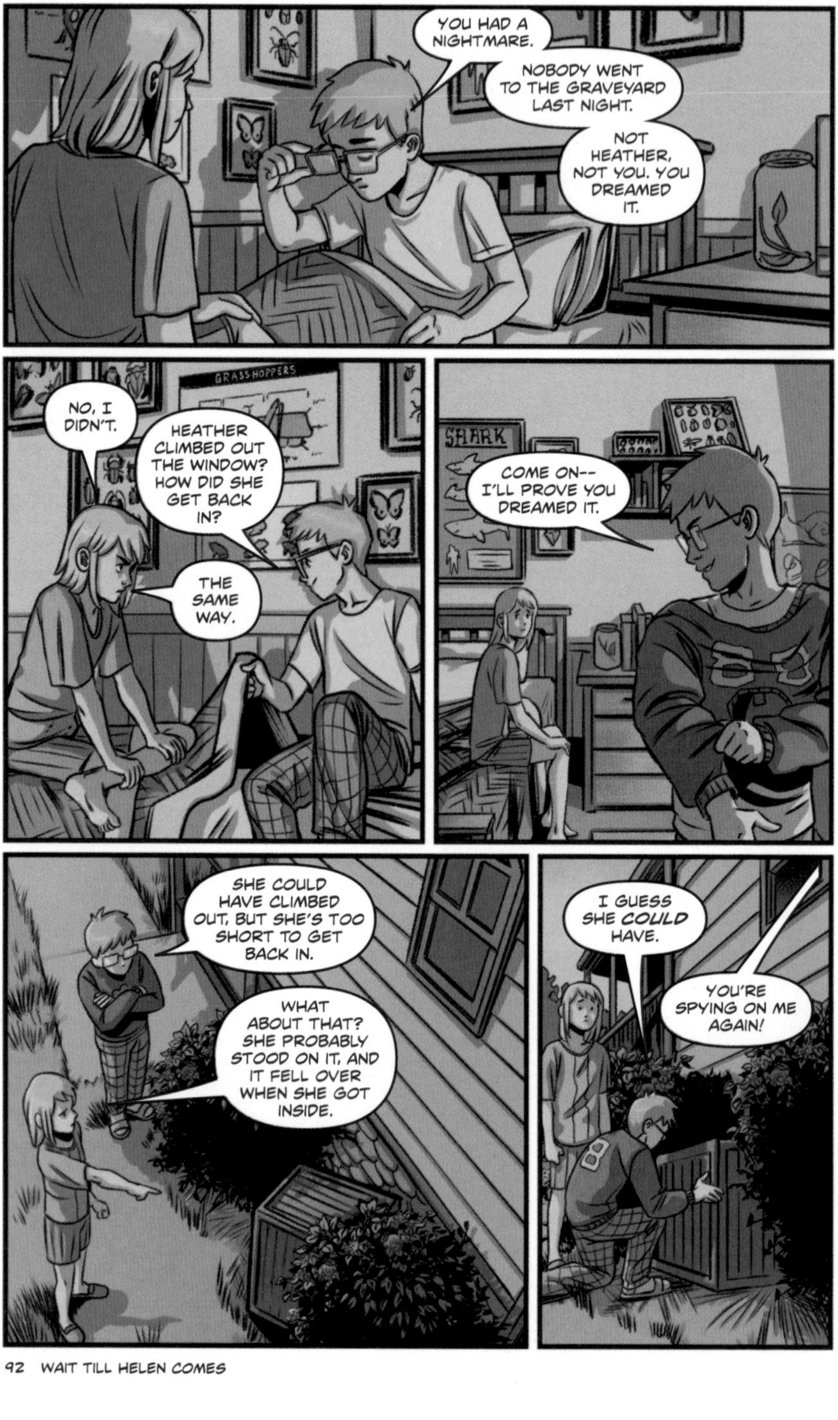
YOU HAD A NIGHTMARE.
NOBODY WENT TO THE GRAVEYARD LAST NIGHT.
NOT HEATHER, NOT YOU. YOU DREAMED IT.
GRASSHOPPERS
NO, I DIDN'T.
HEATHER CLIMBED OUT THE WINDOW? HOW DID SHE GET BACK IN?
THE SAME WAY.
SHARK
COME ON-- I'LL PROVE YOU DREAMED IT.
SHE COULD HAVE CLIMBED OUT, BUT SHE'S TOO SHORT TO GET BACK IN.
WHAT ABOUT THAT? SHE PROBABLY STOOD ON IT, AND IT FELL OVER WHEN SHE GOT INSIDE.
I GUESS SHE *COULD* HAVE.
YOU'RE SPYING ON ME AGAIN!

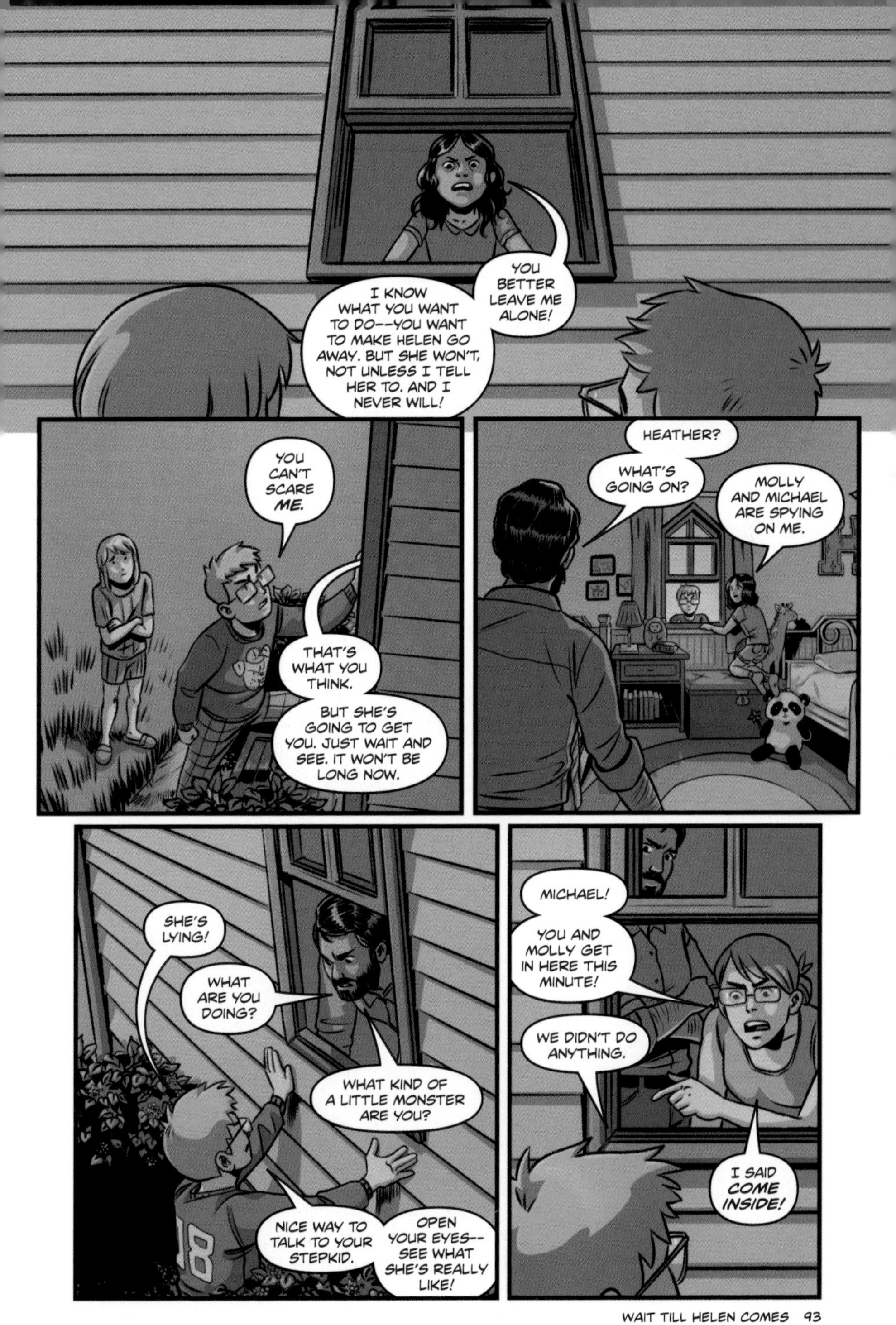
YOU BETTER LEAVE ME ALONE!
I KNOW WHAT YOU WANT TO DO--YOU WANT TO MAKE HELEN GO AWAY. BUT SHE WON'T, NOT UNLESS I TELL HER TO. AND I NEVER WILL!
YOU CAN'T SCARE ME.
THAT'S WHAT YOU THINK.
BUT SHE'S GOING TO GET YOU. JUST WAIT AND SEE. IT WON'T BE LONG NOW.
HEATHER?
WHAT'S GOING ON?
MOLLY AND MICHAEL ARE SPYING ON ME.
SHE'S LYING!
WHAT ARE YOU DOING?
WHAT KIND OF A LITTLE MONSTER ARE YOU?
NICE WAY TO TALK TO YOUR STEPKID.
OPEN YOUR EYES--SEE WHAT SHE'S REALLY LIKE!
MICHAEL!
YOU AND MOLLY GET IN HERE THIS MINUTE!
WE DIDN'T DO ANYTHING.
I SAID COME INSIDE!

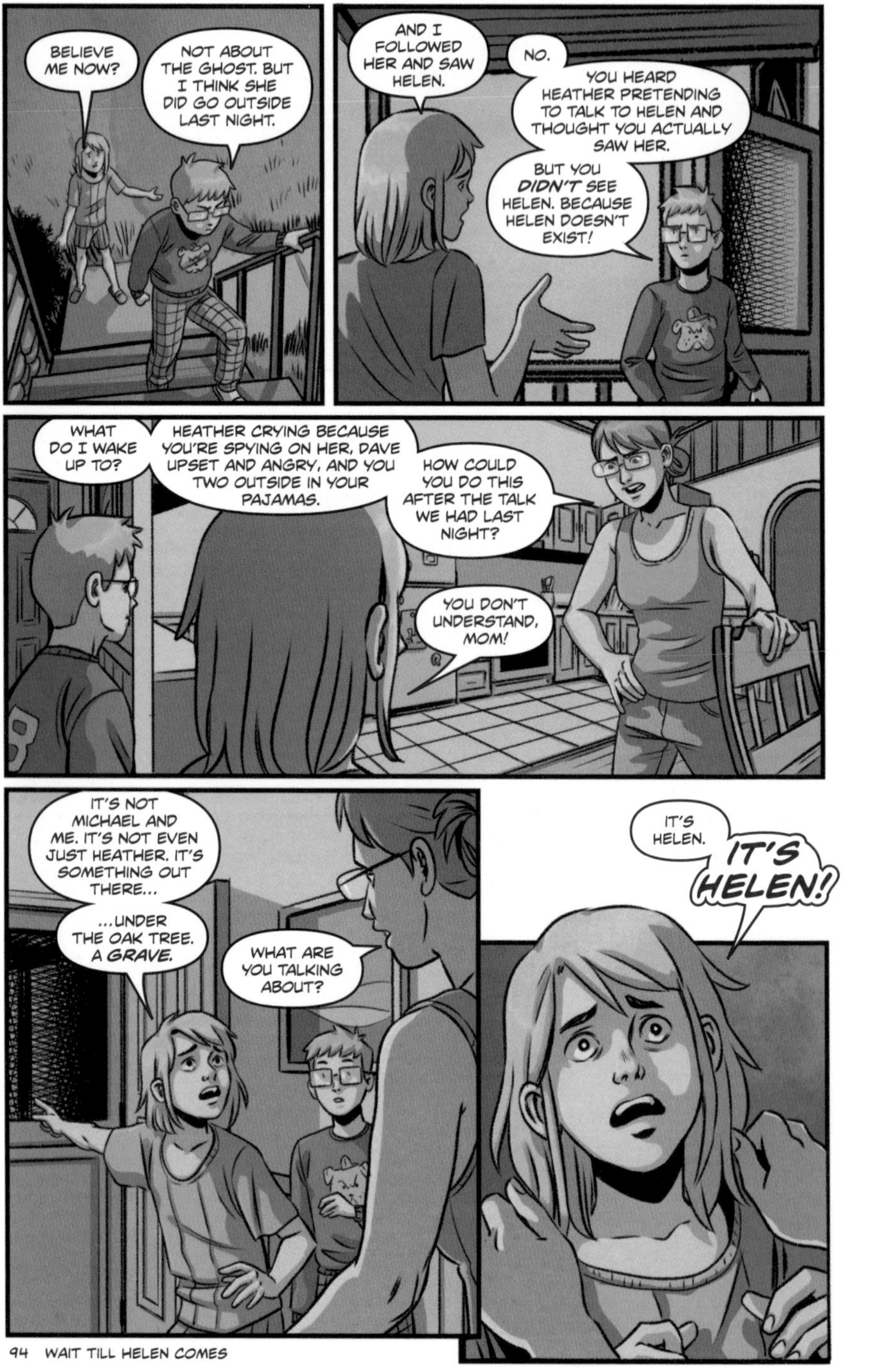
BELIEVE ME NOW?
NOT ABOUT THE GHOST. BUT I THINK SHE DID GO OUTSIDE LAST NIGHT.
AND I FOLLOWED HER AND SAW HELEN.
NO.
YOU HEARD HEATHER PRETENDING TO TALK TO HELEN AND THOUGHT YOU ACTUALLY SAW HER.
BUT YOU *DIDN'T* SEE HELEN. BECAUSE HELEN DOESN'T EXIST!
WHAT DO I WAKE UP TO?
HEATHER CRYING BECAUSE YOU'RE SPYING ON HER, DAVE UPSET AND ANGRY, AND YOU TWO OUTSIDE IN YOUR PAJAMAS.
HOW COULD YOU DO THIS AFTER THE TALK WE HAD LAST NIGHT?
YOU DON'T UNDERSTAND, MOM!
IT'S NOT MICHAEL AND ME. IT'S NOT EVEN JUST HEATHER. IT'S SOMETHING OUT THERE...
...UNDER THE OAK TREE. A *GRAVE.*
WHAT ARE YOU TALKING ABOUT?
IT'S HELEN.
IT'S HELEN!

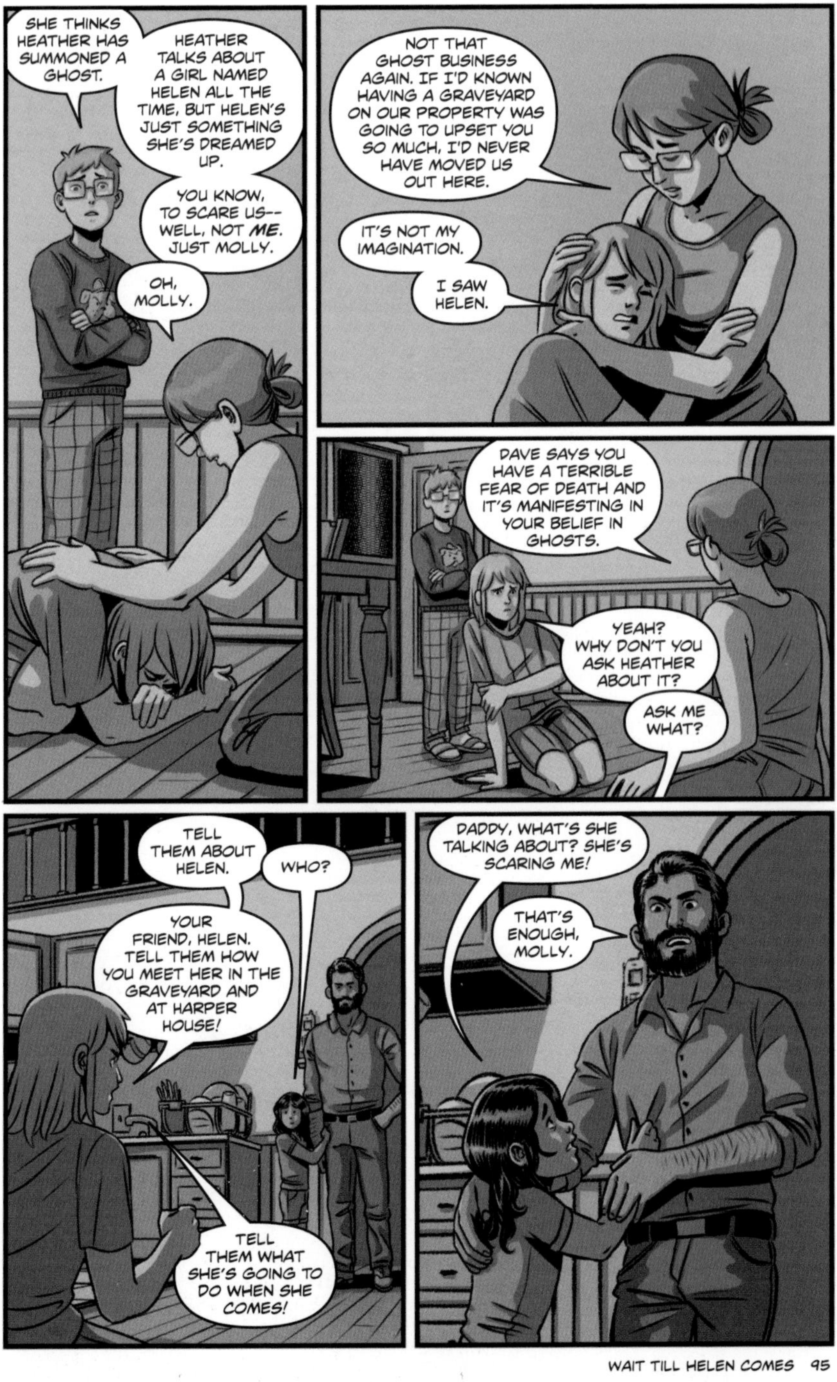
SHE THINKS HEATHER HAS SUMMONED A GHOST.
HEATHER TALKS ABOUT A GIRL NAMED HELEN ALL THE TIME, BUT HELEN'S JUST SOMETHING SHE'S DREAMED UP.
YOU KNOW, TO SCARE US-- WELL, NOT ***ME***. JUST MOLLY.
OH, MOLLY.
NOT THAT GHOST BUSINESS AGAIN. IF I'D KNOWN HAVING A GRAVEYARD ON OUR PROPERTY WAS GOING TO UPSET YOU SO MUCH, I'D NEVER HAVE MOVED US OUT HERE.
IT'S NOT MY IMAGINATION.
I SAW HELEN.
DAVE SAYS YOU HAVE A TERRIBLE FEAR OF DEATH AND IT'S MANIFESTING IN YOUR BELIEF IN GHOSTS.
YEAH? WHY DON'T YOU ASK HEATHER ABOUT IT?
ASK ME WHAT?
TELL THEM ABOUT HELEN.
WHO?
YOUR FRIEND, HELEN. TELL THEM HOW YOU MEET HER IN THE GRAVEYARD AND AT HARPER HOUSE!
TELL THEM WHAT SHE'S GOING TO DO WHEN SHE COMES!
DADDY, WHAT'S SHE TALKING ABOUT? SHE'S SCARING ME!
THAT'S ENOUGH, MOLLY.

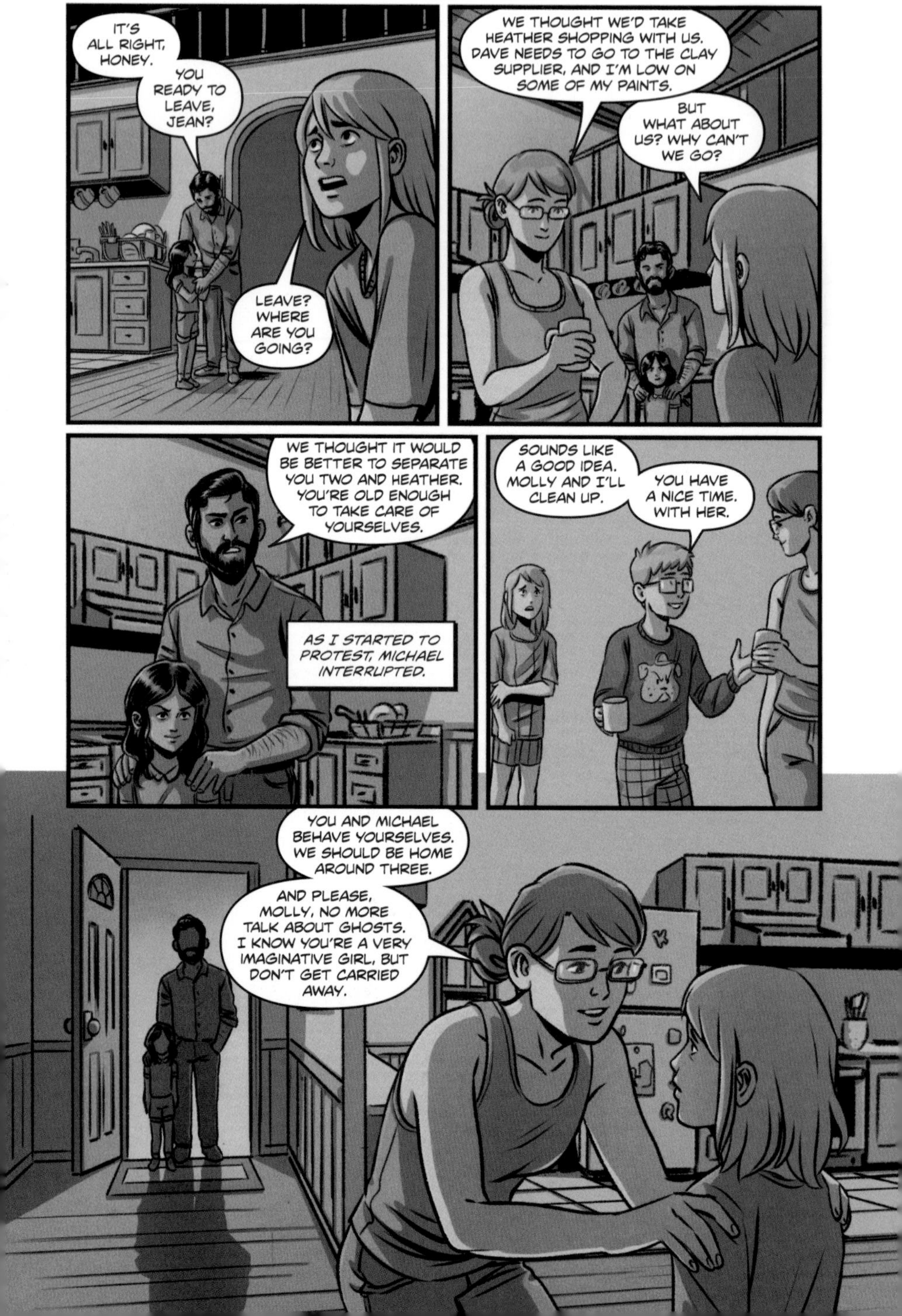
IT'S ALL RIGHT, HONEY.
YOU READY TO LEAVE, JEAN?
LEAVE? WHERE ARE YOU GOING?
WE THOUGHT WE'D TAKE HEATHER SHOPPING WITH US. DAVE NEEDS TO GO TO THE CLAY SUPPLIER, AND I'M LOW ON SOME OF MY PAINTS.
BUT WHAT ABOUT US? WHY CAN'T WE GO?
WE THOUGHT IT WOULD BE BETTER TO SEPARATE YOU TWO AND HEATHER. YOU'RE OLD ENOUGH TO TAKE CARE OF YOURSELVES.
AS I STARTED TO PROTEST, MICHAEL INTERRUPTED.
SOUNDS LIKE A GOOD IDEA. MOLLY AND I'LL CLEAN UP.
YOU HAVE A NICE TIME. WITH HER.
YOU AND MICHAEL BEHAVE YOURSELVES. WE SHOULD BE HOME AROUND THREE.
AND PLEASE, MOLLY, NO MORE TALK ABOUT GHOSTS. I KNOW YOU'RE A VERY IMAGINATIVE GIRL, BUT DON'T GET CARRIED AWAY.

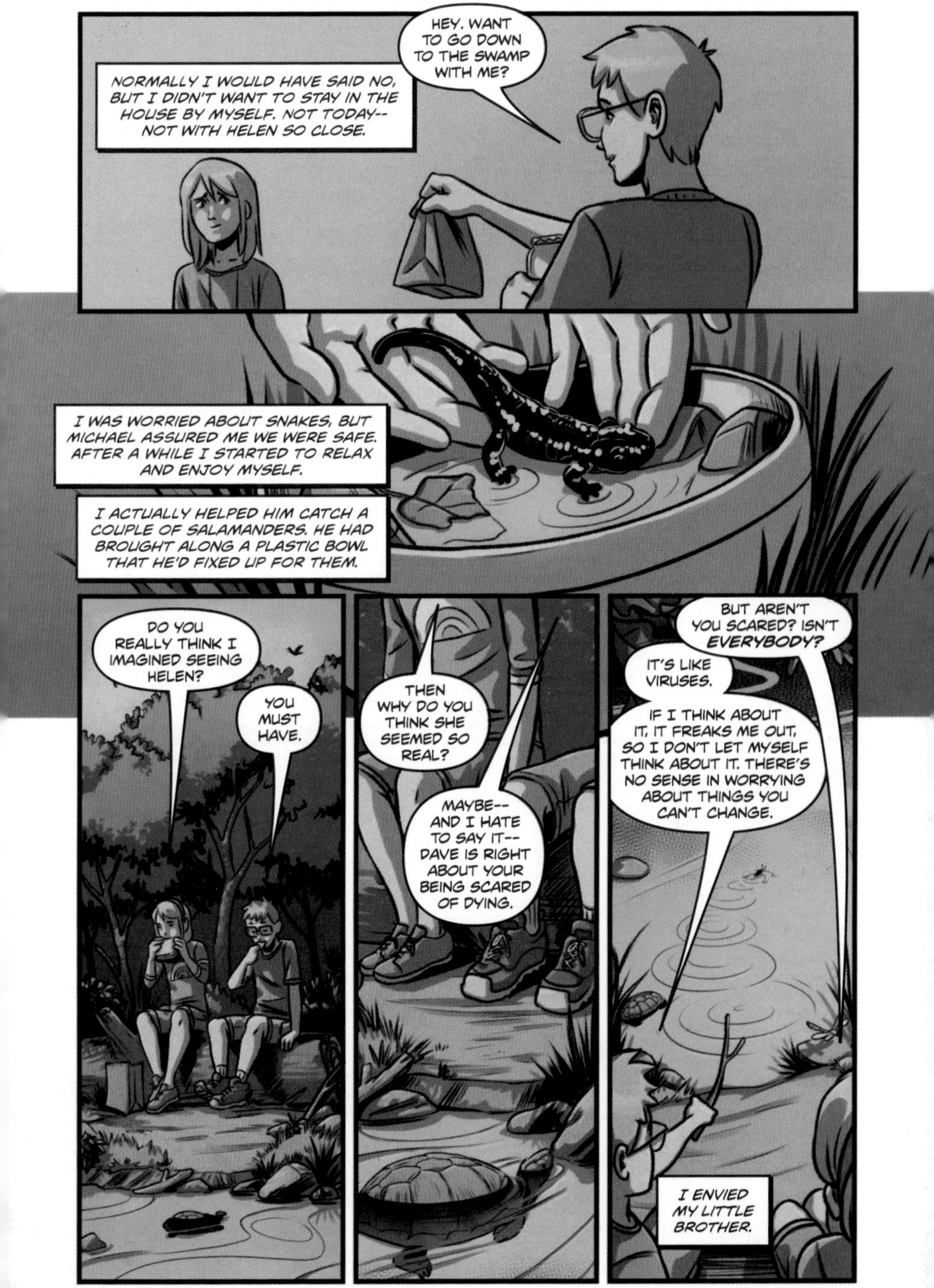
NORMALLY I WOULD HAVE SAID NO, BUT I DIDN'T WANT TO STAY IN THE HOUSE BY MYSELF. NOT TODAY-- NOT WITH HELEN SO CLOSE.
HEY. WANT TO GO DOWN TO THE SWAMP WITH ME?
I WAS WORRIED ABOUT SNAKES, BUT MICHAEL ASSURED ME WE WERE SAFE. AFTER A WHILE I STARTED TO RELAX AND ENJOY MYSELF.
I ACTUALLY HELPED HIM CATCH A COUPLE OF SALAMANDERS. HE HAD BROUGHT ALONG A PLASTIC BOWL THAT HE'D FIXED UP FOR THEM.
DO YOU REALLY THINK I IMAGINED SEEING HELEN?
YOU MUST HAVE.
THEN WHY DO YOU THINK SHE SEEMED SO REAL?
MAYBE-- AND I HATE TO SAY IT-- DAVE IS RIGHT ABOUT YOUR BEING SCARED OF DYING.
BUT AREN'T YOU SCARED? ISN'T **EVERYBODY?**
IT'S LIKE VIRUSES.
IF I THINK ABOUT IT, IT FREAKS ME OUT, SO I DON'T LET MYSELF THINK ABOUT IT. THERE'S NO SENSE IN WORRYING ABOUT THINGS YOU CAN'T CHANGE.
I ENVIED MY LITTLE BROTHER.

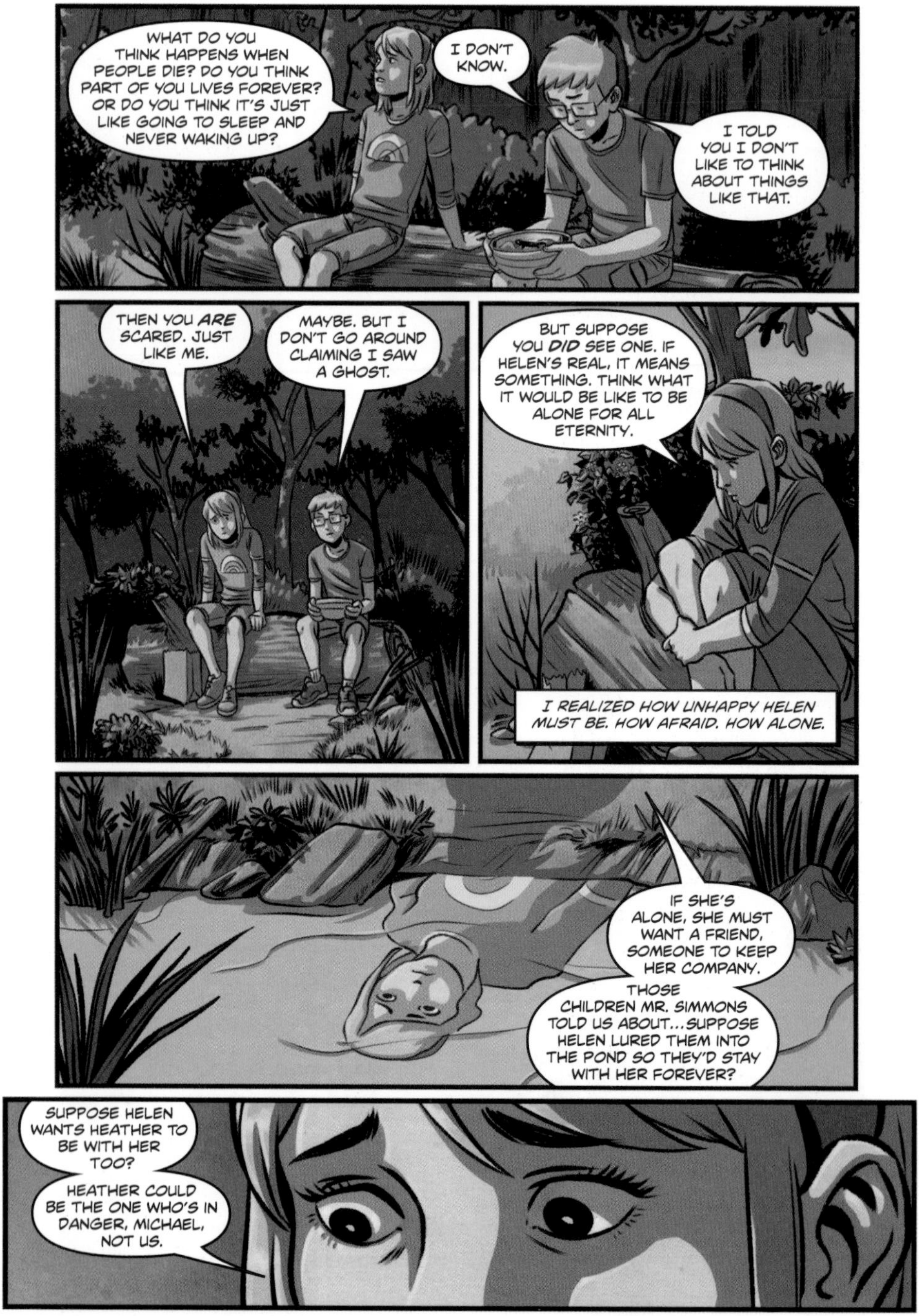

WHAT DO YOU THINK HAPPENS WHEN PEOPLE DIE? DO YOU THINK PART OF YOU LIVES FOREVER? OR DO YOU THINK IT'S JUST LIKE GOING TO SLEEP AND NEVER WAKING UP?
I DON'T KNOW.
I TOLD YOU I DON'T LIKE TO THINK ABOUT THINGS LIKE THAT.
THEN YOU ***ARE*** SCARED. JUST LIKE ME.
MAYBE. BUT I DON'T GO AROUND CLAIMING I SAW A GHOST.
BUT SUPPOSE YOU ***DID*** SEE ONE. IF HELEN'S REAL, IT MEANS SOMETHING. THINK WHAT IT WOULD BE LIKE TO BE ALONE FOR ALL ETERNITY.
I REALIZED HOW UNHAPPY HELEN MUST BE. HOW AFRAID. HOW ALONE.
IF SHE'S ALONE, SHE MUST WANT A FRIEND, SOMEONE TO KEEP HER COMPANY.
THOSE CHILDREN MR. SIMMONS TOLD US ABOUT... SUPPOSE HELEN LURED THEM INTO THE POND SO THEY'D STAY WITH HER FOREVER?
SUPPOSE HELEN WANTS HEATHER TO BE WITH HER TOO?
HEATHER COULD BE THE ONE WHO'S IN DANGER, MICHAEL, NOT US.

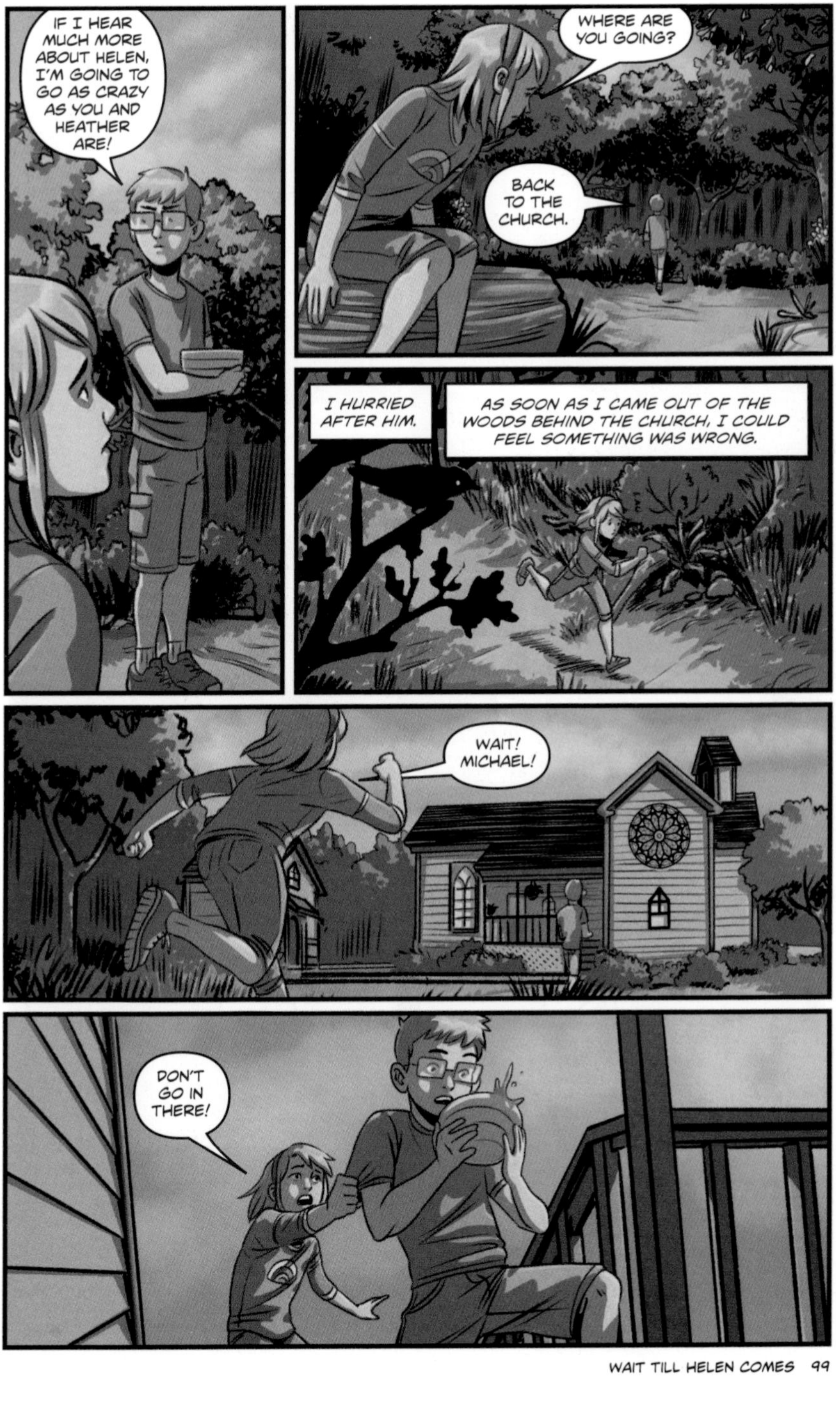
IF I HEAR MUCH MORE ABOUT HELEN, I'M GOING TO GO AS CRAZY AS YOU AND HEATHER ARE!
WHERE ARE YOU GOING?
BACK TO THE CHURCH.
I HURRIED AFTER HIM.
AS SOON AS I CAME OUT OF THE WOODS BEHIND THE CHURCH, I COULD FEEL SOMETHING WAS WRONG.
WAIT! MICHAEL!
DON'T GO IN THERE!

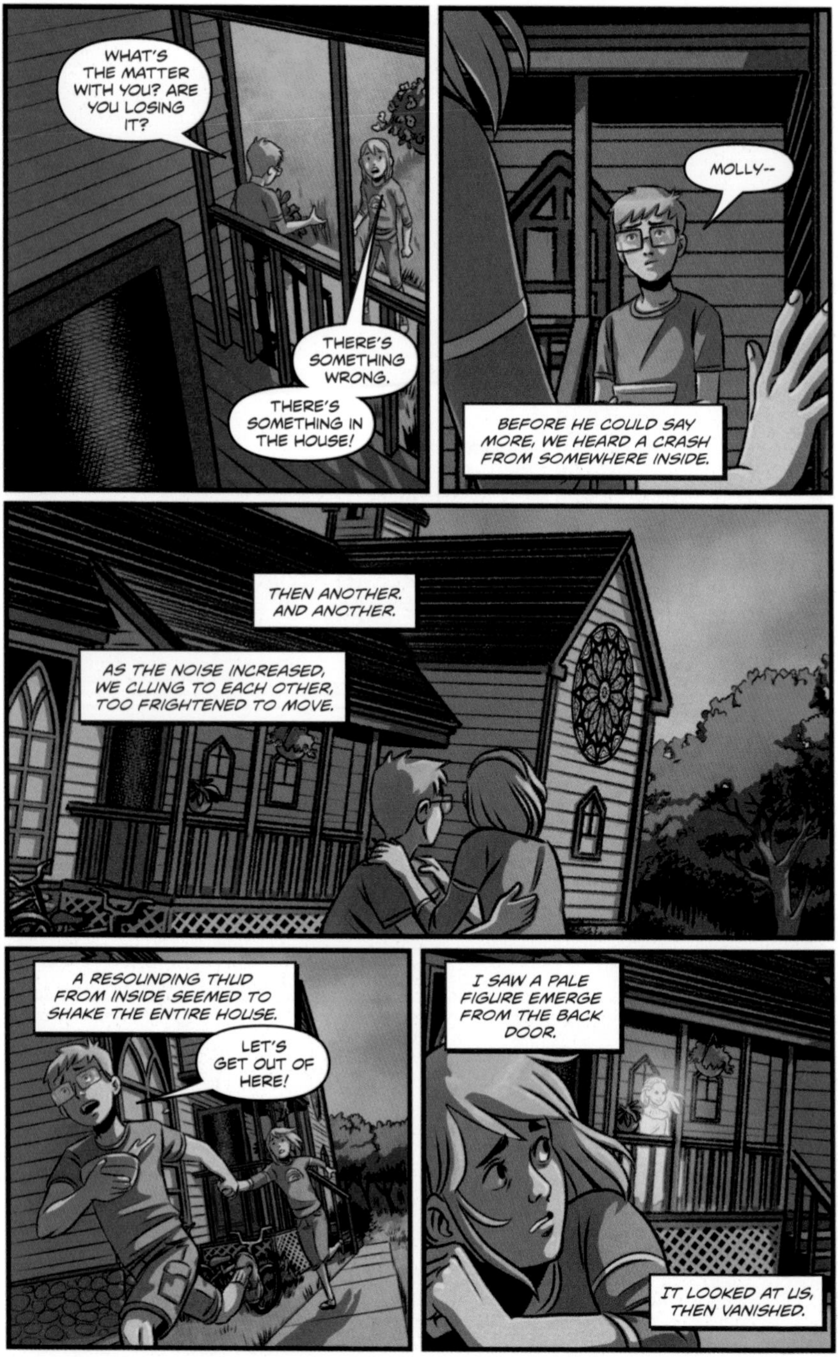
WHAT'S THE MATTER WITH YOU? ARE YOU LOSING IT?
THERE'S SOMETHING WRONG.
THERE'S SOMETHING IN THE HOUSE!
MOLLY--
BEFORE HE COULD SAY MORE, WE HEARD A CRASH FROM SOMEWHERE INSIDE.
THEN ANOTHER. AND ANOTHER.
AS THE NOISE INCREASED, WE CLUNG TO EACH OTHER, TOO FRIGHTENED TO MOVE.
A RESOUNDING THUD FROM INSIDE SEEMED TO SHAKE THE ENTIRE HOUSE.
LET'S GET OUT OF HERE!
I SAW A PALE FIGURE EMERGE FROM THE BACK DOOR.
IT LOOKED AT US, THEN VANISHED.

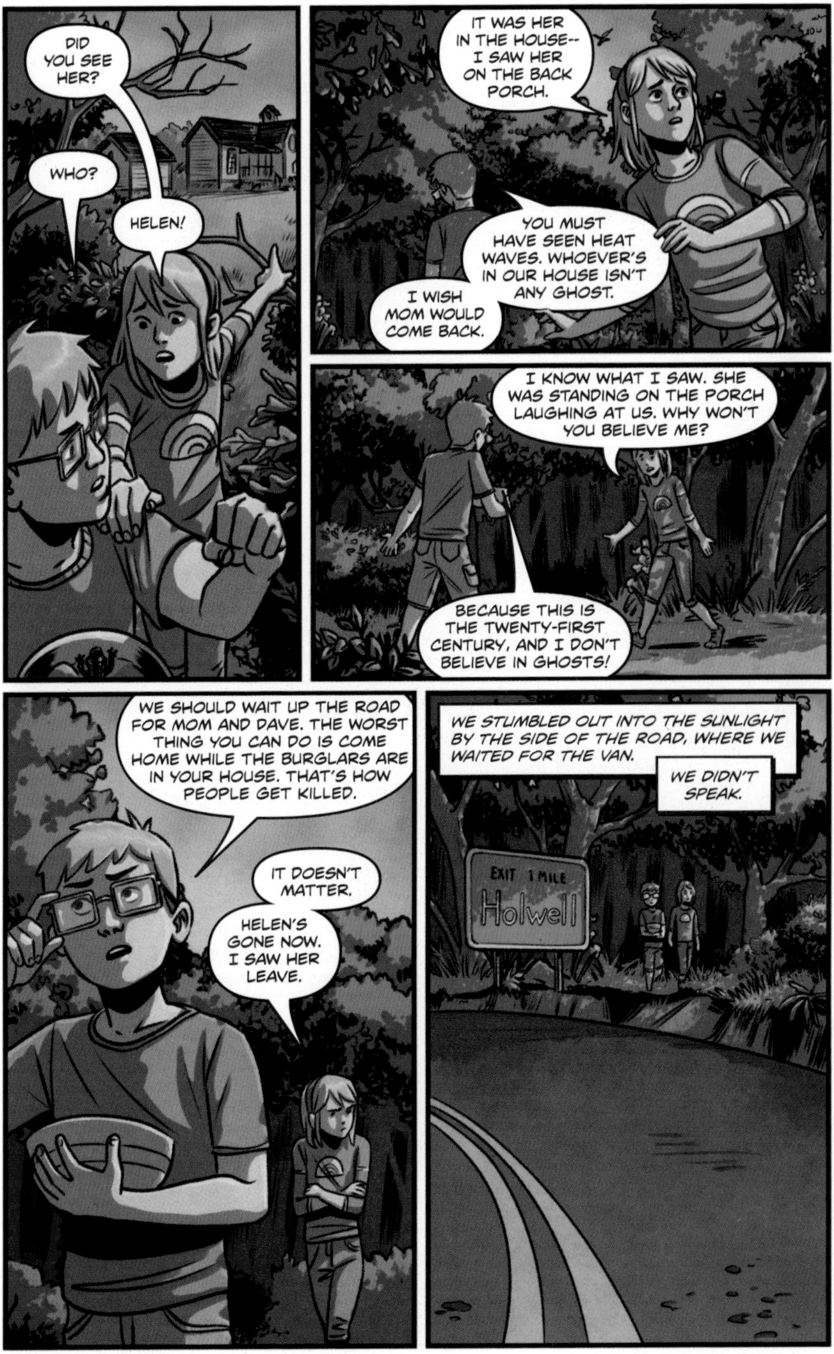
DID YOU SEE HER?
WHO?
HELEN!
IT WAS HER IN THE HOUSE-- I SAW HER ON THE BACK PORCH.
YOU MUST HAVE SEEN HEAT WAVES. WHOEVER'S IN OUR HOUSE ISN'T ANY GHOST.
I WISH MOM WOULD COME BACK.
I KNOW WHAT I SAW. SHE WAS STANDING ON THE PORCH LAUGHING AT US. WHY WON'T YOU BELIEVE ME?
BECAUSE THIS IS THE TWENTY-FIRST CENTURY, AND I DON'T BELIEVE IN GHOSTS!
WE SHOULD WAIT UP THE ROAD FOR MOM AND DAVE. THE WORST THING YOU CAN DO IS COME HOME WHILE THE BURGLARS ARE IN YOUR HOUSE. THAT'S HOW PEOPLE GET KILLED.
IT DOESN'T MATTER.
HELEN'S GONE NOW. I SAW HER LEAVE.
WE STUMBLED OUT INTO THE SUNLIGHT BY THE SIDE OF THE ROAD, WHERE WE WAITED FOR THE VAN.
WE DIDN'T SPEAK.
EXIT 1 MILE
Holwell

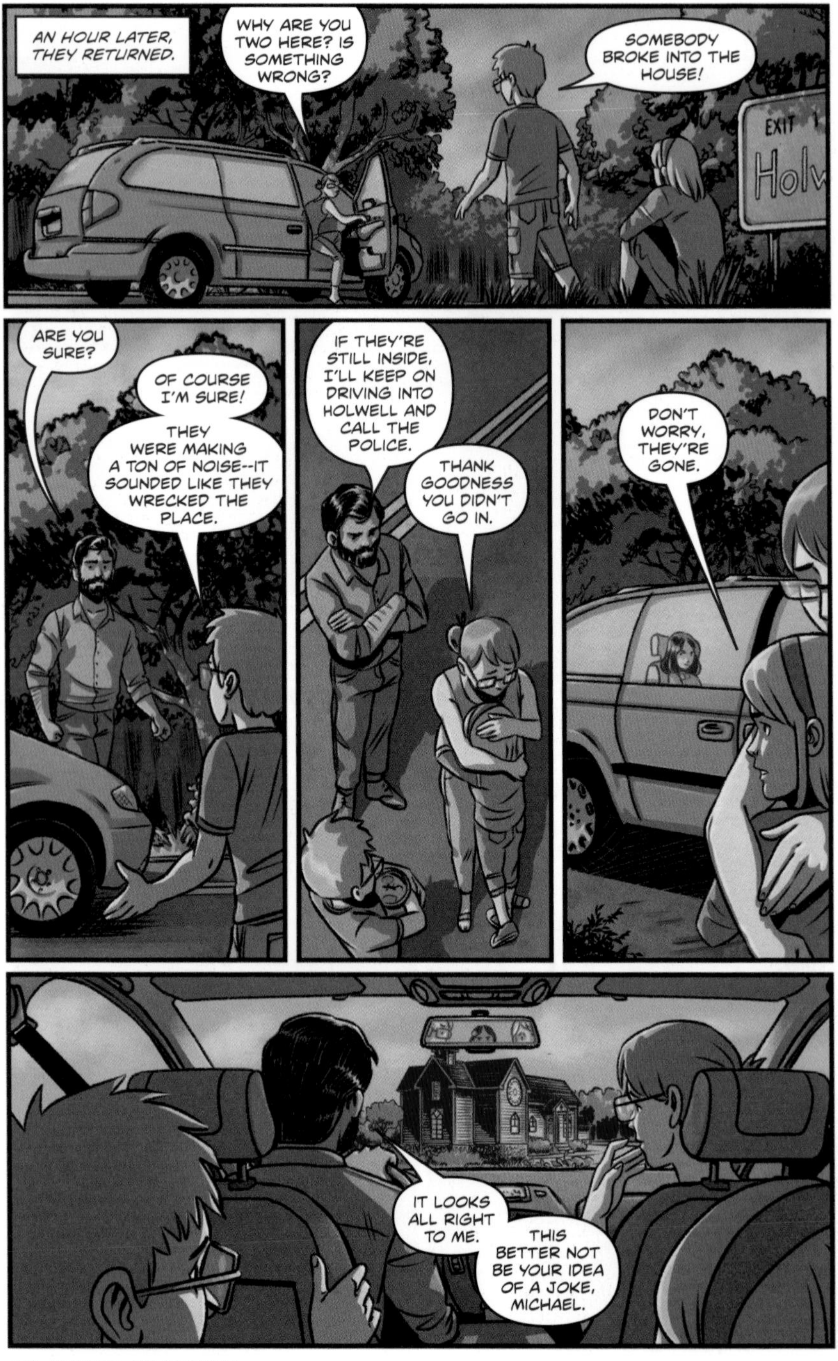
AN HOUR LATER, THEY RETURNED.
WHY ARE YOU TWO HERE? IS SOMETHING WRONG?
SOMEBODY BROKE INTO THE HOUSE!
EXIT
Holw
ARE YOU SURE?
OF COURSE I'M SURE!
THEY WERE MAKING A TON OF NOISE--IT SOUNDED LIKE THEY WRECKED THE PLACE.
IF THEY'RE STILL INSIDE, I'LL KEEP ON DRIVING INTO HOLWELL AND CALL THE POLICE.
THANK GOODNESS YOU DIDN'T GO IN.
DON'T WORRY, THEY'RE GONE.
IT LOOKS ALL RIGHT TO ME.
THIS BETTER NOT BE YOUR IDEA OF A JOKE, MICHAEL.

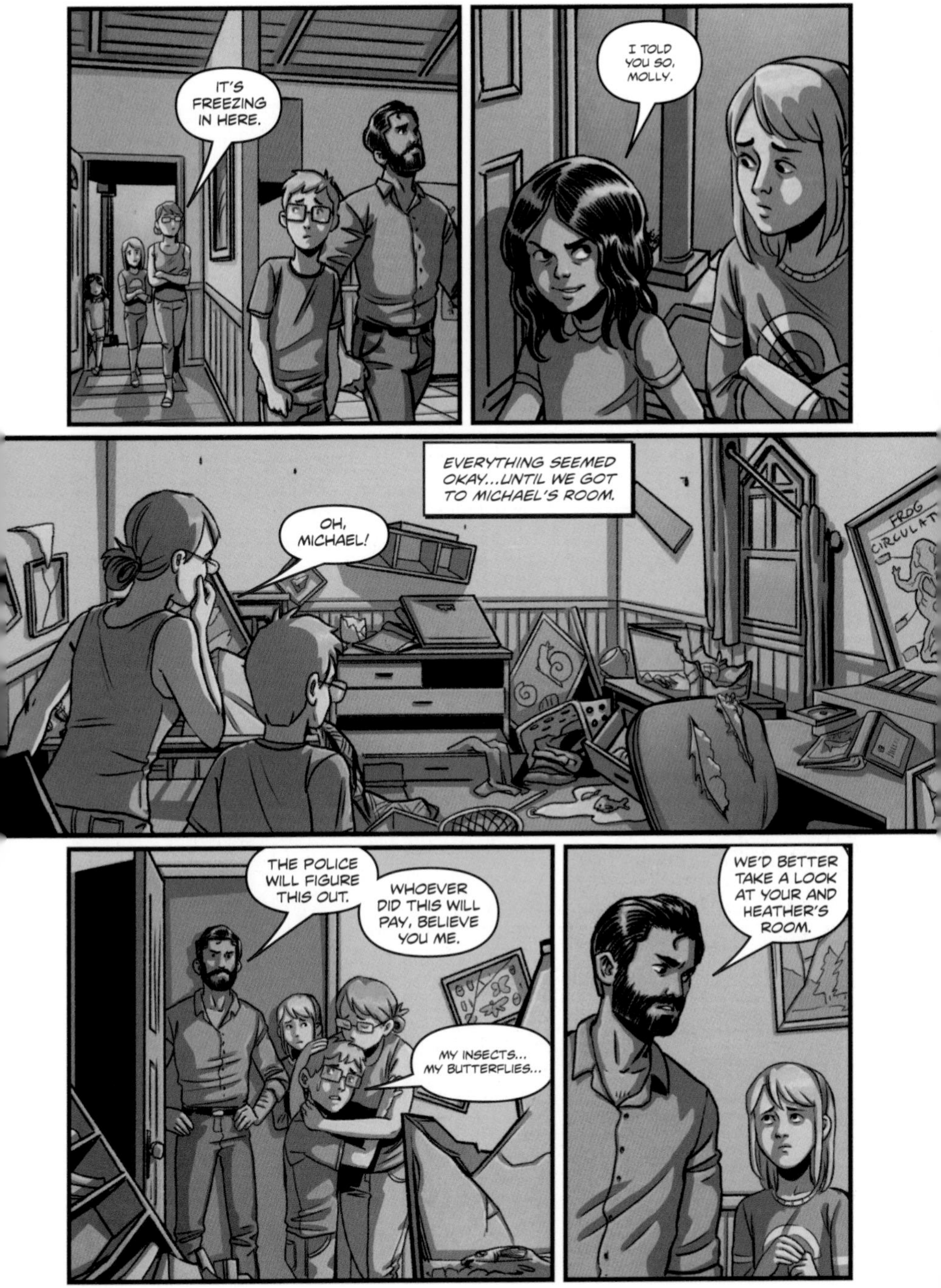
IT'S FREEZING IN HERE.
I TOLD YOU SO, MOLLY.
EVERYTHING SEEMED OKAY...UNTIL WE GOT TO MICHAEL'S ROOM.
OH, MICHAEL!
FROG CIRCULAT
THE POLICE WILL FIGURE THIS OUT.
WHOEVER DID THIS WILL PAY, BELIEVE YOU ME.
MY INSECTS... MY BUTTERFLIES...
WE'D BETTER TAKE A LOOK AT YOUR AND HEATHER'S ROOM.

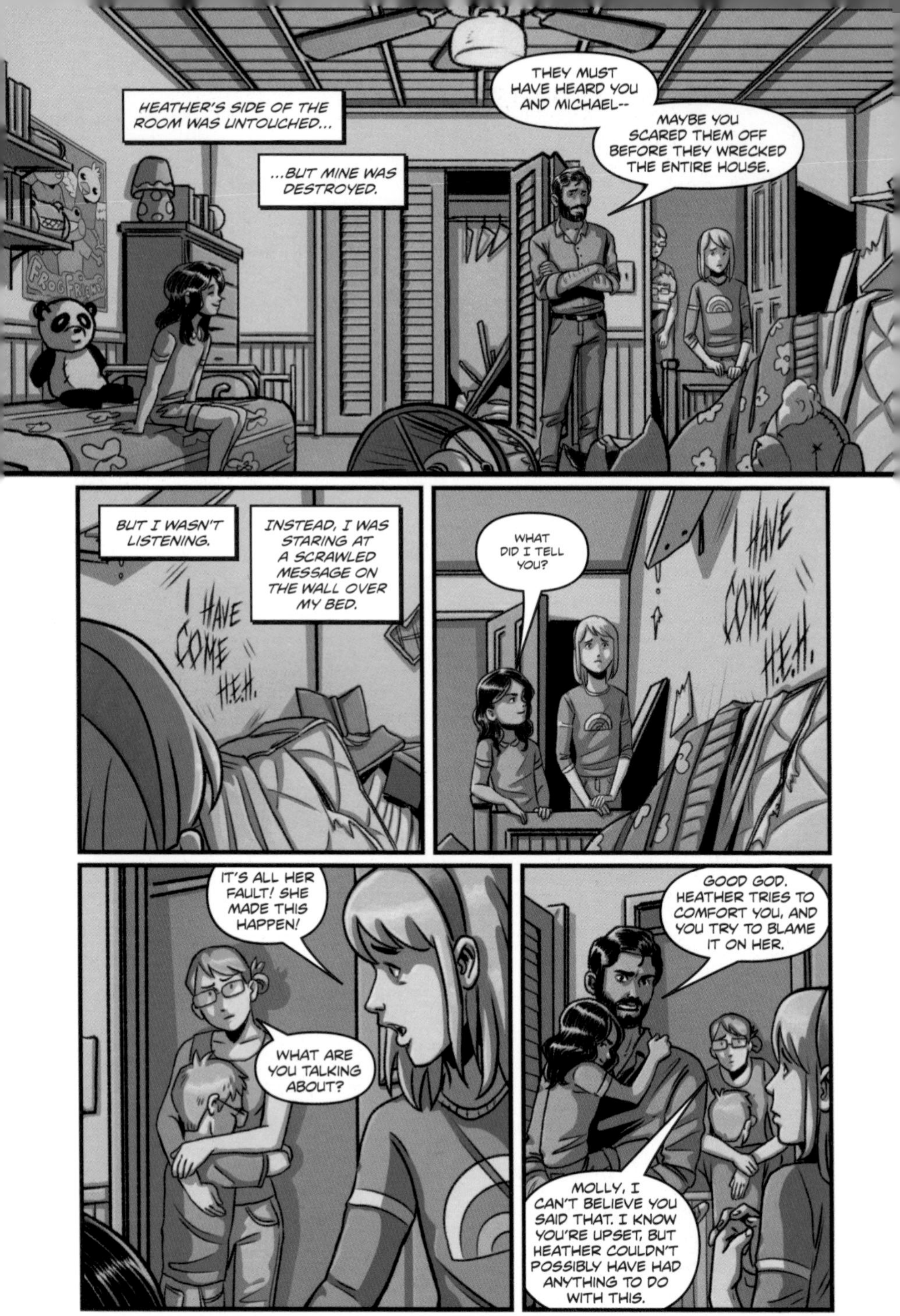
HEATHER'S SIDE OF THE ROOM WAS UNTOUCHED...
...BUT MINE WAS DESTROYED.
THEY MUST HAVE HEARD YOU AND MICHAEL--
MAYBE YOU SCARED THEM OFF BEFORE THEY WRECKED THE ENTIRE HOUSE.
FROG FRIENDS
BUT I WASN'T LISTENING.
INSTEAD, I WAS STARING AT A SCRAWLED MESSAGE ON THE WALL OVER MY BED.
I HAVE COME H.E.H.
WHAT DID I TELL YOU?
I HAVE COME H.E.H.
IT'S ALL HER FAULT! SHE MADE THIS HAPPEN!
WHAT ARE YOU TALKING ABOUT?
GOOD GOD. HEATHER TRIES TO COMFORT YOU, AND YOU TRY TO BLAME IT ON HER.
MOLLY, I CAN'T BELIEVE YOU SAID THAT. I KNOW YOU'RE UPSET, BUT HEATHER COULDN'T POSSIBLY HAVE HAD ANYTHING TO DO WITH THIS.

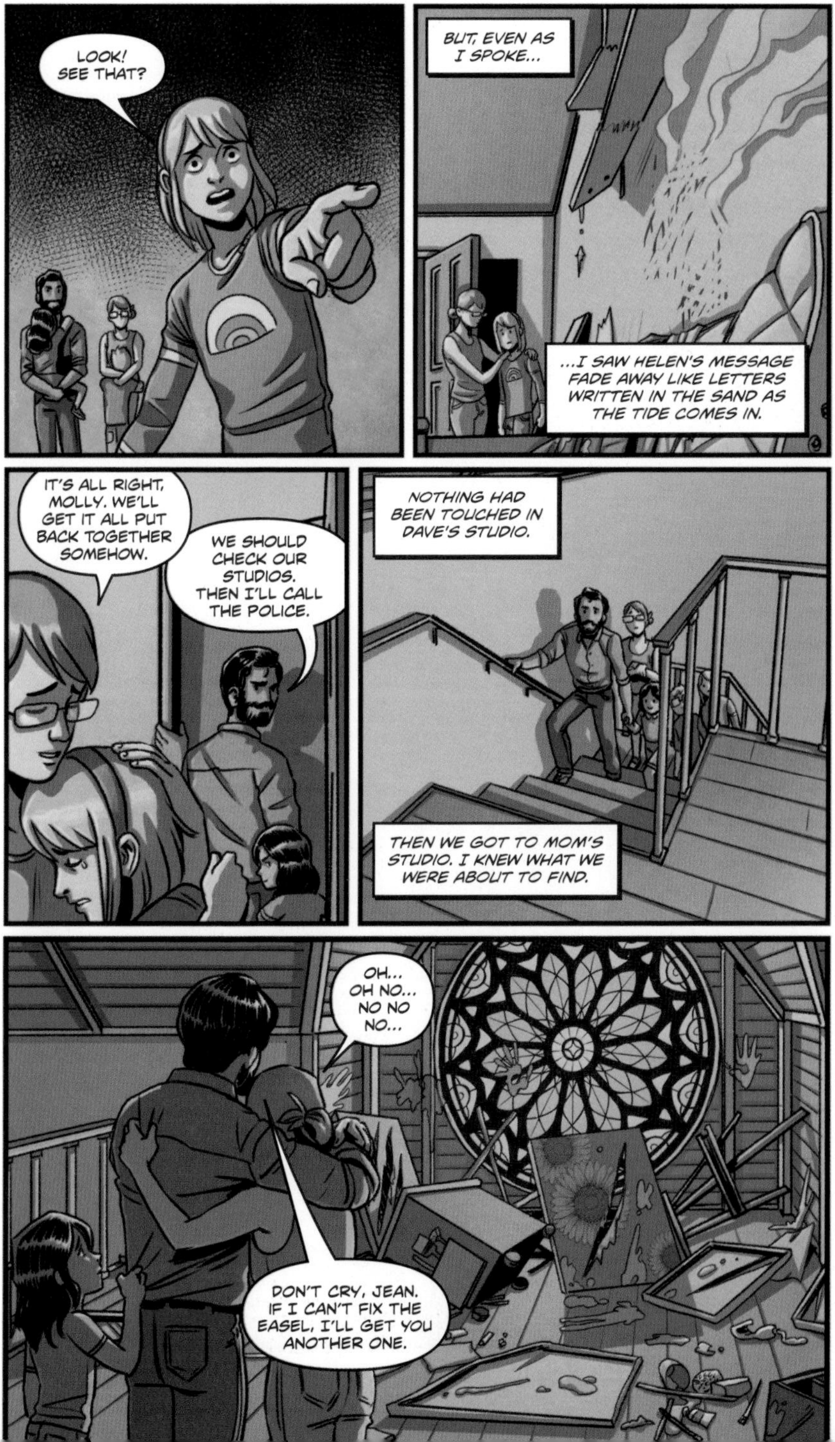
LOOK! SEE THAT?
BUT, EVEN AS I SPOKE...
...I SAW HELEN'S MESSAGE FADE AWAY LIKE LETTERS WRITTEN IN THE SAND AS THE TIDE COMES IN.
IT'S ALL RIGHT, MOLLY. WE'LL GET IT ALL PUT BACK TOGETHER SOMEHOW.
WE SHOULD CHECK OUR STUDIOS. THEN I'LL CALL THE POLICE.
NOTHING HAD BEEN TOUCHED IN DAVE'S STUDIO.
THEN WE GOT TO MOM'S STUDIO. I KNEW WHAT WE WERE ABOUT TO FIND.
OH... OH NO... NO NO NO...
DON'T CRY, JEAN. IF I CAN'T FIX THE EASEL, I'LL GET YOU ANOTHER ONE.

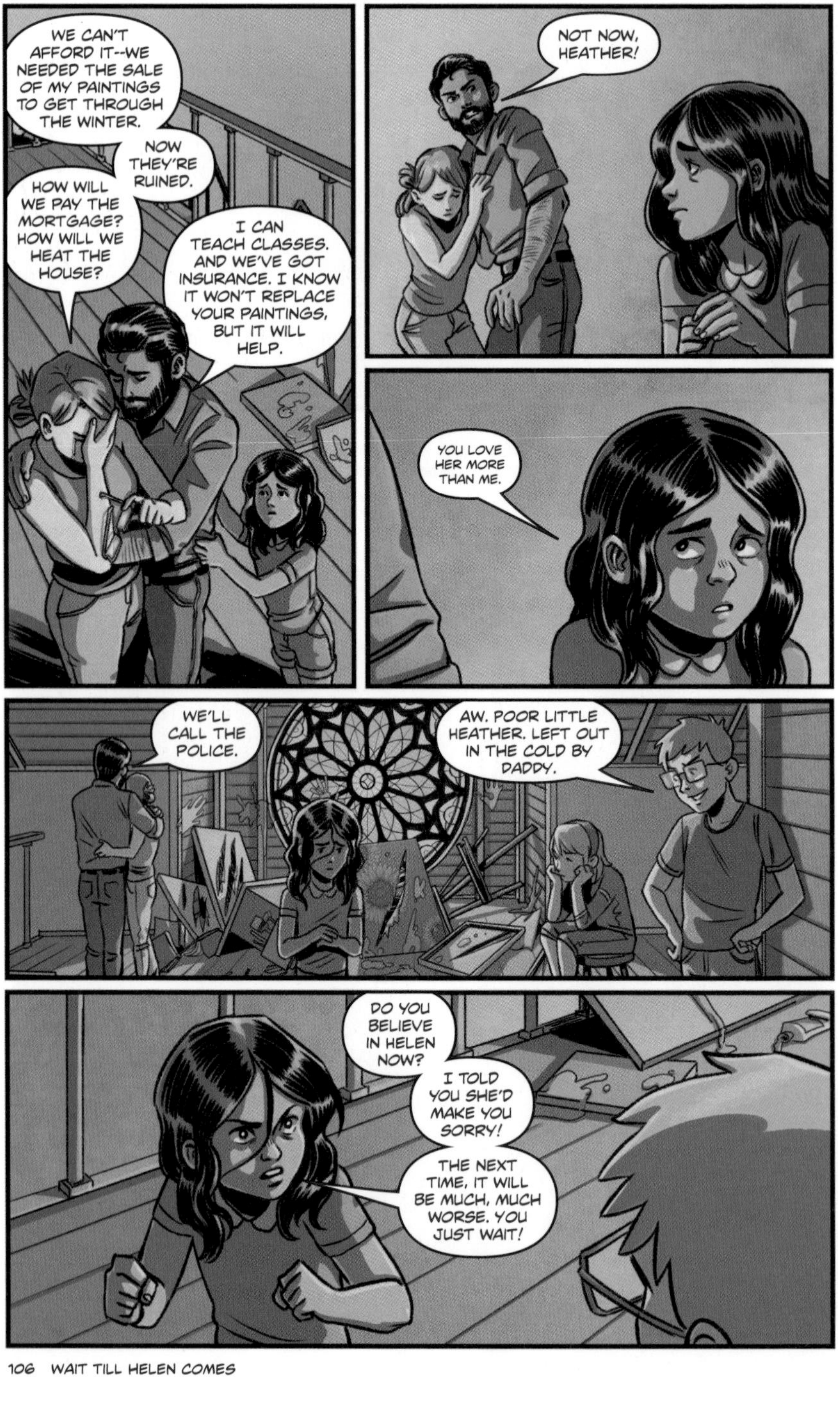
WE CAN'T AFFORD IT--WE NEEDED THE SALE OF MY PAINTINGS TO GET THROUGH THE WINTER.
NOW THEY'RE RUINED.
HOW WILL WE PAY THE MORTGAGE? HOW WILL WE HEAT THE HOUSE?
I CAN TEACH CLASSES. AND WE'VE GOT INSURANCE. I KNOW IT WON'T REPLACE YOUR PAINTINGS, BUT IT WILL HELP.
NOT NOW, HEATHER!
YOU LOVE HER MORE THAN ME.
WE'LL CALL THE POLICE.
AW. POOR LITTLE HEATHER. LEFT OUT IN THE COLD BY DADDY.
DO YOU BELIEVE IN HELEN NOW?
I TOLD YOU SHE'D MAKE YOU SORRY!
THE NEXT TIME, IT WILL BE MUCH, MUCH WORSE. YOU JUST WAIT!

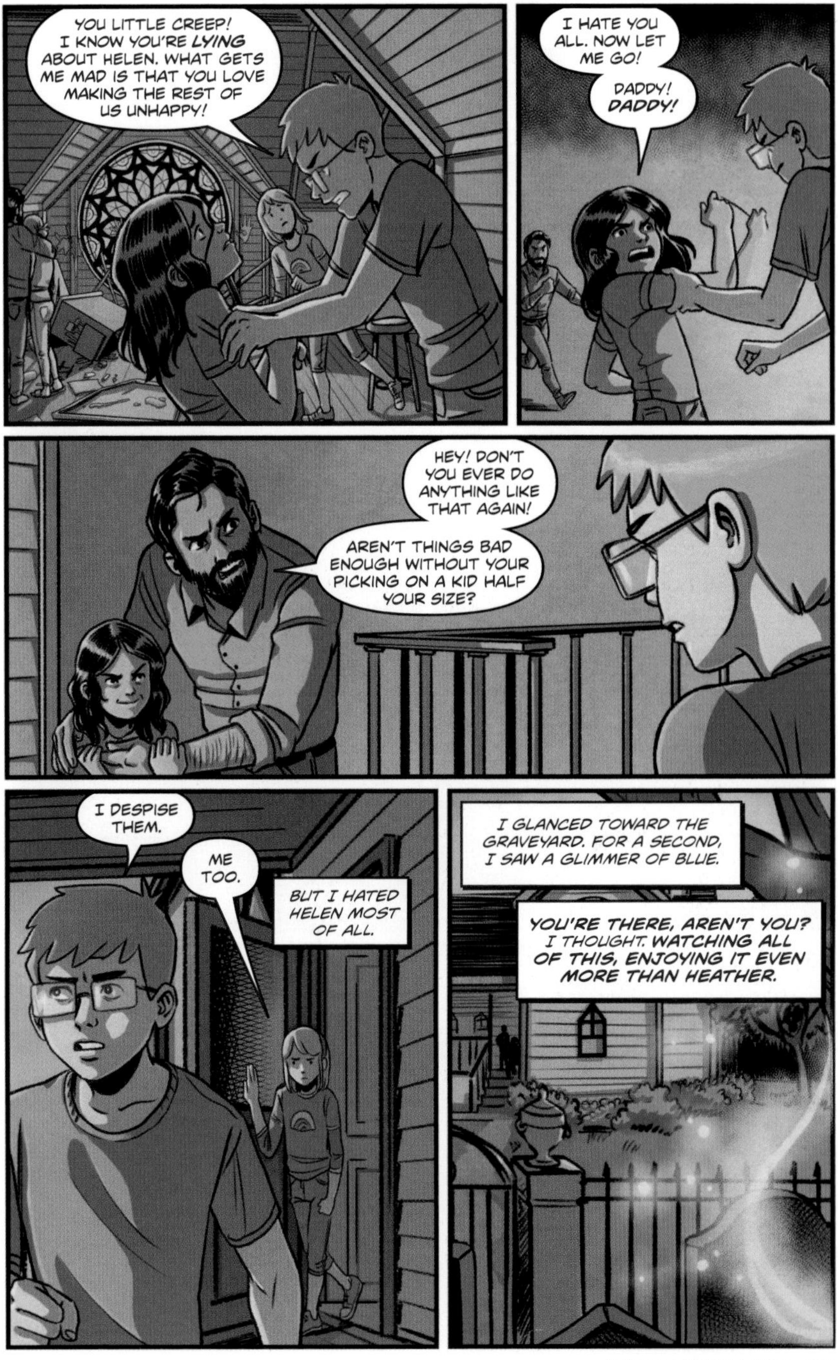
YOU LITTLE CREEP! I KNOW YOU'RE LYING ABOUT HELEN. WHAT GETS ME MAD IS THAT YOU LOVE MAKING THE REST OF US UNHAPPY!
I HATE YOU ALL. NOW LET ME GO!
DADDY! DADDY!
HEY! DON'T YOU EVER DO ANYTHING LIKE THAT AGAIN!
AREN'T THINGS BAD ENOUGH WITHOUT YOUR PICKING ON A KID HALF YOUR SIZE?
I DESPISE THEM.
ME TOO.
BUT I HATED HELEN MOST OF ALL.
I GLANCED TOWARD THE GRAVEYARD. FOR A SECOND, I SAW A GLIMMER OF BLUE.
YOU'RE THERE, AREN'T YOU? I THOUGHT. WATCHING ALL OF THIS, ENJOYING IT EVEN MORE THAN HEATHER.

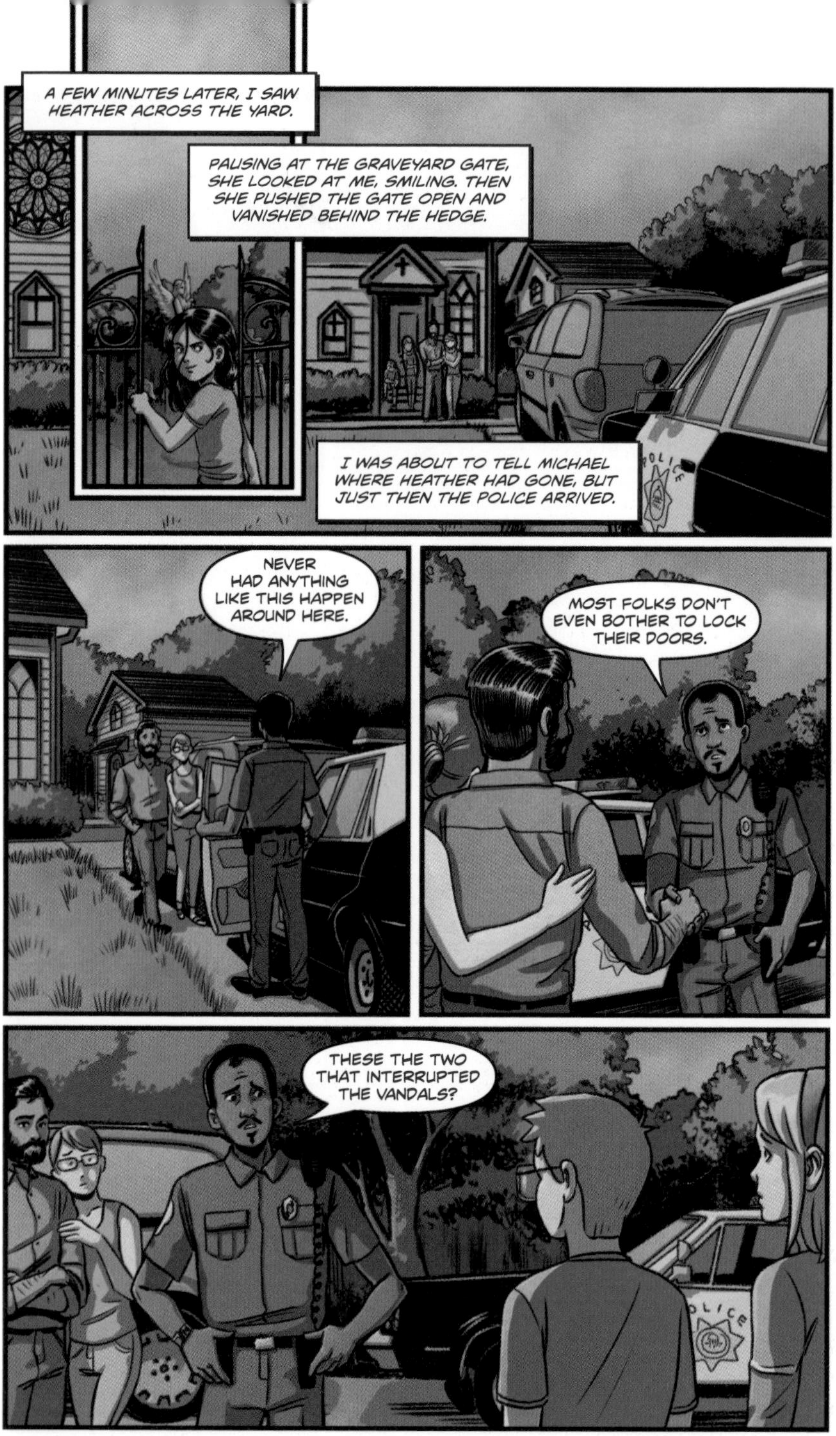
A FEW MINUTES LATER, I SAW HEATHER ACROSS THE YARD.
PAUSING AT THE GRAVEYARD GATE, SHE LOOKED AT ME, SMILING. THEN SHE PUSHED THE GATE OPEN AND VANISHED BEHIND THE HEDGE.
I WAS ABOUT TO TELL MICHAEL WHERE HEATHER HAD GONE, BUT JUST THEN THE POLICE ARRIVED.
NEVER HAD ANYTHING LIKE THIS HAPPEN AROUND HERE.
MOST FOLKS DON'T EVEN BOTHER TO LOCK THEIR DOORS.
THESE THE TWO THAT INTERRUPTED THE VANDALS?

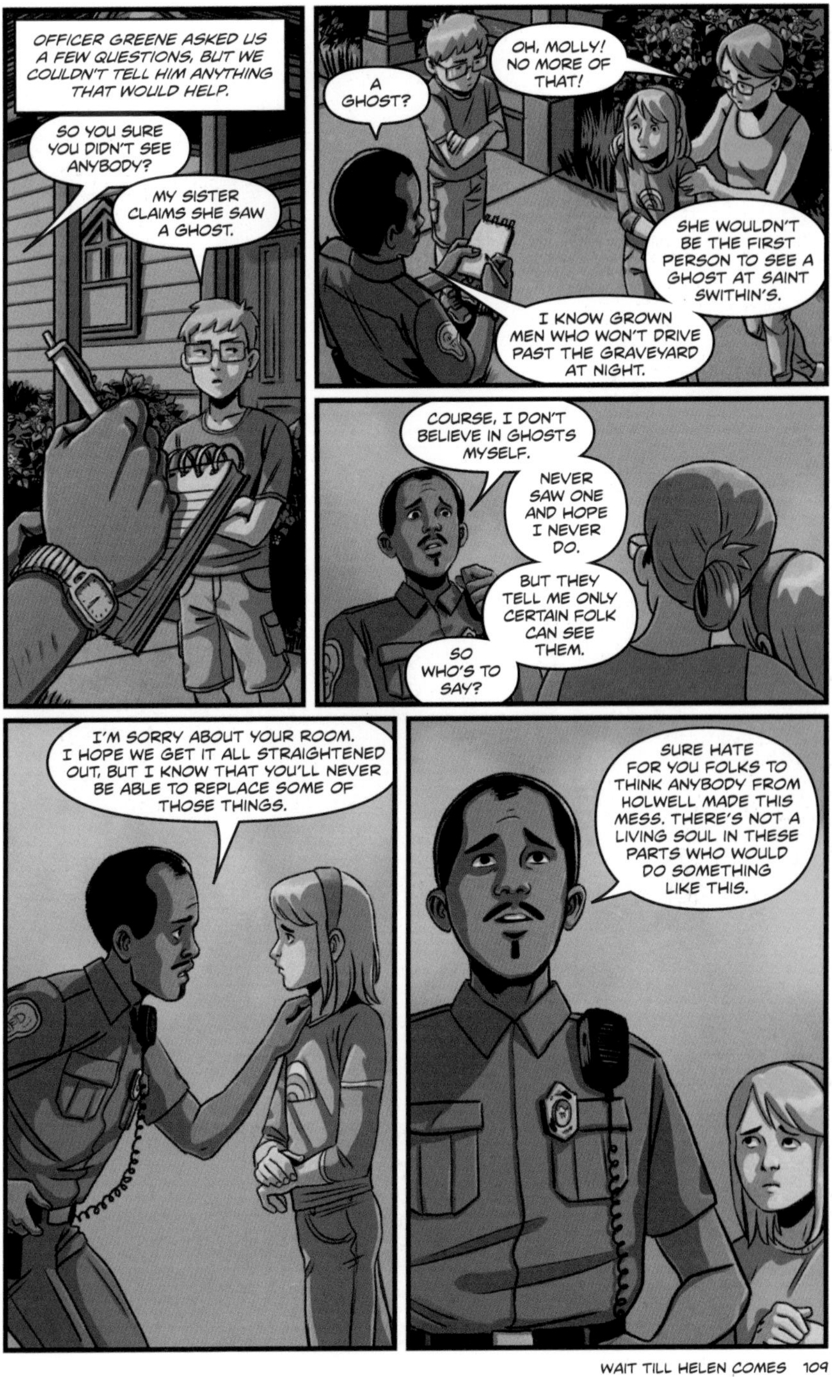
OFFICER GREENE ASKED US A FEW QUESTIONS, BUT WE COULDN'T TELL HIM ANYTHING THAT WOULD HELP.
SO YOU SURE YOU DIDN'T SEE ANYBODY?
MY SISTER CLAIMS SHE SAW A GHOST.
A GHOST?
OH, MOLLY! NO MORE OF THAT!
SHE WOULDN'T BE THE FIRST PERSON TO SEE A GHOST AT SAINT SWITHIN'S.
I KNOW GROWN MEN WHO WON'T DRIVE PAST THE GRAVEYARD AT NIGHT.
COURSE, I DON'T BELIEVE IN GHOSTS MYSELF.
NEVER SAW ONE AND HOPE I NEVER DO.
BUT THEY TELL ME ONLY CERTAIN FOLK CAN SEE THEM.
SO WHO'S TO SAY?
I'M SORRY ABOUT YOUR ROOM. I HOPE WE GET IT ALL STRAIGHTENED OUT, BUT I KNOW THAT YOU'LL NEVER BE ABLE TO REPLACE SOME OF THOSE THINGS.
SURE HATE FOR YOU FOLKS TO THINK ANYBODY FROM HOLWELL MADE THIS MESS. THERE'S NOT A LIVING SOUL IN THESE PARTS WHO WOULD DO SOMETHING LIKE THIS.

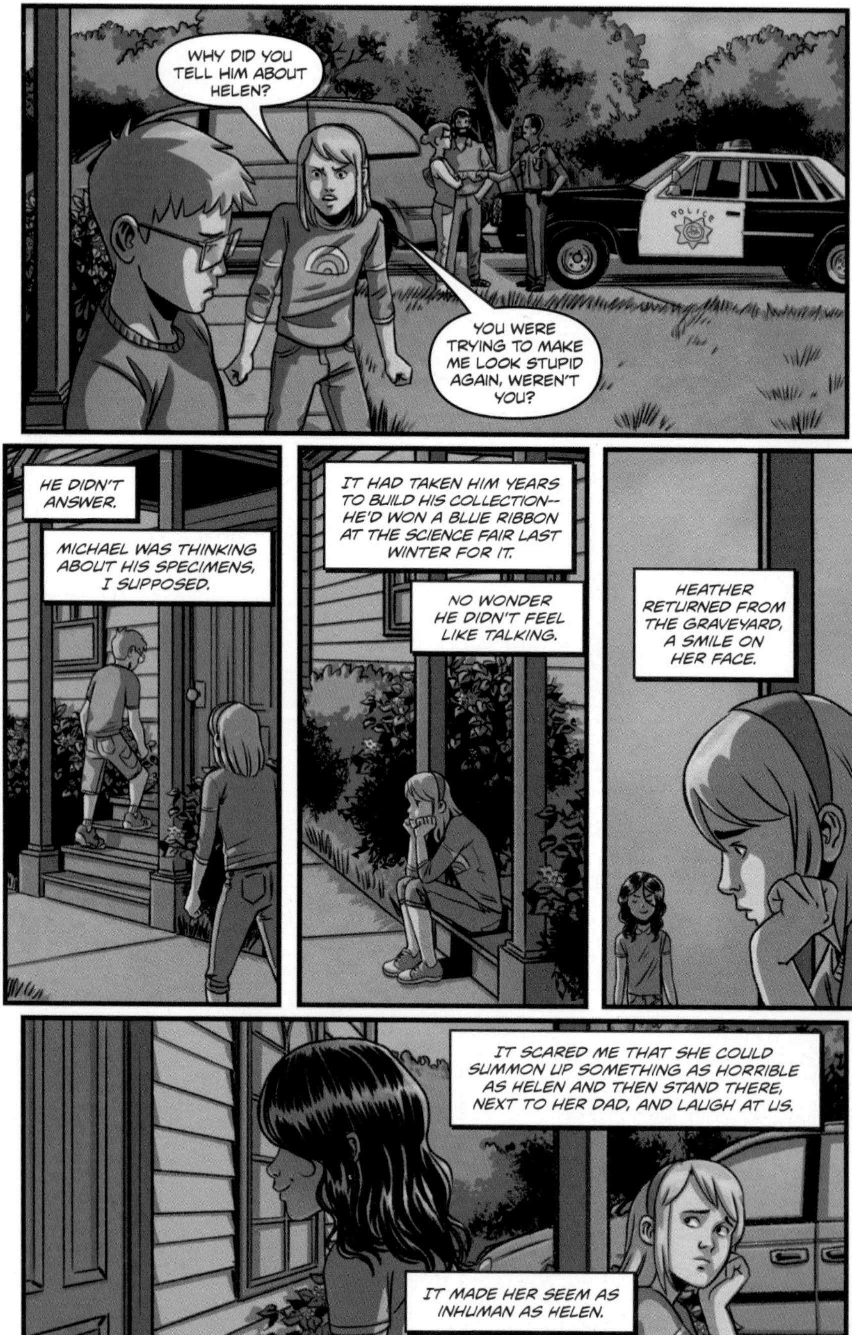
WHY DID YOU TELL HIM ABOUT HELEN?
YOU WERE TRYING TO MAKE ME LOOK STUPID AGAIN, WEREN'T YOU?
HE DIDN'T ANSWER.
MICHAEL WAS THINKING ABOUT HIS SPECIMENS, I SUPPOSED.
IT HAD TAKEN HIM YEARS TO BUILD HIS COLLECTION-- HE'D WON A BLUE RIBBON AT THE SCIENCE FAIR LAST WINTER FOR IT.
NO WONDER HE DIDN'T FEEL LIKE TALKING.
HEATHER RETURNED FROM THE GRAVEYARD, A SMILE ON HER FACE.
IT SCARED ME THAT SHE COULD SUMMON UP SOMETHING AS HORRIBLE AS HELEN AND THEN STAND THERE, NEXT TO HER DAD, AND LAUGH AT US.
IT MADE HER SEEM AS INHUMAN AS HELEN.

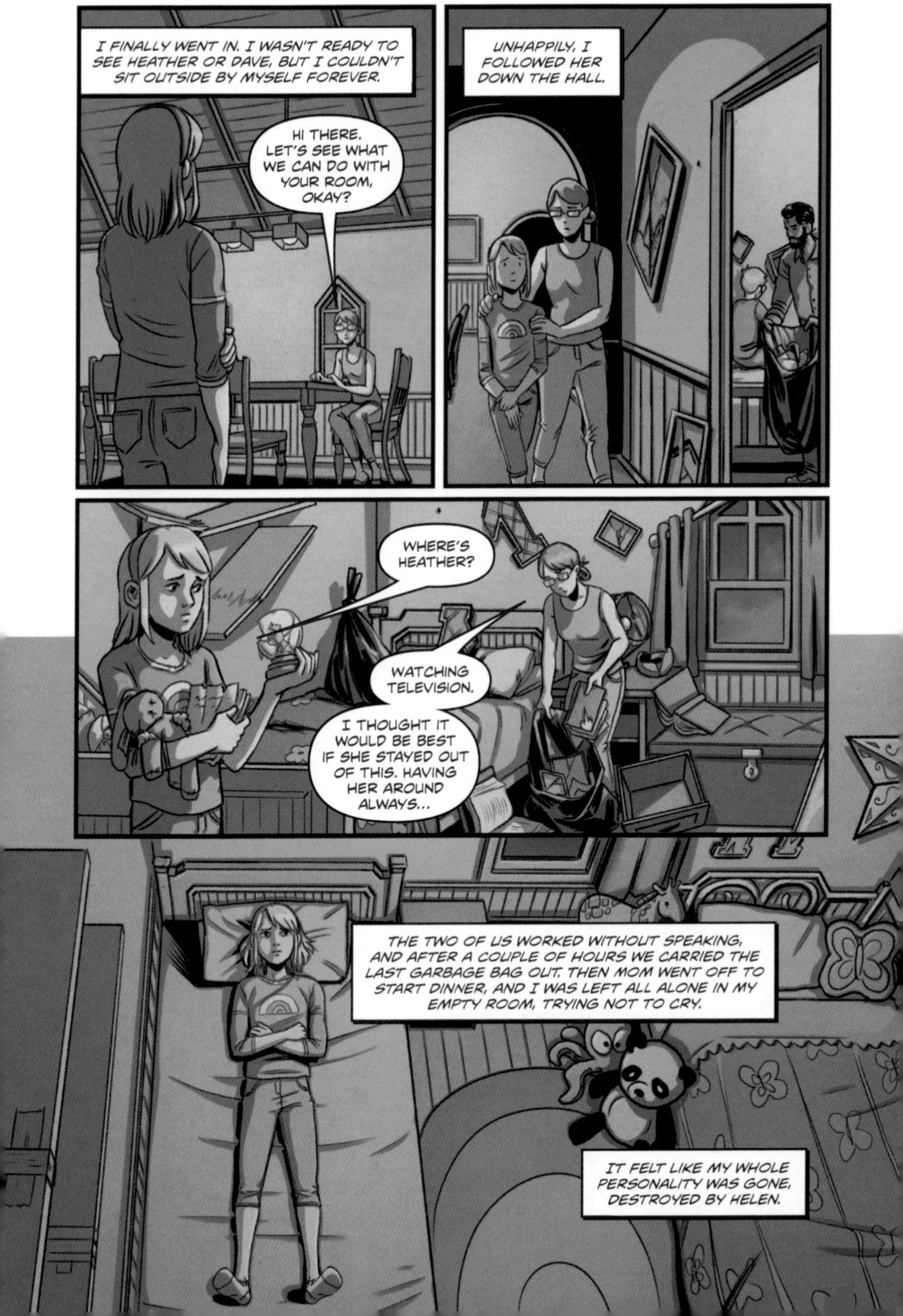
I FINALLY WENT IN. I WASN'T READY TO SEE HEATHER OR DAVE, BUT I COULDN'T SIT OUTSIDE BY MYSELF FOREVER.
HI THERE. LET'S SEE WHAT WE CAN DO WITH YOUR ROOM, OKAY?
UNHAPPILY, I FOLLOWED HER DOWN THE HALL.
WHERE'S HEATHER?
WATCHING TELEVISION.
I THOUGHT IT WOULD BE BEST IF SHE STAYED OUT OF THIS. HAVING HER AROUND ALWAYS...
THE TWO OF US WORKED WITHOUT SPEAKING, AND AFTER A COUPLE OF HOURS WE CARRIED THE LAST GARBAGE BAG OUT. THEN MOM WENT OFF TO START DINNER, AND I WAS LEFT ALL ALONE IN MY EMPTY ROOM, TRYING NOT TO CRY.
IT FELT LIKE MY WHOLE PERSONALITY WAS GONE, DESTROYED BY HELEN.

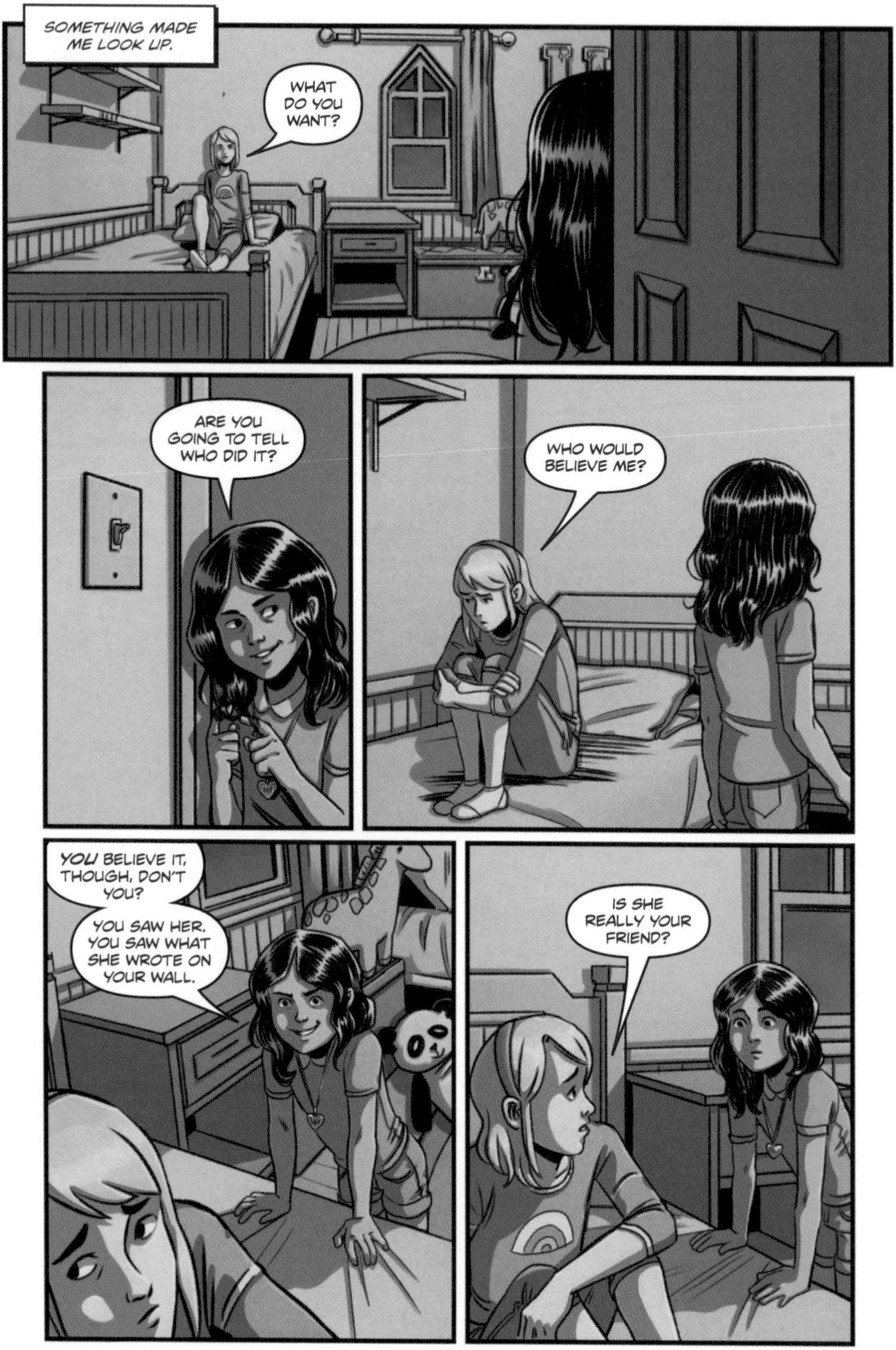
SOMETHING MADE ME LOOK UP.
WHAT DO YOU WANT?
ARE YOU GOING TO TELL WHO DID IT?
WHO WOULD BELIEVE ME?
YOU BELIEVE IT, THOUGH, DON'T YOU?
YOU SAW HER. YOU SAW WHAT SHE WROTE ON YOUR WALL.
IS SHE REALLY YOUR FRIEND?

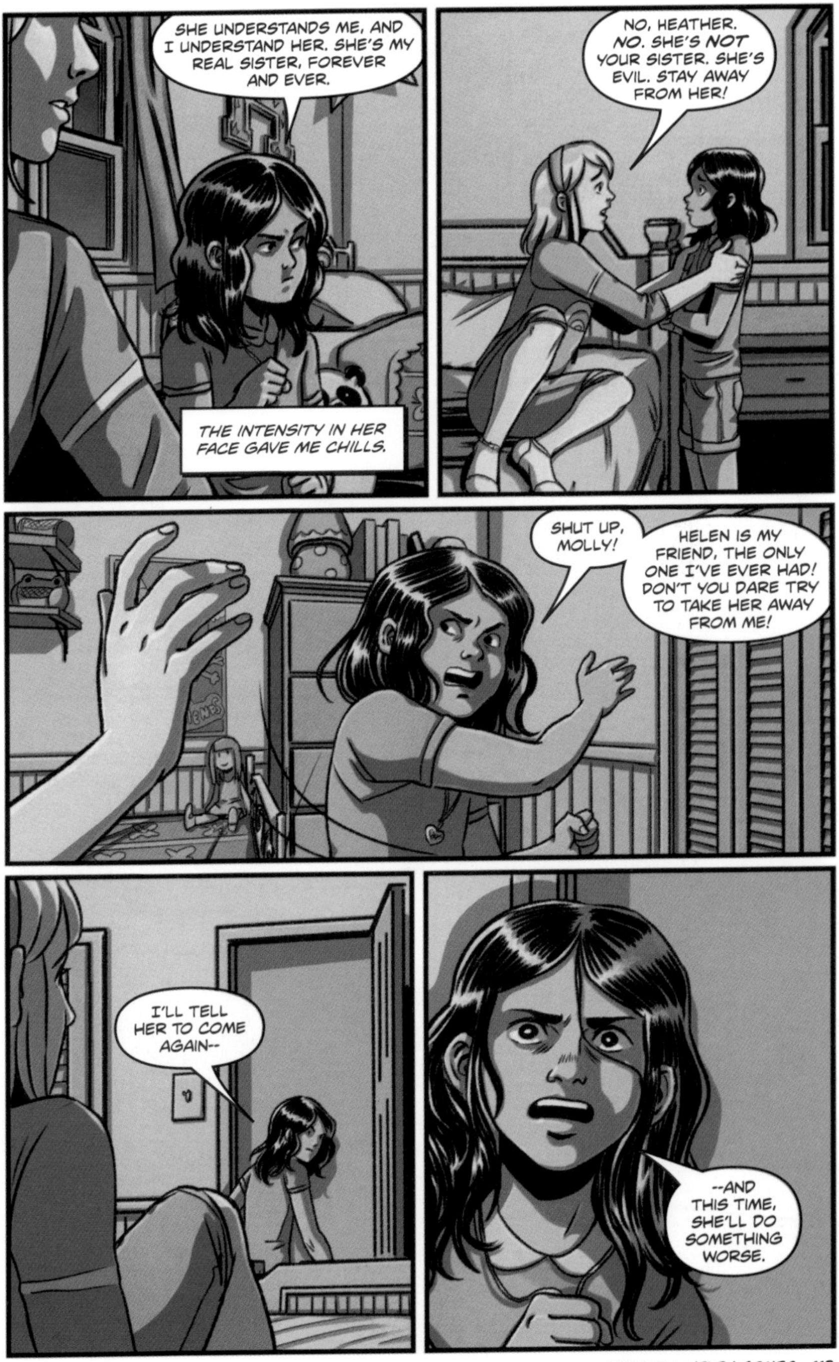
SHE UNDERSTANDS ME, AND I UNDERSTAND HER. SHE'S MY REAL SISTER, FOREVER AND EVER.
THE INTENSITY IN HER FACE GAVE ME CHILLS.
NO, HEATHER. *NO*. SHE'S *NOT* YOUR SISTER. SHE'S EVIL. STAY AWAY FROM HER!
SHUT UP, MOLLY!
HELEN IS MY FRIEND, THE ONLY ONE I'VE EVER HAD! DON'T YOU DARE TRY TO TAKE HER AWAY FROM ME!
I'LL TELL HER TO COME AGAIN--
--AND THIS TIME, SHE'LL DO SOMETHING WORSE.

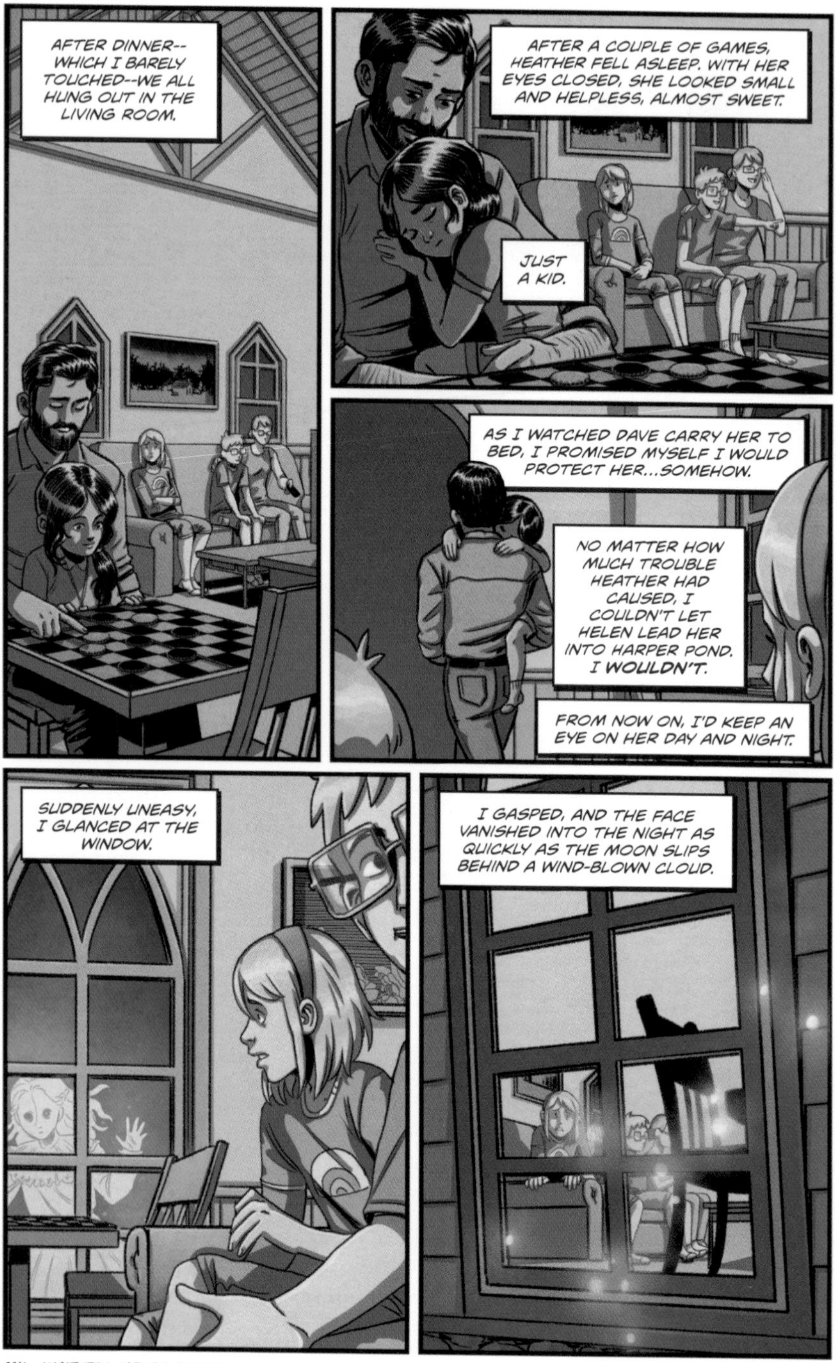
AFTER DINNER--WHICH I BARELY TOUCHED--WE ALL HUNG OUT IN THE LIVING ROOM.
AFTER A COUPLE OF GAMES, HEATHER FELL ASLEEP. WITH HER EYES CLOSED, SHE LOOKED SMALL AND HELPLESS, ALMOST SWEET.
JUST A KID.
AS I WATCHED DAVE CARRY HER TO BED, I PROMISED MYSELF I WOULD PROTECT HER...SOMEHOW.
NO MATTER HOW MUCH TROUBLE HEATHER HAD CAUSED, I COULDN'T LET HELEN LEAD HER INTO HARPER POND. I **WOULDN'T**.
FROM NOW ON, I'D KEEP AN EYE ON HER DAY AND NIGHT.
SUDDENLY UNEASY, I GLANCED AT THE WINDOW.
I GASPED, AND THE FACE VANISHED INTO THE NIGHT AS QUICKLY AS THE MOON SLIPS BEHIND A WIND-BLOWN CLOUD.

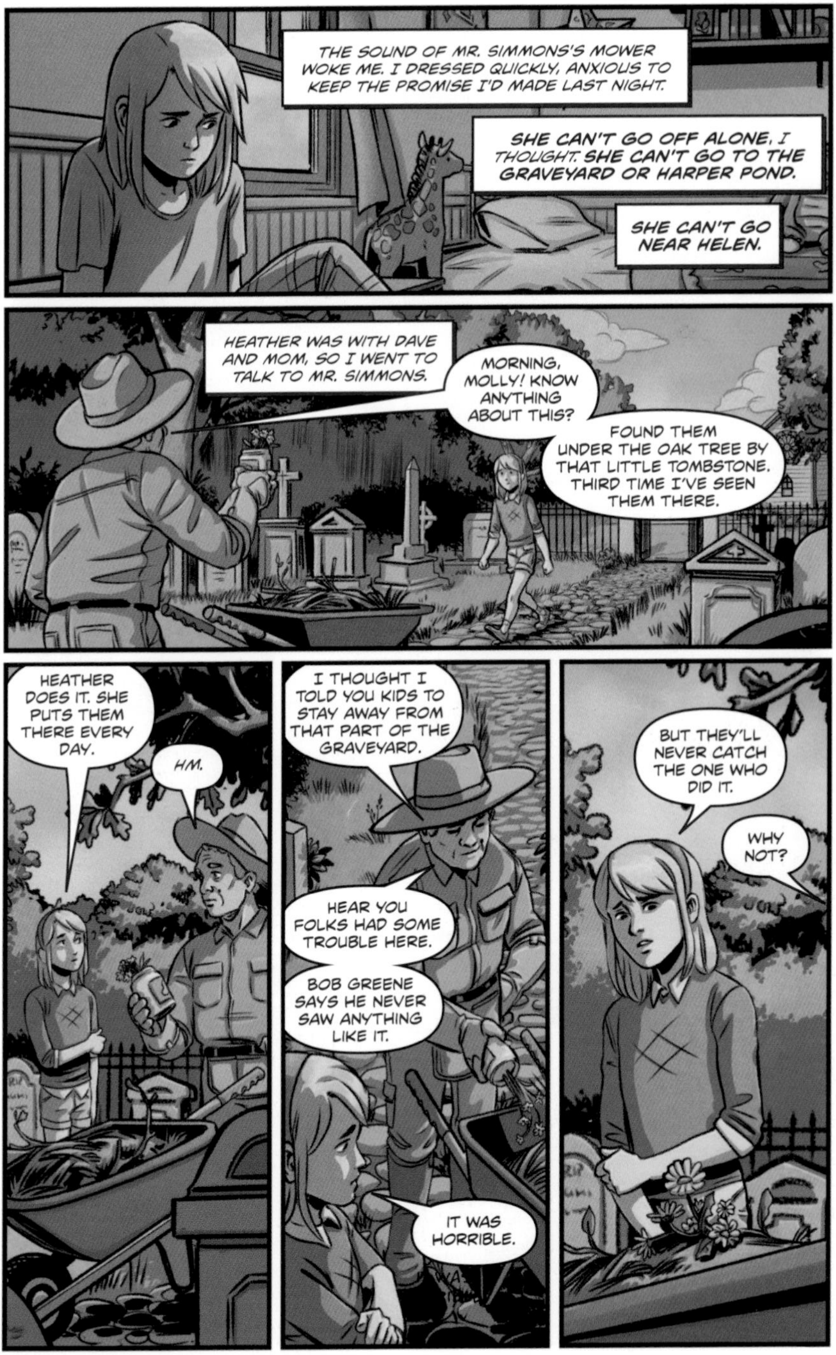
THE SOUND OF MR. SIMMONS'S MOWER WOKE ME. I DRESSED QUICKLY, ANXIOUS TO KEEP THE PROMISE I'D MADE LAST NIGHT.
SHE CAN'T GO OFF ALONE, I THOUGHT. SHE CAN'T GO TO THE GRAVEYARD OR HARPER POND.
SHE CAN'T GO NEAR HELEN.
HEATHER WAS WITH DAVE AND MOM, SO I WENT TO TALK TO MR. SIMMONS.
MORNING, MOLLY! KNOW ANYTHING ABOUT THIS?
FOUND THEM UNDER THE OAK TREE BY THAT LITTLE TOMBSTONE. THIRD TIME I'VE SEEN THEM THERE.
HEATHER DOES IT. SHE PUTS THEM THERE EVERY DAY.
HM.
I THOUGHT I TOLD YOU KIDS TO STAY AWAY FROM THAT PART OF THE GRAVEYARD.
HEAR YOU FOLKS HAD SOME TROUBLE HERE.
BOB GREENE SAYS HE NEVER SAW ANYTHING LIKE IT.
IT WAS HORRIBLE.
BUT THEY'LL NEVER CATCH THE ONE WHO DID IT.
WHY NOT?

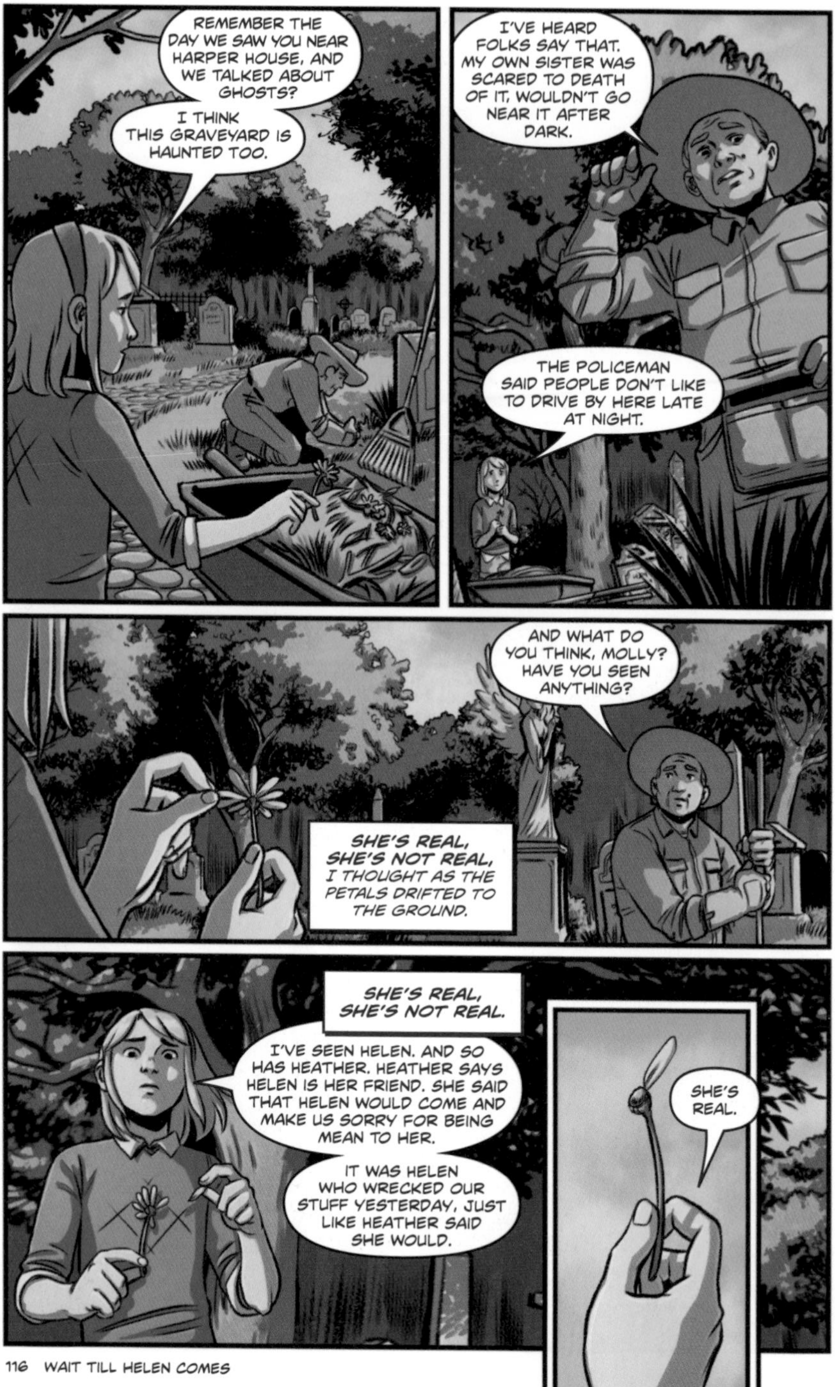
REMEMBER THE DAY WE SAW YOU NEAR HARPER HOUSE, AND WE TALKED ABOUT GHOSTS?
I THINK THIS GRAVEYARD IS HAUNTED TOO.
I'VE HEARD FOLKS SAY THAT. MY OWN SISTER WAS SCARED TO DEATH OF IT, WOULDN'T GO NEAR IT AFTER DARK.
THE POLICEMAN SAID PEOPLE DON'T LIKE TO DRIVE BY HERE LATE AT NIGHT.
AND WHAT DO YOU THINK, MOLLY? HAVE YOU SEEN ANYTHING?
SHE'S REAL, SHE'S NOT REAL, I THOUGHT AS THE PETALS DRIFTED TO THE GROUND.
SHE'S REAL, SHE'S NOT REAL.
I'VE SEEN HELEN. AND SO HAS HEATHER. HEATHER SAYS HELEN IS HER FRIEND. SHE SAID THAT HELEN WOULD COME AND MAKE US SORRY FOR BEING MEAN TO HER.
IT WAS HELEN WHO WRECKED OUR STUFF YESTERDAY, JUST LIKE HEATHER SAID SHE WOULD.
SHE'S REAL.

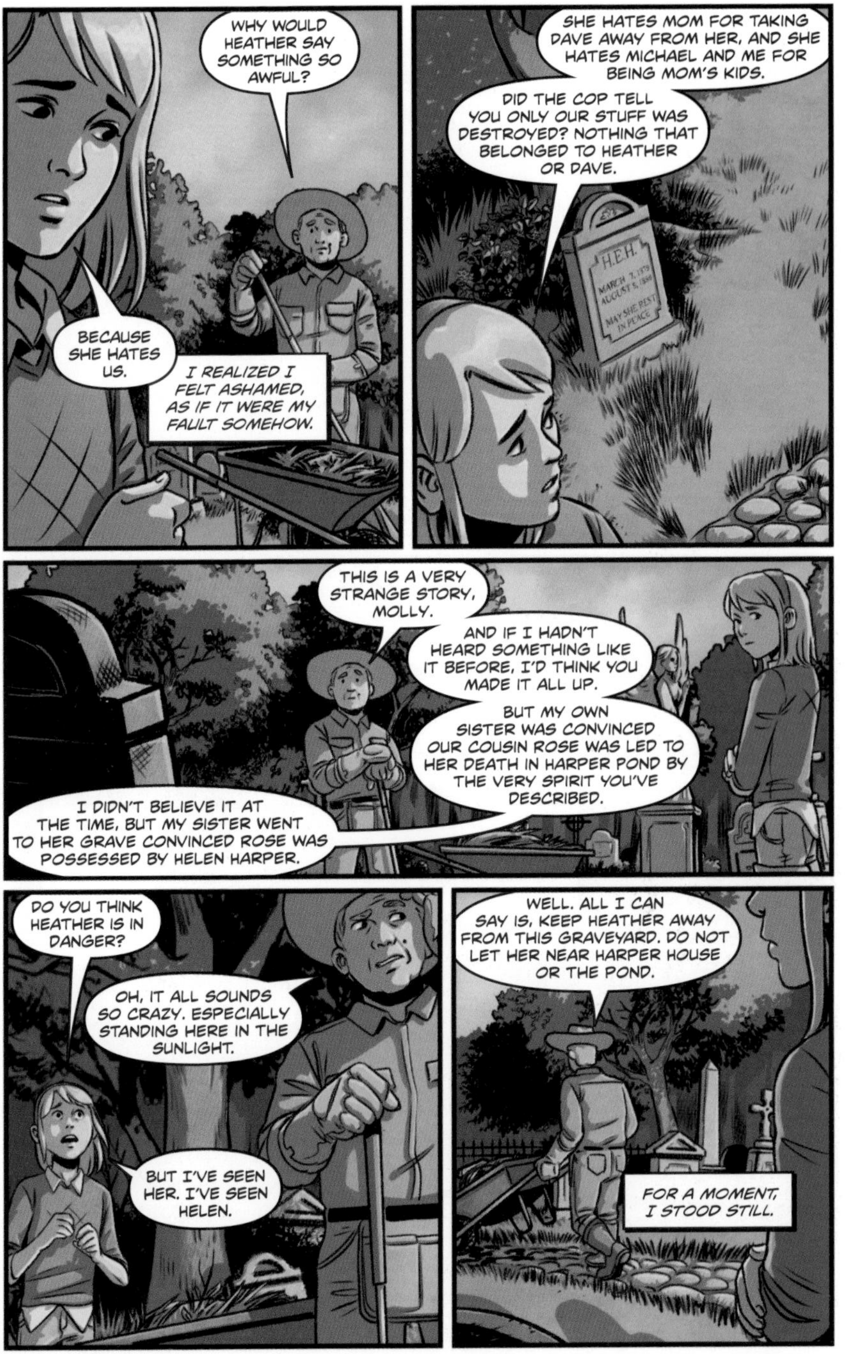
WHY WOULD HEATHER SAY SOMETHING SO AWFUL?
BECAUSE SHE HATES US.
I REALIZED I FELT ASHAMED, AS IF IT WERE MY FAULT SOMEHOW.
SHE HATES MOM FOR TAKING DAVE AWAY FROM HER, AND SHE HATES MICHAEL AND ME FOR BEING MOM'S KIDS.
DID THE COP TELL YOU ONLY OUR STUFF WAS DESTROYED? NOTHING THAT BELONGED TO HEATHER OR DAVE.
H.E.H.
MAY SHE REST IN PEACE
THIS IS A VERY STRANGE STORY, MOLLY.
AND IF I HADN'T HEARD SOMETHING LIKE IT BEFORE, I'D THINK YOU MADE IT ALL UP.
BUT MY OWN SISTER WAS CONVINCED OUR COUSIN ROSE WAS LED TO HER DEATH IN HARPER POND BY THE VERY SPIRIT YOU'VE DESCRIBED.
I DIDN'T BELIEVE IT AT THE TIME, BUT MY SISTER WENT TO HER GRAVE CONVINCED ROSE WAS POSSESSED BY HELEN HARPER.
DO YOU THINK HEATHER IS IN DANGER?
OH, IT ALL SOUNDS SO CRAZY. ESPECIALLY STANDING HERE IN THE SUNLIGHT.
BUT I'VE SEEN HER. I'VE SEEN HELEN.
WELL. ALL I CAN SAY IS, KEEP HEATHER AWAY FROM THIS GRAVEYARD. DO NOT LET HER NEAR HARPER HOUSE OR THE POND.
FOR A MOMENT, I STOOD STILL.

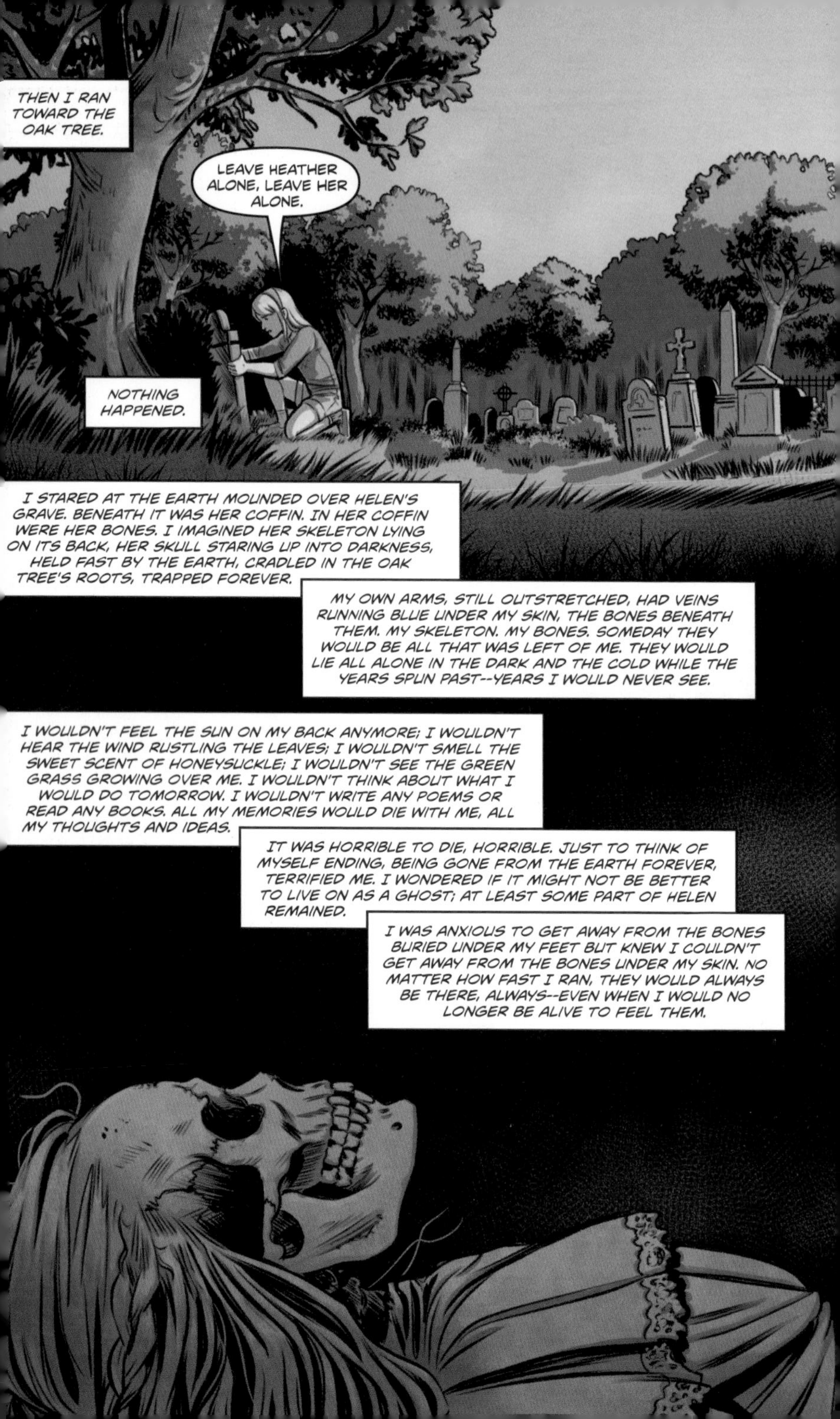
THEN I RAN TOWARD THE OAK TREE.
LEAVE HEATHER ALONE, LEAVE HER ALONE.
NOTHING HAPPENED.
I STARED AT THE EARTH MOUNDED OVER HELEN'S GRAVE. BENEATH IT WAS HER COFFIN. IN HER COFFIN WERE HER BONES. I IMAGINED HER SKELETON LYING ON ITS BACK, HER SKULL STARING UP INTO DARKNESS, HELD FAST BY THE EARTH, CRADLED IN THE OAK TREE'S ROOTS, TRAPPED FOREVER.
MY OWN ARMS, STILL OUTSTRETCHED, HAD VEINS RUNNING BLUE UNDER MY SKIN, THE BONES BENEATH THEM. MY SKELETON. MY BONES. SOMEDAY THEY WOULD BE ALL THAT WAS LEFT OF ME. THEY WOULD LIE ALL ALONE IN THE DARK AND THE COLD WHILE THE YEARS SPUN PAST--YEARS I WOULD NEVER SEE.
I WOULDN'T FEEL THE SUN ON MY BACK ANYMORE; I WOULDN'T HEAR THE WIND RUSTLING THE LEAVES; I WOULDN'T SMELL THE SWEET SCENT OF HONEYSUCKLE; I WOULDN'T SEE THE GREEN GRASS GROWING OVER ME. I WOULDN'T THINK ABOUT WHAT I WOULD DO TOMORROW. I WOULDN'T WRITE ANY POEMS OR READ ANY BOOKS. ALL MY MEMORIES WOULD DIE WITH ME, ALL MY THOUGHTS AND IDEAS.
IT WAS HORRIBLE TO DIE, HORRIBLE. JUST TO THINK OF MYSELF ENDING, BEING GONE FROM THE EARTH FOREVER, TERRIFIED ME. I WONDERED IF IT MIGHT NOT BE BETTER TO LIVE ON AS A GHOST; AT LEAST SOME PART OF HELEN REMAINED.
I WAS ANXIOUS TO GET AWAY FROM THE BONES BURIED UNDER MY FEET BUT KNEW I COULDN'T GET AWAY FROM THE BONES UNDER MY SKIN. NO MATTER HOW FAST I RAN, THEY WOULD ALWAYS BE THERE, ALWAYS--EVEN WHEN I WOULD NO LONGER BE ALIVE TO FEEL THEM.

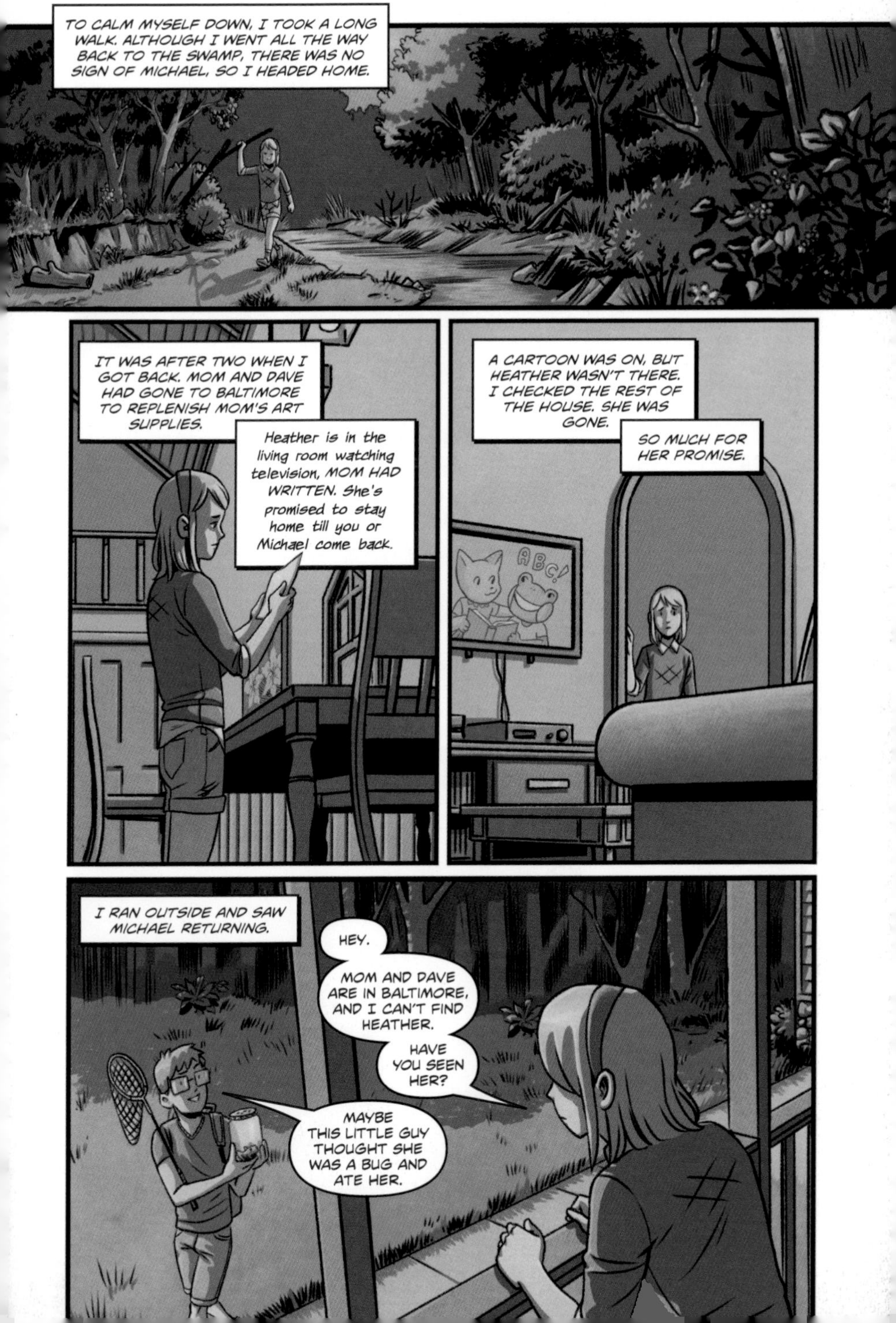
TO CALM MYSELF DOWN, I TOOK A LONG WALK. ALTHOUGH I WENT ALL THE WAY BACK TO THE SWAMP, THERE WAS NO SIGN OF MICHAEL, SO I HEADED HOME.
IT WAS AFTER TWO WHEN I GOT BACK. MOM AND DAVE HAD GONE TO BALTIMORE TO REPLENISH MOM'S ART SUPPLIES.
Heather is in the living room watching television, MOM HAD WRITTEN. She's promised to stay home till you or Michael come back.
A CARTOON WAS ON, BUT HEATHER WASN'T THERE. I CHECKED THE REST OF THE HOUSE. SHE WAS GONE.
SO MUCH FOR HER PROMISE.
ABC!
I RAN OUTSIDE AND SAW MICHAEL RETURNING.
HEY.
MOM AND DAVE ARE IN BALTIMORE, AND I CAN'T FIND HEATHER.
HAVE YOU SEEN HER?
MAYBE THIS LITTLE GUY THOUGHT SHE WAS A BUG AND ATE HER.

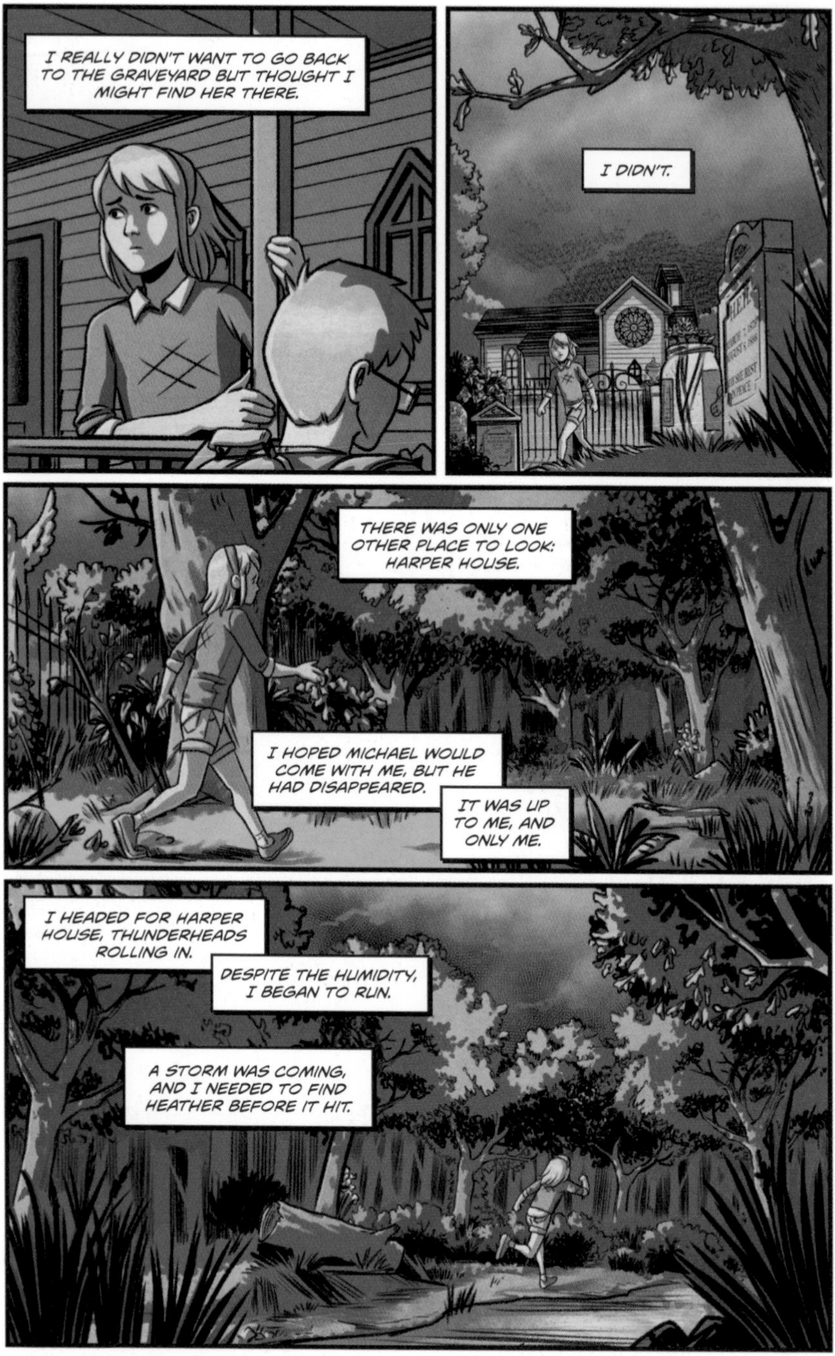
I REALLY DIDN'T WANT TO GO BACK TO THE GRAVEYARD BUT THOUGHT I MIGHT FIND HER THERE.
I DIDN'T.
THERE WAS ONLY ONE OTHER PLACE TO LOOK: HARPER HOUSE.
I HOPED MICHAEL WOULD COME WITH ME, BUT HE HAD DISAPPEARED.
IT WAS UP TO ME, AND ONLY ME.
I HEADED FOR HARPER HOUSE, THUNDERHEADS ROLLING IN.
DESPITE THE HUMIDITY, I BEGAN TO RUN.
A STORM WAS COMING, AND I NEEDED TO FIND HEATHER BEFORE IT HIT.

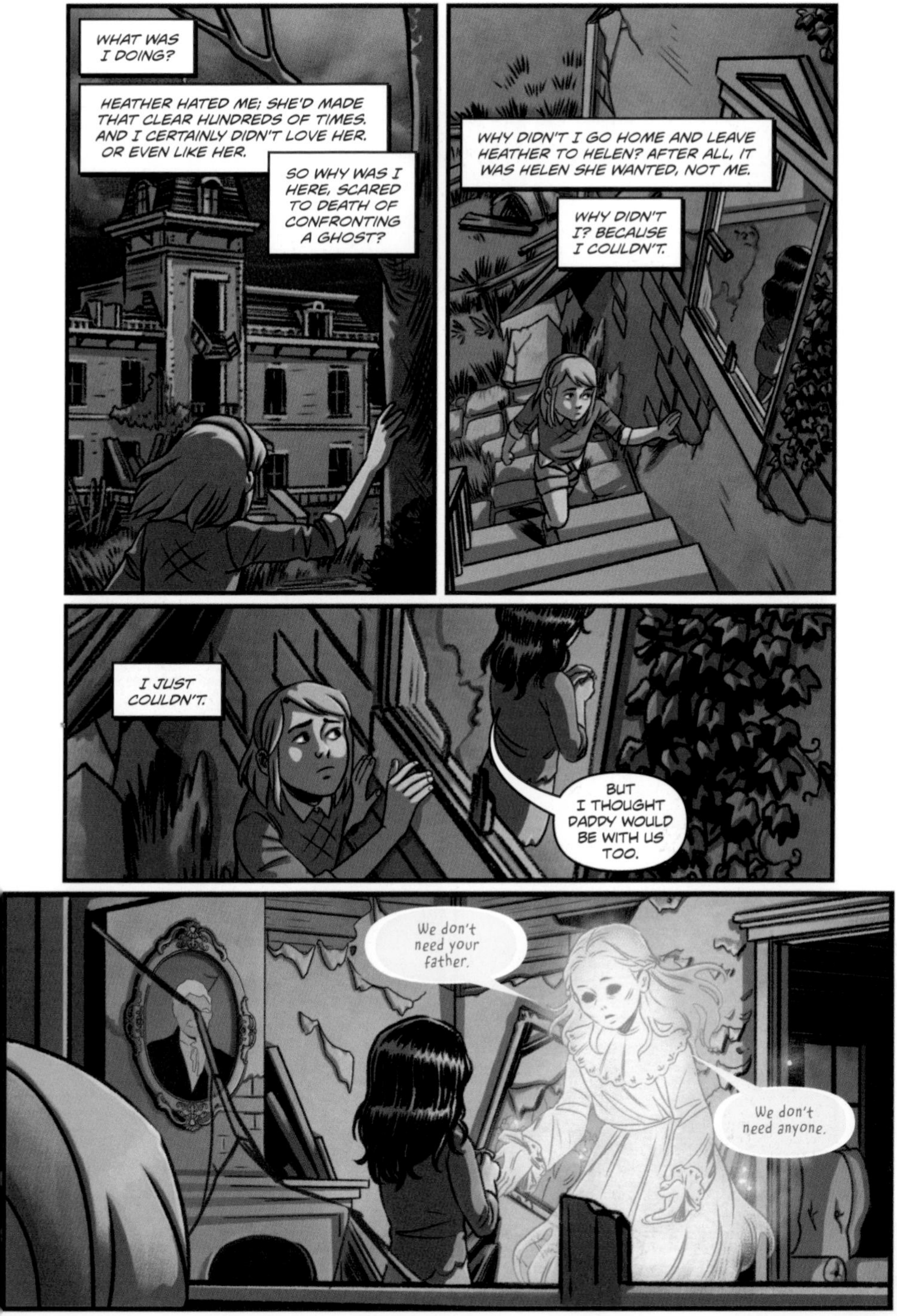

WHAT WAS I DOING?
HEATHER HATED ME; SHE'D MADE THAT CLEAR HUNDREDS OF TIMES. AND I CERTAINLY DIDN'T LOVE HER. OR EVEN LIKE HER.
SO WHY WAS I HERE, SCARED TO DEATH OF CONFRONTING A GHOST?
WHY DIDN'T I GO HOME AND LEAVE HEATHER TO HELEN? AFTER ALL, IT WAS HELEN SHE WANTED, NOT ME.
WHY DIDN'T I? BECAUSE I COULDN'T.
I JUST COULDN'T.
BUT I THOUGHT DADDY WOULD BE WITH US TOO.
We don't need your father.
We don't need anyone.

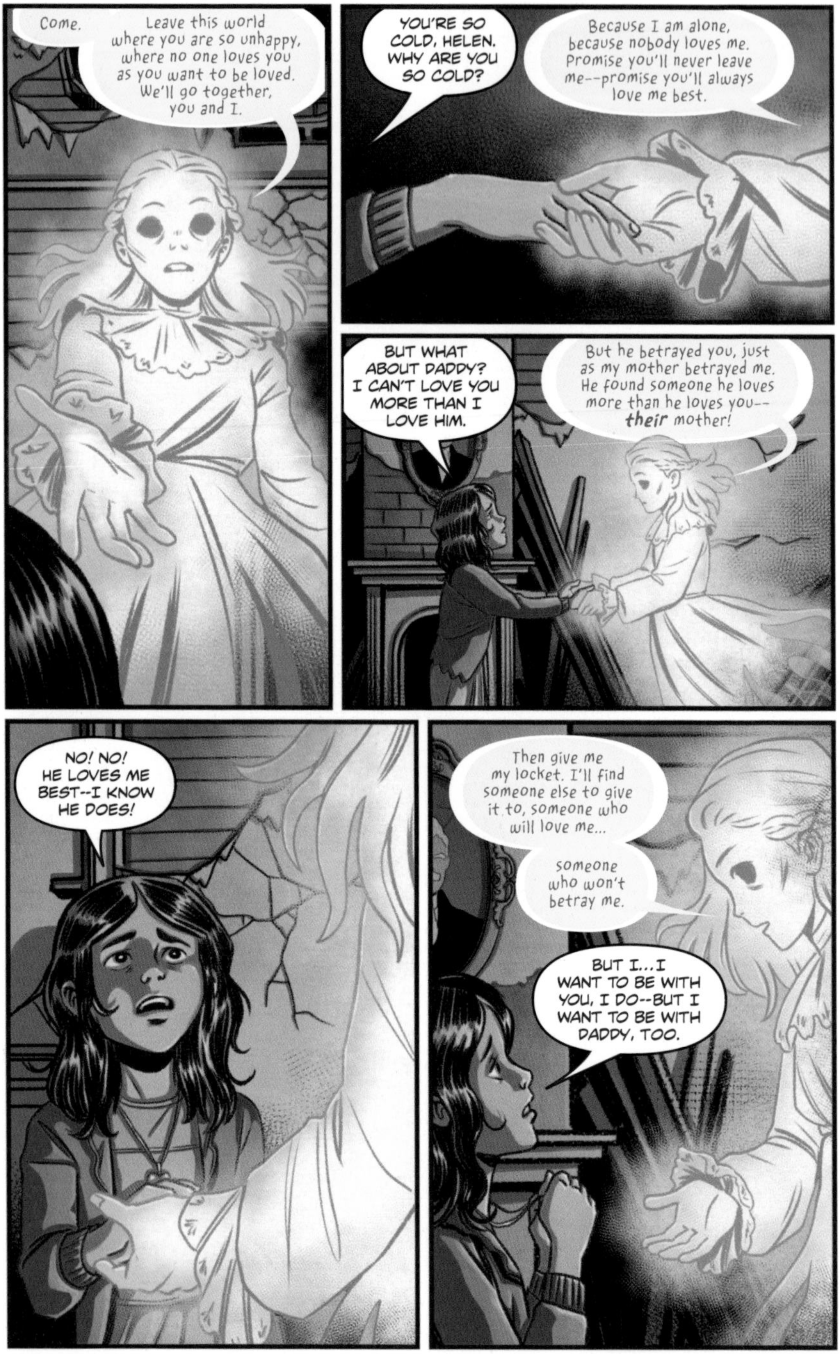
Come.
Leave this world where you are so unhappy, where no one loves you as you want to be loved. We'll go together, you and I.
YOU'RE SO COLD, HELEN. WHY ARE YOU SO COLD?
Because I am alone, because nobody loves me. Promise you'll never leave me--promise you'll always love me best.
BUT WHAT ABOUT DADDY? I CAN'T LOVE YOU MORE THAN I LOVE HIM.
But he betrayed you, just as my mother betrayed me. He found someone he loves more than he loves you--*their* mother!
NO! NO! HE LOVES ME BEST--I KNOW HE DOES!
Then give me my locket. I'll find someone else to give it to, someone who will love me...
someone who won't betray me.
BUT I...I WANT TO BE WITH YOU, I DO--BUT I WANT TO BE WITH DADDY, TOO.

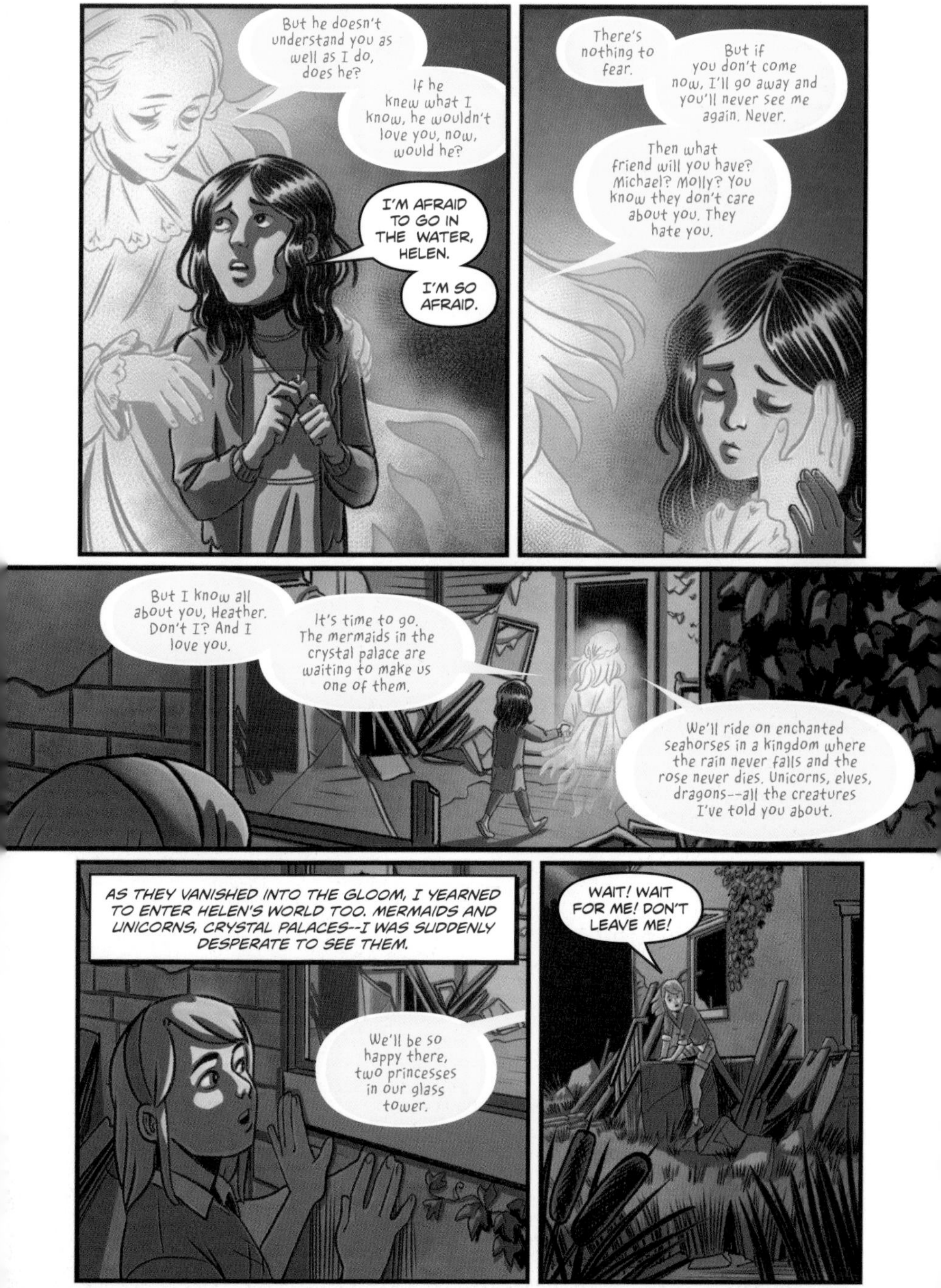
But he doesn't understand you as well as I do, does he?
If he knew what I know, he wouldn't love you, now, would he?
I'M AFRAID TO GO IN THE WATER, HELEN.
I'M SO AFRAID.
There's nothing to fear.
But if you don't come now, I'll go away and you'll never see me again. Never.
Then what friend will you have? Michael? Molly? You know they don't care about you. They hate you.
But I know all about you, Heather. Don't I? And I love you.
It's time to go. The mermaids in the crystal palace are waiting to make us one of them.
We'll ride on enchanted seahorses in a kingdom where the rain never falls and the rose never dies. Unicorns, elves, dragons--all the creatures I've told you about.
AS THEY VANISHED INTO THE GLOOM, I YEARNED TO ENTER HELEN'S WORLD TOO. MERMAIDS AND UNICORNS, CRYSTAL PALACES--I WAS SUDDENLY DESPERATE TO SEE THEM.
We'll be so happy there, two princesses in our glass tower.
WAIT! WAIT FOR ME! DON'T LEAVE ME!

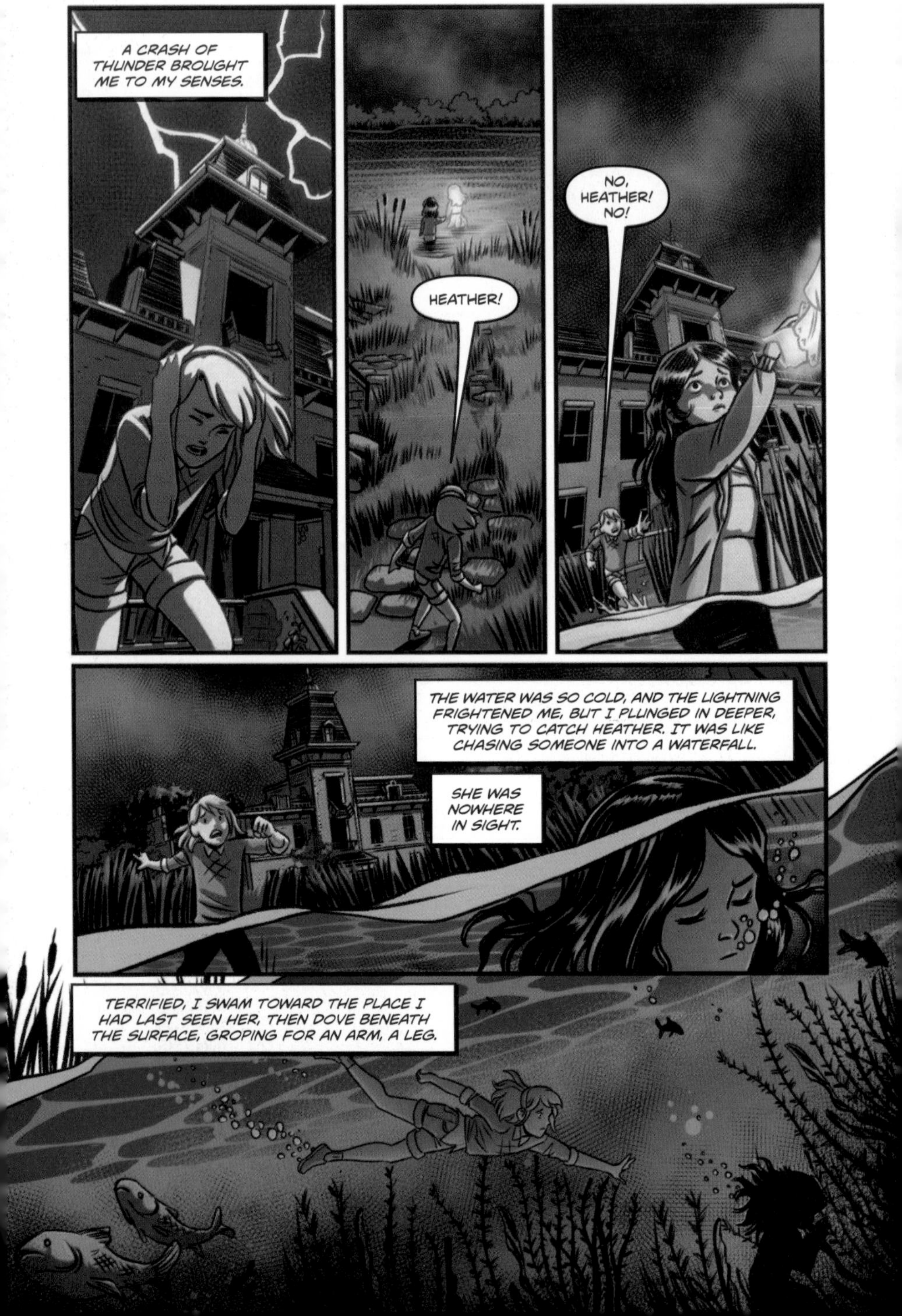
A CRASH OF THUNDER BROUGHT ME TO MY SENSES.
HEATHER!
NO, HEATHER! NO!
THE WATER WAS SO COLD, AND THE LIGHTNING FRIGHTENED ME, BUT I PLUNGED IN DEEPER, TRYING TO CATCH HEATHER. IT WAS LIKE CHASING SOMEONE INTO A WATERFALL.
SHE WAS NOWHERE IN SIGHT.
TERRIFIED, I SWAM TOWARD THE PLACE I HAD LAST SEEN HER, THEN DOVE BENEATH THE SURFACE, GROPING FOR AN ARM, A LEG.

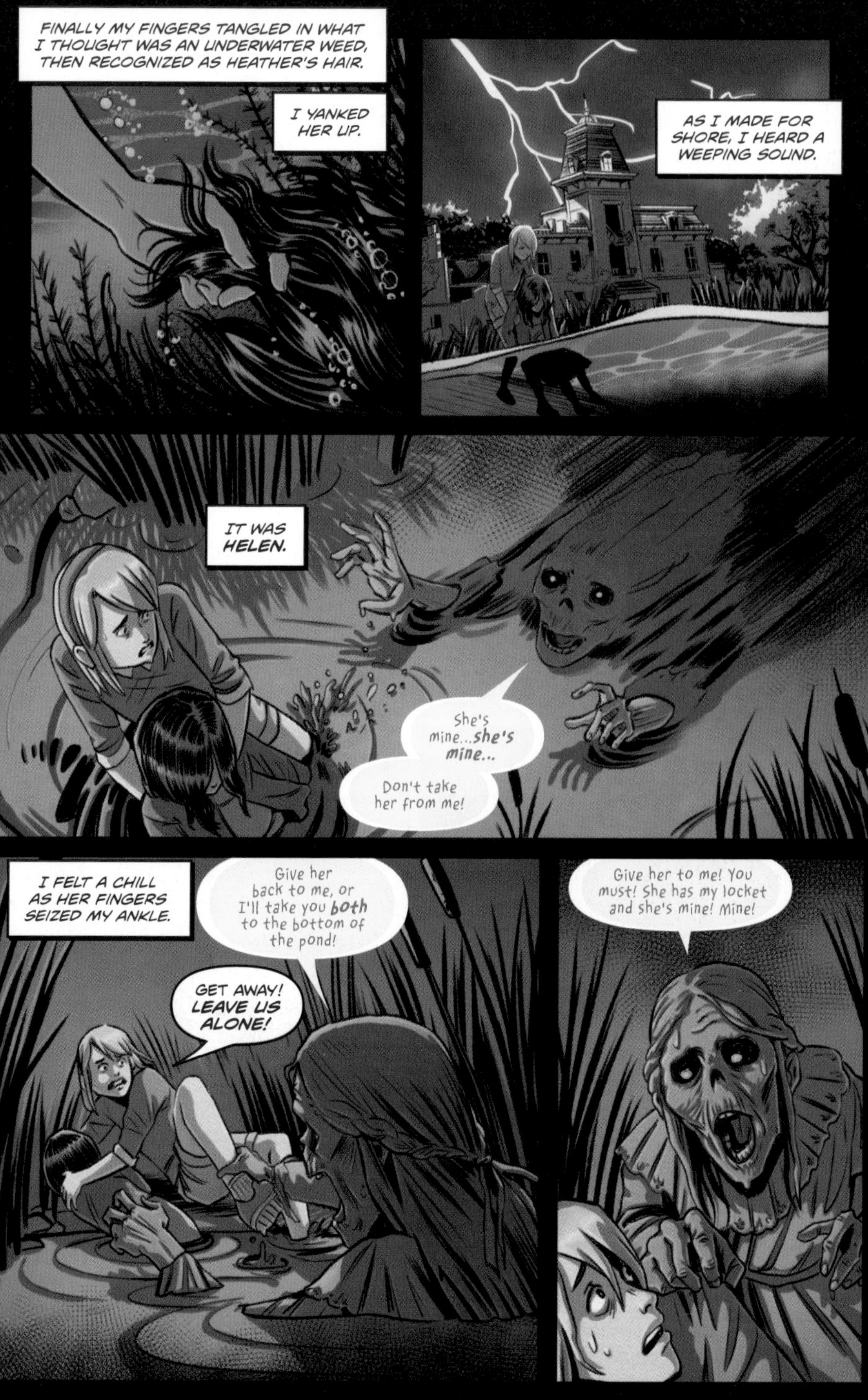
FINALLY MY FINGERS TANGLED IN WHAT I THOUGHT WAS AN UNDERWATER WEED, THEN RECOGNIZED AS HEATHER'S HAIR.
I YANKED HER UP.
AS I MADE FOR SHORE, I HEARD A WEEPING SOUND.
IT WAS HELEN.
She's mine...she's mine...
Don't take her from me!
I FELT A CHILL AS HER FINGERS SEIZED MY ANKLE.
Give her back to me, or I'll take you both to the bottom of the pond!
GET AWAY! LEAVE US ALONE!
Give her to me! You must! She has my locket and she's mine! Mine!

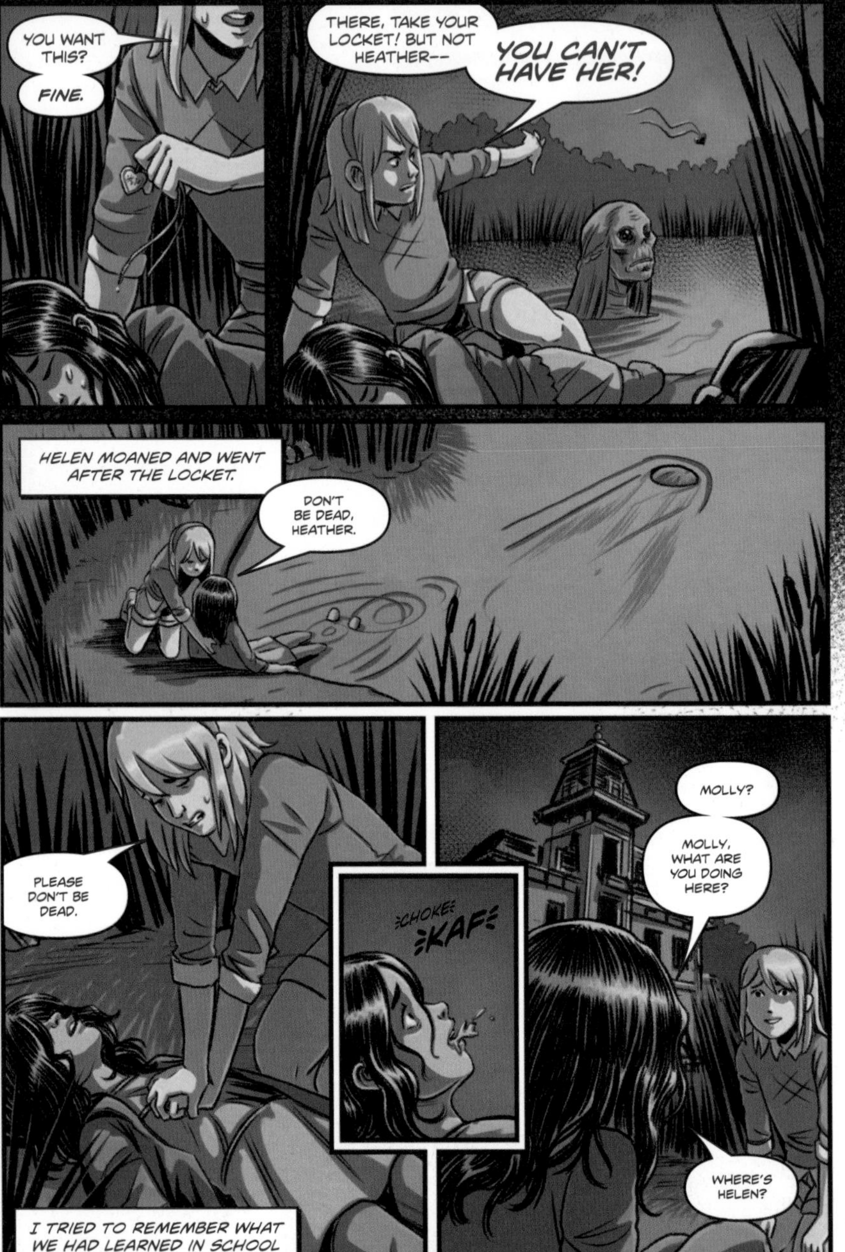
YOU WANT THIS?
FINE.
THERE, TAKE YOUR LOCKET! BUT NOT HEATHER--
YOU CAN'T HAVE HER!
HELEN MOANED AND WENT AFTER THE LOCKET.
DON'T BE DEAD, HEATHER.
PLEASE DON'T BE DEAD.
I TRIED TO REMEMBER WHAT WE HAD LEARNED IN SCHOOL ABOUT MOUTH-TO-MOUTH RESUSCITATION. BREATHE, I THOUGHT, BREATHE!
CHOKE
KAF
MOLLY?
MOLLY, WHAT ARE YOU DOING HERE?
WHERE'S HELEN?

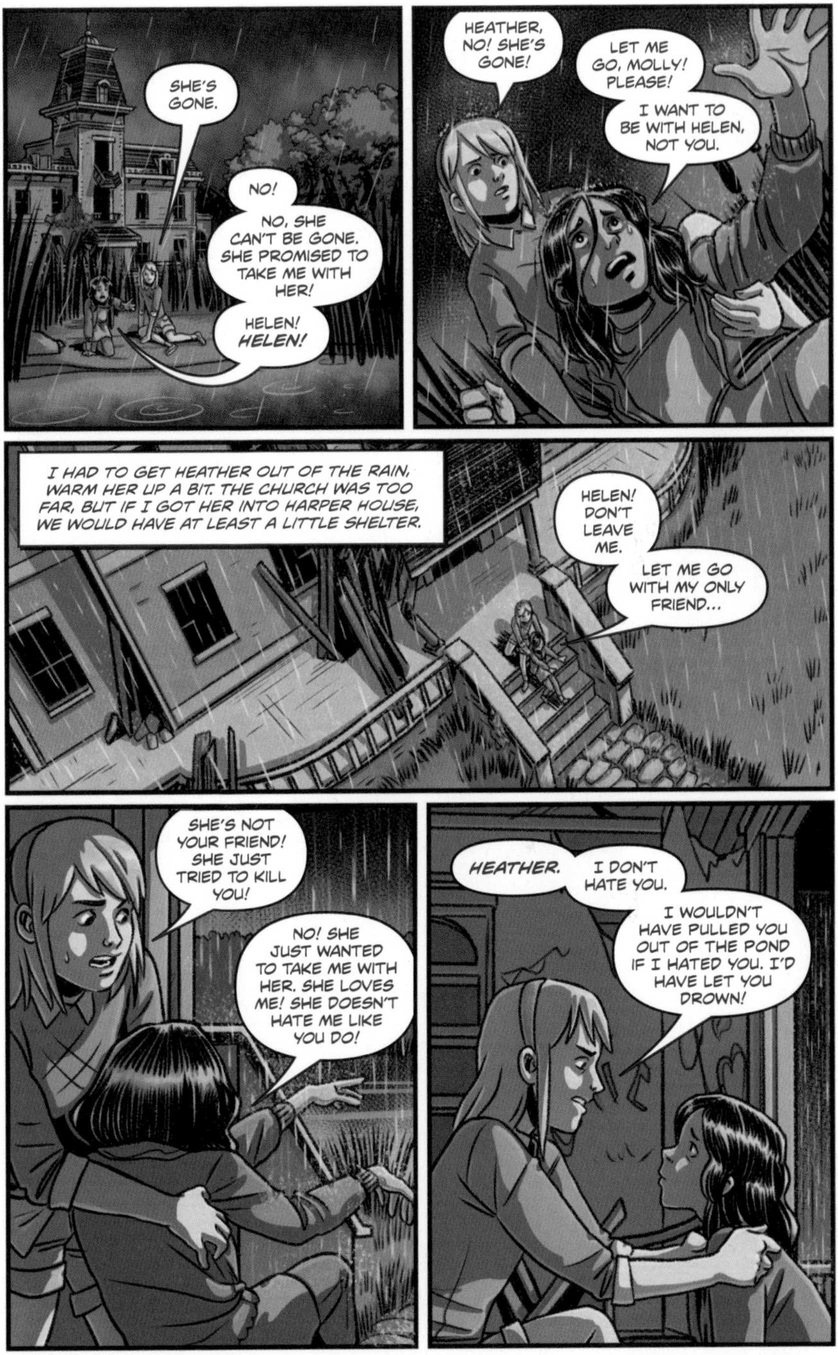
SHE'S GONE.
NO!
NO, SHE CAN'T BE GONE. SHE PROMISED TO TAKE ME WITH HER!
HELEN! *HELEN!*
HEATHER, NO! SHE'S GONE!
LET ME GO, MOLLY! PLEASE!
I WANT TO BE WITH HELEN, NOT YOU.
I HAD TO GET HEATHER OUT OF THE RAIN, WARM HER UP A BIT. THE CHURCH WAS TOO FAR, BUT IF I GOT HER INTO HARPER HOUSE, WE WOULD HAVE AT LEAST A LITTLE SHELTER.
HELEN! DON'T LEAVE ME.
LET ME GO WITH MY ONLY FRIEND...
SHE'S NOT YOUR FRIEND! SHE JUST TRIED TO KILL YOU!
NO! SHE JUST WANTED TO TAKE ME WITH HER. SHE LOVES ME! SHE DOESN'T HATE ME LIKE YOU DO!
HEATHER.
I DON'T HATE YOU.
I WOULDN'T HAVE PULLED YOU OUT OF THE POND IF I HATED YOU. I'D HAVE LET YOU DROWN!

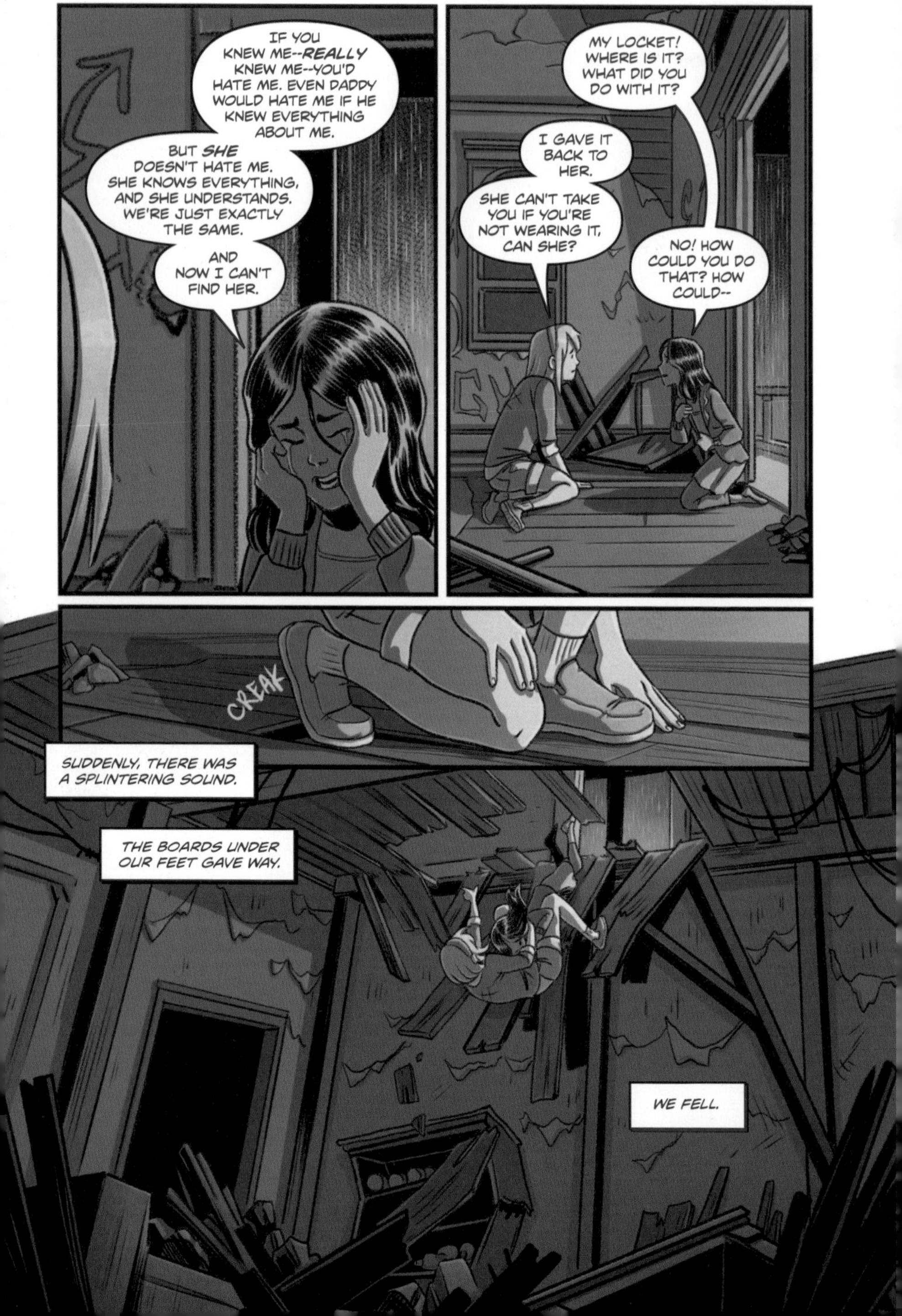

IF YOU KNEW ME--REALLY KNEW ME--YOU'D HATE ME. EVEN DADDY WOULD HATE ME IF HE KNEW EVERYTHING ABOUT ME.
BUT SHE DOESN'T HATE ME. SHE KNOWS EVERYTHING, AND SHE UNDERSTANDS. WE'RE JUST EXACTLY THE SAME.
AND NOW I CAN'T FIND HER.
MY LOCKET! WHERE IS IT? WHAT DID YOU DO WITH IT?
I GAVE IT BACK TO HER.
SHE CAN'T TAKE YOU IF YOU'RE NOT WEARING IT, CAN SHE?
NO! HOW COULD YOU DO THAT? HOW COULD--
CREAK
SUDDENLY, THERE WAS A SPLINTERING SOUND.
THE BOARDS UNDER OUR FEET GAVE WAY.
WE FELL.

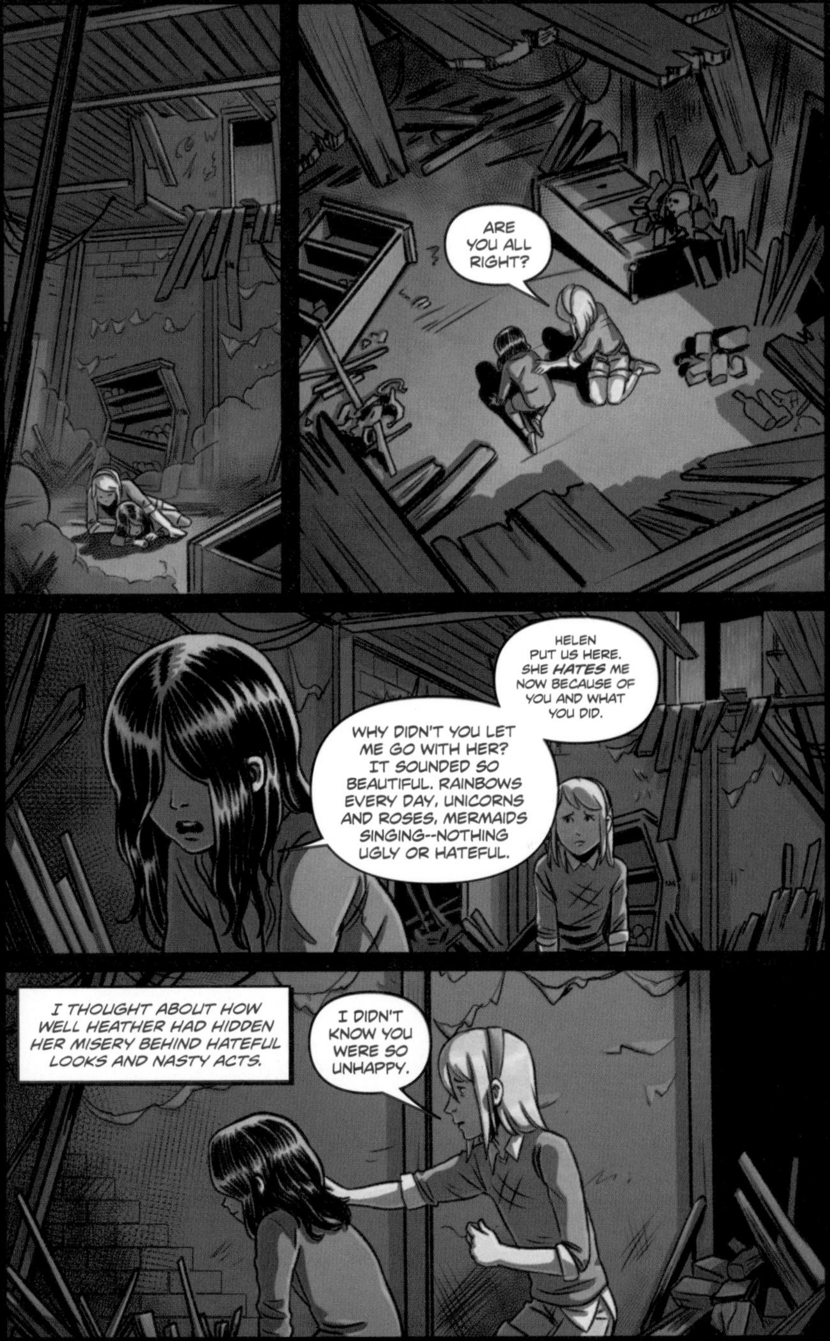
ARE YOU ALL RIGHT?
HELEN PUT US HERE. SHE HATES ME NOW BECAUSE OF YOU AND WHAT YOU DID.
WHY DIDN'T YOU LET ME GO WITH HER? IT SOUNDED SO BEAUTIFUL. RAINBOWS EVERY DAY, UNICORNS AND ROSES, MERMAIDS SINGING--NOTHING UGLY OR HATEFUL.
I THOUGHT ABOUT HOW WELL HEATHER HAD HIDDEN HER MISERY BEHIND HATEFUL LOOKS AND NASTY ACTS.
I DIDN'T KNOW YOU WERE SO UNHAPPY.

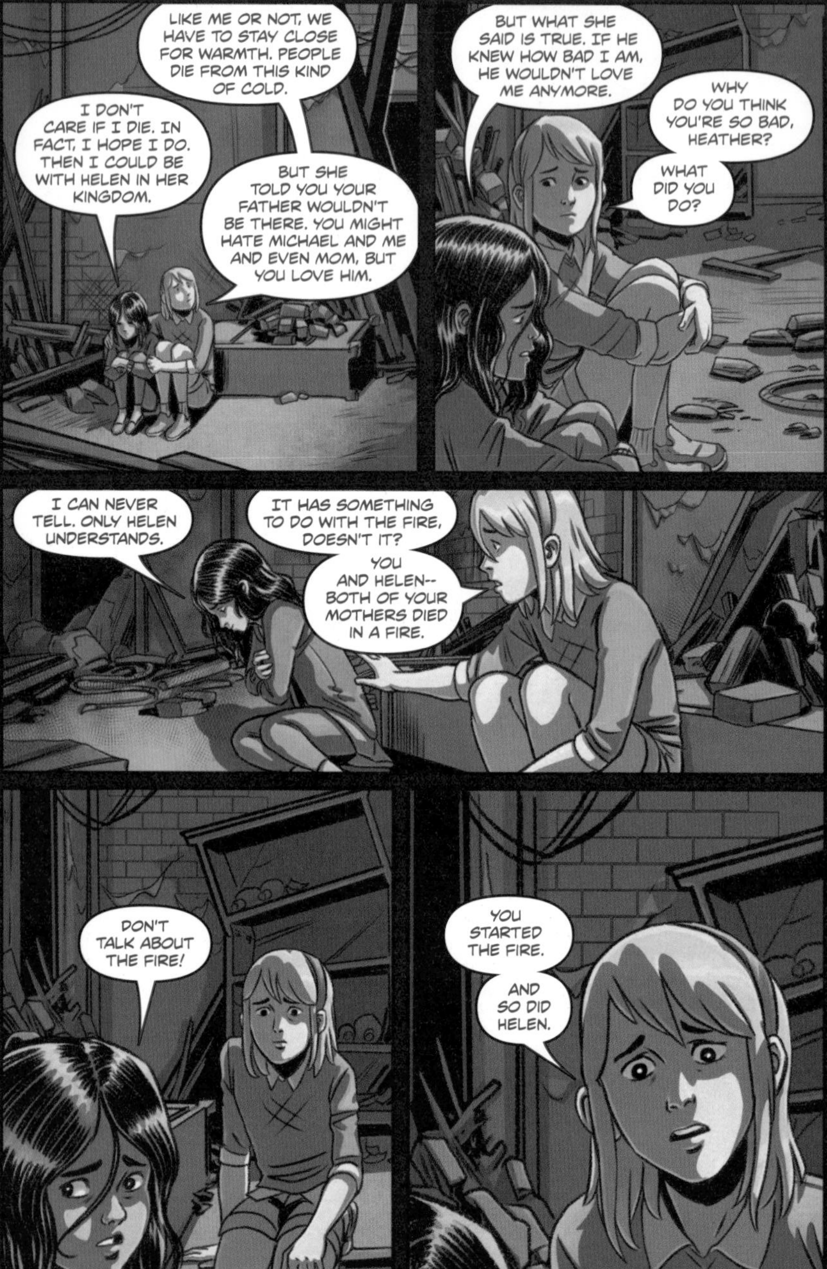
I DON'T CARE IF I DIE. IN FACT, I HOPE I DO. THEN I COULD BE WITH HELEN IN HER KINGDOM.
LIKE ME OR NOT, WE HAVE TO STAY CLOSE FOR WARMTH. PEOPLE DIE FROM THIS KIND OF COLD.
BUT SHE TOLD YOU YOUR FATHER WOULDN'T BE THERE. YOU MIGHT HATE MICHAEL AND ME AND EVEN MOM, BUT YOU LOVE HIM.
BUT WHAT SHE SAID IS TRUE. IF HE KNEW HOW BAD I AM, HE WOULDN'T LOVE ME ANYMORE.
WHY DO YOU THINK YOU'RE SO BAD, HEATHER?
WHAT DID YOU DO?
I CAN NEVER TELL. ONLY HELEN UNDERSTANDS.
IT HAS SOMETHING TO DO WITH THE FIRE, DOESN'T IT?
YOU AND HELEN-- BOTH OF YOUR MOTHERS DIED IN A FIRE.
DON'T TALK ABOUT THE FIRE!
YOU STARTED THE FIRE.
AND SO DID HELEN.

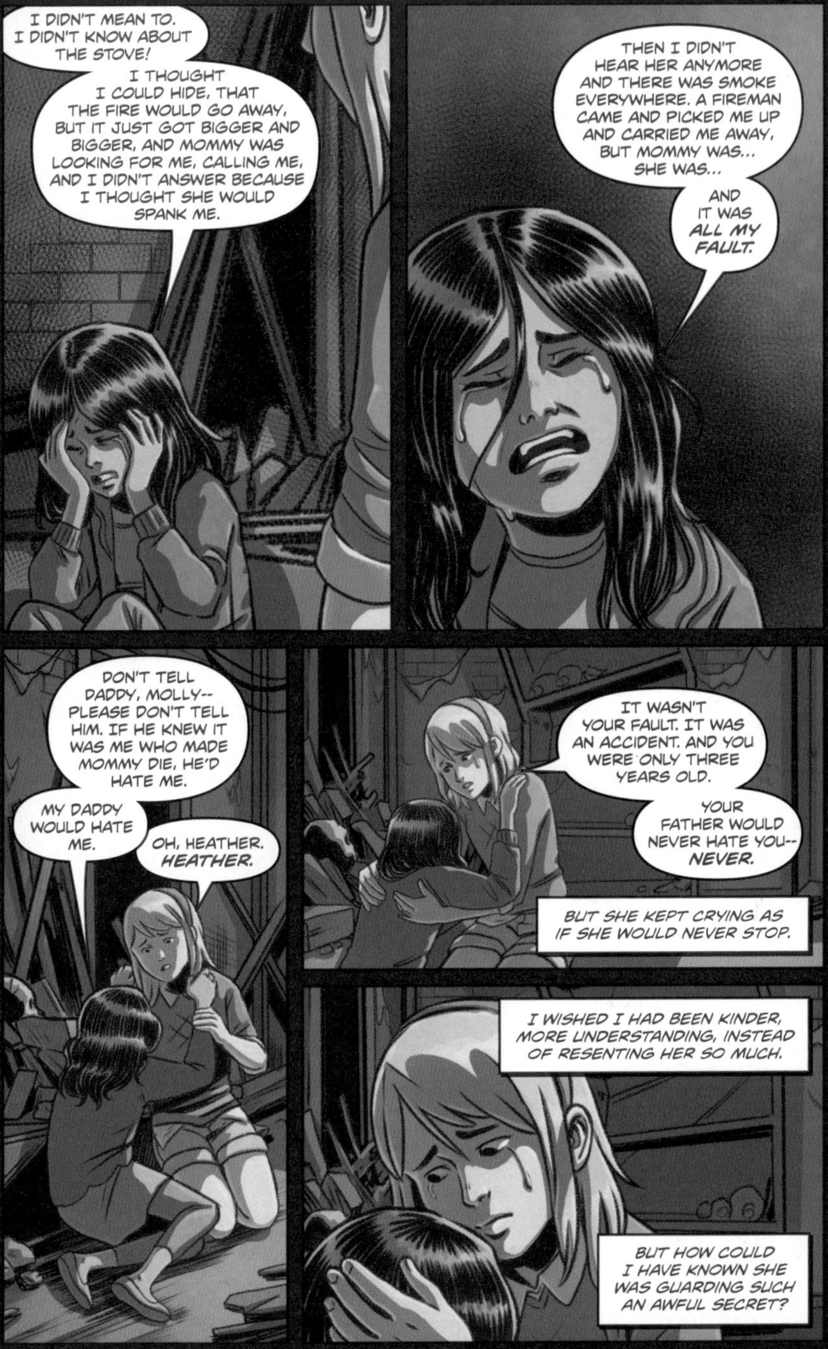
I DIDN'T MEAN TO. I DIDN'T KNOW ABOUT THE STOVE!
I THOUGHT I COULD HIDE, THAT THE FIRE WOULD GO AWAY, BUT IT JUST GOT BIGGER AND BIGGER, AND MOMMY WAS LOOKING FOR ME, CALLING ME, AND I DIDN'T ANSWER BECAUSE I THOUGHT SHE WOULD SPANK ME.
THEN I DIDN'T HEAR HER ANYMORE AND THERE WAS SMOKE EVERYWHERE. A FIREMAN CAME AND PICKED ME UP AND CARRIED ME AWAY, BUT MOMMY WAS... SHE WAS...
AND IT WAS *ALL MY FAULT.*
DON'T TELL DADDY, MOLLY-- PLEASE DON'T TELL HIM. IF HE KNEW IT WAS ME WHO MADE MOMMY DIE, HE'D HATE ME.
MY DADDY WOULD HATE ME.
OH, HEATHER. *HEATHER.*
IT WASN'T YOUR FAULT. IT WAS AN ACCIDENT. AND YOU WERE ONLY THREE YEARS OLD.
YOUR FATHER WOULD NEVER HATE YOU-- *NEVER.*
BUT SHE KEPT CRYING AS IF SHE WOULD NEVER STOP.
I WISHED I HAD BEEN KINDER, MORE UNDERSTANDING, INSTEAD OF RESENTING HER SO MUCH.
BUT HOW COULD I HAVE KNOWN SHE WAS GUARDING SUCH AN AWFUL SECRET?

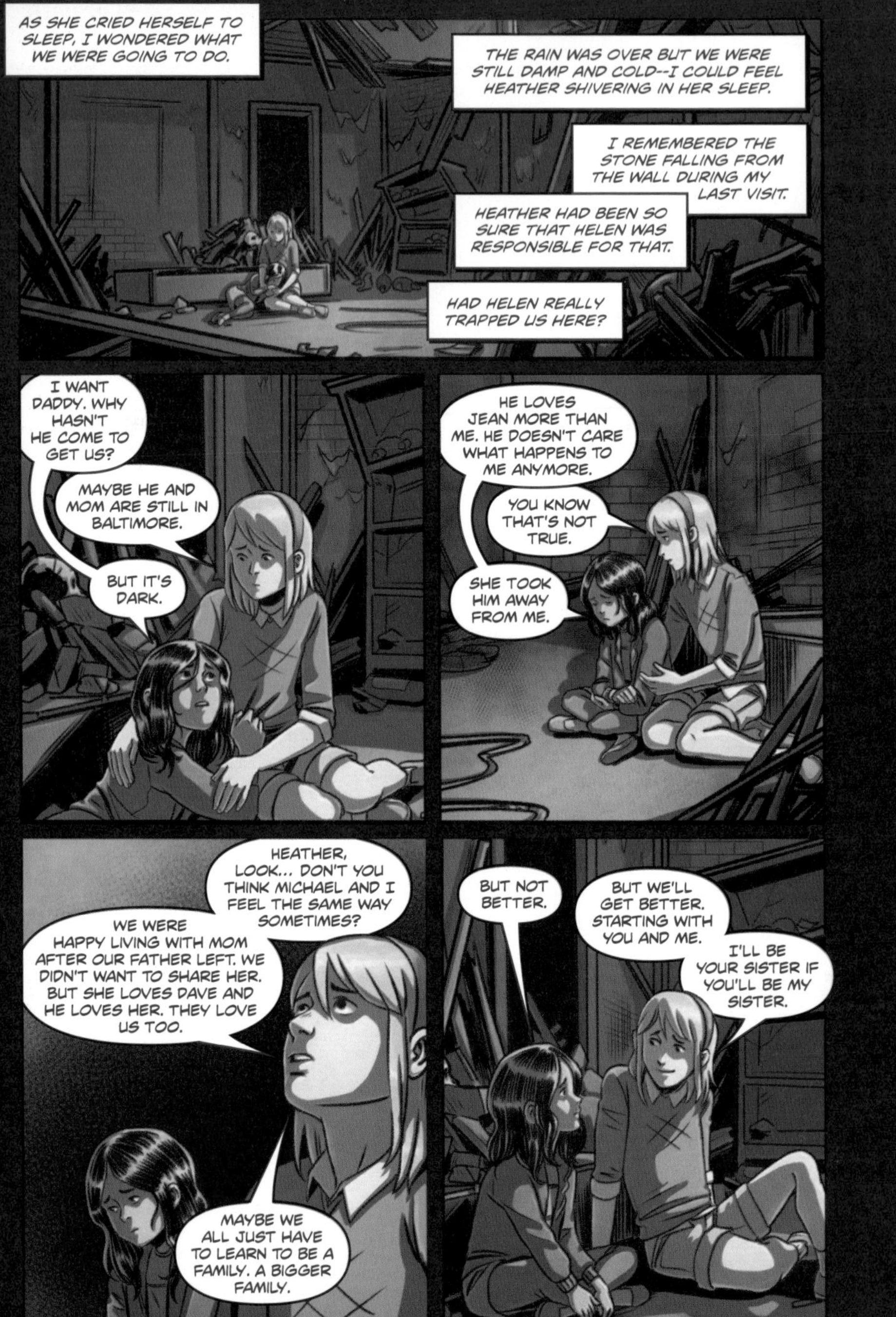
AS SHE CRIED HERSELF TO SLEEP, I WONDERED WHAT WE WERE GOING TO DO.
THE RAIN WAS OVER BUT WE WERE STILL DAMP AND COLD--I COULD FEEL HEATHER SHIVERING IN HER SLEEP.
I REMEMBERED THE STONE FALLING FROM THE WALL DURING MY LAST VISIT.
HEATHER HAD BEEN SO SURE THAT HELEN WAS RESPONSIBLE FOR THAT.
HAD HELEN REALLY TRAPPED US HERE?
I WANT DADDY. WHY HASN'T HE COME TO GET US?
MAYBE HE AND MOM ARE STILL IN BALTIMORE.
BUT IT'S DARK.
HE LOVES JEAN MORE THAN ME. HE DOESN'T CARE WHAT HAPPENS TO ME ANYMORE.
YOU KNOW THAT'S NOT TRUE.
SHE TOOK HIM AWAY FROM ME.
HEATHER, LOOK... DON'T YOU THINK MICHAEL AND I FEEL THE SAME WAY SOMETIMES?
WE WERE HAPPY LIVING WITH MOM AFTER OUR FATHER LEFT. WE DIDN'T WANT TO SHARE HER. BUT SHE LOVES DAVE AND HE LOVES HER. THEY LOVE US TOO.
MAYBE WE ALL JUST HAVE TO LEARN TO BE A FAMILY. A BIGGER FAMILY.
BUT NOT BETTER.
BUT WE'LL GET BETTER. STARTING WITH YOU AND ME.
I'LL BE YOUR SISTER IF YOU'LL BE MY SISTER.

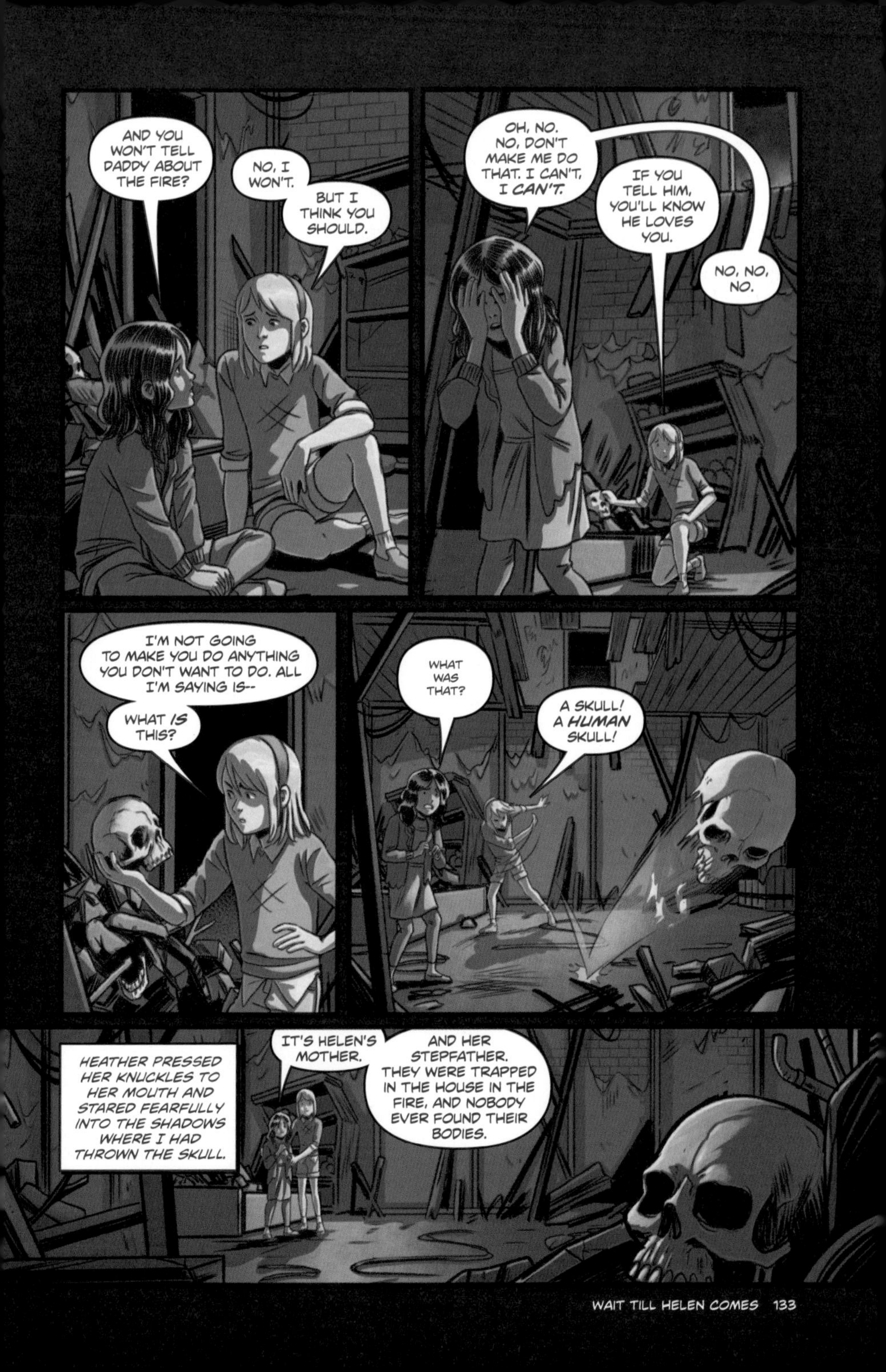
AND YOU WON'T TELL DADDY ABOUT THE FIRE?
NO, I WON'T.
BUT I THINK YOU SHOULD.
OH, NO. NO, DON'T MAKE ME DO THAT. I CAN'T, I *CAN'T.*
IF YOU TELL HIM, YOU'LL KNOW HE LOVES YOU.
NO, NO, NO.
I'M NOT GOING TO MAKE YOU DO ANYTHING YOU DON'T WANT TO DO. ALL I'M SAYING IS--
WHAT *IS* THIS?
WHAT WAS THAT?
A SKULL! A *HUMAN* SKULL!
HEATHER PRESSED HER KNUCKLES TO HER MOUTH AND STARED FEARFULLY INTO THE SHADOWS WHERE I HAD THROWN THE SKULL.
IT'S HELEN'S MOTHER.
AND HER STEPFATHER. THEY WERE TRAPPED IN THE HOUSE IN THE FIRE, AND NOBODY EVER FOUND THEIR BODIES.

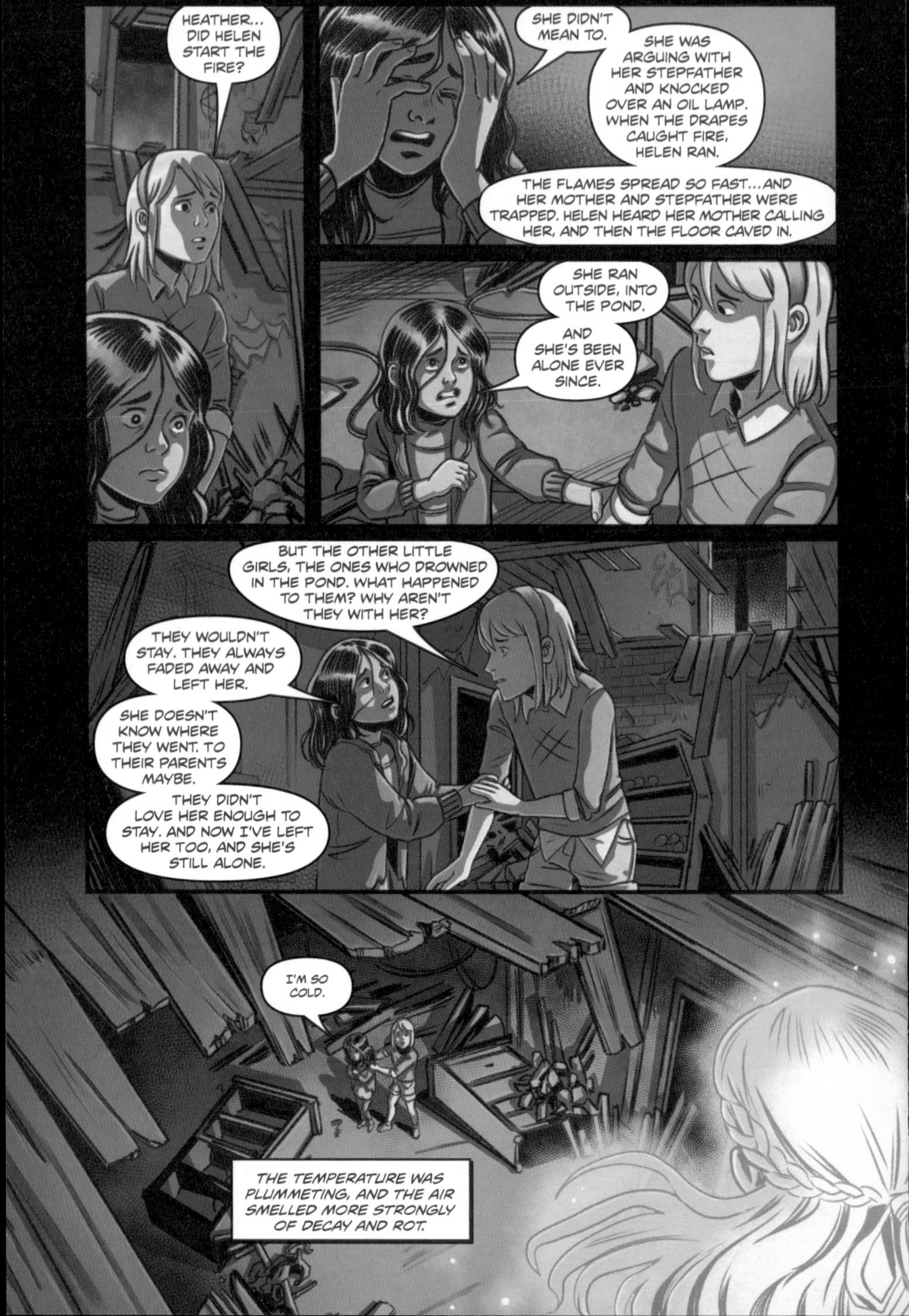
HEATHER... DID HELEN START THE FIRE?
SHE DIDN'T MEAN TO.
SHE WAS ARGUING WITH HER STEPFATHER AND KNOCKED OVER AN OIL LAMP. WHEN THE DRAPES CAUGHT FIRE, HELEN RAN.
THE FLAMES SPREAD SO FAST...AND HER MOTHER AND STEPFATHER WERE TRAPPED. HELEN HEARD HER MOTHER CALLING HER, AND THEN THE FLOOR CAVED IN.
SHE RAN OUTSIDE, INTO THE POND.
AND SHE'S BEEN ALONE EVER SINCE.
BUT THE OTHER LITTLE GIRLS, THE ONES WHO DROWNED IN THE POND. WHAT HAPPENED TO THEM? WHY AREN'T THEY WITH HER?
THEY WOULDN'T STAY. THEY ALWAYS FADED AWAY AND LEFT HER.
SHE DOESN'T KNOW WHERE THEY WENT. TO THEIR PARENTS MAYBE.
THEY DIDN'T LOVE HER ENOUGH TO STAY. AND NOW I'VE LEFT HER TOO, AND SHE'S STILL ALONE.
I'M SO COLD.
THE TEMPERATURE WAS PLUMMETING, AND THE AIR SMELLED MORE STRONGLY OF DECAY AND ROT.

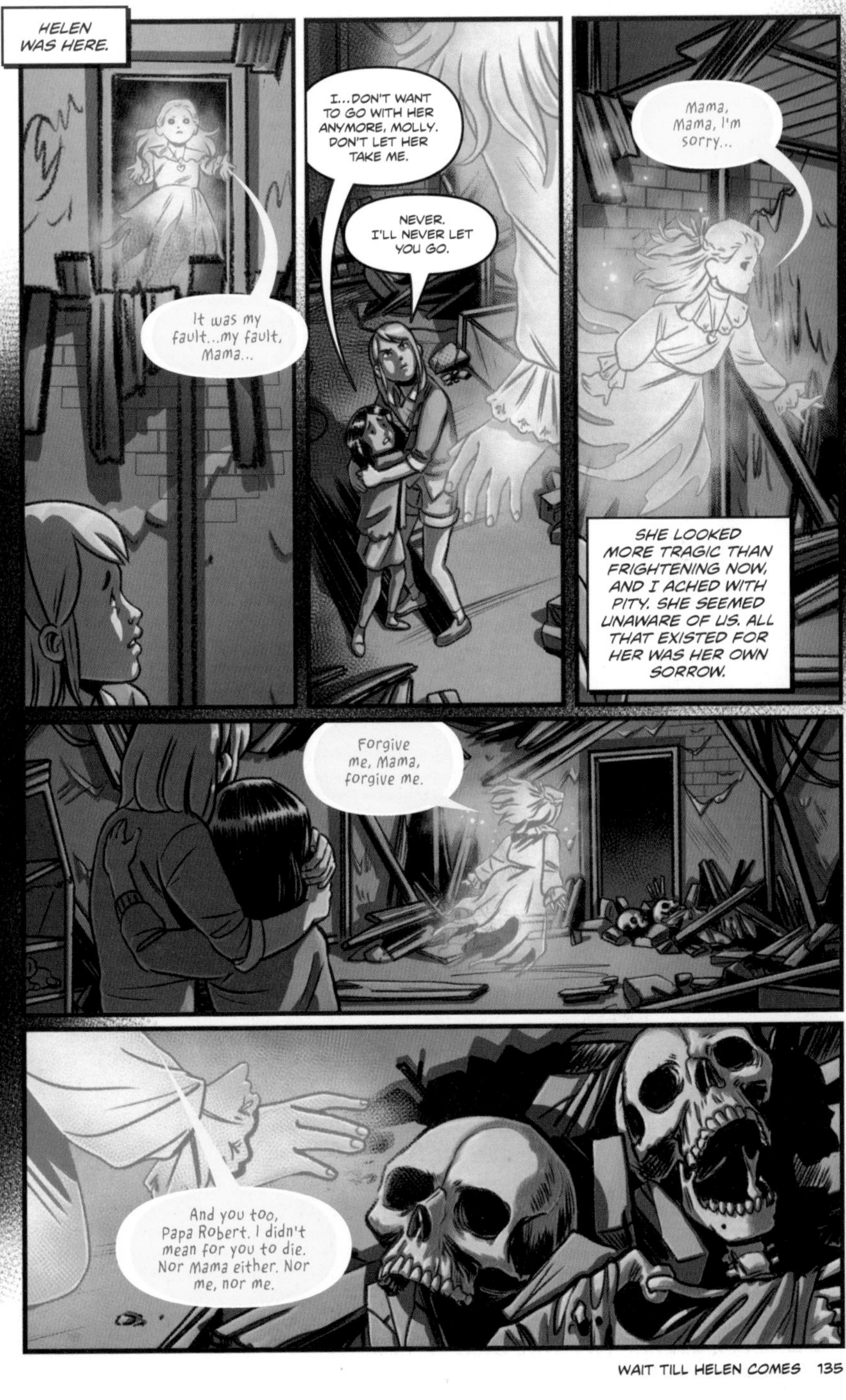
HELEN WAS HERE.
It was my fault...my fault, Mama...
I...DON'T WANT TO GO WITH HER ANYMORE, MOLLY. DON'T LET HER TAKE ME.
NEVER. I'LL NEVER LET YOU GO.
Mama, Mama, I'm sorry...
SHE LOOKED MORE TRAGIC THAN FRIGHTENING NOW, AND I ACHED WITH PITY. SHE SEEMED UNAWARE OF US. ALL THAT EXISTED FOR HER WAS HER OWN SORROW.
Forgive me, Mama, forgive me.
And you too, Papa Robert. I didn't mean for you to die. Nor Mama either. Nor me, nor me.

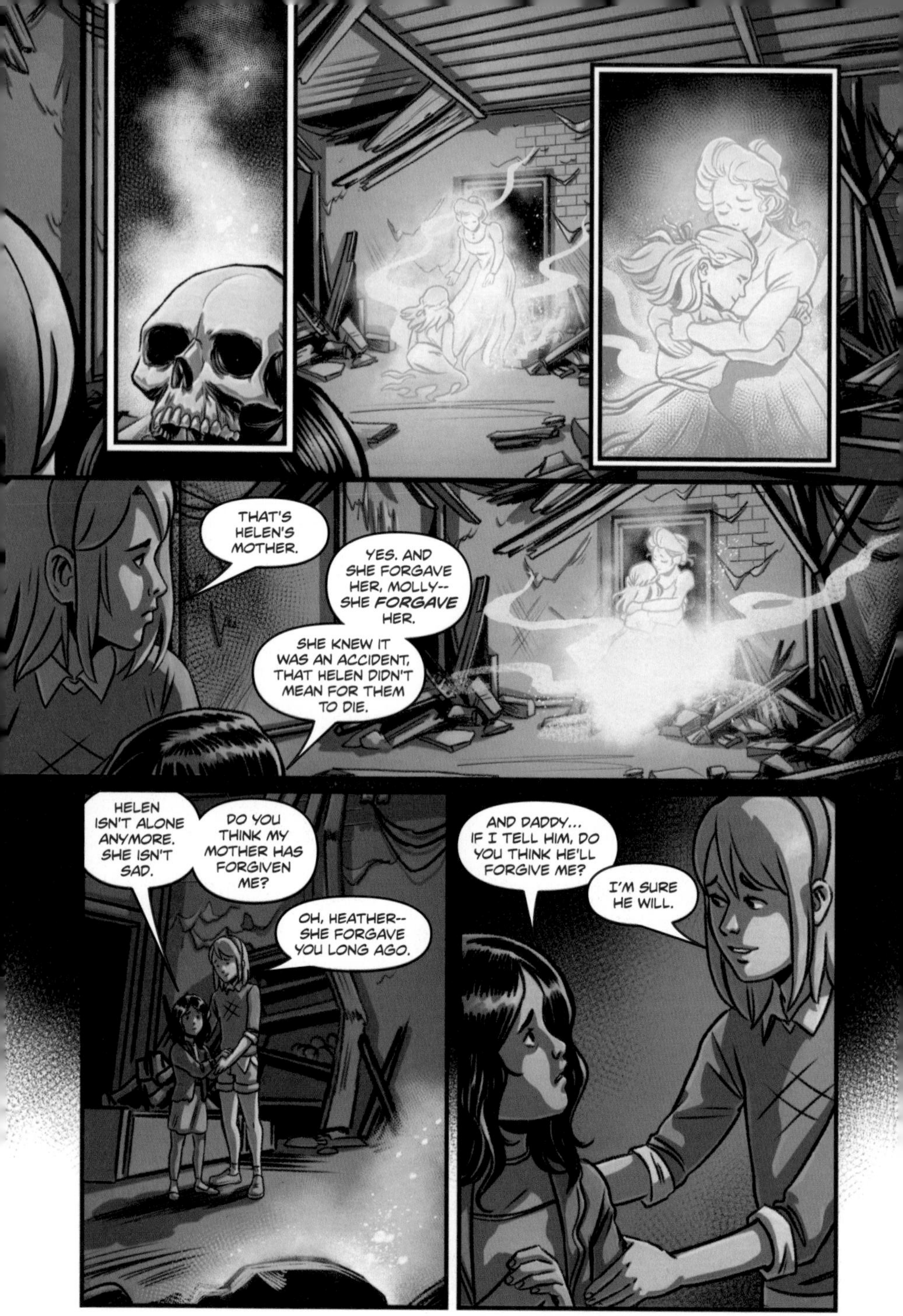
THAT'S HELEN'S MOTHER.
YES. AND SHE FORGAVE HER, MOLLY-- SHE *FORGAVE* HER.
SHE KNEW IT WAS AN ACCIDENT, THAT HELEN DIDN'T MEAN FOR THEM TO DIE.
HELEN ISN'T ALONE ANYMORE. SHE ISN'T SAD.
DO YOU THINK MY MOTHER HAS FORGIVEN ME?
OH, HEATHER-- SHE FORGAVE YOU LONG AGO.
AND DADDY... IF I TELL HIM, DO YOU THINK HE'LL FORGIVE ME?
I'M SURE HE WILL.

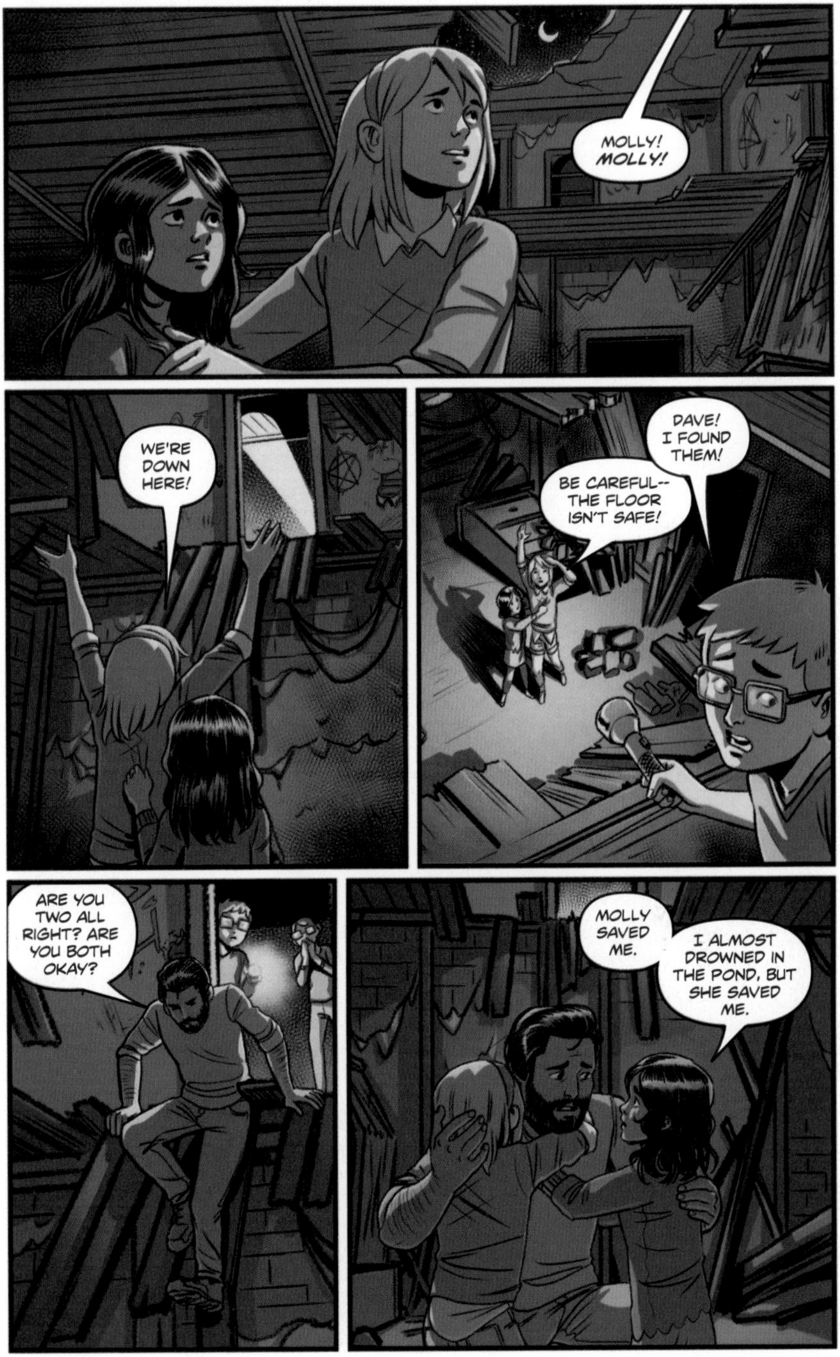
MOLLY! MOLLY!
WE'RE DOWN HERE!
DAVE! I FOUND THEM!
BE CAREFUL-- THE FLOOR ISN'T SAFE!
ARE YOU TWO ALL RIGHT? ARE YOU BOTH OKAY?
MOLLY SAVED ME.
I ALMOST DROWNED IN THE POND, BUT SHE SAVED ME.

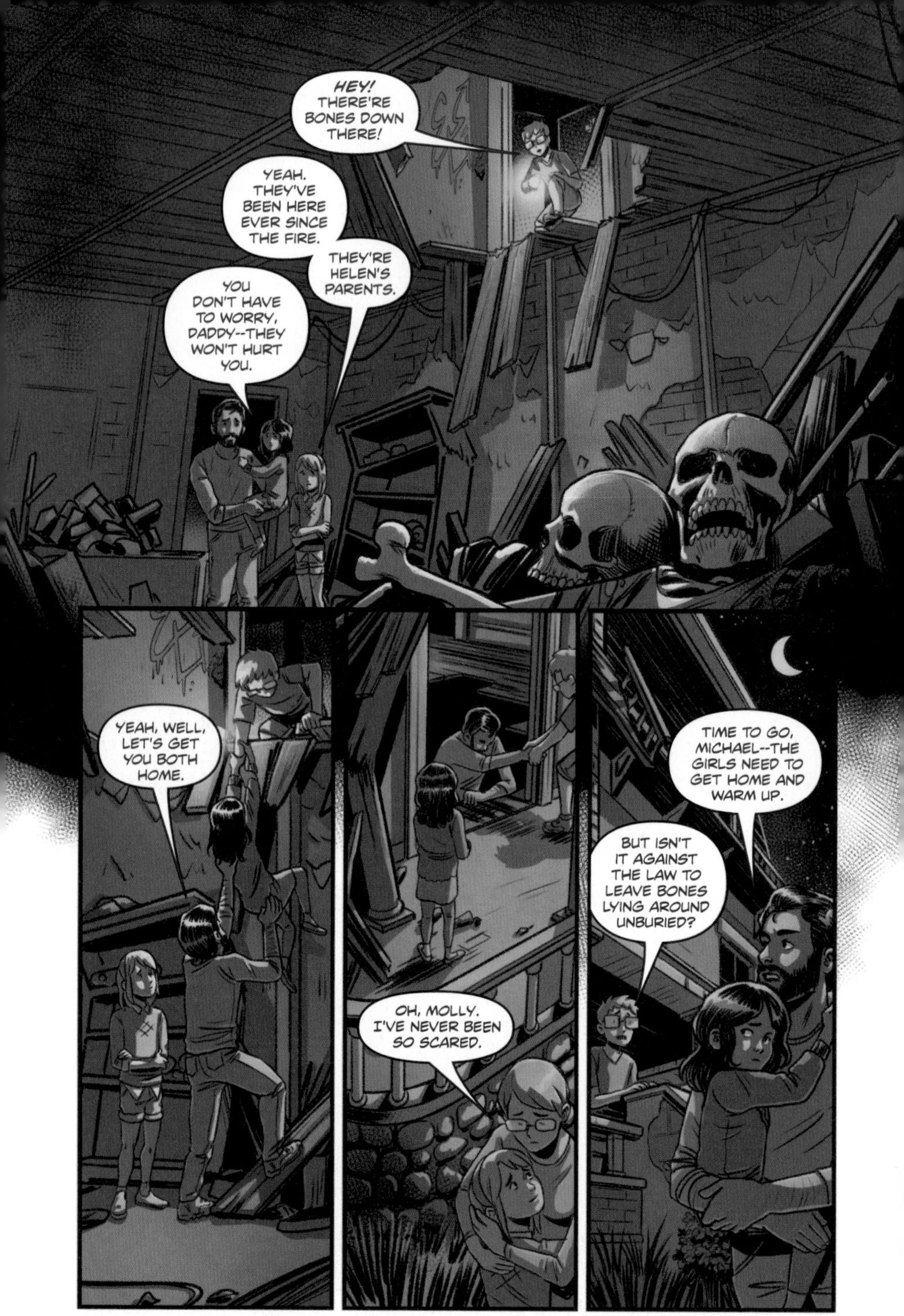
HEY! THERE'RE BONES DOWN THERE!
YEAH. THEY'VE BEEN HERE EVER SINCE THE FIRE.
THEY'RE HELEN'S PARENTS.
YOU DON'T HAVE TO WORRY, DADDY--THEY WON'T HURT YOU.
YEAH, WELL, LET'S GET YOU BOTH HOME.
OH, MOLLY. I'VE NEVER BEEN SO SCARED.
TIME TO GO, MICHAEL--THE GIRLS NEED TO GET HOME AND WARM UP.
BUT ISN'T IT AGAINST THE LAW TO LEAVE BONES LYING AROUND UNBURIED?

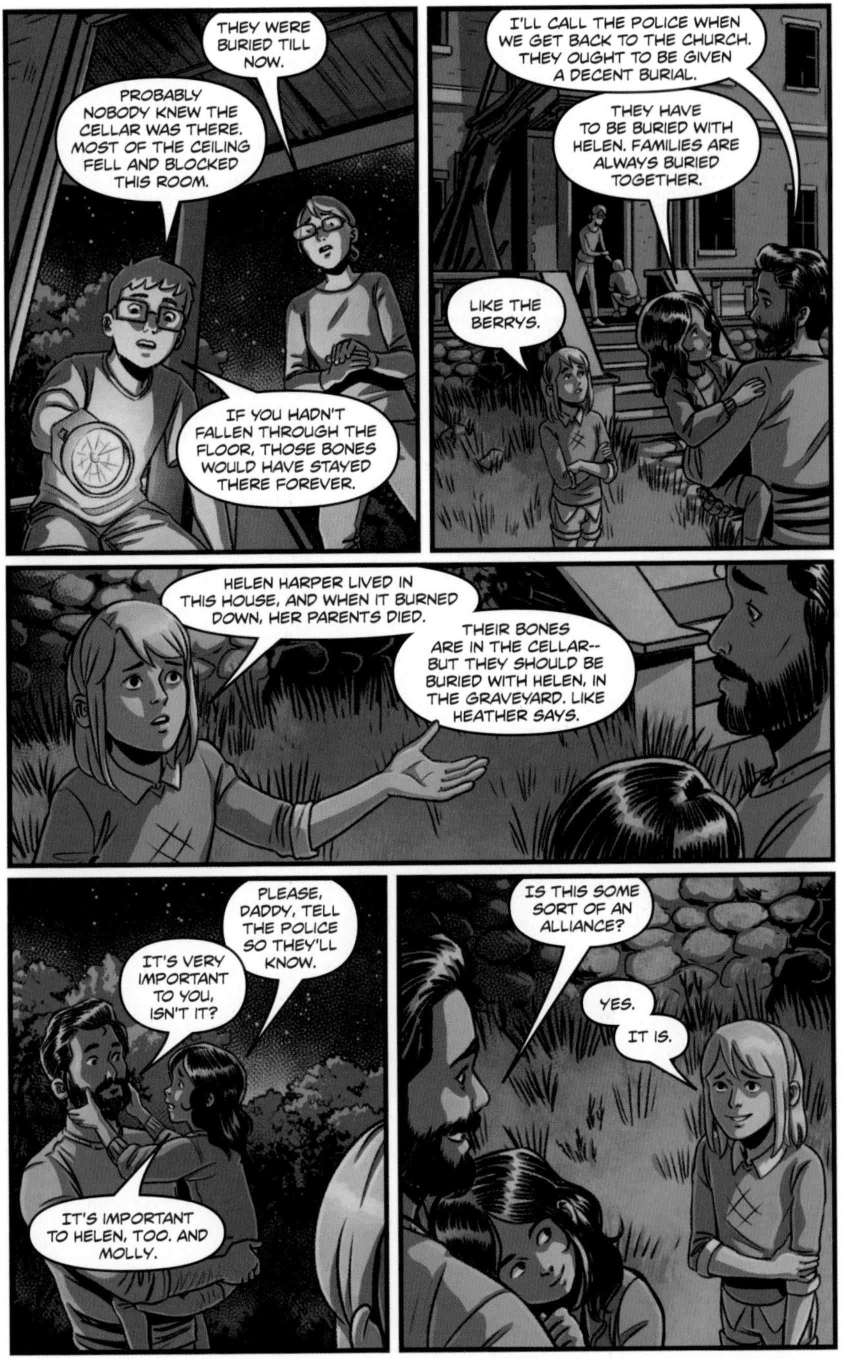
THEY WERE BURIED TILL NOW.
PROBABLY NOBODY KNEW THE CELLAR WAS THERE. MOST OF THE CEILING FELL AND BLOCKED THIS ROOM.
IF YOU HADN'T FALLEN THROUGH THE FLOOR, THOSE BONES WOULD HAVE STAYED THERE FOREVER.
I'LL CALL THE POLICE WHEN WE GET BACK TO THE CHURCH. THEY OUGHT TO BE GIVEN A DECENT BURIAL.
THEY HAVE TO BE BURIED WITH HELEN. FAMILIES ARE ALWAYS BURIED TOGETHER.
LIKE THE BERRYS.
HELEN HARPER LIVED IN THIS HOUSE, AND WHEN IT BURNED DOWN, HER PARENTS DIED.
THEIR BONES ARE IN THE CELLAR-- BUT THEY SHOULD BE BURIED WITH HELEN, IN THE GRAVEYARD. LIKE HEATHER SAYS.
PLEASE, DADDY, TELL THE POLICE SO THEY'LL KNOW.
IT'S VERY IMPORTANT TO YOU, ISN'T IT?
IT'S IMPORTANT TO HELEN, TOO. AND MOLLY.
IS THIS SOME SORT OF AN ALLIANCE?
YES.
IT IS.

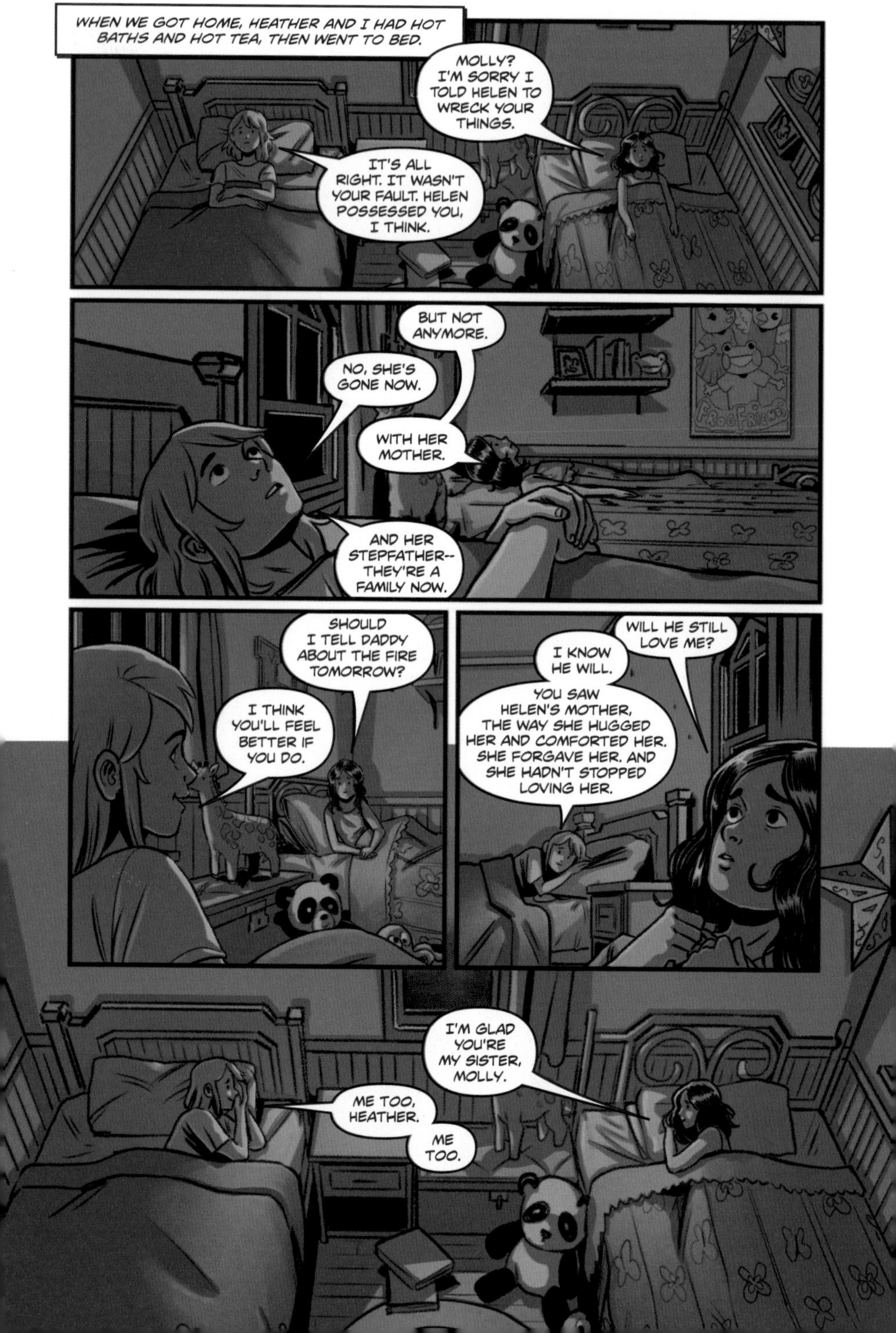
WHEN WE GOT HOME, HEATHER AND I HAD HOT BATHS AND HOT TEA, THEN WENT TO BED.
MOLLY? I'M SORRY I TOLD HELEN TO WRECK YOUR THINGS.
IT'S ALL RIGHT. IT WASN'T YOUR FAULT. HELEN POSSESSED YOU, I THINK.
NO, SHE'S GONE NOW.
BUT NOT ANYMORE.
WITH HER MOTHER.
AND HER STEPFATHER-- THEY'RE A FAMILY NOW.
SHOULD I TELL DADDY ABOUT THE FIRE TOMORROW?
I THINK YOU'LL FEEL BETTER IF YOU DO.
WILL HE STILL LOVE ME?
I KNOW HE WILL.
YOU SAW HELEN'S MOTHER, THE WAY SHE HUGGED HER AND COMFORTED HER. SHE FORGAVE HER. AND SHE HADN'T STOPPED LOVING HER.
I'M GLAD YOU'RE MY SISTER, MOLLY.
ME TOO, HEATHER.
ME TOO.

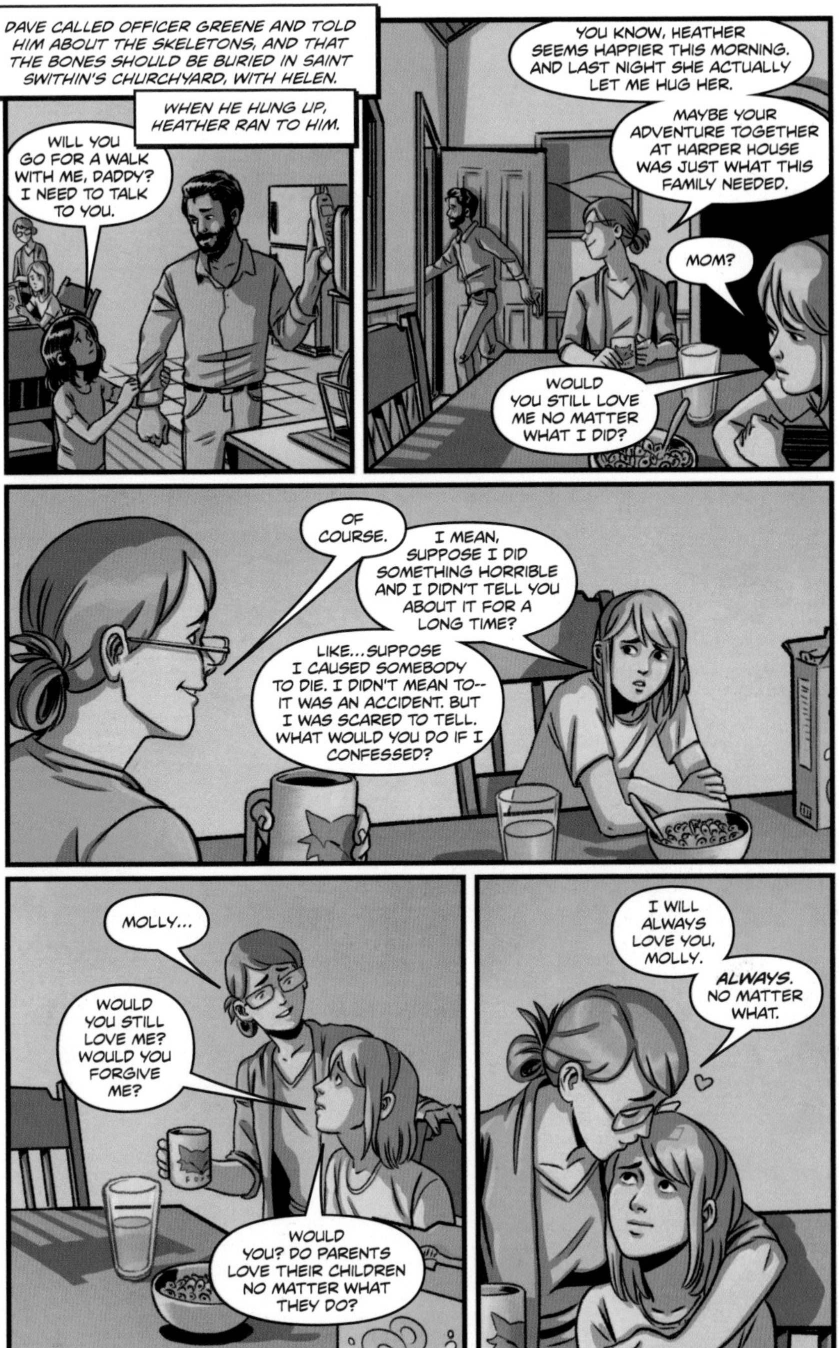

DAVE CALLED OFFICER GREENE AND TOLD HIM ABOUT THE SKELETONS, AND THAT THE BONES SHOULD BE BURIED IN SAINT SWITHIN'S CHURCHYARD, WITH HELEN.
WHEN HE HUNG UP, HEATHER RAN TO HIM.
WILL YOU GO FOR A WALK WITH ME, DADDY? I NEED TO TALK TO YOU.
YOU KNOW, HEATHER SEEMS HAPPIER THIS MORNING. AND LAST NIGHT SHE ACTUALLY LET ME HUG HER.
MAYBE YOUR ADVENTURE TOGETHER AT HARPER HOUSE WAS JUST WHAT THIS FAMILY NEEDED.
MOM?
WOULD YOU STILL LOVE ME NO MATTER WHAT I DID?
OF COURSE.
I MEAN, SUPPOSE I DID SOMETHING HORRIBLE AND I DIDN'T TELL YOU ABOUT IT FOR A LONG TIME?
LIKE... SUPPOSE I CAUSED SOMEBODY TO DIE. I DIDN'T MEAN TO-- IT WAS AN ACCIDENT. BUT I WAS SCARED TO TELL. WHAT WOULD YOU DO IF I CONFESSED?
MOLLY...
WOULD YOU STILL LOVE ME? WOULD YOU FORGIVE ME?
WOULD YOU? DO PARENTS LOVE THEIR CHILDREN NO MATTER WHAT THEY DO?
I WILL ALWAYS LOVE YOU, MOLLY.
ALWAYS. NO MATTER WHAT.

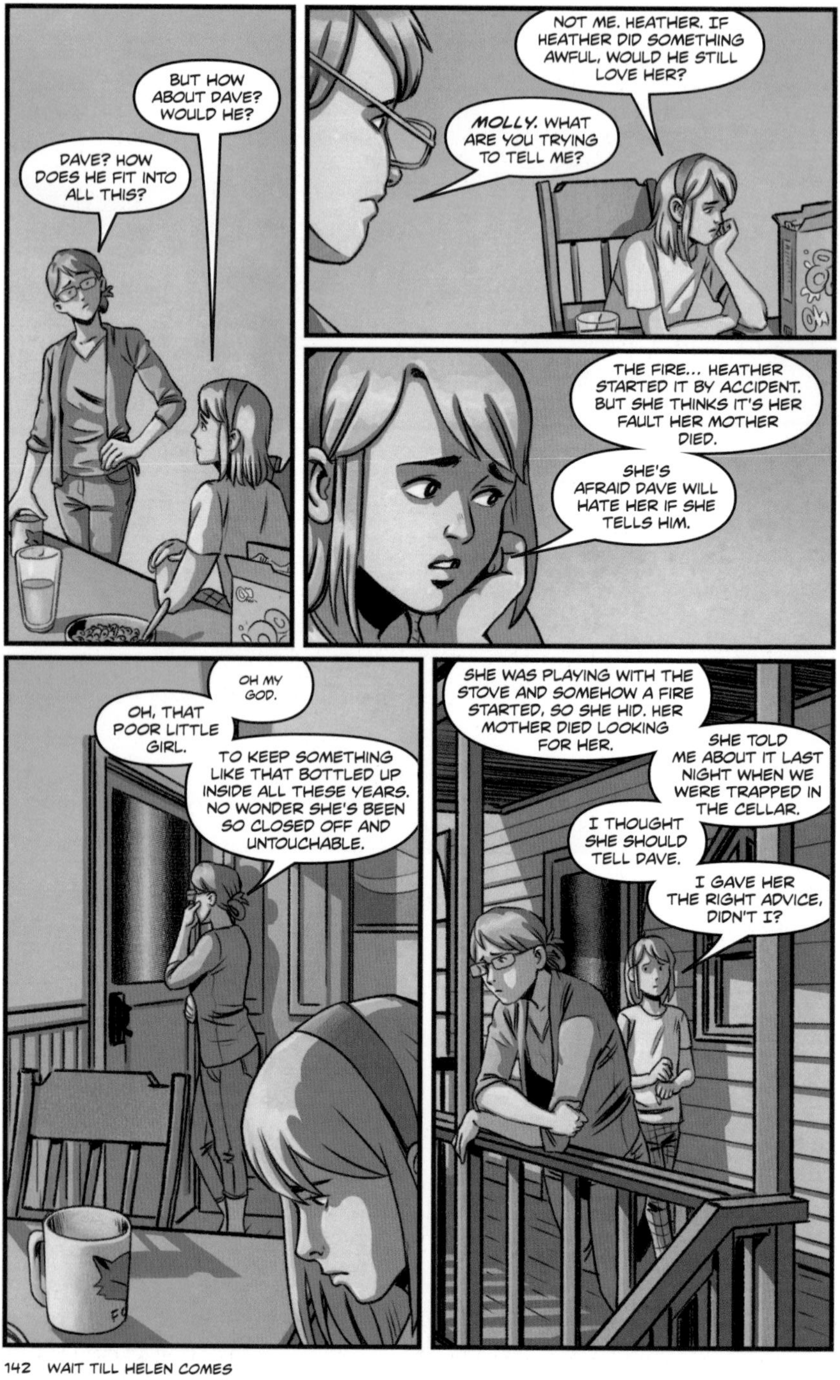
BUT HOW ABOUT DAVE? WOULD HE?
DAVE? HOW DOES HE FIT INTO ALL THIS?
NOT ME. HEATHER. IF HEATHER DID SOMETHING AWFUL, WOULD HE STILL LOVE HER?
MOLLY. WHAT ARE YOU TRYING TO TELL ME?
THE FIRE... HEATHER STARTED IT BY ACCIDENT. BUT SHE THINKS IT'S HER FAULT HER MOTHER DIED.
SHE'S AFRAID DAVE WILL HATE HER IF SHE TELLS HIM.
OH MY GOD.
OH, THAT POOR LITTLE GIRL.
TO KEEP SOMETHING LIKE THAT BOTTLED UP INSIDE ALL THESE YEARS. NO WONDER SHE'S BEEN SO CLOSED OFF AND UNTOUCHABLE.
SHE WAS PLAYING WITH THE STOVE AND SOMEHOW A FIRE STARTED, SO SHE HID. HER MOTHER DIED LOOKING FOR HER.
SHE TOLD ME ABOUT IT LAST NIGHT WHEN WE WERE TRAPPED IN THE CELLAR.
I THOUGHT SHE SHOULD TELL DAVE.
I GAVE HER THE RIGHT ADVICE, DIDN'T I?

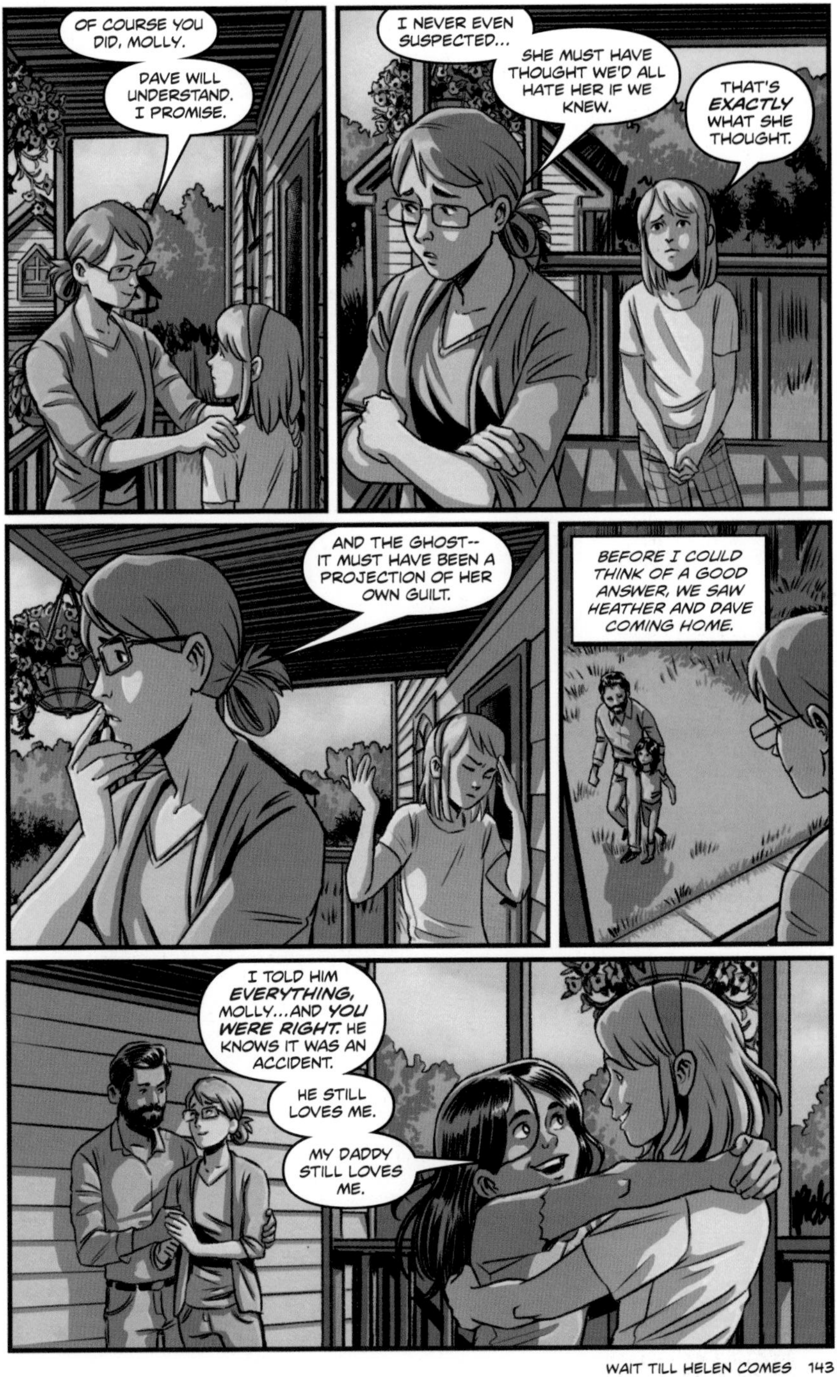
OF COURSE YOU DID, MOLLY.
DAVE WILL UNDERSTAND. I PROMISE.
I NEVER EVEN SUSPECTED...
SHE MUST HAVE THOUGHT WE'D ALL HATE HER IF WE KNEW.
THAT'S EXACTLY WHAT SHE THOUGHT.
AND THE GHOST-- IT MUST HAVE BEEN A PROJECTION OF HER OWN GUILT.
BEFORE I COULD THINK OF A GOOD ANSWER, WE SAW HEATHER AND DAVE COMING HOME.
I TOLD HIM EVERYTHING, MOLLY...AND YOU WERE RIGHT. HE KNOWS IT WAS AN ACCIDENT.
HE STILL LOVES ME.
MY DADDY STILL LOVES ME.

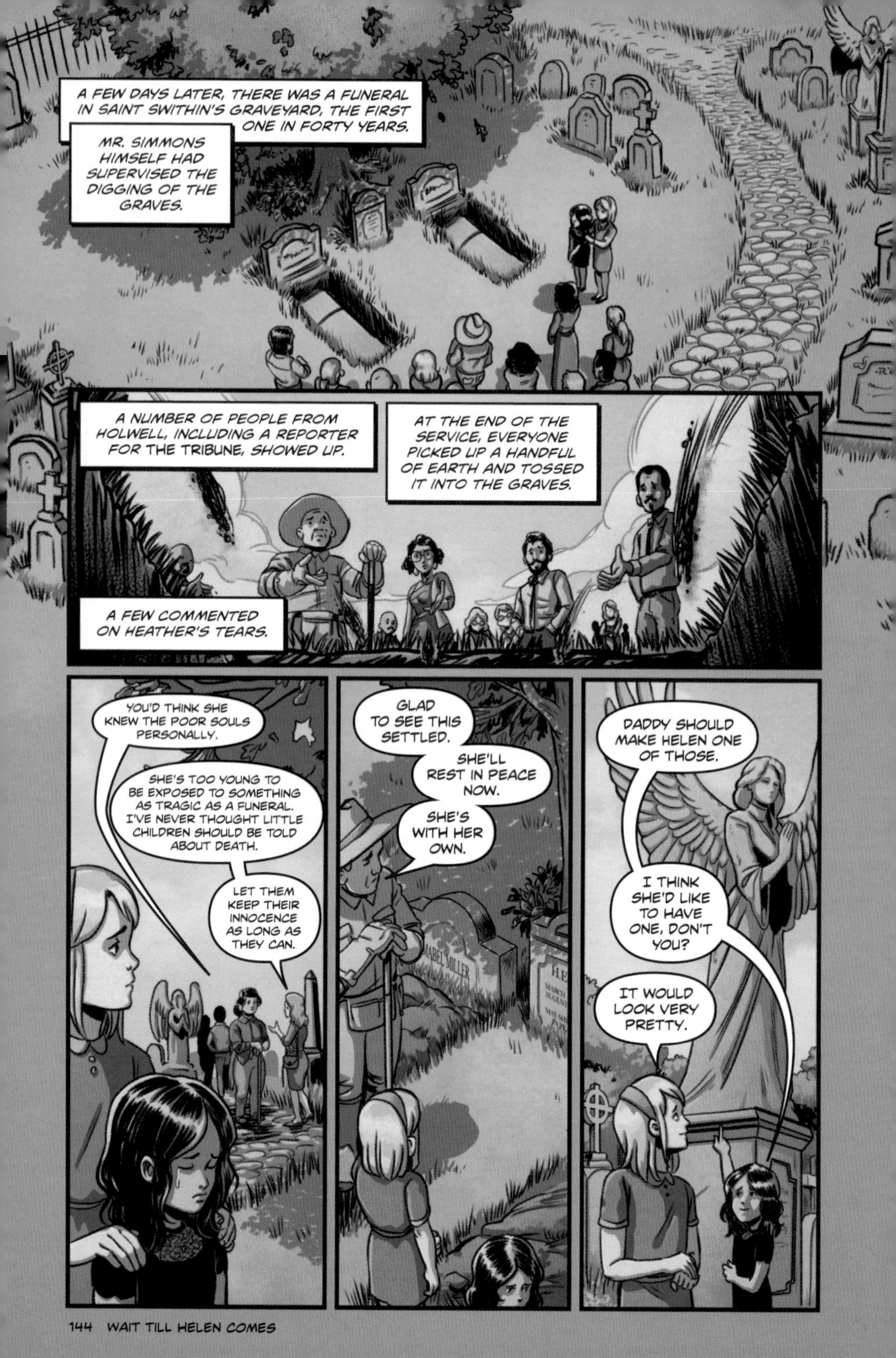
A FEW DAYS LATER, THERE WAS A FUNERAL IN SAINT SWITHIN'S GRAVEYARD, THE FIRST ONE IN FORTY YEARS.
MR. SIMMONS HIMSELF HAD SUPERVISED THE DIGGING OF THE GRAVES.
A NUMBER OF PEOPLE FROM HOLWELL, INCLUDING A REPORTER FOR THE TRIBUNE, SHOWED UP.
AT THE END OF THE SERVICE, EVERYONE PICKED UP A HANDFUL OF EARTH AND TOSSED IT INTO THE GRAVES.
A FEW COMMENTED ON HEATHER'S TEARS.
YOU'D THINK SHE KNEW THE POOR SOULS PERSONALLY.
SHE'S TOO YOUNG TO BE EXPOSED TO SOMETHING AS TRAGIC AS A FUNERAL. I'VE NEVER THOUGHT LITTLE CHILDREN SHOULD BE TOLD ABOUT DEATH.
LET THEM KEEP THEIR INNOCENCE AS LONG AS THEY CAN.
GLAD TO SEE THIS SETTLED.
SHE'LL REST IN PEACE NOW.
SHE'S WITH HER OWN.
MABEL MILLER
DADDY SHOULD MAKE HELEN ONE OF THOSE.
I THINK SHE'D LIKE TO HAVE ONE, DON'T YOU?
IT WOULD LOOK VERY PRETTY.

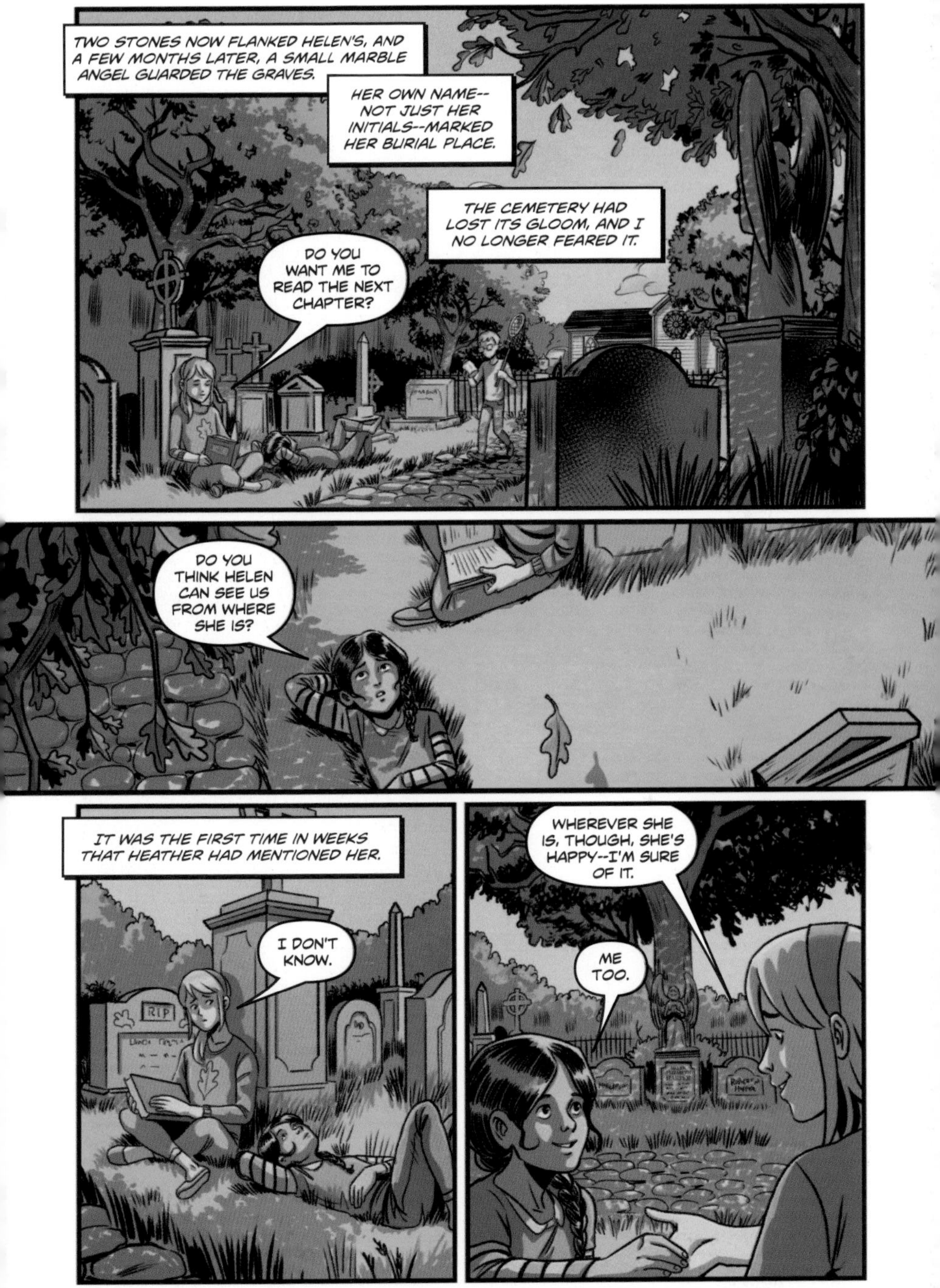
TWO STONES NOW FLANKED HELEN'S, AND A FEW MONTHS LATER, A SMALL MARBLE ANGEL GUARDED THE GRAVES.
HER OWN NAME--NOT JUST HER INITIALS--MARKED HER BURIAL PLACE.
THE CEMETERY HAD LOST ITS GLOOM, AND I NO LONGER FEARED IT.
DO YOU WANT ME TO READ THE NEXT CHAPTER?
DO YOU THINK HELEN CAN SEE US FROM WHERE SHE IS?
IT WAS THE FIRST TIME IN WEEKS THAT HEATHER HAD MENTIONED HER.
I DON'T KNOW.
RIP
WHEREVER SHE IS, THOUGH, SHE'S HAPPY--I'M SURE OF IT.
ME TOO.

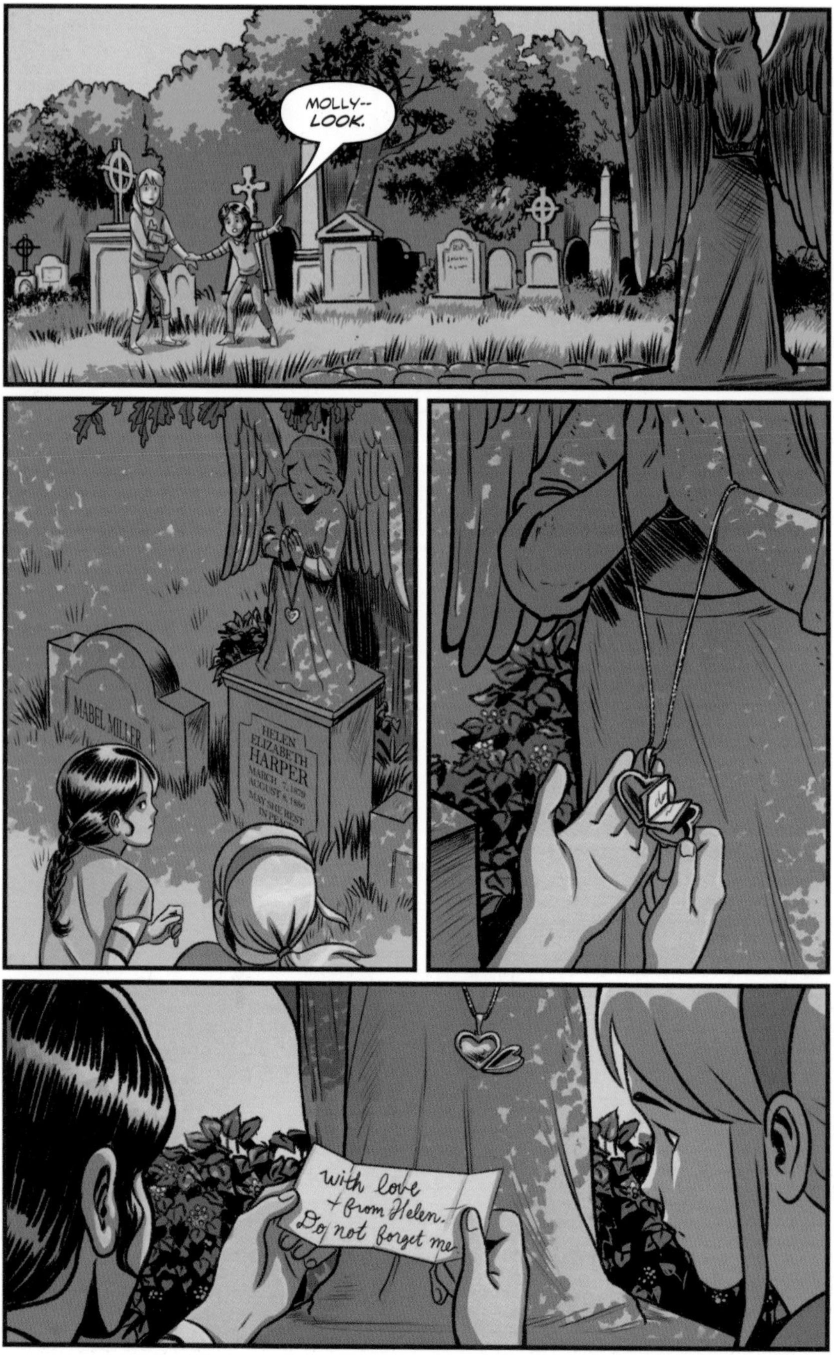
MOLLY-- LOOK.
MABEL MILLER
HELEN ELIZABETH HARPER
MAY SHE REST
with love + from Helen. Do not forget me

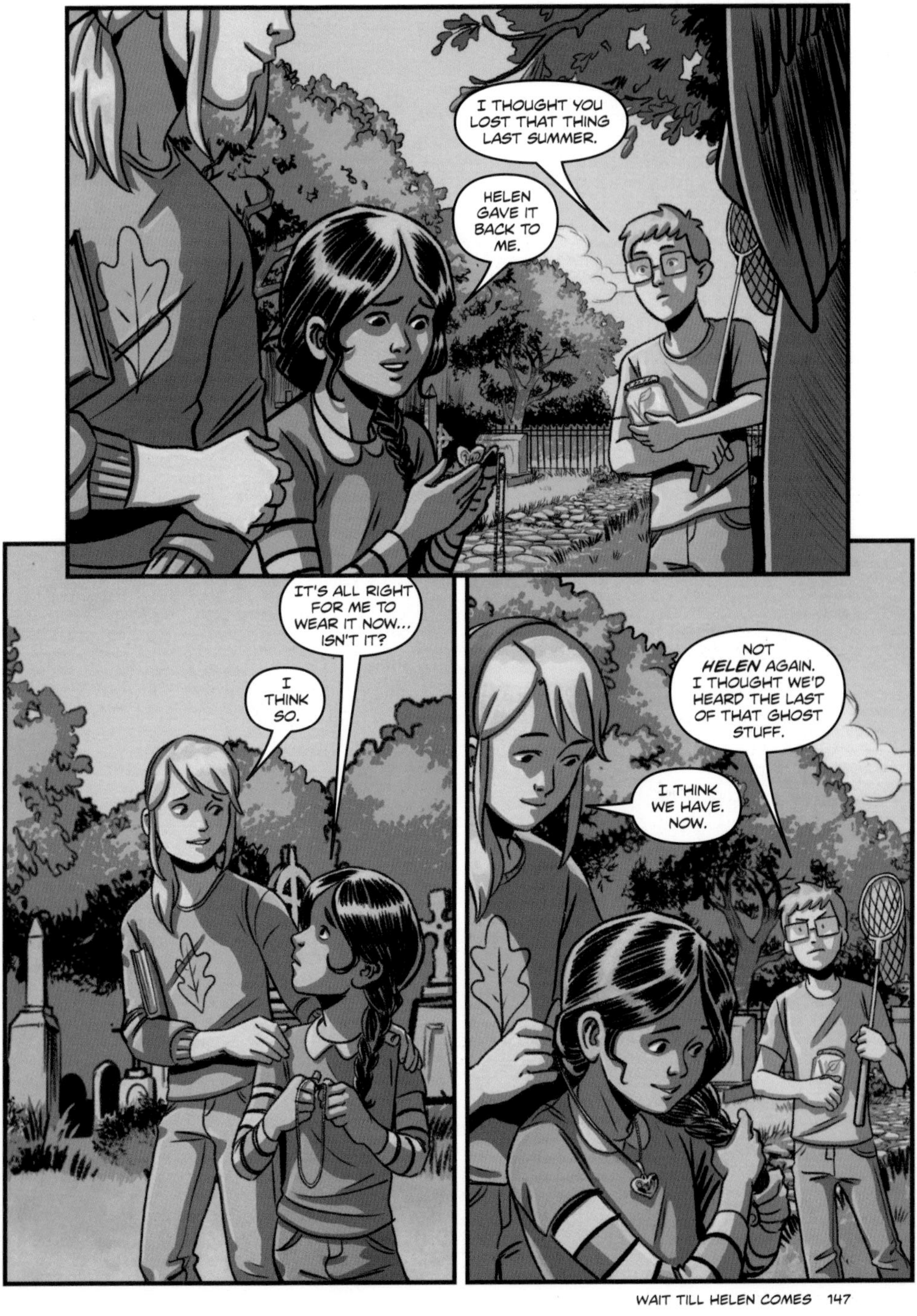
I THOUGHT YOU LOST THAT THING LAST SUMMER.
HELEN GAVE IT BACK TO ME.
IT'S ALL RIGHT FOR ME TO WEAR IT NOW... ISN'T IT?
I THINK SO.
NOT *HELEN* AGAIN. I THOUGHT WE'D HEARD THE LAST OF THAT GHOST STUFF.
I THINK WE HAVE. NOW.

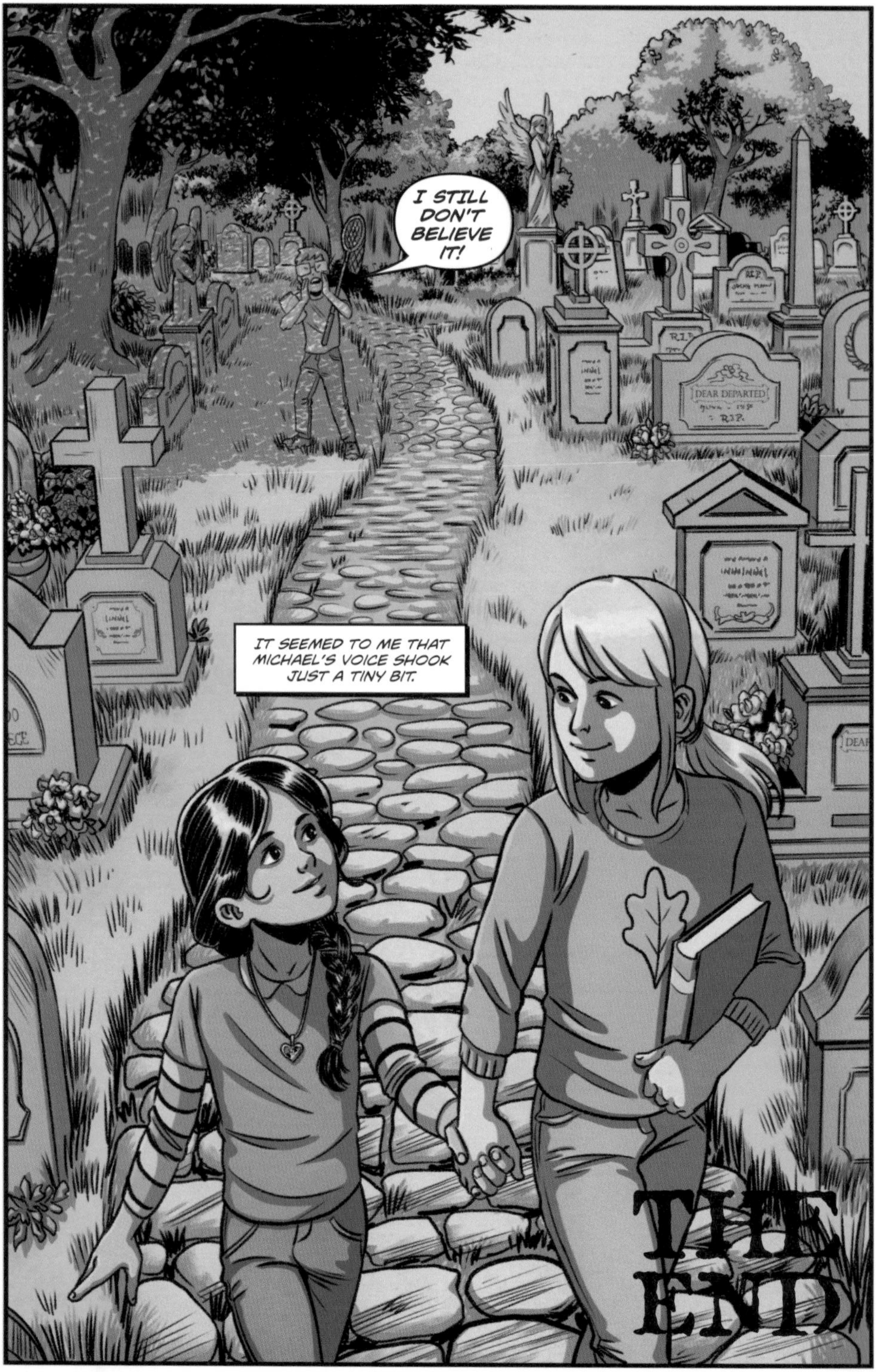
I STILL DON'T BELIEVE IT!
IT SEEMED TO ME THAT MICHAEL'S VOICE SHOOK JUST A TINY BIT.
DEAR DEPARTED
THE END

More stories by Mary Downing Hahn

What We Saw
The Thirteenth Cat
The Puppet's Payback and Other Chilling Tales
Guest
The Girl in the Locked Room
One for Sorrow
Took
Where I Belong
Mister Death's Blue-Eyed Girls
The Doll in the Garden
Closed for the Season
The Ghost of Crutchfield Hall
Deep and Dark and Dangerous
Witch Catcher
The Old Willis Place
Hear the Wind Blow
Anna on the Farm
Promises to the Dead
Anna All Year Round
As Ever, Gordy
Following My Own Footsteps
The Gentleman Outlaw and Me
Look for Me by Moonlight
Time for Andrew
The Wind Blows Backward
Stepping on the Cracks
The Spanish Kidnapping Disaster
The Dead Man in Indian Creek
December Stillness
Following the Mystery Man
Tallahassee Higgins
Wait Till Helen Comes
The Jellyfish Season
Daphne's Book
The Time of the Witch
The Sara Summer

The Creative Team

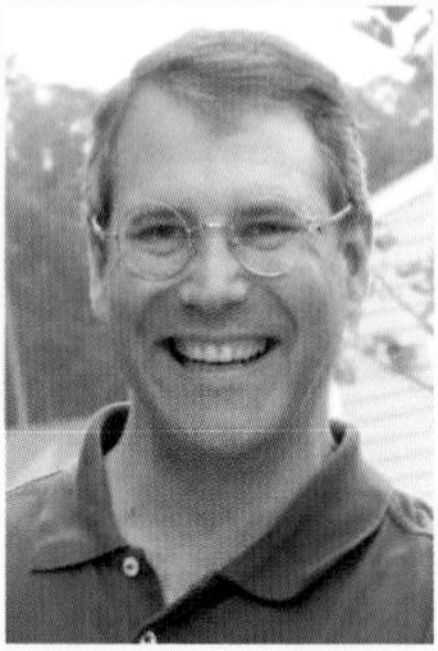
Photo by Scott Peterson

Scott Peterson is the editor of Detective Comics, DC Comics' flagship title; writer of *Batman: Gotham Adventures*; and co-creator of not one, but two new Batgirl comics. He has written children's books, animation, webcomics, music reviews, and novels and is the author of the acclaimed original graphic novel *Truckus Maximus*. He lives in the Pacific Northwest with his wife, children's author Melissa Wiley, and their children.

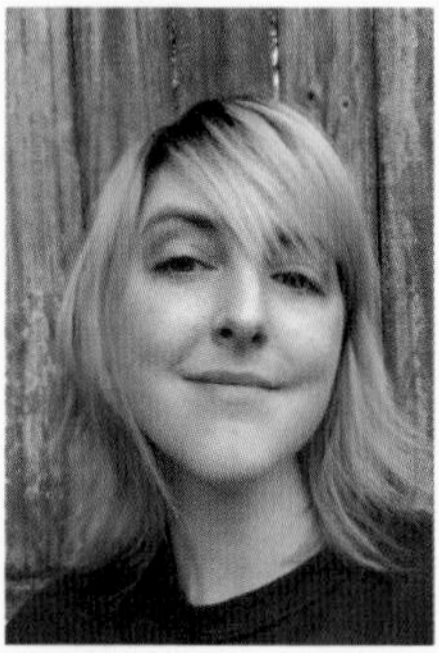
Photo by Meredith Laxton

Meredith Laxton is an illustrator, comic artist, and proud parent of two chubby cats. Prior to creating comics full-time, Meredith worked in the video game industry creating artwork and graphics for both indie and major studios. Their most notable published work includes titles such as *MPLS Sound*, *The Crow: Hark The Herald*, and *Charlie's Spot* #1–4. They are based in Savannah, Georgia.

Photo by Russ Badgett

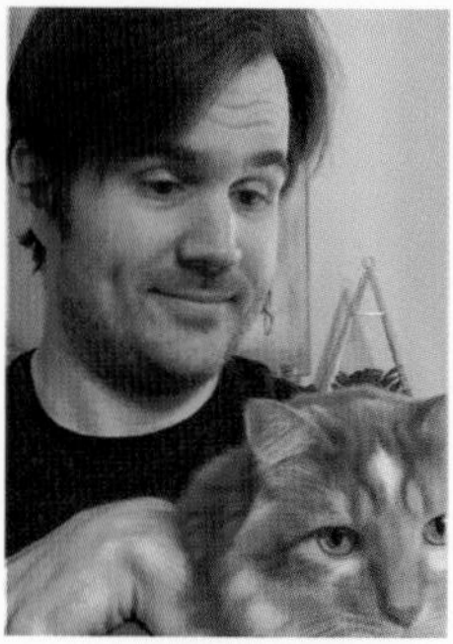

Russ Badgett has been making comics for several years, recently shifting toward color as his primary focus of study and practice. Titles of previous note include *Bloody Hel* as well as cover colors for IDW's *Ghostbusters: Answer the Call*. He currently resides in the hilly part of Texas.

Photo by Morgan Martinez

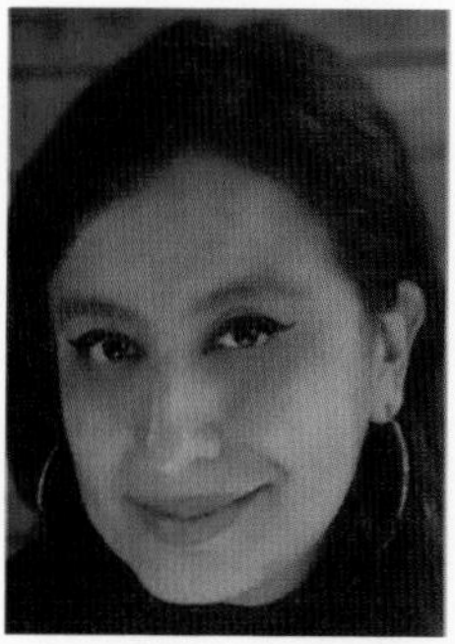

Morgan Martinez has worked in comics since 2011, lettering everything from *Teen Titans Go!* for DC Comics to acclaimed indies such as *Heathen*, *The Curie Society*, and John Leguizamo's *Freak*. When she isn't working on comics, Morgan's interests include writing, drawing, gaming, queer rights, trans liberation, and being as unserious as circumstances allow. She lives in the South Bronx with her wife and their cat, Darcy.

Read more graphic novels
by Mary Downing Hahn!

MARY DOWNING HAHN
Took
A Ghost Story
Adapted by
Scott Peterson,
Jen Vaughn
and Hank Jones

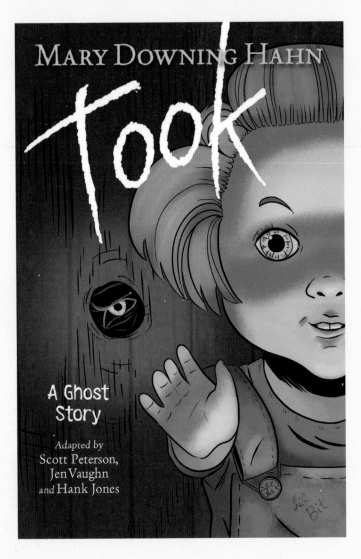